#1 NEW YORK TIMES BESTSELLING AUTHOR
MARY HIGGINS CLARK
A NOVEL
KISS THE GIRLS AND MAKE THEM CRY
D0017138
LIBRARY

$8.99 U.S.
$11.99 CAN.

After thrilling readers for more than forty years,
#1 *New York Times* bestselling author

MARY HIGGINS CLARK

was "A FLAWLESS STORYTELLER"
(*The Washington Post Book World*).

Don't miss the Under Suspicion series
from the Queen of Suspense and her
unstoppable partner in crime, Alafair Burke!

Look for these other stand-alone novels
from the Queen of Suspense

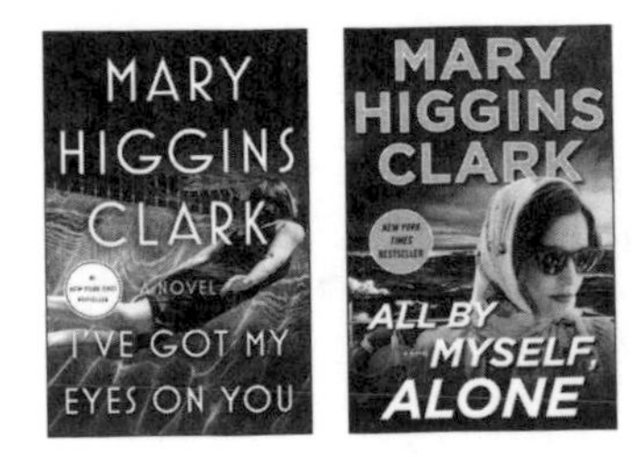

ISBN 978-1-5011-7177-2 $8.99 U.S./$11.99 Can.

Nobody wrote mysteries better than
the Queen of Suspense!
After thrilling readers for forty years,
#1 *New York Times* bestselling author

MARY HIGGINS CLARK

will always be "a flawless storyteller"
(*The Washington Post Book World*).

Praise for *KISS THE GIRLS AND MAKE THEM CRY*

"Mary Higgins Clark, the 'Queen of Suspense,' captivates her readers with another thrilling read, demonstrating how when big businesses with money and power are being jeopardized they will go to any length to protect their assets no matter the consequences."

—*New York Journal of Books*

"Mary Higgins Clark has written a timely and electrifying thriller that will keep readers on the edge of their seats. . . . Fans will find themselves turning the pages as fast as they can to keep up with the pace of the unfolding narrative, and will not be disappointed."

—*Bookreporter*

"Clark's usual mixture now updated, with surprising and welcome assurance, for a new generation of imperiled women."

—*Kirkus Reviews*

"[A] roller-coaster ride until the very last page."

—Midwest Book Review

"Timely and tense, *Kiss the Girls and Make Them Cry* compels the reader's attention—possibly strongly enough to make it a one-sitting read."

—*Fredericksburg Free-Lance Star*

Praise for *YOU DON'T OWN ME*

"The suspense, intrigue, and powerful characters this duo's fans have come to expect are all here; readers will be absorbed by the twists the tale takes and the new subplots that unexpectedly emerge."

—*Booklist*

Praise for *I'VE GOT MY EYES ON YOU*

"Clark—as always—ratchets up the suspense before the big reveal. . . . Superior storytelling."

—*Richmond Times-Dispatch*

Praise for *EVERY BREATH YOU TAKE*

"Mary Higgins Clark and Alafair Burke take the reader on another gripping journey. . . . Powerful."

—*New York Journal of Books*

Praise for *ALL BY MYSELF, ALONE*

"Murders and men missing at sea provide Alvirah and Willy dangerous excitement and ample opportunities to further test their amateur sleuthing skills. The tried-and-true whodunit formula benefits from Alvirah and Willy's down-home charm."

—*Booklist*

"An example of the classic closed-setting mystery . . . *All By Myself, Alone* guarantees a pleasurable cruise through its pages."

—*Richmond Times-Dispatch*

Praise for *THE SLEEPING BEAUTY KILLER*

"A clever plot and a cast of intriguing characters, whose actions and agendas are easily misconstrued . . . The authors keep Laurie and the reader grasping for answers till the end."

—*Publishers Weekly*

Praise for *AS TIME GOES BY*

"Once again, Mary Higgins Clark validates her title as 'Queen of Suspense.'" —*New York Journal of Books*

Praise for *ALL DRESSED IN WHITE*

"An explosive mix of family drama, secrets, rivalry, money and deception . . . For those who enjoy escaping into a fine mystery, it's the perfect hot read for chilly nights."

—*Richmond Times-Dispatch*

Praise for *THE MELODY LINGERS ON*

"A summer list would be lacking without one from Mary Higgins Clark." —*New York Post*

"Clark, whose novels and short stories have entertained her fans for forty years, proves again that she's a master of plot twists and sympathetic portrayals of strong damsels in serious distress. *The Melody Lingers On* is no exception, and the octogenarian Clark continues to shine." —*Richmond Times-Dispatch*

Praise for *DEATH WEARS A BEAUTY MASK AND OTHER STORIES*

"This collection nicely illustrates Clark's range and superlative storytelling talent." —*Publishers Weekly*

Praise for *THE CINDERELLA MURDER*

"Fans of MWA Grand Master Clark will find plenty of intrigue and excitement in this contemporary thriller. . . . Clark keeps readers guessing and in suspense." —*Publishers Weekly*

"This serendipitous series launch, or continuation, will satisfy Clark's legion of fans and may well win her some new ones."

—*Kirkus Reviews*

Praise for *I'VE GOT YOU UNDER MY SKIN*

"Score another winner for the woman who has been nicknamed—with good cause—the queen of suspense."

—*Richmond Times-Dispatch*

"Clark's books keep getting better. The suspense she manages to generate will keep readers up all night. Her writing style is always approachable, her characters are finely limned, and her plots are believable. *I've Got You Under My Skin* is a shining example of all these strengths." —*Bookreporter*

Praise for *DADDY'S GONE A HUNTING*

"Multi-layered, highly suspenseful . . . Mary Higgins Clark has penned yet another mystery that will keep her at the top of the suspense writers list for a very long time. . . . This one is not to be missed." —*Bookreporter*

"Clark still delivers a delicious mystery. . . . Her tautly interwoven story lines, colorful characters, and suspenseful twists will enthrall readers." —*Library Journal*

ALSO BY MARY HIGGINS CLARK

I've Got My Eyes on You
All By Myself, Alone
As Time Goes By
The Melody Lingers On
Death Wears a Beauty Mask and Other Stories
I've Got You Under My Skin
Daddy's Gone A Hunting
The Lost Years
The Magical Christmas Horse
(Illustrated by Wendell Minor)
I'll Walk Alone
The Shadow of Your Smile
Just Take My Heart
Where Are You Now?
Ghost Ship (Illustrated by Wendell Minor)
I Heard That Song Before
Two Little Girls in Blue
No Place Like Home
Nighttime Is My Time
The Second Time Around
Kitchen Privileges
Mount Vernon Love Story
Daddy's Little Girl
On the Street Where You Live
Before I Say Good-Bye
We'll Meet Again
All Through the Night
You Belong to Me
Pretend You Don't See Her
My Gal Sunday
Moonlight Becomes You
Silent Night

Let Me Call You Sweetheart
The Lottery Winner
Remember Me
I'll Be Seeing You
All Around the Town
Loves Music, Loves to Dance
The Anastasia Syndrome and Other Stories
While My Pretty One Sleeps
Weep No More, My Lady
Stillwatch
A Cry in the Night
The Cradle Will Fall
A Stranger Is Watching
Where Are the Children?

BY MARY HIGGINS CLARK AND
CAROL HIGGINS CLARK

Dashing Through the Snow
Santa Cruise
The Christmas Thief
He Sees You When You're Sleeping
Deck the Halls

BY MARY HIGGINS CLARK AND
ALAFAIR BURKE

You Don't Own Me
Every Breath You Take
The Sleeping Beauty Killer
All Dressed in White
The Cinderella Murder

MARY HIGGINS CLARK

A NOVEL

KISS THE GIRLS AND MAKE THEM CRY

Pocket Books
New York London Toronto Sydney New Delhi

Pocket Books
An Imprint of Simon & Schuster, Inc.
1230 Avenue of the Americas
New York, NY 10020

This Pocket Books paperback edition September 2020

POCKET and colophon are registered trademarks of Simon & Schuster, Inc.

For information about special discounts for bulk purchases, please contact Simon & Schuster Special Sales at 1-866-506-1949 or business@simonandschuster.com.

The Simon & Schuster Speakers Bureau can bring authors to your live event. For more information or to book an event, contact the Simon & Schuster Speakers Bureau at 1-866-248-3049 or visit our website at www.simonspeakers.com.

Manufactured in the United States of America

10 9 8 7 6 5 4 3 2 1

ISBN 978-1-5011-7177-2
ISBN 978-1-5011-7171-0 (ebook)

In loving memory of
John Conheeney,
My Spouse Extraordinaire

Acknowledgments

And once again we have written the words "The end" at the close of the new book.

Trying to tell a good tale is both a challenge and a joy.

My desire is to have my reader engrossed in the first chapter and satisfied when reading the epilogue.

Now to thank the indispensable people who have made this possible.

Michael Korda, my editor for over forty years who has continued to be my guiding light. Thank you again, Michael.

Marysue Rucci, editor-in-chief of Simon & Schuster, whose observations and suggestions never fail to make the story better.

Kevin Wilder for his sage advice about detectives and law enforcement.

My son, Dave, who worked with me word by word until the end.

My daughter-in-law, Sharon, for her invaluable assistance in copyediting.

Last but certainly not least all my dear readers. I hope you enjoy reading this story as much as I enjoyed writing it.

Cheers and blessings,
Mary

Prologue

October 12

Gina Kane stretched in her window seat. Her latest prayer had been answered. The door of the jumbo jet was closing and the flight attendants were preparing for takeoff. The middle of the three seats on her side was empty and would remain that way for the sixteen-hour direct flight from Hong Kong to JFK in New York City.

Her second piece of luck was the passenger on the other side of the empty seat. Immediately after buckling himself in, he had taken two Ambien. His eyes were already closed and would remain that way for the next eight hours. That was perfect. She wanted time to think, not make small talk.

It was a trip her parents had spent over a year planning, and they were so excited when they called her to say they had sent in the deposit and were "committed to going." She remembered her mother saying, as they often did, "We want to do this before we get too old."

The notion of either of them getting old had seemed so foreign. Both were outdoors enthusiasts, always hiking, walking, and biking. But at her mother's annual physical, her doctor had spotted an "abnormality." It was shocking, an inoperable cancerous tumor. She went from being the picture of health to gone in four months.

It was after the funeral that Dad brought up the trip. "I'm going to cancel. When I see the other couples from the hiking club together, it will be too depressing to do it alone." Gina had made her decision on the spot. "Dad, you're going, and you're not going to be there alone. I'm going with you." They had spent ten days hiking through small villages in mountainous Nepal. After flying with her to Hong Kong, he had taken the direct flight to Miami.

It had been so easy to see and choose the right thing to do. Her father had thoroughly enjoyed the trip. She had as well. She had never once second-guessed her decision to go.

But where was that ability to decide and plow forward when it came to Ted? He was such a good guy. Both of them were thirty-two. He was absolutely certain that she was the person he wanted to spend his life with. Although disappointed that they would be apart for so long, he had encouraged her to accompany her father. "Family should always come first." It was a line he had said to her many times as they went to gatherings with his bewildering array of relatives.

All that time to think and she was no closer to knowing what to say to Ted. He had a right to know where they were going. *How many times can I say, "I just need a little more time"*?

As usual, her reflection ended in a stalemate. Longing for any distraction, she opened her iPad and entered the password for her email. The screen immediately filled with "new" messages, ninety-four in total. She typed several keystrokes to make the screen display the emails by the name of the sender. There was no response from CRyan. Surprised and disappointed, she hit NEW, typed in CRyan's address, and began writing:

> Hi C, I hope you received the email I sent ten days ago. I'm very interested in hearing about your "terrible experience." Please be in touch at your earliest convenience. Best regards, Gina.

Before pressing SEND, she added her phone number after her name.

The only other email she opened was from Ted. She was sure it would say that he had made a plan for them to meet for dinner. And talk. It was with a mixture of relief and disappointment that she read his note.

> Hi Gina,
>
> I've been counting the days until I get to see you. I'm sorry to say I'm going to have to keep counting. I leave tonight for a special project the bank put me on. Will be in LA for at least a week. I can't tell you how disappointed I am.

I promise to make it up to you when I get back. Call you tomorrow.

All my love now,
Ted

A voice came over the PA announcing they had been cleared for takeoff and ordering that all electronic devices be powered down. She closed her iPad, yawned, and propped her pillow between her head and the side of the cabin.

The email from ten days earlier, the one that would put her life in danger, remained on her mind as she slowly dozed off.

Part I

1

Gina's apartment was on 82nd Street and West End Avenue. Her mother and father had given it to her after they retired and moved to Florida. Spacious, with two bedrooms and a decent-size kitchen, it was the envy of her friends, many of whom were crammed into tiny one-bedrooms and studios.

After dropping her bags in her bedroom, she checked her watch. 11:30 p.m. in New York; 8:30 p.m. in California. She decided it would be a good time to call Ted. He answered on the first ring.

"Well hello, stranger." His tone was deep and loving, giving Gina a rush of warmth. "I can't tell you how much I've missed you."

"I've missed you, too."

"It's killing me that I'm stuck in LA for a week."

They chatted for a few minutes. He finished by saying, "I know you just got in and you're probably exhausted. I have a bunch of meetings planned. I'll call you when things calm down."

"It's a deal," she said.

"Love you."

"Love you, too."

As she hung up the phone, Gina realized that Ted's unexpected trip to California was a mixed blessing. On the one hand she wanted to see him. On the other it was a relief to not have to have a conversation she was not ready for.

Stepping out of the shower at five-thirty in the morning, Gina was pleasantly surprised at how she felt so good. She had slept for almost eight hours on the plane and another four after arriving home. She wasn't feeling any of the dreaded jet lag most people experience after a long west to east flight.

She was eager to get back to work. After graduating from Boston College with a major in Journalism, she had been thrilled to land a job as a desk assistant at a suburban newspaper on Long Island. Budget cutbacks had forced the paper to let many of their senior writers go. Within a year she was writing feature stories.

Her articles on business and finance caught the eye of the editor of *Your Money*. She happily made the switch to the brash new upstart and had loved every minute of her seven years there. But the declining interest in print publications and slowing advertising revenue had taken their toll. In the three years since *Your Money* had folded, she had been a freelancer.

While part of her enjoyed the freedom to pursue the

stories that interested her, another part missed the steady paycheck and health care that came along with being an employee. She was free to choose what she wanted to write about, but at the end of the day somebody had to buy her story.

Empire Review had been a lifesaver. While visiting her parents in Florida, friends of theirs told Gina about being horrified that their eighteen-year-old grandson had been branded during a hazing ritual at his college fraternity. Using a hot iron, Greek letters had been burned into the back of his upper thigh.

Complaints to the university's administration were going unanswered. Big donors among the alumni had threatened to withhold contributions if there was a clampdown on the "Greek Life" community.

Empire Review had agreed to the story immediately. They gave her a hefty advance and a generous travel and expense budget. *ER*'s exposé caused a sensation. It was covered by the national evening news programs and even prompted a segment on *60 Minutes*.

The success of the fraternity story had given her high visibility as an investigative journalist. She was inundated with "tips" emails from would-be whistle-blowers and people who claimed to have knowledge of major scandals. A few of them had resulted in stories she had pursued and published. The trick was distinguishing between providers of genuine leads versus crackpots, disgruntled former employees, and conspiracy theorists.

Gina glanced at her watch. She was scheduled to meet with the magazine's editor in chief the next day. Charles Maynard typically began the conversation with "So Gina, what do we want to write about next?" She had a little over twenty-four hours to come up with a good answer.

She dressed quickly, choosing jeans and a warm turtleneck sweater. After touching up her makeup, she glanced at her full-length mirror. She looked like the early pictures of her mother, who had been homecoming queen at Michigan State. Wideset eyes, more green than hazel, and classic features. Auburn shoulder-length hair made her look even taller than her five foot, seven inch frame.

Satisfied with her appearance, she put a frozen bagel in the toaster and made a cup of coffee. When it was ready, she brought her plate and cup to the table by the living room window. She had a view of the morning sun that was barely peaking over the horizon. It was the time of day when she keenly felt the death of her mother and experienced the feeling of time rushing by too quickly.

Settling at the table, her favorite place to work, she opened her laptop and watched a wave of unread emails unfold on her screen.

Her first glance was at the new emails that had arrived since she had checked while on the plane. Nothing urgent. More importantly, nothing from CRyan.

Next she scanned through the ones that had arrived over the last week and a half, when she had been in one of the few remaining places on earth where WiFi service was not available.

- A note from a woman in Atlanta who claimed she had proof that the recycled rubber being used in school playgrounds was making children sick.
- A request to speak the following month at the ASJA, American Society of Journalists and Authors.
- An email from a man who claimed he had in his possession the portion of President Kennedy's skull that had gone missing after the autopsy.

Even though she probably could have recited its content, she went back and clicked on the email she had received the day she left on her vacation.

> Hi Gina, I don't believe we ever met when we were at Boston College. I finished a few years apart from you. Right after I graduated, I went to work at REL News. I had a terrible experience with one of the higher-ups. (And I wasn't the only one.) Now they're afraid I'll talk about it. I've been approached about a settlement offer. I don't want to put more in an email. Can we arrange to meet?

When she had seen the name CRyan on an email, she had tried to remember why the name was familiar. Had there been a Courtney Ryan at school?

Gina reread the email twice, pushing herself to see if there was anything she had missed. REL News was a Wall Street darling among media companies. Its headquarters were at 55th Street and Avenue of the Americas, or Sixth Avenue as most New Yorkers still called it. In a span of twenty years it had grown from a small group of cable TV stations to a national powerhouse. Its ratings had surpassed CNN and were growing ever closer to the market leader, Fox. Its unofficial motto was "REaL News, not the other kind."

The first subject that had come to her mind was sexual harassment. Hold on, she had thought. You don't even know if "CRyan" is a man or a woman. You're a reporter. Don't get ahead of yourself. Get the facts. There had been only one way to find out. She looked again at the response she had sent.

> Hi Mr./Ms. Ryan, I'm very interested in talking to you about the "terrible experience" you referred to. I'll be out of the country without access to email, but I'll be back on October 13. As you probably know, I live and work in New York City. Where are you? Looking forward to hearing from you. Best, Gina.

She had difficulty focusing as she scrolled through other emails. I had really hoped to have more than this, she said to herself as her mind drifted to tomorrow's meeting at the magazine.

Maybe she left a message, Gina thought optimistically. Her cell phone had been down to one bar when she boarded her flight. It was dead by the time she landed in New York. In the email she gave CRyan her number.

Gina walked quickly into her bedroom, removed her phone from the charger, and brought it back to the kitchen. She tapped the phone to wake it up. A quick glance revealed several messages, but none from unfamiliar numbers.

The first was from her best friend Lisa. "Hi girlfriend. Welcome back. Looking forward to hearing all about your trip. I hope we're still on for dinner tonight. We have to go to a dive restaurant in the Village called the Bird's Nest. I have a great new case. A slip and fall. My client fell on ice cubes dropped by the bartender when he was shaking martinis. Broke her leg in three places. I want to scope out the joint."

Gina chuckled as she listened. Dinner with Lisa was always fun.

The other messages were solicitations, which she immediately deleted.

2

Gina took the subway four stops to 14th Street. From there she walked the three blocks to the Fisk Building. The third through seventh floors were rented by the magazine.

"Good morning," the security guard said as she walked through the detection scanner. A spate of recent threats had led to a policy change at the magazine: "All employees and visitors go through the security line. No exceptions."

Gina entered the elevator and pushed 7, the floor reserved for the executive and editorial staff. As she stepped out, a friendly voice greeted her. "Hi Gina. Welcome back." Jane Patwell, a longtime administrative assistant, held out her hand. Fifty years old, a little stocky, and always lamenting her dress size, Jane said, "Mr. Maynard will see you in his office."

She lowered her voice to a conspiratorial whisper. "He has some good-looking guy with him. I don't know who he is."

Jane was a born matchmaker. It irritated Gina that

Jane was always trying to find someone for her. She was tempted to say, "Maybe he's a serial killer." Instead she smiled without replying. She followed Jane to the large corner office that was the domain of Charlie Maynard, the magazine's longtime editor in chief.

Charlie was not at his desk. He was seated at his favorite spot, the conference table by the window, a cell phone stuck in his ear. About five feet nine, Charlie had a protruding paunch and cherubic face. Graying hair was combed sideways over his skull. Reading glasses were raised on his forehead. In front of Gina a colleague of Charlie's once asked him what he did for exercise. Quoting George Burns, Charlie responded, "I make it a point to walk to the funerals of my friends who jog."

He waved when he saw Gina and pointed to the chair opposite him. Next to him was the good-looking guy Jane had referred to.

As she walked to the table, the newcomer stood up and extended his hand. "Geoffrey Whitehurst," he said with a slight British accent. He was about six feet tall, with even features dominated by piercing dark brown eyes and equally dark brown hair. Combined with his face and athletic build his manner suggested an air of authority.

"Gina Kane," she said, feeling that he already knew her name. He looks mid to late thirties, she thought, as she sat in the chair he had pulled out for her.

Charlie clicked to end the phone conversation. Turning to him, she said, "Charlie, I'm so sorry I missed your birthday while I was away."

"Don't worry, Gina. Seventy is the new fifty. We all had a great time. I see you've met Geoffrey. Let me tell you why he's here."

"Gina, before Charlie begins," Geoffrey intervened, "I want to say I'm a big fan of your work."

"Thank you," Gina said, wondering what would come next. What came was a shock.

"After over forty-five years in the magazine business, I've decided to call it quits. My wife wants us to spend more time on the West Coast with the grandkids and I've agreed. Geoff is in the process of taking over for me and he'll be working with you from now on. The change will be announced next week and I will appreciate your keeping this confidential until then."

He paused to give Gina time to let his decision sink in, then added, "We were fortunate to snatch Geoff away from the Time Warner group. Until now he's spent most of his career in London."

"Congratulations to both of you, Charlie and Geoffrey," Gina said automatically. She took comfort in the fact that Geoffrey had already said he liked her work.

"Please call me Geoff," he said briskly.

Charlie continued. "Gina, your investigations usually run several months to completion. That's why I invited Geoff here for the initial meeting." Clearing his throat, he said, "So, Gina, what do we want to write about next?"

"I have a couple of ideas," Gina said as she pulled a small notebook from her purse, "and would like to hear what you think." The statement was addressed to both of them. "I've exchanged a series of emails with a former aide to a New York State senator. The aide and the senator are currently retired. The aide claims she has evidence of bid rigging and granting contracts in exchange for cash payments and other favors. But there's a problem with this one. The aide wants twenty-five thousand dollars upfront to go on the record and tell her story."

Geoff jumped in first. "My experience is that people who want to be paid to share what they know are not generally reliable. They embellish and sensationalize the story because they want the money and publicity."

Charlie chuckled. "I think even the most avid fans of Albany corruption are starting to find the subject tiresome. And I agree that paying a source is rarely a good idea."

Gesturing toward Gina's notebook, Charlie asked, "What else have you got?"

"Okay," Gina said while flipping the page. "A longtime employee in the Admissions Office at Yale reached out to me. He claims that the Ivy League schools are sharing with each other the amount of aid they plan to offer individual applicants."

"Why is that a problem?" Geoff asked.

"Because it's right on the edge of price fixing and collusion. The student is the loser. It's similar in some ways to when Silicon Valley companies made a gentleman's agreement to not poach each other's engineers. The result was that companies profited because they did not have to pay more to keep their top talent. The engineers earned less than they would have if they could have sold their talents to the highest bidder."

"I believe there are eight Ivy League schools, is that right?" Geoff asked.

"Yes," Charlie said, "and they average about six thousand undergrads. So that's forty-eight thousand of the country's twenty million college students. I'm not sure many of our readers are going to care about a handful of Ivy Leaguers who might have gotten stiffed on their aid package. If you ask me, I think they're wasting their money on those overpriced places."

Charlie had grown up in Philadelphia and gone to Penn State. His allegiance to state schools never wavered.

What a great way to make an impression on the new boss, Gina thought while flipping the page. Trying to sound animated, she said, "This next one is literally at square one." She told them about receiving the email about the "terrible experience" at REL News and the response she had sent.

"So it's been ten days since you answered the email and you haven't gotten a reply?" Charlie asked.

"Yes, eleven counting today."

"This CRyan who sent the email. Have you been able to find out anything about her? Is she credible?" Geoff inquired.

"I agree with your assumption that CRyan is a woman, but we can't be sure of that. Of course the first thing that came to mind when I read this is that it may be a MeToo situation. No, I don't know anything more about her than she put in the email. My instinct tells me this is worth pursuing."

Geoff looked at Charlie. "What do you think?"

"If I were you, I'd be very interested in finding out what CRyan has to say," Charlie answered. "And it will be much easier to get her to tell her story before she reaches a settlement agreement."

"Okay, Gina, get to work on it," Geoff affirmed. "Wherever she is, and I'm also confident we're dealing with a 'she,' go *meet* with her. I want to hear your personal impressions of her."

As Gina walked down the hallway to the elevator, she whispered to herself, "Please don't let CRyan turn out to be a psycho!"

3

Ordinarily Gina would have taken time to absorb and appreciate the sights and sounds of the city she loved. Stepping into the subway car, she smiled as she remembered her freshman year roommate. Marcie was from a small town in Ohio. She asked if it had been "hard" growing up in New York City. Gina had been shocked by the question; she had mastered the subway and bus systems and loved the freedom of navigating them alone by the time she was twelve. She asked Marcie if it had been *hard* growing up in a place where you had to depend on your parents every time you wanted to go somewhere.

She stopped at the small grocery store on the corner of Broadway and picked up milk and some sandwich makings. Surprised that there was no line at the Starbucks next door, she popped in and ordered her favorite, a vanilla latte. As she walked the block and a half to her apartment, her mind was on the daunting task ahead of her.

After putting away the groceries, she carried the latte to the kitchen table and tapped her computer to rouse it from sleep mode. She clicked on the CRyan email. It had been sent from a Google account, but that really didn't matter. After numerous violations the tech companies were under extreme pressure to safeguard the privacy of their users. There's no way Google will lift a finger to help me find CRyan, she thought.

Gina reread the only part of the email that offered a clue; *I don't believe we ever met when we were at Boston College. I finished a few years apart from you.*

CRyan obviously knows the year I graduated, Gina thought, and we were on campus together at some point. A *few* means more than one, but it has to be less than four or we would never have been in school at the same time. So that means CRyan graduated either two to three years *before* me or two to three years *after* me.

Gina sat back in her chair and took a sip of her latte. When she was working on the branding iron story, the Southern university had gotten wind of her investigation. They had fought her every step of the way when she sought contact information for fraternity members and faculty advisors.

But those were different circumstances. Boston College was not a target. This was not about them. And she was only asking them to identify the owner of one email address.

If it were only that easy, she thought. If they didn't have that CRyan email address on file, she would be forced to make a much bigger request. Privacy rules being what they were—"Oh well," she said out loud. "Only one way to find out."

4

"Boston College Alumni Affairs, how may I help you?" The male voice on the other end of the line sounded crisp and efficient. Gina guessed she was speaking to someone in his fifties.

"Hello, my name is Gina Kane. I graduated BC ten years ago. May I ask who I'm speaking to?"

"My name is Rob Mannion."

"It's nice to make your acquaintance, Mr. Mannion—"

"Please call me Rob."

"Thank you, Rob. I'm hoping you can help me with some information."

"If you are seeking the arrangements for the reunion classes, they are posted on our website. I can give you the address."

"No, that's not why I'm calling. I'm trying to get in touch with someone who was at the college around the time I was."

"I might be able to help you. What is that person's name and what was the graduation year?"

"That's where I'm having a problem," Gina said. "I

don't have the person's full name. All I have is an email address. I'm hoping you can—"

"Why don't you send the person an email and ask for the name?"

Gina tried to keep her frustration out of her voice. "I assure you I did think of that." She was uncertain about how much to share during this conversation. Some people were excited by the prospect of talking to a reporter; others clammed up. "My question is, if I give you an email address, can you tell me if you have information about the owner of that email address?"

"I don't believe our policy permits me to share that type of information."

"I understand that," Gina said, "but that's not what I'm asking. Even if you *can't* share it with me, I only want to know if you *have* that information in your possession."

"This is very unusual," Rob said, "but I'll check. Give me a moment to get into that database. What year did the person you're asking about graduate?"

"I'm not sure," Gina replied, "but I have reason to believe it was in one of the following six years." She read him the years CRyan most likely graduated.

"I'll have to look up each year individually," Rob sighed, his level of irritation apparent.

"I really appreciate your help," Gina said warmly.

"Okay, it's coming on my screen now. No to the first year, no to the second, no to the third, no to the fourth, fifth, and sixth. I'm sorry. It appears I won't be able to assist you."

"Generally speaking, do you have current emails for alumni?"

"We try our best to maintain updated contact information. But for the most part we are reliant on the individual alumnus or alumna to keep us informed. If they begin using a new email address and discontinue the one we have, then the answer is no. The same applies for addresses and phone numbers."

"Do you still have the last year I asked you to check on your screen?"

"I do."

"Can you tell me how many students with the last name 'Ryan' graduated that year?"

"Ms. Kane, a large percent of our students are of Irish ancestry."

"I know," Gina replied. "I'm one of them."

"This call is taking an awfully long time, Ms. Kane."

"Please call me Gina. And Rob, I really appreciate your patience. Before we hang up, I want to talk to you about the mailings I received regarding this year's fund-raising campaign."

"How kind of you," Rob replied with more enthusiasm.

Fifteen minutes later Rob had emailed her spreadsheets of the last name "Ryan" from the six years she had requested. A $3,000 contribution had been charged to her MasterCard.

5

Gina combed through the spreadsheets Rob had sent her. To the right of each student's name—Last, First, and Middle—there were columns for different pieces of information: Date of Birth, Home Address, Employer, Email, Phone Number, Spouse's Name. She quickly verified that Rob had been correct when he told her none of these students listed the email address she was seeking.

Using the Cut and Paste tools she put the names on a new spreadsheet. Across the six graduation years there were seventy-one, with slightly more females than males.

She then selected each Ryan whose first name began with "C" and moved them to the top of her list. There were fourteen: Carl, Carley, Casey, Catherine, Charles, Charlie, Charlotte, Chloe, Christa, Christina, Christopher, Clarissa, Clyde, and Curtiss.

Gina printed the list and used her highlighter to accentuate the women's names. Not sure about "Casey," she checked the middle name. It was "Riley." That one could also go either way, she thought. She added "Casey" to her list of women.

She paused a moment as a troubling thought went through her mind. Her friend Sharon's email address was "S" followed by her last name. But "Sharon" was her friend's middle name; "Eleanor" was her first name. If she were searching these records for Sharon, she would be looking under the wrong name. "Please let your first name begin with 'C,' Ms. Ryan," she whispered to herself.

Gina wondered if Facebook could help narrow her search. She tried the first name on her highlighted list: Carley Ryan. Predictably, there were dozens of women and a few men with that name. She typed in "Carley Ryan, Boston College." There were four matches, but none appeared to be in the age range she was seeking. She tried again, using "Carley Ryan, REL News," but nothing came up.

She was about to try the same exercise with the next name on her list, Casey, when she paused. CRyan by her own words had a "terrible experience" while working at REL News. If that had happened to Gina, would she include a mention of REL on *her* Facebook account? Probably not. And someone who had a bad experience might just want to disappear. Or she might be one of those people who just don't like using social media.

Gina debated but then dismissed the idea of sending an email to each of the nine women. CRyan for whatever reason had chosen not to respond to the email Gina had sent a week and a half ago. Why would she answer if she sent her one today? She picked up her phone and began dialing the phone number for Carley Ryan.

"Hello." The woman who answered the phone sounded middle-aged.

"Hello, is this Mrs. Ryan?"

"Yes, it is."

"My name is Gina Kane. I graduated Boston College in 2008."

"Did you know my daughter, Carley? She was class of 2006."

"Honestly, I don't recall meeting Carley. I'm researching for an article about Boston College graduates from that time period who went on to work in the news business. Did Carley ever work for one of the TV networks such as REL News?"

"Oh, not my Carley," the woman said with a small laugh. "Carley believes watching TV is a waste of time. She's an instructor with Outward Bound. She's currently leading a canoeing trip in Colorado."

After scratching Carley from her list, Gina looked at the remaining names and phone numbers. There was no way to tell which numbers were those of the graduates versus the parents.

She dialed again. Casey answered on the first ring and explained she had gone straight to law school and then been hired by a firm in Chicago. Another dead end.

She next left a message for Catherine.

Charlie turned out to be a male who was an accountant.

The number for Charlotte was preceded by 011. The address column listed a street in London, England. Gina checked her watch. England was five hours ahead. Not too late to call. The phone was answered on the second ring by a middle-aged woman with a British accent. She explained that immediately after graduation her daughter Charlotte had accepted a position with Lloyd's of London and had been at the firm ever since.

Gina left a message for Chloe.

Clarissa's mother explained in agonizing detail that her daughter had married her high school sweetheart, had four beautiful children, and had only worked for one year in Pittsburgh before becoming a stay-at-home mother. She added that this was in stark contrast to her experience. "I worked for almost ten years before I decided to have a family. Even though it worked for Clarissa, don't you agree that it makes more sense for women to work at least five years to establish their careers, to build their self-confidence before rushing into a commitment? I tried to tell Clarissa, but do you think she would listen to me? Of course not. I—"

A return call from Chloe gave Gina a merciful excuse to end the conversation. Chloe had gone straight to medical school and now had a fellowship at the Cleveland Clinic.

The number for Christa had been disconnected.

Courtney answered while on her lunch break. She had gotten her master's and gone straight into teaching.

Trying not to feel discouraged, Gina looked at the only two remaining names, Catherine and Christina. Not sure what to do next, she got up and made herself a sandwich.

6

Feeling invigorated after lunch, Gina looked at the address information for each of the former students. The most recent for Christina was Winnetka, Illinois, an upscale suburb about fifteen miles from Chicago. She checked the telephone area codes for Winnetka, 224 and 847. Christina's phone number on the spreadsheet began with 224.

Hoping against hope, she dialed that number. A cheery voice answered with a robust hello. Gina's now practiced opening explained the reason she was calling.

Christina's friendly tone quickly morphed into an angry rant. "So you're calling me to help you write a story about how wonderful Boston College is. Skip your stupid story and write about this. My parents met when they were undergrads at BC. You couldn't find two more loyal alums. They gave money every year, volunteered for a slew of committees. I did the same after I got out. And then five years later my younger brother applies. Top ten percent in his class. Captain of the lacrosse team. Involved in every activity. An all around great kid and they turn him down. 'We had so many qualified applicants from your area' was all they would say. After all my parents and I did! Do me a favor. Lose my number."

The sound of the phone being slammed down signaled the end of the call. Gina chuckled to herself. If Christina had stayed on the phone a moment longer, she could have given her Rob Mannion's number. I'm sure the two of them would have a wonderful conversation, she thought.

Gina stared out the window. She was hitting nothing but blind alleys. Peachtree City, Georgia, was the address Rob had provided for Catherine Ryan. But when she searched the online databases for that area, none of the Catherine Ryans she found matched the age of the woman she was looking for.

She wasn't sure what to do. If Catherine Ryan was the "CRyan" she was searching for, she could give her a little more time to respond to the voice mail message she had left. But something told her to press on, to try to figure out another way to get in touch with Catherine.

It occurred to her that Rob had said they updated their records as the graduates kept them informed regarding new addresses and phone numbers. Did that mean they deleted the old addresses? Or might BC still have Catherine's parents' address?

She was put through to Rob's line, and he answered on the first ring. When she identified herself, his voice became terse. “In less than a minute I have a conference call.”

Gina knew she had to be quick. “Catherine Ryan’s most recent address showed her living in Georgia. Trying to find her was a dead end. I’m hoping to locate her parents. Would you have her original address, her home address when she was an undergrad?”

“I’ll have to check an older database. Let me see if I can find it now before I have to start dialing.”

She heard him under his breath mumbling the spelling of Catherine Ryan’s name as he typed. “Okay, it’s opening. Here we go. 40 Forest Drive, Danbury, Connecticut.

“And with that, I have to say goodbye.”

7

Gina went to an online site and found a listing for a Justin and Elizabeth Ryan in Danbury. The street address matched what Rob had given her. Their ages were sixty-five and sixty-three. That was about right for parents whose child was in her early thirties, Gina thought. Her reporter's instinct told her it would be better to drive to Danbury than to reach out to them by phone.

The ride on the crisp autumn day was pleasant and not crowded with traffic. Thank God for Waze, she thought as the directions app guided her rental car out of the city to a pleasant suburban area in southern Connecticut with upscale homes on wide lots.

When she rang the bell, a white-haired woman in her late sixties answered. At first cautious when she read Gina's card, she warmed up and explained that she and her husband had bought the house less than a year ago from the Ryan family and didn't have their new address.

So much for the accuracy of online databases, Gina thought. But as she turned away, she noticed a FOR SALE sign on a neighbor's lawn. The sign caused her to turn back while the new owner was still standing at the door.

"One last question," she promised. "Did you buy this house through a Realtor?"

"Yes, we did."

"Do you remember the name of the Realtor?"

"Yes, I can give you his card."

According to Waze the broker was a mile away. It was five o'clock. Hoping that he was still in the office, Gina forced herself to stay within ten miles of the speed limit as she hurried across town.

The office was on a main street surrounded by a dry cleaner, delicatessen, hair salon, and sporting goods store. Pictures of houses were prominently displayed in the window. Keeping her fingers crossed, she tried the door handle and was relieved to find it open. She stepped inside just as a stocky, balding man of about sixty came from a back room.

He was obviously disappointed that she was not house hunting, but when she mentioned the Ryans, he became expansive, even loquacious. "Nice family," he began. "Known them ever since the kids were babies. Hated to see them leave, but Elizabeth's arthritis was getting worse. They finally decided they needed to do something about it and started looking around. Debated about the Naples and Sarasota areas but ended up in Palm Beach. Good decision if you ask me. They showed me the pictures of the condominium they were planning to buy. I told them in my opinion, even though I've only visited the area a few times, they were getting it at a good price. Newly remodeled, big rooms, second bath off the guest bedroom. What more could anyone want? Hated to see them go. Good people, if you get my drift."

The agent stopped for breath and Gina managed to get a word in. "By any chance, do you remember the names of their children?"

"Oh, let's see. I swear I'm getting old. Used to be that names popped right into my head. No more. It takes a while." Frowning, he paused. "Wait a minute. I'm starting to remember. Both really good-looking kids. They must be in their late twenties by now. Let's see. Okay, I've got it. Their son is Andrew. The daughter is Catherine. They called her Cathy."

"Do you remember how she spells her name? I mean was it with a 'C' or a 'K'?"

"That I'm sure of. It was with a 'C.' C-A-T-H-E-R-I-N-E."

"C" Ryan, Gina thought. At least it was the right initial.

Three minutes later she managed to get the Ryans' address in Palm Beach and their phone number.

She walked out to her car, started it, and paused.

Rather than call now with the possibility of background traffic noise making it hard to hear, or going through areas with spotty cell service, Gina decided to wait until she was home to make the call. This time the distance to Danbury felt longer, and she had to remind herself that she had gotten up early and it had been a long day.

It was seven-fifteen when she got back to her apartment. Gratefully, she poured herself a glass of wine, settled on a chair in the dinette area, and reached for her land line phone.

The call was answered by a man's voice saying, "Ryan residence."

Gina repeated what she had told the real estate agent, that she had gone to Boston College with Cathy and was hoping to speak to her. There was a long pause before Andrew Ryan asked, "Were you a friend of my sister?"

"Not a close friend, but I do want to get in touch with her."

"Then you don't know that Cathy died in an accident last week, when she was on vacation in Aruba."

Gina gasped. "No, I didn't know that. I'm so terribly sorry."

"Thank you. Of course, we're all in shock. It was the last thing we could have expected. Cathy was always very careful, and she was a very good swimmer."

"I'd like to tell you more about the reason I'm calling. But I understand if this is not a good time. If you prefer, I can call back—"

"Now is okay. How can I help you?"

Gina hesitated for only a moment. "I'm a journalist and I had hoped to talk to Cathy about a story I'm working on. Before I go into it, I have to ask, did she ever work at REL News?"

"Yes, she did."

"How long was she there?"

"Three years. And then she left for a job at a magazine publisher in Atlanta."

"When was the last time you saw or heard from Cathy?"

"About two weeks ago. It was our mother's birthday so both of us came down to Palm Beach for the weekend to celebrate."

"What was the date of the birthday?"

When Andrew Ryan answered, Gina did a quick calculation.

"I received an email from Cathy the day of your mother's birthday. Let me read it to you."

Andrew listened as she read the email. Gina explained how she had been about to leave on a trip and had encouraged Cathy to get in touch with her when she returned.

"And she never contacted you after that initial email?"

"No, she didn't. But I've gone to great lengths to try to find her."

There was a long silence before he said, "I sensed something was not right with Cathy the night of the birthday. She was very quiet. She said she wanted to talk to me about something, but then said, 'Let's do it when I get back from Aruba.' She was going there for five days."

"Do you know if she stayed in touch with any of her coworkers from her days at REL News?"

"I'm pretty sure she kept up with a few people after she left."

"Would you happen to know their names?"

"There was one in the New York area. I'm blanking

on her name. Maybe I can find it. I went down to Aruba after the accident and picked up Cathy's personal items including her cell phone and laptop. I'll go through them. I know I'll recognize her name if I see it."

"I'd really appreciate that."

"Give me your number. I'll call you as soon as I find something."

They exchanged cell phone numbers. Then Andrew asked her quietly, "Do you have any idea what my sister was referring to when she wrote 'terrible experience'?"

"Not yet. But I intend to find out."

8

After speaking with Andrew Ryan, Gina sat for long minutes reviewing the conversation in her mind. There were so many more questions she wanted to ask him. She grabbed a pad and began to jot notes.

Cathy started at REL News right out of college. She would have been twenty-two. Her brother said she worked there for three years before leaving. So the "terrible experience" happened when she was twenty-two to twenty-five. Very young and vulnerable, Gina thought.

She hadn't thought to ask about the particulars of her accident. He mentioned that she was a good swimmer, so it must have been in the water? It happened in Aruba. Was she there with a boyfriend? girlfriends? alone?

Aruba, wasn't that where Natalee Holloway's family had such a hard time finding out what happened when she disappeared after going there on a high school graduation trip?

Was there an investigation? If by any chance this was *not* an accident, how should she follow up?

Gina pushed the chair back and got up. She remembered that she was to meet Lisa at the Bird's Nest in another twenty minutes.

She jumped into the bedroom and quickly changed her clothes. She grabbed a pair of black slacks, a black tank top, and her favorite black-and-white print jacket and hurried out.

The subway ride to the West Village took only twenty minutes. When she opened the door of the restaurant, Lisa was seated at a small table facing the bar.

Lisa jumped up to meet her. "I missed my buddy when you were on vacation," she said. "In case you're wondering, I got this table because I want to watch that bartender make drinks and see if any ice hits the floor."

"And has any?" Gina asked.

"Not so far. Enough about ice cubes. Tell me about Nepal over a glass of wine."

"It will take the whole bottle," Gina said. "To begin, the trip to Nepal was fabulous. I think it did my father a world of good to be with his old friends. He's still brokenhearted about losing my mother."

"Very understandable," Lisa said. "I loved your mother."

Gina took a sip of the wine, hesitated, and then began. "The day I left for Nepal I received an email that may be the next article I'm hoping to write." She filled Lisa in on the details.

"A fatal accident of this kind," Lisa said. "To put it crassly, that's a lucky break for whoever was trying to settle a lawsuit with her. Maybe too lucky?"

"That's the same question I've asked myself. Of course it could be a coincidence, but on the other hand, it happened so quickly after Cathy Ryan sent me the email."

"What's your next step?"

"I need to get an okay from my new boss to go down to Aruba and do my own investigating."

"Will the magazine pay your expenses?"

"I'll find out later this week."

Lisa smiled. "In my next life I want your job."

"Enough about what I'm doing, what's going on with you?"

"More of the same. Ambulance chasing." Lisa filled her in on new cases that she had been assigned since Gina had last seen her. A client walking down Fifth Avenue had been hit in the head by a windblown piece of construction debris and sustained a mild concussion. "They're paying a lot more for concussions nowadays after all the publicity from football players. That will be an easy one." Another client was exiting the subway via a revolving door made of metal bars. "The door got stuck halfway. My client walked into it and broke his nose. He insists he was sober. But I wonder what he was doing until three o'clock in the morning if he wasn't drinking."

Lisa glanced over at the bar as she heard the sound of a drink being shaken. "So far, no ice on the floor," she observed wryly.

9

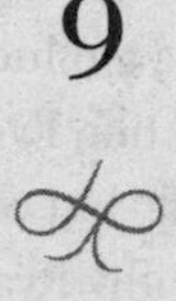

At 6:50 the next morning, as Gina stretched and tried to keep her eyes open, her cell phone rang. The name on the screen was Andrew Ryan.

"I hope I'm not calling too early," he said. "I'm about to board my flight back to Boston. I want to follow up on yesterday's conversation."

"I'm fine to talk now," Gina said as she reached for the notebook she always kept on her night table. "Thanks for getting back to me so quickly."

"Meg Williamson is one of the people from REL News that Cathy kept in touch with."

"Meg Williamson," she said as she jotted the information. "Any contact info on her?"

"No, I couldn't find her on Cathy's computer or cell phone. The name literally just jumped into my head while I was driving to the airport. When I get to Boston, I'll call my mother and ask her to try to find it."

"That's great. Thanks so much. Any luck on remembering anybody else at REL News Cathy stayed in touch with?"

"Not yet, but I'll talk to my mother. We'll keep working on it."

"Thank you again. If you have any more time, I have some questions I thought of after we spoke."

"I've got about five minutes. Fire away."

"When Cathy went to Aruba, was she alone or with friends?"

"She went alone."

"Do you know if she was planning to meet anybody there?"

"Not that I know of. She said she just wanted a little R&R on her own."

"Aruba's pretty far to go for a few days of vacation. Any idea why she chose to go there?"

"None. She loved doing anything and everything near or in the water. Scuba diving, snorkeling, windsurfing."

"You told me Cathy died in 'an accident.'"

"Yes, she had an accident while on a Jet Ski."

"What happened?"

"The Aruba police called the day after the accident to tell my parents that the Jet Ski Cathy was riding had crashed into a boat in the harbor. She was thrown from the ski."

"Did she drown or die from the impact of the crash?"

"It's not clear which."

"I hate to even ask the question. Did they do an autopsy?"

"No. We asked about that. When they told us it would take two to three weeks, we decided against it. I know she had massive head trauma. The collision almost certainly knocked her unconscious. Cathy had on a life jacket, but she was lying facedown in the water for several minutes before anyone got to her."

"I'm sorry to ask this, but do you know if she had any alcohol in her system?"

"The police report said there was a strong odor of alcoholic beverage on her body."

"As far as you know, did she have a drinking problem?"

"Absolutely not. She was a social drinker. One or two drinks at a gathering. Occasionally three. I never saw her drunk."

Gina made a mental note to talk to a pathologist she had befriended to help her make sense of the police report.

"Was she riding alone or with a group?"

"It was a tour. There were three or four other skiers and a guide."

"Do you know if the police interviewed the other people on the tour?"

"They said they did. The police report said they all admitted they had been drinking at lunch."

Admitted, Gina thought to herself. They make it sound as if they were doing something criminal.

"Did the police speak to the outfit that provided the Jet Skis?"

"They did. Predictably, the proprietor claimed all of his Jet Skis were in excellent working order."

"Did *you* speak to the person who rented her the Jet Ski?"

"No. I'll admit to feeling shell-shocked when I was down there. It's a terrible feeling to open drawers and move your sister's personal items into her suitcase. The last thing I wanted to do was talk to the people who provided the ski."

"I can certainly understand that. I'm sorry to be asking you all these questions."

"It's okay. Let's keep going."

"Did anybody examine the ski after the accident?"

"I didn't think to ask about that. I don't know if any experts looked at it."

"Did the police report reach any conclusions regarding what happened?"

"It attributed the accident to operator error. It said Cathy probably panicked after inadvertently putting the ski on full throttle. Her panic likely was made worse because she had consumed a large amount of alcohol in a short time before the accident."

"Were you given a copy of the police report?"

"Yes, I was."

"Would you be willing to share that with me?"

"Of course. I had it scanned. I'm calling you on my cell. Text me your email address and I'll send the report."

"If you can get me some recent pictures of Cathy, that would be helpful."

"I'll see what I can find and send them along with the police report. Do you really think that Cathy's death was not an accident?"

"I'm not sure what to think. But there's one thing I

can say. I don't like coincidences. A powerful corporation was negotiating with, maybe pressuring somebody to accept a settlement. That person may have been reluctant. And all of a sudden that person dies in an accident. In my opinion, that's too much of a coincidence."

"My God, to think anyone would have deliberately killed my sister! They're calling my group number to board. I'm sure we will speak again."

"We will. Have a nice flight."

The connection ended.

10

After showering and getting dressed, Gina, laptop under her arm, walked to the corner and ordered a vanilla latte from Starbucks. When she was writing her articles, she preferred the solitude and quiet of her apartment. But when she was answering emails and doing research, she enjoyed the background noise the coffeehouse never failed to provide.

Settling at a table near the center of the store, she woke up her computer and started to educate herself about Aruba. The little knowledge she had was the result of reading and watching reports of the Natalee Holloway murder.

Her first stop was Wikipedia. As she read, she jotted notes.

> 18 miles north of Venezuela. In what's often referred to as "Dutch Caribbean." Constituent country of the Kingdom of the Netherlands. Sandy white beaches. Population

100,000. Popular with tourists because very little rainfall.

A fact caught the attention of the history buff in her.

Peter Stuyvesant in 1642 was appointed governor before being sent to his new post in New Amsterdam which would later be renamed New York City.

Switching over to a travel site, she found direct flights from JFK to Aruba. She could go round trip for $666. And the hotels were very reasonable. She definitely wanted to book the hotel Cathy Ryan stayed in. She wrote herself a reminder to get that information from Andrew.

Gina took a long sip of her coffee, savoring the sensation of the hot liquid passing downward from her throat. She thought to herself, I'm pretty sure I have enough to convince *ER* to send me down to Aruba. But I'd love to be able to tell them how, if at all, Meg Williamson fits into the story.

With a little luck, Gina thought, she would get Meg's number later in the day from Mrs. Ryan. She wanted to be completely thought out on what she would say to Meg before she made contact. Did Meg work at REL News for all or a portion of the three years Cathy Ryan was there? How close are/were Cathy and Meg? Did Meg even know that Cathy died two weeks ago? Did Meg also have a "terrible experience" at REL News? If no, did Cathy share anything about her experience with Meg? Or if Meg had accepted a settlement, would she even speak to Gina?

She opened her email and hit NEW. After a few keystrokes, Geoff's name appeared. *Hi Geoff, I have some updates on the REL News situation I want to share with you. Are you free for a meet?*

Thirty seconds later his response chimed in. *Tied up until 4. Can you come then?*

Okay. See you at 4.

11

Back in the apartment, on the chance that Geoff would give her an immediate okay, Gina pulled a few warm-weather clothes from her closet and laid them on her bed. She knew that if she ended up going, she would be there for two or three overnights, so it was not hard to put together everything she would need. She made a mental note to pick up some sunblock.

While Gina waited, she went online and reread news accounts of the Natalee Holloway murder. For all I know, she thought, I might be interacting with some of the same locals who worked on Natalee's case. What struck her was that Natalee's parents had had to wait so long to find out what happened to their daughter and for an arrest to be made. Any doubt about the role of Joran van der Sloot, a resident she had met down there, played in her murder was erased when, a few years later, he killed another young woman.

A text message arrived from Andrew Ryan. His mother had found Meg Williamson's number.

Great! Gina thought as she picked up her phone and started dialing. She decided to tweak the approach she had used when she was trying to find CRyan. After five rings and no answer an electronic voice identified the number she had dialed and invited her to leave a message. "Hi, my name is Gina Kane. I'm a print journalist. I'm writing an article about women who have gone to work for broadcast media companies over the last ten to fifteen years. I understand you worked at REL News. I'd love to speak with you. Please give me a call. My cell number is . . ."

12

Meg Williamson did not go into work at the PR firm in White Plains that morning. Instead she took her six-year-old daughter, Jillian, directly to the pediatrician. Jillian had been coughing during the night and had a slight fever. When they got home, Meg went through her phone messages. When she listened to the one from Gina Kane, she gasped and played it again.

Terrified, she knew what she had to do. For the first time in almost two years, she dialed the number Michael Carter had given her. He answered on the first ring. "What is it, Meg?"

"I just received a message on my phone. I wrote it down to make sure I got it right." She read him Gina's message.

"First thing. Give me her name and the number she wanted you to use to call her back." Meg gave him both. There was a long pause. Then, in a slow, deliberate voice Carter said, "I know how these reporters work. They reach out to a lot of people, but they end up interviewing only a handful of them. Ignore the message. Let her interview somebody else. You did the right thing. If she attempts to contact you again, call me."

"Of course, I will," Meg responded quickly. "I promise—" The call had been disconnected.

13

In high school and college Gina had been very casual about arriving on time. When a class was taught in a lecture hall, she would often slink into a seat in the back row to avoid the attention of the professor. Her experience as a journalist had made her the opposite. She was now not only punctual; she always arrived early for her appointments. At 3:45 she was in the downstairs lobby of *Empire Review* with the guard announcing her arrival.

When she exited the elevator, Jane Patwell was waiting to greet her. "It's just as well you came early," she said. "Geoff's last appointment ended early. He's ready to see you now."

She paused and added, "Gina, you look so pretty. I love that slacks suit. You should always wear blue. I mean especially that deep rich shade."

Gina knew what Jane was driving at. She thinks I'm dressing up for Geoff, she thought, amused. Am I? she asked herself with a smile.

Jane knocked on Geoff's door and opened it as he called, "Come in."

When he saw it was Gina, he stood up quickly and motioned her to the table by the window.

"Now that it's your show, how's it going?" she asked as she settled into a chair.

"Hectic, but all in all very good. Now, tell me, what's new at REL News?"

Gina quickly summarized her eventually successful attempt to find Cathy Ryan, her conversation with Andrew, and Cathy's untimely death on the Jet Ski. She explained that she was in the early stages of pursuing a lead on a woman who worked with Cathy at REL News.

Geoff paused, deep in thought. "I have a feeling you're going to tell me that the Jet Ski incident might not have been an accident."

"Precisely," Gina said. "The only way to find out what really happened is for me to go down there, stay at the same hotel, meet whoever rented her the Jet Ski, and the investigator who worked on her case. Basically, just start asking questions."

"When can you leave?"

"There's an afternoon flight tomorrow from JFK straight to Aruba. I think I'll need two to three days on the ground there."

"Will a three-thousand-dollar advance for expenses be sufficient?"

"Yes."

"Book your flight. I'll take care of the advance."

As she walked to the door he called to her. "Gina, if you're right, and I think you are, someone went through an awful lot of trouble to arrange Cathy Ryan's death to make it look like an accident. Be careful down there."

14

I never thought I'd be on another trip so quickly, Gina thought as she boarded the JetBlue flight to Aruba. As soon as the Airbus 320 was in the air, she began to read the news accounts she had printed on the Holloway case.

On a high school graduation trip to Aruba eighteen-year-old Natalee Holloway had disappeared. . . .

Gina's overall impression was that the local police had stonewalled the FBI's attempts to investigate the disappearance. If they stiff-armed the FBI, she thought, I can only imagine what they'll try to do to me.

The email from Andrew Ryan, with several attachments, had arrived last evening. Along with the police report, Andrew had included several photos of Cathy, explaining in the email that these were the most recent he could find.

Gina studied the pictures. One was on a beach. A smiling Cathy was standing next to a surfboard that was as tall as she was. Because she was the only one in the picture, it was hard to determine her height. A blue one-piece bathing suit hugged her trim, athletic body. Her long dark brown hair fell almost to her shoulders. Dimples were visible in a broad smile accentuated by exceptionally white teeth. Slightly round facial features suggested a certain tomboy quality.

A second photo showed Cathy sitting at a table. A cake with lit candles was visible on the lower left. Gina wondered if this was taken at their mother's birthday party just before Cathy left for Aruba. Cathy looked different. Her smile looked forced; the corners of her mouth barely turned up. Although she was looking at the camera, she appeared distracted, as if her mind was far away.

Next Gina removed the police report and reread it carefully. She wasn't concerned that she would not be able to meet Peter van Riper, the patrol officer who had responded to the call about an accident at the pier. She was told he was away on vacation.

She was far more interested in talking to Hans Werimus, the investigator who had conducted the interviews and who had reached the conclusion that Cathy's death was the result of an accident. Werimus had agreed to see her on Thursday. That gave her the balance of today and tomorrow to meet the others on her list.

Aruba delivered on its reputation for good weather. It was sunny and seventy-seven degrees when Gina left the airport and boarded a taxi for the twenty-minute ride to the hotel.

They weren't kidding when they described this island as desertlike, she thought to herself. The gently rolling hills were mostly brown. From her research she knew that the best beaches and water conditions were on the northwest side of the island, where she would be staying. The other side was for the most part undeveloped.

The Americana Hotel was busy during this week in October. From the information Andrew had sent her she knew that Cathy had stayed in Room 514. While registering at the desk, she asked if that room was available. The young woman clerk eyed her suspiciously. "Is there any reason you want that particular room?"

Not wanting to tip her hand, Gina replied, "My mother was born on May 14. I've always considered five and fourteen to be lucky numbers."

"Well, your numbers continue to be lucky. I'm putting you in Room 514."

Gina refused help from the bellhop. She only had one small suitcase and it was on rollers.

Not knowing what to expect, she inserted her electronic key into the room door lock. When the light turned green, she turned the door handle and stepped into the spacious L-shaped room.

It turned out to be a large corner room with floor-to-ceiling windows offering a view of the Caribbean. A gentle, salty breeze off the water was blowing through the open windows. The king-size bed was positioned to capture the setting sun. Night tables were on either side of the bed. The wall unit housed the television and had three sets of drawers on each side below it. A newspaper and a booklet bearing the hotel's logo were on the countertop.

Gina tried to imagine what it must have been like for Andrew Ryan to come into this room and collect his sister's clothes and toiletries, knowing that the reality of her death had barely set in.

Trying to shake off those thoughts, she unpacked her things and glanced at her watch. 7:30. No wonder she was hungry. She had skipped lunch, and the snack on the plane had been minimal.

Gina briefly touched up her hair and changed into a pair of summer-weight slacks and a short-sleeve shirt. She started to reach for the latest edition of *ER* from her travel bag, but instead grabbed the newspaper and the hotel booklet. Friends often asked her if she felt uncomfortable going to dinner alone. Her answer was "Quite the opposite." Being raised as an only child had made her not only comfortable with it but fond of time spent losing herself in a book or a magazine article. There was nothing lonely about solitude; it was an opportunity.

The hotel dining room was about half-filled. She accepted the maître d's offer of a table in the corner. As she followed him, she overheard several conversations in English. One older couple was speaking a foreign language that she assumed was Dutch.

There were two tables opposite hers, each occupied by a couple who appeared to be in their early to mid thirties. One pair clinked glasses, and she smiled at the conclusion of the toast he made. The only word she could hear was "beginning." The other couple leaned across the table and kissed, lingering for a moment before they settled back in their chairs. Honeymooners, she guessed.

She glanced over the wall of windows, past the pool, and studied the timeless, gentle motion of the blue-green Caribbean water. Given license to wander, her mind settled on the memory of her favorite picture of her parents. It was taken while they were on their honeymoon at the Southampton Princess in Bermuda.

Next she browsed the *Aruba Daily*, the island's only English-language newspaper. There were no stories about any crimes committed on the island.

While eating, Gina casually glanced at the activities sheet that had been left on the wall unit in her room. *All activities can be arranged by the hotel concierge.* There was a daily trip for those interested in scuba diving, as well as lessons for beginners. There were three different snorkeling trips that would ferry guests to a reef just offshore. A *See Aruba in a Day* excursion would leave early the next morning and include breakfast and lunch.

The next item attracted her full attention.

> Jet Skiers Delight! Four hours of fun! Our expert guide will lead you on a 90-minute trip along our beautiful coastline, stopping to point out historic and other fascinating destinations. Break for one hour for lunch at the famous Tierra Mar restaurant on the water. After a quick ride back to our beach,

> enjoy another hour of fun on your own on our state-of-the-art Jet Ski. Must be 16 years of age or older to operate ski.

Change of plans, Gina thought to herself. Her original idea had been to rent a car and drive to the Jet Ski location and then to the restaurant. Why not experience for herself what Cathy was doing up until the last moments of her life?

On her way back to her room she stopped at the concierge desk and made a reservation for the next day's Jet Ski tour. A hotel jitney would provide free transportation to the ski rental facility. "Yes," she was told, "there are taxis available if you prefer not to take the jitney." She could tell that the concierge found it odd, even suspicious, that she wanted to get to the concession early.

It was only nine-thirty, but she decided to go right to bed. She clicked off the light and allowed her eyes to adjust to the darkness. A faint glow of moonlight made the shapes of the furniture in the room barely visible. She tried to imagine what thoughts had been in her head as Cathy Ryan drifted off to sleep for the very last time.

15

Gina opened her eyes and glanced around the room. For a moment she was startled and didn't know where she was. Everything looked so different from the small inns and tents they had stayed in during the hiking trip. "You're not in Kansas anymore, Dorothy," she joked to herself as she glanced out the window at the sun slowly rising over the Atlantic.

The small bedside alarm clock showed 6:45 a.m.

She slipped on jogging clothes and a sun visor and went for a thirty-minute run along the main road. When she got back to her room, she carried her laptop to the small desk in the corner of the room. Fourteen NEW messages greeted her, nothing from Meg Williamson. The only message she opened was from Ted.

> Hey there. I didn't call last night because I wanted to make sure I didn't wake you up. Hard to describe how much I miss you. Even if I tried, I'd fall short. It's tough being

in love with a writer! LOL. LA is oven hot. Enjoy but be careful in Aruba. Love you to death. Ted

Gina sighed and got up from her chair. Why can't I feel about him the way he feels about me? It would be so much easier, she thought, if I was as sure about him as he is about me. She headed into the bathroom and ran water for a shower. She would go to the business office to print the pictures of Cathy before going to breakfast. Maybe the waiters would have more time to chat if she got there early.

The breakfast room was almost empty when she entered. Two waitresses appeared to be on duty. A young couple wearing clothing more suited for a colder climate was finishing their meal. They're probably headed to the airport and back to wherever, Gina thought.

Gina had a choice to serve herself at the buffet or order from the menu. The buffet looked tempting, but it would reduce her chance to naturally interact with the waiters. Seating herself at a table near the window, she slid the pictures she'd printed of Cathy out of her beach bag and put them on the table.

As she readied herself to talk to anyone who might remember meeting Cathy two weeks ago, she tried to focus on what information would be most helpful to her. According to Andrew, Cathy had come here alone. Cathy might have kept quiet about a plan to meet someone here, possibly whoever was negotiating with her on behalf of REL News. But why would the REL News negotiator go through the trouble to traipse all the way down to Aruba when it would have been much easier to see Cathy in Atlanta?

Another possibility was that the negotiator might have surprised Cathy with his or her presence here. If Cathy put off talking to him by saying that she was going to Palm Beach and then Aruba for a few days, it would not have been hard to find the hotel where she was staying. As Gina knew well, newspeople were very good at getting sources to share confidential information.

A waitress in a crisp short-sleeve white shirt and tight-fitting black pants came to her table carrying a pot. "Anna" was on the nameplate clipped to her breast pocket. "Yes," Gina replied to her offer of coffee. As she was pouring, Gina pointed to the pictures of Cathy on the table.

"My friend stayed at this hotel about two weeks ago. By any chance do you recognize and remember her?"

"We have so many guests," Anna started to say. She glanced at the picture, and her expression quickly changed, becoming more serious.

"Your friend is the woman who died in the accident. I'm so sorry."

"Thank you. So am I," Gina replied. "I believe my friend, Cathy, might have met someone at the hotel just before," she paused, "her accident. I'm trying to figure out who that might have been. Do you recall Cathy spending time with anyone?"

"No. She was like you. By herself. I waited on her at

dinner once. She was very nice. Very polite. I remember she asked for a table apart from the other guests. She brought a magazine to her table. But I never saw her reading it. She just stared out the window at the water."

"If you remember anything about Cathy, please be in touch," Gina asked, dropping her voice as she handed over her card.

"Of course, I will," Anna promised. "It was so sad about your friend. She was so young and so pretty."

"Yes, she was," Gina said. "Now, one last favor. Would you ask the other waitress to come over and take my order? I want to ask her about Cathy."

As it turned out the other waitress had no recollection of Cathy.

The cab ride to the Jet Ski rental took about five minutes. She told the driver she would not need a ride back to the hotel.

Gina walked from the parking area across a path of wooden planks that zigzagged its way to a small office. The walls were lined with pictures of past clients, presumably happy renters. The bulletin board behind the counter suggested that Paradise Rentals offered a little bit of everything. In addition to the Jet Skis, small sailboats were available, as well as SUPs, stand-up paddleboards.

The couple in front of her finished paying for their sailboat, and the man behind the counter turned to Gina. "Good morning, do you have a reservation?"

He appeared to be about sixty. His deeply tanned face was creased with wrinkles. Thinning gray hair was combed backward and hung behind a baseball cap. Gina guessed him to be the proprietor as she recognized his face in most of the pictures on the wall.

As the owner, he'd likely be suspicious of anyone asking questions about an accident involving one of his rentals, Gina decided.

"Yes," she replied. "I'm with the tour group from the Americana Hotel."

"You're early," he said, glancing at his watch.

"I know. I thought it would be nice if someone could take a little extra time to familiarize me with the ski before I took off. I've never ridden one before."

He sighed. "Go outside to the right and down to the gas dock. Klaus will tell you what to do."

Gina left the office, glanced to her right, and saw a hunched-over teenager putting gas in one of the skis. She walked over to him and he looked up, his glance lingering on her long, shapely legs. His thick blond hair hung halfway over his ears. Deep blue eyes stood out behind a handsome face. A Speedo bathing suit was the only cover of a slender but well-muscled torso.

"Are you Klaus?" Gina asked.

"Yes, I am," he said, his English revealing a distinct German accent.

"Your boss said you could help me out. Before I go on the tour at eleven o'clock, I want to learn a little about how these things work."

"Don't worry. They're easy to operate. Are you from the Americana Hotel? I'll be leading your tour."

"Are you the guide on all the tours?"

"Peter and I used to split them until he quit last month. Now I do them all until they hire somebody else."

"I understand that in the middle of a tour a woman named Cathy Ryan was killed in an accident two weeks ago. Were you her tour guide?"

Klaus put his head down and glanced over at the office, where the owner was leading a family toward the sailboats, before he spoke softly. "There's a bar called the Silly Parrot about a kilometer south of your hotel. Tonight at six-thirty. We can talk there."

Klaus then raised the volume of his voice as the owner approached. "Don't worry. We get plenty of first-timers using our skis. Just follow a few basic rules and you'll be fine."

16

About fifteen minutes later the jitney from the hotel arrived. Two couples who appeared to be in their late twenties or early thirties and a man in his fifties got off and walked down to the boathouse. After they checked in, introductions were made. The couples were honeymooners from Minneapolis and Cleveland. The man, who introduced himself as Richie, asked, "So Gina, are you here by yourself?"

This is the last thing I need, she thought. A little white lie will nip this in the bud. "Yes, for now. My fiancé will arrive tomorrow."

"Lucky him," Richie said, obviously trying to conceal his disappointment.

Klaus came over, introduced himself as the tour guide, and asked the group to follow him. He climbed onto a ski while the others remained on the pier. "Anything you want to keep dry, put in here," he said while pointing to a small saddlebag behind the seat. "Although you will be riding on several different models, the controls are in the same place." He flipped a switch to start the ski. "It's in neutral now. When you put it in forward gear, turn your right hand grip to speed up, let go of the grip to slow down. A few basic rules of the road . . ."

"Is there a brake?" the honeymooner from Minneapolis asked.

"No brakes," Klaus said, smiling. "As soon as you stop giving it gas, the water will slow you quickly down."

Fifteen minutes later they were speeding along the coast. From the lead position Klaus put his hand up, signaling everyone to slow down. Pointing to the remains of a fort, he shared information about the early days of the Dutch settlers on the island and their interaction with the Caiquetio Indians of the Arawak tribe from Venezuela.

Gina was enjoying herself. She experienced an ounce of guilt, but only for an instant, knowing that she would bill this tour to the magazine as part of her research.

After three more stops they pulled in to a pier next to the Tierra Mar restaurant. Fishing boats and yachts of various sizes bobbed gently in their slips.

Gina remembered from the guidebook that this was where the tour would break for lunch. She thought of Cathy Ryan docking her ski, going inside for what would be her last meal.

They fetched their personal items from the saddlebag on each ski and followed Klaus into the restaurant. A table for seven had been reserved. It was just to the right of the bar and enjoyed a view of the azure-blue water and the coastline. Richie was quick to take the seat next to

Gina. Her telling him that she was engaged had not delivered the intended message.

The waiter insisted that everyone try their world-famous piña coladas. After some hesitation they all nodded and decided to go along. Klaus alone demurred in favor of a Coke.

Everyone ordered fish, and twenty minutes later they unanimously raved that it was very good. The waiter came over and without being asked began refilling the piña colada glasses. Gina held her hand over her glass and asked for an iced tea. The newlyweds looked at each other, shrugged, and accepted their second cocktails. "In for a penny, in for a pound," Richie said as he watched the creamy white liquid inch up inside his glass.

Gina asked Klaus, "Do they always reserve this table for the Jet Ski tour?"

"Whenever we have six people on the tour, which is almost always, they save this table for us," he replied.

After lunch Klaus led them back to Paradise Rentals. "We stayed a little overtime at lunch," he announced. "You can ride on your own now. Please have the skis back in forty-five minutes."

The four newlyweds took off in a race to the open ocean. Gina decided to head in. She wanted time by herself. She was relieved when, after hesitating, Richie gunned his ski in the opposite direction from the others. If he had been hoping she would follow his lead, he was sorely disappointed.

17

The atmosphere was quiet on the jitney ride back to the hotel. A long day in the hot sun and the two piña coladas had taken their toll on both sets of newlyweds. Although it was only a ten-minute ride, they appeared to be dozing. The couple from Minnesota was in the seat in front of Gina. His head leaned against the window while her head rested against his shoulder. A bright red sunburn was apparent on the back of his neck and upper back. He should have used a little more sunblock on that Viking skin, Gina decided.

Back in her room she set her iPhone alarm to wake her at 4:30. Within minutes she was fast asleep.

She was out on the water heading for the open sea. The Jet Ski was skimming quickly and effortlessly across the glassy calm water. To the right of her was Klaus, his blond hair trailing behind him. He waved and she smiled back at him. To her left and slightly behind her was Ted. She looked back at him and his face was anguished. He was shouting something, but she couldn't make out what he was yelling. "Out" was all she heard. She turned her head forward and Klaus was no longer to her right. Directly in front of her, barely twenty yards away, was a small yacht. She was going to crash into it. She thought of trying to jump off the ski, but there was not enough time. Her heart racing, her mouth open wide, she began to scream.

Gina opened her eyes. Both hands were clenched in fists, gripping her pillow. She was breathing heavily, as if she had just completed a run around Central Park. Small beads of sweat were on her forehead. She lay still for a minute, thankful for the safety of her hotel room. She wished Ted was in the room with her. Or her father. Someone to hold and to be held by.

Her iPhone began to chime its wake-up tone.

18

The concierge spotted Gina walking across the lobby. "I see you're headed out. Would you like a taxi?"

"No thanks," Gina said. "Just to be sure. I'm meeting a friend for a drink at the Silly Parrot. I can walk there in about fifteen minutes. Correct?"

"Yes. Ten to fifteen minutes," he said, pointing out and to his right. "You can walk along the road, but it's a nicer walk along the beach."

"The beach it is," Gina said as she put on her sunglasses and headed outside.

The concierge waited until Gina was out of sight and then disappeared into his small office beyond the luggage room. Removing the piece of paper from his wallet, he began dialing the number for the second time that day.

The phone was answered after one ring. The greeting was the same as this morning. "Talk to me."

"Gina Kane asked the waitresses at breakfast about Cathy Ryan—"

"We already discussed that," the voice interrupted. "Tell me what I don't know."

"All right. Miss Kane went on the Jet Ski tour this afternoon. She's now going to meet somebody at a nearby bar, the Silly Parrot."

"Keep me informed" was the response before the connection was ended.

The concierge smiled as he slipped the paper with the phone number back into his wallet. It was easy to tolerate the rude American on the other end of the phone as he thought about how he would spend the $2,000 that would be wired to his bank account.

19

Gina was lost in thought as she walked, beach bag in hand, across the smooth white sand. She was crossing what appeared to be a public beach. Parents had dropped their towels and staked their umbrellas close to the water where they could keep a close eye on their young children. Two boys who she guessed to be about thirteen were skillfully tossing a Frisbee back and forth. A group of young couples, two on each side, were enjoying a game of beach volleyball.

She thought about her parents. High school sweethearts. He had gone to the all-boys Catholic high school in Oradell, New Jersey. Her mother went to the all-girls sister school. They would hold dances, "mixers," her mom and dad called them, which were supervised by parents who got roped into being chaperones.

Gina never tired of her father telling the story. "I'm sixteen years old, a junior, and I'm standing with a group of my friends from the track team. I look across the gym and I see this beautiful girl talking to her girlfriends. We made eye contact for just a second. But she smiled at me and went back to talking. To this day I don't know where

I found the courage to go over and introduce myself." He would always add with a laugh, "I really would have felt like a fool if she was smiling at the guy behind me, but luckily the thought never occurred to me."

Her mother's response was always the same. "Honey, I was really fortunate. The first guy I ever really kissed turned out to be a prince. I got to skip all the frogs!"

Looking down the beach, Gina spotted a large wooden red parrot with one eye in a wink. It sat atop a thatched roof. Beneath the roof was a long bar with high stools. Tables were under the roof for those who preferred shade and on the sand for those who had not had enough sun. About half of the tables were occupied.

A waitress in a bikini approached her. "Just one?" she asked.

"No, I'm meeting someone."

"Would you like to sit at the bar?"

Gina looked around. A table near the pool was unoccupied, as were the tables closest to it. Pointing, she asked, "Okay if I have that one?"

"Sure," the waitress replied, leading her over. "Do you know what you'd like to drink?"

"A sparkling water for now. I'll order something when my friend gets here."

Gina reached into her beach bag and pulled out the small notebook she always carried. She did a scribble with her pen to make sure it worked.

She saw Klaus enter the bar area from the street side.

She put her arm up and waved. He nodded and made his way over to the table.

"You made it. Thank you," he said.

"I'm the one who should thank you," she replied.

Seeing the waitress headed their way, Gina said, "I'm buying. What will you have?"

Distracted for a moment by the waitress's bikini, Klaus ordered a Heineken. His eyes lingered on her as she made her way back to the bar.

"Don't worry," Gina said, "you'll see her again when she brings our drinks."

"Was I that obvious?" he asked sheepishly.

"Yes, but if she didn't want men to look, she wouldn't wear that outfit."

Relieved, he laughed.

"So Klaus, do you have a last name?" Gina asked with a smile.

"Yes," he replied. "Webber, with two Bs."

"Where are you from?"

"Hamburg, Germany."

"Your English is excellent. Did you grow up speaking it?"

"My mother worked as a translator. She spoke English to me all the time. She said it will help me someday when I pick a career. She was right."

"How old are you?"

"Nineteen."

"That's pretty young to already know what kind of work you want to do."

"In Germany it's different. In America it seems like everybody goes to college whether it makes sense to go or not. In Germany if you go to a good technical high school and do well on the finishing exam, you can get an excellent job."

"Are you talking about the job at Paradise Rentals?"

His broad laugh revealed two rows of even white teeth. "Of course not. You're American, yes?"

"I am. From New York City."

"You know BMW, the German carmaker, yes?"

"Of course."

"In Woodcliff Lake, New Jersey, which is near New York City, BMW has its American headquarters. Every year they bring in trainees from around the world. They teach them to repair and design their products, and then send them to countries all over the world. Some of the trainees are college graduates; others like me went to technical high schools."

"That certainly makes a lot of sense. In the United States so many young people are saddled with hundreds of thousands in student debt and they can't even find a job. So at BMW, you are going to learn to work on their cars?"

"No, motorcycles are my specialty. I've been riding them since I was fourteen. I built my first bike myself. The Japanese sell the most motorcycles, but BMW and Harley-Davidson make the best ones."

"Okay. You went to high school in Hamburg. You're going to work for BMW. How did you end up in Aruba?"

"The BMW training program begins in September.

I've always been interested in Jet Skis. For me they are like motorcycles that go on the water. I bought a couple old ones. Took them apart. Put them back together to see how they worked. I was looking at a magazine that advertises Jet Skis. There were ads in the back. One of the ads was for a technician to work at Paradise Rentals. I applied, they accepted, and I started here two months ago. I am honest. I told them I would leave in August."

"Klaus, I appreciate the opportunity to learn about your background. You may be the perfect person to help me."

"Help you do what?"

"When I first met you at the gas dock and asked about Cathy Ryan, you didn't want to talk to me there. Why not?"

"Before I answer, can I ask, are you with the American police?"

"No."

"The Aruba police?"

"No, I'm a journalist."

"A reporter?"

Gina was uncertain about how much to share with him. "Yes, you could say I'm a reporter. I'm investigating an American company. A number of the employees had bad experiences when they worked at that company. I want to find those former employees and learn what happened to them."

"And Cathy Ryan was one of these employees?"

"Yes, she was. I assume you were the tour guide the day Cathy came to Paradise Rentals."

Klaus nodded.

“Tell me everything you remember about her.”

“I meet a lot of people at the shop, but she is easy to remember.”

“Why?”

“Because, not like you, she was a very experienced rider.”

“How do you know that?”

“You may have noticed that the skis at the shop are made by different manufacturers.”

“I didn’t, but go on.”

“After I gave Cathy’s tour the instruction on how to operate the skis, she noticed the newest Kawasaki model that was recently added to the fleet. She said she had ridden the others and asked if she could try that one.”

“And what did you say?”

“I said yes. The others on the tour didn’t care which ski they rode.”

“Aside from being knowledgeable about skis, do you remember anything about her mood? Was she happy? Sad?”

“She was friendly, but quiet. She didn’t smile much. She reminded me a little bit of you.”

“Me?” Gina asked, surprised.

“Yes. There were three guys thirties age in the group. They tried to get her to talk. She wasn’t rude, but she made it clear she wanted to be on her own.”

“Did the tour go to lunch at the Tierra Mar restaurant, the same one we went to?”

“Yes.”

"Did you sit at the same table?"

"Yes. Is that important?"

"It might be. Klaus, it will be easier if I tell you what I am trying to do. Can I trust you to keep this conversation confidential?"

He nodded.

"The Aruba authorities conducted an investigation of Cathy Ryan's death." Gesturing to her bag, she said, "I've read the police report. They quickly concluded it was an accident caused by operator error and that Cathy was drunk at the time of the collision. In other words, it was entirely Cathy's fault. I have reason to believe that it may not have been an accident."

Klaus took a long sip from his beer. "I want to help you if I can."

"Did you see the accident happen?"

"A little bit. I was last to leave the restaurant. I meet with the manager to make sure the names on the reservation are the same as those people on the tour. I was just walking outside when I heard someone yelling. I looked and saw Cathy smash into the yacht."

"What did you do?"

"I ran to my ski and rode out to try to help."

"Did the people on the yacht try to help her?"

"I saw the man and woman. They were very old. Maybe seventy-five years. They could not help. They told me they called the police."

"Where were the other people on the tour?"

"They had started to ride back toward the shop. As you

know, the skis are very loud. Unless they turned around to look, they would not know about Cathy."

"What happened next?"

"When I got to Cathy, she was not conscious. Her face was down in the water. She was floating because she was wearing her vest. I pulled her on the seat of my ski and I came back to the dock. Very quickly a police car came, followed by an ambulance. They started pushing on her chest." His face took on a pained expression. "Then they put her on a bed, put a mask over her face, and carried her to the ambulance. I could tell they believed it was too late."

"When you were with her, did she ever regain consciousness?"

"No."

"The police report concluded that Cathy panicked. She kept accelerating until she hit the yacht."

"That is very surprising."

"Why do you say that?"

"Because we have so many beginners rent the skis. And so many idiots who all they want to do is race. Cathy was experienced and careful. She was not the type to panic."

"Klaus, when we were at the lunch table today, I couldn't see our skis from where we were sitting. If someone wanted Cathy to have an accident on her ski, is there something he could do to it?"

"You mean, *sabotage it*?"

"Yes."

Klaus exhaled. "The ski is designed to lose power when you release the hand grip with your right hand. You could put a small cover with a spring on the hand grip to cause it to stay at full power even after you let go."

"What would you do if the ski you were riding kept going at top speed even after you released the grip?"

"It's a strange situation. The safest thing, and the smart thing, would be to jump off the ski. You would hit the water hard, but you would be okay. I would probably spend a few seconds trying to fix the grip that was stuck."

"Would you be looking at the grip?"

"Probably."

"And that means not looking at what's ahead of you?"

"Again, probably yes."

"Do you know what happened to Cathy's Jet Ski after the accident?"

"It was badly broken apart. I saw pieces in the water when I rode to help Cathy."

"Do you know if anyone examined the ski after the accident?"

"I don't know. The police spoke to me for a few minutes on the dock before the ambulance took Cathy away. They told me to go back to Paradise Rentals and wait. An investigator would speak to me there."

"Did you—?"

"Before I left the dock, the police told me to phone the shop. I told the owner what happened. I also told him to tell the others on the tour to wait at the shop. The investigator wanted to speak to them also."

"Did the investigator interview all of you together?"

"In the beginning, no. He spoke to me and the owner.

He wanted to know if the ski Cathy was riding had any problems before the accident. I told him honestly no."

"And then he questioned the other riders?"

"Yes. None of them saw the accident. They had already ridden away. He was very interested in what happened at lunch and how much everyone had to drink."

"Was the restaurant pushing their 'world-famous piña coladas' like they were today?"

Klaus smiled. "Yes. The same as today."

"The police report states that everyone, including Cathy, drank a lot at lunch and that likely played a role in the accident."

"That's not correct. I had nothing to drink. And Cathy had very little."

"The restaurant bill that was added to her room charge shows she had two piña coladas. It's in the police report."

"When the waiter came around with more drinks, Cathy's glass was still halfway. Before she could say no, it was refilled. When we were getting ready to leave at the end of lunch, I noticed her glass was still to the top."

Klaus took the last sip of his beer and looked at his watch.

Gina said, "Klaus, I can't tell you how grateful I am. You've been very helpful." She reached into her bag for her card. "This has my cell phone and email address. If you can think of anything else—"

"I will contact you. Thank you for the beer."

20

Back in her hotel room Gina was too preoccupied to appreciate the beauty of the sunset. The bright orange ball had disappeared below the horizon. A yellow glow illuminated the puffy clouds before slowly fading into a peaceful twilight.

Her appointment with Inspector Werimus was at ten-thirty the next morning. It would be about a twenty-five-minute ride to police headquarters according to Google Maps.

Gina's initial plan to investigate Cathy Ryan's death included tracking down and speaking to each of the people who were on the Jet Ski tour with her the day of the accident. Their names were in the police report. Four were from the United States and one was from Canada. It wouldn't be hard to find them.

But what was she hoping to learn from them that she didn't already know from Klaus? Gina asked herself. If Cathy had any inkling that she was in danger, it was unlikely she would have shared it with anyone on the ski tour, or for that matter anyone at the hotel.

When she returned from meeting with Klaus, Gina spoke to the concierge. After confessing that he really shouldn't be sharing guest information, he revealed that when Cathy had her accident she had two more days on her hotel reservation. He told Gina he had no idea how Cathy intended to spend the remaining time. The only activity she had booked through the hotel was the ski tour.

There was only one other person in Aruba that Gina thought might be helpful to her. The owner of Paradise Rentals. She was annoyed at herself for not asking Klaus what happened to the ski after the accident. Maybe he didn't know. But the owner certainly would.

Gina considered but then passed on the idea of trying to talk to the owner tomorrow morning before her ten-thirty appointment. She might be in a better position to ask him questions after she met with the investigator.

For perhaps the tenth time that day she glanced at her phone hoping to see a voice mail or text from Meg Williamson. Undaunted, she opened her laptop and waited for her email to download. Scanning through it, she was disappointed to see no response from Meg. "It's the squeaky wheel that gets the grease," she said to herself as she phoned and left another message for Meg and then sent her another email.

Her mood brightened when she read the email from her father. He had been to the movies and also raved about a new restaurant that had just opened.

She felt relieved. In previous emails and phone conversations, he always wanted to talk about what she was doing, what story she was working on, how things were going with Ted. After telling him, she would ask, "Dad, enough about me. What have you been up to?" His answer was usually a vague "Don't worry about me. I'm okay." She whispered a prayer of thanks that he had so many friends in the community and that they were including him in their plans.

21

The Aruba police station was in the heart of Oranjestad, a city of thirty thousand people. The boxy, Spanish colonial–style building had a soft vanilla color exterior. Three rows of chairs were on either side of a center aisle where Gina entered. Directly ahead of her a uniformed policeman was seated behind a formidable wooden desk.

As Gina approached, the policeman had his head down reading the paper in front of him. Twenty seconds passed. Unsure about how to get his attention, she cleared her throat with a little more volume than was necessary. It worked.

She could now read the nameplate on his lapel. Knudsen looked up and apologized. Before he could continue, she said, "My name is Gina Kane. I am here to see Inspector Hans Werimus."

Pushing a clipboard in her direction, he asked her to sign in. "I have an appointment with him at ten-thirty."

"Please take a seat. I will let him know you are here."

Gina turned around, walked a few steps to the first

row of chairs, and sat down. Knudsen took several minutes to finish reading the apparently captivating report in front of him. She considered but decided against another attention-getting throat clearing. Her patience was finally rewarded when Knudsen picked up the phone and began dialing.

Thirty minutes passed. There was no point going over the police report again. She had nearly committed it to memory. She glanced at her watch. Almost eleven o'clock. The slow-turning wheels of justice, she thought to herself.

She heard the phone ring on Knudsen's desk. He answered and quickly put it back down. "Ms. Gina Kane," he said, making eye contact with her. He pointed to his left indicating a route she should follow around his desk. A man was waiting for her at the end of a long hallway. He was well over six feet tall. Gina remembered reading someplace that the Dutch were among the tallest people in the world; the average male was over six feet.

"Follow me, please," he said as he led her around a corner into an area of eight cubicles that were separated by shoulder-high partitions. From nearby voices she could tell that at least some of the cubicles were occupied.

Stopping at the second cubicle, the inspector pulled a desk chair around to face outward, gesturing toward a smaller chair. "Please sit," he said. "I'm sorry. We are a little cramped for space."

"I appreciate your taking the time to meet with me, Inspector Werimus. I have several questions I want to ask—"

"Before we go forward, Ms. Kane, I want to clear up a

possible misunderstanding. I am Inspector Andrew Tice. Inspector Werimus was dispatched to work on an emergency case and will be unavailable for the next several days."

"Frankly, that is very disappointing," Gina said, dropping her notebook on her lap. "I flew all the way down from New York to meet him."

"I am sorry for any inconvenience. Sometimes these things can't be avoided. Perhaps I can answer your questions."

"Perhaps," Gina said, with an edge of sarcasm in her tone.

Tice opened a drawer on his side of the desk and removed a file. "Before we begin, Ms. Kane, I am interested in learning more about why you are interested in this case. You told my colleague you are a writer?" he said, glancing at the file.

"That's correct."

"Of fiction?"

"No. What I do for a living, does that really matter?"

"It might," he said with a condescending smile. "Tell me, are you an attorney?"

"No, I'm not."

"You say you are a writer—"

"I am a writer," Gina responded with a condescending smile of her own.

"Very well. Are you a writer who works for a law firm?"

Gina decided to change tactics. "Inspector Tice, I have no affiliation with a law firm. But the more questions you ask, the more I'm tempted to consult with one. Can we get to my questions now?"

"I'm sorry, Ms. Kane. People from the United States have a fondness for filing lawsuits whenever something goes wrong. Lawsuits create bad publicity. Aruba is a small country that is very dependent on tourism, much of it from the United States. I will be happy to answer your questions."

Gina stared without seeing out the window of her cab as she headed back toward her hotel. She lamented the waste of time it had been to go to police headquarters. Tice knew very little that was not in the police report. Gina had challenged him on the patrol officer's finding that there was "a strong odor of alcoholic beverage" on Cathy's body. "Cathy Ryan had been facedown in the water for as much as two minutes. Can you explain to me how the officer would have been able to smell 'an alcoholic beverage' under those circumstances?"

"I cannot. But it would not have been in his report unless he observed it at the scene."

"So Patrol Officer van Riper noted the 'strong odor of alcoholic beverage' based on what he observed at the dock. Did he make this observation before or after learning that Cathy Ryan had been served alcohol at the restaurant?"

"I don't know the answer to that. I'm sorry."

So am I, Gina had thought.

Tice had stood by the accuracy of the report that

stated Cathy had consumed two drinks at lunch. Gina had been reluctant to name Klaus as her source of different information. If I drag him into this now, he might not be there if I need him later, she thought.

The only area where Tice had been somewhat helpful was telling her what happened to the ski after the accident. "The inspection concluded that the ski was in good working order before the accident, which was caused by operator error," he had told her. "It would then have been released to Paradise Rentals, its rightful owner."

"So the police transported the ski from the dock where the accident took place back to the rental shop?"

"No," he said. "We are not a delivery service. The owner of the ski would be responsible for retrieving it and transporting it to wherever he chose."

"And you don't know what Paradise Rentals did with the ski?"

"No, why would I?"

You're not interested in what happened to Cathy Ryan's ski, but I am, she thought.

"Excuse me," she called, raising her voice in an attempt to get the attention of the taxi driver.

He turned down the radio.

"Slight change of plans," she said as she gave him the address of the rental shop.

22

The owner was on the phone when Gina returned to the rental shop's small boathouse office. He was finalizing an order for four kayaks for the afternoon on the following day. Before entering, she had glanced down at the docks near the gas pump. There was no sign of Klaus and the Jet Skis were not in their dock slips. Probably leading today's tour, she thought.

Placing the phone down, the owner turned to Gina. "Can I help you?"

"Yes, you can," she said, "Mr. . . . ?"

"De Vries," he answered, pointing to a framed license hanging on the wall behind the counter.

"This is your place, Mr. De Vries?"

"For the last twenty-five years, yes," he said, smiling.

"Two and a half weeks ago, a young woman named Cathy Ryan was killed while riding a Jet Ski that was rented here."

"Are you a lawyer?" De Vries asked, the smile having been replaced by an angry stare.

Here we go again, Gina thought to herself. She spent the next two minutes assuring him that she did not work for a law firm, had no interest in suing him, and that she was convinced that the ski he had rented to Cathy was in good working order *when she rented it.*

"I want to find out what happened to the ski after the accident. The police said they released it to you. Did you bring it back here to your shop?"

"Of course not," he said. "How stupid do you think I am?"

"It was your property—"

"I know who it belonged to. You were on the ski tour yesterday. Am I right?"

"Yes."

"How would it look if you walked down to the dock and saw a wrecked ski? You'd ask, 'What happened?' I'd say, 'No big deal. A young lady who rented from us got killed when she crashed into a yacht in the harbor. But I'm sure you'll have a nice ride today.'"

"Okay," Gina said. "I understand why you wouldn't want to bring it back here. What did you do with it?"

"I called a carting service and told them to take it to the dump."

"You didn't want one of your people to look at it, to see if—"

"To see if what? The police told me the young lady, who by the way was drunk, had panicked and caused the accident. What was I supposed to look at?"

"Do you know what dump they took it to?"

"There's only one in this area, but you won't find the ski there."

"Why not?"

"Because it was over two weeks ago. I'm sure by now it's been crushed."

23

A little *crushed* was how Gina felt the next morning as she buckled her seatbelt for the almost five-hour flight from Aruba to JFK. Leaving nothing to chance, she had rented a car and made the thirty-five-minute drive to the dump site that served the central part of the island. The sound of trucks going in and out had been punctuated every ten minutes by the high-pitched whine of a compactor and the crunching of its contents. A supervisor on-site had confirmed that items made from metal—cars, appliances, and yes, a Jet Ski—would be routed to the compactor to be crushed and sold for scrap. Typically, it took three days from arrival for a metal item to make its journey to the compactor. Nothing would remain of a Jet Ski that had been dumped almost three weeks ago.

The Airbus 320 accelerated down the runway and began its ascent over the blue-green waters below. The hydraulic hum signaled that the wheels had tucked inside the bowels of the aircraft. Gina stared out the window, lost in thought. "Stalemate" was the word running through her head. Her gut told her that she was on the right track. Someone had wanted Cathy Ryan dead and had made it look like an accident. But the Cathy Ryan trail, at least in Aruba, was cold. She was forced to pin her hopes on Meg Williamson, who for whatever reason was not responding to the messages she had left.

She had emailed Geoff to schedule a date to fill him in on what she had learned during her time in Aruba. His response had surprised her. He was traveling the early part of next week. If she wasn't too tired, could she meet him this afternoon? Gina had accepted.

She now faced a daunting task. Find a way to convince Geoff that the REL News story had legs at a time when she herself was uncertain about how to go forward.

At least tonight will be fun, she thought. Gina had agreed to Lisa's suggestion that they were overdue for a TGIF dinner. After the last few days in Aruba, I could use a few laughs, she thought as she started to write notes for her meeting at the magazine.

24

Geoff expected her at three-thirty. That gave her time to toss her few summer outfits on top of the washing machine and unpack her toiletries. It also gave her an opportunity to call her father. When she had tried to reach him before she left for Aruba, she had only got his answering machine, and he had not replied. The faint feeling of uneasiness was released by his message. "Hi. Sorry I missed your call."

There was an unexpectedly buoyant sound in his voice. Welcome, but surprising. Her "Hi Dad" was immediately interrupted by his question "How was Aruba?"

"Better weather than New York. What about Florida?"

"It's been raining the last few days."

"Too bad. How have you been keeping yourself busy?"

"Oh, catching up on a few movies." Gina knew that her father hated to go to the movies alone. "Who did you go with?" she asked.

"A new neighbor who is a movie buff."

"Good for you."

"So how is your latest story going?"

She briefly filled him in on her progress or lack thereof. She followed her usual practice of not naming the company she was investigating. They chatted for a few minutes more. It was only after they disconnected that she realized her father had not mentioned the name of the new neighbor. She dismissed the thought as she put on a winter jacket and wrapped a scarf around her neck. It was time to head to the subway and a meeting with Geoff.

Thirty minutes later, when she arrived at *Empire*, Jane as usual was the one to greet her. "Always glad to see you. The boss said to send you in when you get here," she told her.

Gina knew she wasn't late, but even so she quickened her step until she was at Geoff's office. She knocked on the door and opened it when he called, "Come in, Gina."

He was seated at the table by the window again. She wondered if, just like Charles Maynard, he preferred it to his desk for small meetings. "Tell me about your vacation in Aruba," he suggested. Shocked, Gina stared at him. Did he really consider her trip a vacation?

But then he raised his eyebrows. "My too subtle British sense of humor. Forgive me, Gina. Now, tell me what happened there."

Gina explained her attempt to replicate Cathy Ryan's stay in Aruba; the same hotel room and Jet Ski tour. She carefully summarized the conversations she'd had, up to and including her visit to the dump site.

"Geoff, the key is the control device on the ski Cathy was using," she said. "Was it tampered with while she was having lunch with her group? Klaus from the ski shop said that would have been easy to do."

She continued. "It certainly appears that the Aruba police were determined to present Cathy's death as nothing but an unfortunate accident. Inadvertently or deliberately they allowed the evidence to be destroyed."

"Where do we go from here?"

"Cathy's brother mentioned the name of a friend from REL News she kept in contact with. Her name is Meg Williamson. I left several messages for her. I'm waiting to hear back."

"I'd say it's obvious that's the place to start," Geoff said wryly.

He stood up. It was clear to Gina that the meeting was over.

"I'll get on it right away," she told him. "Is there any place quiet I can make a phone call?"

"I'll ask Jane to put you in the small conference room."

"Don't bother. I know the way."

Two minutes later, closing the door behind her, keeping her fingers crossed, Gina dialed Meg Williamson's number. After four rings it went to voice mail.

25

"Mommy, why don't you answer the phone?" Jillian asked. Meg inadvertently put her fingers to her lips in a gesture of *shhhh*, then smiled self-consciously. "I can tell it's one of those calls from people trying to sell us something," she explained, even as she recognized Gina Kane's number from the earlier messages.

"Or saying that we won something, but only it's not true," Jillian replied as she left the living room and headed to the library, which was set up for her to do homework there.

Meg's eyes followed her six-year-old's progress. Jillian misses nothing, she thought fondly. And that's another reason I don't like her to be around when *he* phones.

She had told him about the phone messages from Gina. He had ordered her to ignore them. She had followed his instructions, but the phone calls were persisting. How long were they going to keep up?

26

After her attempt to reach Meg Williamson by phone, Gina left the conference room and went home. She had agreed to meet Lisa for dinner, but they had not set a place or time.

She phoned Lisa, who picked up on the first ring.

"Hey, Lisa. Any suggestions about where to go?"

"Any place except where the bartender may let ice cubes fly. The gal who broke her leg has now figured out that she also hurt her neck when she fell."

Gina laughed. "I want to hear all about it over a drink."

"And I want to hear about your sun and fun in Aruba. I'll make a reservation at Villa Cesare for seven-thirty."

Villa Cesare on 86th Street was one of those popular restaurants that was always crowded. Both she and Lisa went there regularly and were on a first name basis with the owner and most of the staff.

"I'll see you there," Gina confirmed. It's so good to have a really close friend, she thought as she put down the phone. And when she goes back a long way, it's even better.

She had been on the worst blind date of her life. It was the older brother of one of the girls in her dorm. He was a Harvard guy and completely full of himself. Her best part of the date was at the bar when he bumped into some Harvard classmates and started talking to them. And just kept on talking. That's when she met Lisa. By coincidence, Lisa, who was a sophomore at Boston University, was on a first date with one of the Harvard classmates. She was as bored as Gina. They started chatting and rescued each other from a disastrous evening. They had been fast friends ever since.

We were both nineteen, Gina thought. That was thirteen years ago. She never wanted to get married young. Well, mission accomplished, as her dad liked to say. Thirty-two no longer qualified as really young.

She put aside that thought. The most important thing right now was to somehow contact Meg Williamson. I've phoned her enough to be sued for harassment, she decided.

Lisa was already at the table sipping an apple martini when she arrived. Gina pulled up a chair and said, "You look down in the mouth, girlfriend. Anything wrong?"

"Nothing wrong. Just thinking about how little problems like drifting ice cubes can cause big problems." Lisa laughed. "So tell me. How was sunny Aruba?"

Gina sighed. "I guess the best way to describe it would be 'complicated.' I don't want to bore you with the details."

"Nothing could be more boring than the seven-hour deposition I sat through today. Come on. Tell me what happened."

Just as she had done with Geoff four hours earlier, Gina recounted the interviews she'd had during her stay on the island, and her conversations with Andrew Ryan. She concluded by saying, "My gut tells me that something serious is going on at REL News. But I don't want to fall into the trap of seeing a conspiracy behind every coincidence."

"Gina, as I told you the one other time we talked about this, when somebody is considering suing a big corporation, then that somebody dies in an accident, that's a huge red flag for me. And this Meg Williamson who's refusing to talk to you, that's another red flag. In her email, didn't Cathy Ryan say something about other victims?"

Gina quickly recited it from memory. "'I had a terrible experience with one of the higher-ups. And I wasn't the only one.'"

Lisa replied, "So either this begins and ends with Ryan and maybe Williamson or—"

Gina finished the sentence for her. "Or this is the tip of the iceberg. There are more victims, maybe a lot more."

Part II

Two Years Earlier

27

It was almost two years ago, on a Friday around five-thirty in the evening. The personnel offices were in a building across the street from the REL studios and newsgathering operation. Michael Carter, a lawyer in Human Resources, had stayed late to finish a project and had been looking forward to the weekend.

The knock on his door was soft. Lauren Pomerantz briefly introduced herself. She was a petite five feet three inches with auburn hair and bright brown eyes. He didn't recall having met her, but she was a familiar face from the company cafeteria. He remembered her appearing very nervous. She had to be persuaded to sit down.

Here we go again, Carter thought. The last time one of the early twenty-somethings knocked on his door it was to complain that there weren't enough gluten-free choices in the cafeteria. He wondered what this one wanted.

"Mr. Carter," she began, "I love my job at REL News. I didn't complain when I did my share of overnight shifts.

I hate that I have to leave. I did the right thing after it happened, but nobody did anything." Tears formed in her eyes and began streaming down her face. "And now I've been assigned to the team that's supposed to go with him to the convention." She convulsed into sobs and buried her head in her hands.

"Hey, it's okay. I want to help you," he said as he waited a few moments to allow her to compose herself. His first instinct was to touch her shoulders or her hands. His training told him: Don't!

"Do you mind if I sit opposite you?" he asked while pulling up a chair.

She shook her head.

"Lauren, let me begin by saying I'm glad you trusted me enough to come and see me. I want to help you. It may be painful for you to talk about, but I need to know what happened."

"You're not going to believe me."

"Before you decide how I'm going to react or what I'm going to do, please give me a chance."

"All right," she said and nodded. "Four weeks ago, on Wednesday the twenty-fourth, I was at my desk and I got a call from Evelyn Simms." Carter recognized the name of Brad Matthews's secretary. "She said Mr. Matthews wanted to personally thank me for the segment I had helped edit on the gun control legislation vote. She asked if I could come to his office after the broadcast that evening. Of course I said yes."

"And you went?" Carter asked.

Lauren nodded. "I stopped in the makeup room on my way. Rosalee wasn't busy, so she gave me a quick touch-up."

"Why did you go there first?"

"I don't know. I keep asking myself that. Even though I already work here, I felt like I was going on a job interview. I admit it. I wanted to look my best."

"Go on."

"At first everything was okay. Mr. Matthews talked about when he got his start at a small cable station in Detroit. I already knew the story but I let him tell it. While he was talking, he got up and closed the door to his office."

"Did you object to him doing that?"

"No. It's his office. He's Brad Matthews. What was I supposed to say?"

"And then what happened?"

"He started talking about teamwork, how important it is in any organization that everyone be a team player, that they have chemistry, that they help and support each other. He asked me if I agreed."

"And you—?"

"What was I supposed to say? Of course, I said yes. He said something about the two of us being friends. I didn't answer. Then he walked over to the window and looked out. He told me he never got tired of looking at the beautiful view of the East River. He pointed at something and waved for me to come over to where he was standing."

Lauren's eyes again filled with tears. To give her time to collect herself, Carter got up, went behind his desk, and brought out two bottles of water. She accepted one, twisted it open, and took a sip.

"So you stood next to him by the window—"

"I looked out to see what he was pointing at. All of a sudden he stepped behind me with his hands on either side of me. Then his fingers were on my forehead, then going down my face." Her breathing quickened as she tried to maintain control. "I could feel him rubbing against me from behind. His hand went down my neck, under my blouse, onto my breasts."

"Did you ask him to stop?"

"I was afraid at first. Then I said, 'What are you doing?' "

"He said, 'I'm being your friend.' And then he licked my neck all the way up the side to my head," she said with a grimace.

Carter was mesmerized. Brad Matthews was the Walter Cronkite of his generation. Some polls identified him as the most trusted man in America. If what he was hearing was true, this would be a bombshell. But it was a big *if*.

"I'm sorry to make you relive this," he said, "but I have to know everything that happened."

"He started to lick me a second time when the phone on his desk rang."

"Did he take the call?"

"He acted like nothing had happened. He left me, went over, and picked up the phone. It was Senator Mc-Connell on the line. His first words were, 'Hey Mitch, what's up?' "

"Did he ask you to stay or to leave?"

"He never even made eye contact. It was as if I was never there. I just walked out of the office. He waved as I left."

Carter remained silent for several seconds. Lauren stared at him and said, "Tell me, Mr. Carter, do you believe me?"

He exhaled. If he'd been at liberty to answer honestly, he'd have said, *No, I don't. I think you're full of crap. But I give you credit for having a very fertile imagination. You're trying to make a name for yourself by making an accusation against one of the most trusted men in America.* But he couldn't say that.

"Ms. Pomerantz, I'll be honest with you. What I believe doesn't matter. It's my job to take what you are saying seriously. What you allege happened between you and Mr. Matthews, by your own account, took place behind closed doors. There were no other witnesses. He is entitled to give his version of events. Reputations are at stake—"

"Reputations," she sneered. "Is that your way of telling me that nobody will believe me over him?"

"Lauren, I didn't say that—"

"You didn't have to. You sent the message without saying it."

"Do you have any evidence to support your account? Any emails, text messages between you and Mr. Matthews?"

"I've got something even better than that, Mr. Carter."

She took out her iPhone and tapped it a few times. After a few seconds, Brad Matthews's distinctive baritone voice was heard saying, "Lauren, come in, have a seat." For the next several minutes Carter listened as the recording confirmed what Pomerantz had described.

"Do you make it a habit to tape your conversations?" he asked.

"Only when I have a good reason."

"Are you taping this conversation?"

"No, should I be?"

"What was your 'good reason' to tape your," he paused to find the right word, "visit to Mr. Matthews's office?"

"It wasn't a *visit*. I was an employee who was called to a meeting by a superior. I'd call that a *summons*. As for my reason to tape, women talk, Mr. Carter. They talk to each other about how they're treated, particularly by the men they work for and with."

Carter stared at Lauren. She was formidable. And tough. And smart. She had to know that any prestigious law firm would salivate to have her as a client and bask in the publicity that would result from taking down Brad Matthews. But she was here talking to him. Why?

"Lauren, I assure you REL News will take your complaint seriously. There's a process—"

"No, it won't."

"Please, Lauren. I've known about this for fifteen minutes and you're already concluding I won't do anything."

"You're not the first person I spoke to."

"I'm not?"

"The day after it happened I went to somebody who I was sure would have the guts and the clout to do something about it. Nothing happened. When I called him a week later to ask what was going on, his first question was 'Do you like working here?' He told me I should focus on doing my job."

"Who did you speak to?"

"Frederick Carlyle, Jr."

Carter sat back in his chair. The son of the company founder was a rising executive. Although he was only forty-five, some believed he would be tapped to one day succeed the CEO, Dick Sherman. Two high-level careers were on the line. And possibly a third potentially high-level career if he played this right.

His own.

Establish a bond with her, he thought to himself. Find out what she's looking for. "Lauren—I hope it's okay if I call you by your first name."

"You've been doing that. It's okay."

"I am genuinely sorry about what happened to you. The last thing I want to see is you get victimized any further. How do you want this to end?"

She started tearing up again. "I love what I do. I love working in television. I don't want to be the next Monica Lewinsky. I know it's not an exact analogy, but I don't want the opening paragraph of my obituary to be about the woman who ended the career of the great Brad Matthews. I want to have a normal life and keep doing the work I love."

Carter could barely contain his excitement as he thought about the opportunity Pomerantz had given him to deal with the highest levels of REL News, as an equal. He pictured himself in the much larger office he would occupy in the not so distant future.

"Lauren, no action I take can undo the hurt you've experienced. If you go to an outside law firm, your name will get leaked out. It always happens. Your picture will be on the front page of the *New York Post*. There is, however, a way for you to get justice and maintain your anonymity."

Ten minutes later Pomerantz had left Carter's office. At his request, before leaving, she had emailed him the recording of her encounter in Brad Matthews's office.

With his feet up on his desk and his hands behind his head, he smiled broadly as he listened to it for the third time.

28

Michael Carter had met Richard Sherman a handful of times since he started at REL News. As recently as last week he had passed the CEO in the hallway. "Hello, Mr. Sherman," Carter had said in his friendliest voice. Sherman had brusquely responded "How are you?" without breaking stride or pausing to hear Carter's reply. It was obvious that Sherman had no idea who Carter was. That's certainly going to change, Carter mused.

Despite his having progressed only to the level of sergeant, Carter prided himself on his ability to think like a general. First and foremost, the accusation—call it what it is, he thought, the proof—that the venerable Brad Matthews was an abuser had to be contained. This would not be easy. REL News was, after all, a news gathering organization. The worst of all scenarios would be if another news organization broke the story about Matthews. REL would lose the opportunity to take the high moral ground, to say that they had acted immediately when they learned about the problem.

The old adage—when more than two people know something, it's no longer a secret—likely held true, Carter thought. If he followed protocol, he would bring the Pomerantz situation to his boss in Human Resources. His boss would take it to the firm's chief counsel, a seventy-year-old attorney who was months away from retirement. In an effort to avoid a blemish at the finale of his career, he would seek guidance from one of the many outside law firms that were retained by the company. All of that would happen before word of the matter got to Dick Sherman, who would ultimately decide how REL News would deal with the crisis.

Or Sherman could hear about it directly from the attorney who had devised a plan that would not only deal with the situation but keep the head count of those in the know to an absolute minimum. It would also make Michael J. Carter an indispensable player in the future of REL News.

His first challenge appeared so simple, but the more he thought about how to make it happen, the more complex it became. If something went wrong, Sherman, in typical CEO fashion, would seek to deny ever having authorized Carter's plan. But Sherman would find it difficult to explain a series of meetings and conversations with Carter that would be necessary to implement the plan. Emails leave a trail. Phone calls and texts leave a trail. If he sent Sherman a typed note through the interoffice mail, he couldn't be certain that Sherman's secretary wouldn't open it before forwarding it to him.

Her desk was just outside his office. She kept his calendar. If asked at a later date, she would know who met with Sherman in his office, including those who did so without an appointment. He wanted to have the initial discussion with Sherman in total anonymity. But how could he do that?

Later that evening, after looking through Sherman's personnel file, he settled on a strategy that he believed would work. During dinner his wife, Beverly, observed, "You seem so distracted tonight. Anything on your mind?"

Carter was tempted to say, *No, dear. I'm just contemplating what's likely to be the most important decision in my life.* Instead he answered, "Sorry. My mind is on a few projects at work. No big deal."

After his wife had gone to bed, he entered his son's room. He kissed him on the forehead and opened his son's computer to look up the Saturday train schedule from Grand Central Terminal to Greenwich, Connecticut. No one would think to examine his son's computer.

He went into the kitchen, opened his briefcase, and deposited the legal pad on the table. Scrawled in pencil were the tasks he had to complete to get ready for the meeting that he hoped would take place tomorrow. On the second page were the terms he would insist on if his plan were approved.

"Mistake," he said to himself as he looked at his precise cursive penmanship on the second page. *His handwriting.* He went over to his computer, typed what he had written, and printed the page.

Satisfied with his preparation, he repacked his briefcase, went into the living room, and turned on the television.

REL News at ten o'clock was just beginning.

29

Knowing tomorrow would be a big day—a huge day—for him, Michael Carter went to bed at eleven o'clock, an hour earlier than usual. It didn't do any good. He was awake to see the soft glow light of the alarm clock register twelve o'clock, then one o'clock, then two o'clock. The speed at which his mind was racing easily overwhelmed any feeling of fatigue that would have eased him to sleep. He resisted the temptation to take an Ambien. The last thing he wanted was to spend the day battling a drug-induced hangover.

He opened his eyes and saw that the normally dark room was light. His wife, Beverly, was no longer in the bed beside him. He glanced at the alarm clock. Seven-fifty-five! Bolting out of bed, he headed for the shower. Grateful for the extra sleep, he made an effort to calm himself down. There was still plenty of time to take care of what he needed to do.

Dressing quickly, he chose a collared shirt, blue jeans, and a pair of running shoes. He wanted to blend in, to look like what he was: a young professional putting in a few extra hours at the office on Saturday.

When he entered the kitchen, Zack was at the table halfway through the French toast he had for breakfast every day of the week. Beverly was at the stove. Her exaggerated greeting was "Well, good morning, sleepyhead."

Zack laughed uproariously, looked at him, and yelled, "You're sleepyhead." He turned to his mother and repeated, "Daddy's sleepyhead." They both laughed even louder at the newly assigned nickname.

How did I marry such a ditz? Carter asked himself as he poured a glass of orange juice. And how can I keep Zack from turning into one? "I'll think about it tomorrow," he mumbled to himself, quoting Scarlett O'Hara's famous line from *Gone with the Wind*. My plate for today is full.

"Are you going to come to my soccer game, Daddy?"

"I hope I can," Carter said, realizing he had forgotten about it. "What time is it?"

"He has the late game today," Beverly answered. "Two-thirty in the Park."

"Something came up at the office yesterday and I have to go in and work on it today." He glanced at his watch. "If I leave now, I should be able to finish it in time to make it to the game."

"You don't want any breakfast?" she asked.

"I'll pick something up on the way to the office," he said as he leaned over and kissed Zack. He gave Beverly the mandatory kiss on the top of her head and five minutes later was out the door.

His first stop was at the Starbucks two blocks from his apartment. It was eight-forty-five. Sherman should be awake by now, he thought.

Busy during the week, the coffee shop had few patrons on Saturday morning. Ten people, all of whom appeared to be alone, were sitting at the tables in the center of the store reading newspapers or staring into laptops while sipping their drinks. Carter identified the one he wanted.

"I'm very sorry to bother you, but I lost my cell phone. Could I possibly borrow yours to make a quick call?" As he finished asking the question, Carter dropped a five-dollar bill on the counter beside the young student in the NYU sweatshirt who had looked up from his laptop.

"You will stay in the store, yes?" the young man with a foreign accent asked.

"I'll be right over there," Carter said while pointing to a quiet corner.

"You don't have to pay me," the student said in heavily accented English as he handed over the phone.

"It's all right," Carter said as he retreated to the corner. After one last glance around to be sure no one was taking notice of him, he dialed the number from memory.

"Hello" was the answer, in a distinctly grouchy tone.

"Am I speaking to Mr. Richard Sherman?"

"Yes. Who the hell are you?"

"My name is Michael Carter. I'm an attorney in Human Resources at REL News—"

"Never heard of you. You better have a good reason for calling me at home on a Saturday."

"I do, sir." He had repeatedly rehearsed the words. "Unless appropriate action is taken immediately, REL News is about to be sued by a young woman employee who has proof that Brad Matthews molested her in his office. There is a narrow window of opportunity to contain the situation. I don't want to say more on the phone. When can we meet?"

Several moments of silence followed. "Can you come to Greenwich?"

"Tell me where and when."

"Do you know the Greenwich train station?"

"I'll be coming by train."

"I'll be in a black Mercedes S550 parked at the northern end of the lot. Twelve o'clock. Be on time."

The call ended before Carter could signal his agreement. He exhaled, having made it over the first hurdle. Without thinking, he put the phone in his pocket and started walking toward the door. He looked across the store to see the student waving and pointing to his empty hand. Stay focused, he thought to himself as he returned the borrowed phone.

30

The Greenwich station was sparsely populated. Michael Carter proceeded out the front door and glanced toward the northern end of the mostly empty parking lot. He didn't see what he was looking for. No point standing out there like a jerk, he thought. He walked back inside and took a seat.

He tried unsuccessfully to focus on the article he was reading. At 11:57 he got up, went outside, and walked slowly toward a lone Mercedes. He was about ten feet away when the driver's-side window rolled down.

"Carter?" Richard Sherman asked.

"Yes, Mr. Sherman. I—"

"Get in," he said, waving him around the car.

31

Michael Carter walked around the car and climbed into the passenger's front seat. He closed the door behind him and put his briefcase between his legs. Sherman was wearing a dark blue sweat suit and gray running shoes. The CEO was known for taking pride in his physical condition. He's probably on his way to or from his trainer, Carter thought.

He was unsure what to do next. Despite all his preparation, he was extremely nervous. Should he let Sherman begin the conversation or should he take the initiative? Sherman did nothing but stare at him, *glare at him* was probably more accurate.

Carter cleared his throat and extended his hand as he said, "Mr. Sherman, I appreciate your agreeing to meet me on such short notice."

Sherman made no move to shake his hand.

"All right," Carter began, trying to make his voice sound more confident than he felt, "at about five o'clock last night an associate producer named Lauren Pomerantz came to my office. She told me about an encounter she had behind closed doors in Brad Matthews's office."

Sherman listened intently as Carter recounted Pomerantz's story. The CEO's reaction was predictable. "It's just a 'he said, she said,'" Sherman growled.

"That was exactly my reaction, Mr. Sherman," Carter replied as he pulled out his cell phone and began swiping and tapping it, "until I heard this."

Carter held the phone in the air between them. Neither man said a word until the recording ended.

"Good God," was Sherman's first reaction. It was followed by "What do we know about Pomerantz?"

Carter pulled a file from the briefcase that was now open on his lap. He savored that he was now part of the *we*. "Unfortunately for us she's a model employee. She's been with the company for three and a half years. All of her annual evaluations have been excellent and resulted in raises. She's had two promotions."

Sherman snapped, "You're a lawyer. This business of taping people in their office without their knowing it. Isn't that illegal?"

"Good point, sir. I researched that last night. Although Pomerantz may have technically violated REL News policy as laid out in the Employee Handbook, that won't help us very much. Arguably, she could be fired for that, but I got the clear impression she's planning to leave the company anyway."

"Good riddance."

"There's another defense or justification she could

offer. REL is a news gathering organization. The fact that the anchor and editor in chief of the country's highest-rated newscast was abusing an employee in his chain of command certainly qualifies as news. She was doing what any reporter would have done while pursuing a story."

Sherman punched his fist on the steering wheel, a reaction Carter noticed with delight.

"If I can be so bold, sir. Lawyers could wrangle hours over whether or not the tape was admissible in a jury trial," he began.

"Kennedy and Edelman would have a field day with it," Sherman pointed out, referring to the popular REL News program that featured two attorneys debating opposite sides of legal cases.

"You bet. But if it ever gets to that point, the damage to the company will have been done." Carter paused for a moment, then continued, "Unless, of course, the situation can be contained."

Sherman looked at him. For the first time his tone of voice was respectful. "Is there any way we can keep word of this from getting out?"

"There is because we caught this so early. As far as I can determine, no trail exists. No emails about Matthews have been sent. I've been working on a plan since Pomerantz left my office last night. The only thing it requires is your approval to put it in motion."

"What is it?"

"Outside of this car, as best I can determine, only four people for certain know about Matthews's behavior: Matthews himself, Pomerantz, and whoever tipped Pomerantz to record what happened in Matthews's office."

"And the fourth?"

"Pomerantz told me she brought the Matthews matter to the attention of Frederick Carlyle, Jr., immediately after the incident happened."

"Daddy's little Freddie, the village idiot," Sherman said. "Did he do anything about it?"

"According to Pomerantz, no. He reminded her that she was lucky to have a job at REL and advised her to get back to work."

A long silence followed. Carter waited for Sherman to break it. "Will Pomerantz keep quiet?"

"I'm confident she will if we give her what she's looking for."

"Money, right?"

"That, too. Do you know your counterparts from CNN and Fox and the other broadcast networks?"

"That's a stupid question."

"Sorry. After she leaves REL News, Pomerantz wants to stay in the industry. Maybe in New York, maybe in Houston, where she's from. A phone call from you could make that happen?"

"Absolutely. How do we know the one who tipped off Pomerantz isn't going to talk?"

"We don't, but the good news is that she's kept quiet so far. Whoever she is, a healthy deposit into her bank account should buy her continued silence."

"And if there are others?"

"There probably are, and we treat them the same way. Instead of sitting back, dreading the day one or several of them and their attorneys call a news conference, we, I should say *I*, find them one by one and settle directly with them."

"What do you mean by 'directly'?"

"Do you really want to know all the details?"

"No, I guess I don't."

Carter could feel the excitement inside him building. He had succeeded in creating the interest. Now he had to close the deal.

"The only chance of our containing the situation is to keep the number of people who know about Matthews to an absolute minimum. That means no talking to REL lawyers or outside counsel."

"Go on."

"I'm going to start with Pomerantz, convince her to settle and sign a nondisclosure agreement."

"You think she'll do it?"

"For two million dollars, I think she will."

"Two million's a lot of money!"

"I know it is. To get her money she's also going to tell me who else knows about Matthews. And let's put this in perspective. How much revenue does Matthews generate for REL every year? Fifty million?"

"About that amount," Sherman muttered, no doubt knowing that the actual number was closer to seventy million.

"In order to do the work I have to do, we can't be seen

talking, and I can't be sitting in my office in Human Resources." He pulled a paper from his briefcase and handed it to Sherman. "You are going to hire the consulting firm of Carter & Associates. The retainer will be an initial one million dollars and two hundred thousand dollars per month for expenses. A wire of twelve million dollars will be sent to my attorney trust account. This money and additional funds I might need will be used to compensate Matthews's victims."

"Why do you need that much when we only know about a few victims?" Sherman demanded.

"Do you want me to come back to you every time I learn about a new victim and say I need more money?"

Sherman saw his point. "That is a lot of money you're expecting me to make available without explanation."

"You're the CEO. I leave that part to you."

Carter reached into his briefcase and pulled out two bags containing the items he had purchased that morning. He had exercised an abundance of caution. Every 7-Eleven and Rite Aid had security cameras recording visual images of customers and their purchases. Buying six phones in one store might raise questions; buying one phone in six different stores would not.

"If something goes wrong, it will be in both of our best interest to have zero record of the contacts between us. No emails, no use of office phones, cell phones, nothing. Do you know what a burner phone is?"

"Are those the ones that got Samsung in trouble because they kept catching fire?"

Carter almost burst out laughing, but then realized the CEO might not be joking. "No, that was something different. Burner phones are completely untraceable. Each phone has a memory capacity of about thirty minutes. When we talk, we'll keep it short and sweet. A quick update on what I've concluded and what I'm working on."

"How do I get more memory when it runs out?"

"You don't. You throw it away and move on to the next phone. I bought each of us three phones to start. I'll get more later if necessary. I have your three numbers. The numbers of my phones are written on this paper," he said as he handed over a sheet.

"Carter, you were pretty confident that I was going to go along with your plan, weren't you?"

"Honestly, I didn't know what you were going to decide. But if you were going to say yes, it made a lot more sense for us to be able to get started after one meeting instead of two."

Sherman stared straight ahead, feeling the rage inside him build. *I have no idea who this guy is, but I have to trust him,* he thought.

"All right, Carter, we're going to play ball together. Give me until Tuesday or Wednesday to get the money flowing your way."

"I'm not quite finished," Carter said smoothly. "There's an outside chance someone could start listening in on our conversations. To protect ourselves, we talk in code. Each victim will be a car model, a Ford, a Chevy, a Mercedes, etc. When talking about money, each million dollars will be a bushel. This code is on the same paper with the burner phone numbers."

"Is that it?"

"Three last things. First is a copy of the resignation letter I'll submit on Monday. Next, as I find out the names of the victims, I'll need access to their personnel files. Call somebody in IT and make access available to Carter & Associates. You'll make a phone call to confirm that my exit package includes keeping my family on the company health-care plan at company expense for two years."

If I ring this jerk's neck and throw him in Long Island Sound, I wonder how long it will take to find his body? Sherman raged to himself. "And the last thing?"

"The only person who knows for sure how many victims there are is Brad Matthews. You, or I, or we have to talk to him to find out. And while we're at it, ask him to kindly stop adding to the list. Think about how you want to handle that one."

"All right, I'll call you in a couple days on one of these damn phones. Now, get out."

Sherman watched Carter exit the car and walk toward the front doors of the station. He thought about the value of the stock that would be awarded to him when the company went public and slammed on the gas pedal, sending the car barreling from the parking area.

32

It was an act of will for Sherman to keep close to the speed limit as he drove the three miles home from the Greenwich train station. He needed to get on his computer. He cursed himself for the way he had screeched the tires in the parking lot. A moment after he slowed, a police cruiser had come around the corner. He was in no mood for a confrontation with a cop.

I'm placing my whole career in the hands of this Carter guy, and I don't know a damn thing about him, he thought. He remembered the name of a detective agency a friend had used when he suspected, correctly, that his wife was having an affair. Caught in the act, she had agreed to a much more reasonable divorce settlement in exchange for keeping the affair quiet.

But if I have them investigate Carter, what am I hoping they'll find? Does it really matter if he was the smartest or dumbest guy in his law school class? He must have a clean background or he never would have been hired by REL. I'm stuck with him, but can I trust him?

Sherman pulled into his garage and clicked the door closed behind him. He hurried through the den, where his wife was on the couch reading a magazine. "Are you finished exercising already?" she asked without looking up.

Not wanting to bother with her questions, he did what he found himself doing more often. Without answering, he just kept going into his office and closed the door behind him.

Please be different from the way I remember it, he pleaded as he searched for the emails sent to him by Frederick Carlyle, Jr. He scanned past the more recent ones until he landed on the one he was looking for. In the subject line Carlyle had written: *Just between us.*

Sherman tapped it open.

> Dick, A young associate producer spoke to me today. She claims she had a me-too encounter with Brad Matthews in his office. Her description was graphic. I told her I'd look into it. How do you want to handle?
> Fred

Sherman clasped his fingers together behind his head. He looked at the date of the email to confirm what he already knew. It had landed in his inbox when his attorney was completing the negotiation on his latest contract. His retirement severance would be thirty million dollars. That number could double if a rumored IPO ever came to fruition. Sixty million dollars. Mega-rich! Even if he dumped his wife and gave her half of it, he'd still have plenty to live the way he wanted to in retirement.

But now everything was up in the air. Three months had elapsed since he had received the email from Junior. The age-old question: *What did he know and when did he know it?*

They'll crucify me for letting so much time go by, he told himself.

33

Michael Carter was barely aware of the gentle clacking of the train on the tracks as he rode back to Grand Central Terminal. He glanced down at the legal pad in front of him. His *To Do* list filled the top sheet. It all felt surreal.

It would have been wrong to say he'd been confident Sherman would approve his plan, even though there were good reasons for him to do so. What Carter hadn't expected was the rush of exhilaration that he was experiencing knowing that the CEO of REL News had put the fate of the company in his hands.

The toughest case is always the first one. If he reached a settlement with Lauren Pomerantz—*when* I settle with Pomerantz, he chastised himself—he could use the lessons learned from that negotiation to help with the subsequent ones. There would be more. How many, he had no way of knowing. Sick puppies like Brad Matthews didn't do this every once in a while, he thought. Matthews had power and access to so many vulnerable young women.

With a little luck there'll be plenty of victims, Carter thought, and plenty of work for me.

His time in the military had taught him that most outcomes are decided before the first shot is fired on the field of battle. The side with superior intelligence, the opponent with the knowledge advantage, almost always prevails. There was no doubt in his mind that Pomerantz, with that recording of her Matthews encounter in her back pocket, had the stronger hand to play in their upcoming negotiation. My best shot, he thought to himself, is to prevent her from realizing that she holds all the cards.

He opened his gym bag and removed Pomerantz's personnel file. Glancing around, he could see that no one was within earshot on the mostly empty train.

After beginning to dial her cell on one of the burner phones, he paused, then clicked the phone off. She was already on edge. Why spook her by calling on an *unavailable* number?

Switching to his iPhone, he punched in her number. Midway through the third ring she answered in a soft, almost fragile voice.

"Lauren, this is Michael Carter. We spoke in my office last night. Before I say anything else, how are you doing?"

"What are you looking for me to say, Mr. Carter? That I'm doing great? Well, I'm not. I'm sure you're not calling on a Saturday afternoon to inquire about my health. What do you want?"

Carter was not accustomed to young women speaking rudely to him. It took effort to keep any hint of irritation out of his voice. "All right, Lauren, let's go right to the reason I called. The first time you reported an incident at the company nothing happened. In the less than twenty-four hours since you came to my office, I have been granted authority to arrange a confidential settlement with you. Part of that settlement will include the guarantee that you will be offered a comparable position in the news business in the city of your choosing."

There was silence on the other end of the line. Carter thought for a moment he might have lost the connection. "Lauren, are you still there?"

"Yes," she answered quietly.

"Good. I'll need tomorrow and Monday to finish some things at my end. Are you free to meet on Tuesday? I'll text you the where and the when."

"Mr. Carter, I want to bring a friend with me. She's not a lawyer. I'd just feel better if—"

"Lauren, listen to me. The authorization I received to settle with you specifies that I deal directly and only with you. I can't change that. Look at it this way. We should have our meeting. Just the two of us. There won't be any pressure on you to sign anything on Tuesday. Let's try to identify what both sides need to reach an acceptable agreement and go forward from there. Does that make sense?"

"I guess so."

"Perfect. Lauren, I believe I've demonstrated that you

can trust me. Promise me that you won't talk about the incident with anyone before we meet on Tuesday."

"I won't" was the reluctant answer.

"I'll be in touch. Goodbye." Carter ended the call as the train slowed to a stop in Grand Central Terminal.

34

Dick Sherman had had a lousy weekend. Over time he had learned to tune out his wife's inane comments and not let her idiotic suggestions about things they should do together bother him, but he found himself snapping at her. The Carter-Matthews situation was never far from his mind. He was about to take his first step to contain the situation, and he was experiencing an emotion that was foreign to him. He was nervous.

The buzzer on his desk sounded. "Mr. Sherman, Mr. Myers is here to see you."

"Send him in," he barked.

For the past eleven years Ed Myers had been the chief financial officer of REL News Corporation. He was the perfect complement to Sherman's skill set. Where Sherman was a genius at picking the types of programs and on-air personalities that drew in audiences, when it came to the dollars, Myers knew how to make the numbers work. Time and again the *Wall Street Journal* and *Forbes* had commended REL News for the bargain prices they had paid as they acquired regional cable systems and built a national powerhouse.

When it came to keeping expenses under control, no one was better than Myers. It was only a slight exaggeration to say that without looking at a computer, he could remember how every dollar in the company was spent. That was Myers's greatest strength; today it might also be Sherman's biggest headache.

"Come in, Ed. How are you? Sit down," Sherman said as he came around the desk to shake hands.

Myers appeared taken aback. As if he couldn't recall Sherman inquiring about how he was doing and thought something was clearly up. "I'm fine, Dick. Thanks."

"Ed, you and I have worked together for a long time. We've faced a lot of tough challenges, but we always found a way to make things work."

"Yes, we have," Myers said, wondering why Sherman, who never told anybody they were doing a good job, was so full of compliments. The thought went through his head, Is he about to fire me?

"Ed, do you trust me?"

"Of course I do. Have I done anything to make you think otherwise?"

"No, you haven't. It's important we trust each other, because I need you to do something and not ask a lot of questions."

"Do what?"

"I need you to wire twelve million dollars to this account," he said while handing him a sheet of paper. "I want it to be there in the next twenty-four to forty-eight hours."

"You're kidding me, right?"

The look on Sherman's face revealed that he was dead serious.

"That's a lot of money to just let slip through the cracks. I have to classify it as something. Can you at least tell me—"

"Ed, I wouldn't be asking you to do this unless it was critically important to the company. Believe me, you don't want to know why. Nobody will question this if you sign off on it. Can you make this happen?"

Myers exhaled as he glanced at the wiring instructions.

"All right, I know better than to ask who Carter & Associates are." Myers took off his glasses, pulled a smooth cloth from his pocket, and began to wipe them. He stared without seeing out the window. "I'm finalizing the numbers the investment bankers will use to calculate the valuation. Twelve million dollars is a lot. Is this a onetime charge or will there be more?"

It was a question Sherman had not anticipated. It was not the time to appear uncertain. "Just this once," he answered, trying to sound confident.

"Then I can bury this in the M and A budget."

"How?" Sherman asked, knowing that Myers was referring to Mergers and Acquisitions.

"I'm not telling you anything you don't know. When we buy other cable systems, we spend a lot of money on due diligence. Most of it goes to outside entities, investment bankers, law firms, and consultants. They scrub the numbers to see if the company is as profitable as it claims to be, check out any legal hurdles, and then make a recommendation regarding how the acquisition would fit into REL."

"You could add the twelve million dollars as an expense incurred in buying those companies?"

"Actually, just the opposite. Sometimes, we do all the homework, kick the tires, and decide XYZ company is not a good fit. Even when no purchase results, a lot of money is spent on due diligence. As long as nobody digs too deep, I could bury it there."

"And if the Street finds out we spent a lot on companies we didn't acquire?"

"Most of the industry analysts are clueless. If they say anything, they'll probably praise us for being cautious with our acquisitions."

"I knew I could count on you, Ed. Get it done."

35

Michael Carter glanced at his watch. 10:50. Lauren Pomerantz, assuming she was on time, would arrive in ten minutes.

The five days since Pomerantz had come to his office had unleashed a whirlwind of activity. An hour earlier his broker at Schwab had called to confirm the arrival by wire of $12 million into the coffers of Carter & Associates. Sherman had been true to his word. He had figured out a way to get the money.

Carter had hoped to spend a few days searching for office space suitable for his new level of responsibility, his new station in life. There hadn't been time. Instead he had gone online the previous morning to a supplier of temporary space, visited the Midtown location an hour later, and signed a one-month lease. The dim office was smaller than he would have liked, the furniture modern and a little on the cheap side. His view out a small window in the corner was of a skyscraper that kept his office permanently in shadow. He had chosen one of the larger offices that had enough room inside for a small conference table. Only two of the four chairs would be needed. Among the shared services was a very attractive, young receptionist, Beatrice, who would phone him when Pomerantz arrived.

It might be just as well, he thought to himself while looking around, to have the meeting here. If Pomerantz saw him in an opulent setting, her financial demands might go up. It was human nature. There was another advantage to keeping the expenses low, at least at the start.

He had reached out to two military buddies he kept in touch with. Both worked in security; one at a credit reporting agency, the other at Verizon Wireless. The information they had provided would prove invaluable, but it didn't come cheap. And when he signed for the space yesterday, he had put forward his personal credit card for the deposit.

A sickening thought had occurred to him as he submitted his resignation letter to REL and committed to the expenses. Suppose Sherman changed his mind and backed out of their deal. Sherman could deny they had ever met. Carter had gone to great lengths to assure there was no record of their meeting. He'd be the one on the hook for the research and office expenses, and he'd have to go begging for his old job back. The arrival of the wired money had put his fear to rest.

On the way to the office he had stopped at a bakery, bought some pastries, and had them sliced. The receptionist, for a fee, had agreed to bring them coffee upon request.

Not sure what else to do, he made one final visit to

Pomerantz's Facebook page. She had posted nothing over the previous five days.

The phone on his desk buzzed. "Mr. Carter, a Ms. Pomerantz is here to see you."

"I'll be right out." Before leaving his office, he glanced at himself in the mirror on the back of the door. He had researched the fashion choices that he hoped would give him an advantage. Skipping the necktie made him more approachable. Supposedly the pale blue of his V-neck sweater suggested dependability and trustworthiness. It made one look honest. His tan slacks communicated passivity and calming. He wasn't sure he believed in all this color communication nonsense, but why take the chance? Maybe Pomerantz believed it. "Showtime," he said to himself as he patted his hair flat by the temples, opened the door, and walked down the hallway.

Lauren Pomerantz said nothing as she followed him down the hall. That was fine with Carter, who preferred that their entire conversation take place within the confines of his office. Her gray sweater covered a striped shirt that was buttoned to the neck. He recalled what he read about wearing gray. The person wants to remain *invisible.* He would be more than happy to oblige her.

"Please sit," Carter said, gesturing toward the conference table. "I can send out for coffee. Are you—"

"No. Thanks."

"Help yourself to a Danish."

"I already ate."

"A water?" he asked.

"Okay," she said, her expression stone-faced.

Carter grabbed two bottles of Poland Spring from the mini-refrigerator behind his desk. Pomerantz had taken the chair with her back to the wall. Carter sat down opposite her and placed one of the bottles in front of her.

"Why arc we here?" she asked abruptly.

Carter was taken aback by her question. "I'm here to do everything I can to make things right for you, to—"

"I'm not talking about that. Why are we *here*, and not at the REL News building?"

"Frankly, Lauren, I wanted to make things as easy as I could for you. The last thing I wanted was for you to bump into the person who caused you so much anguish."

Lauren was silent. She looked around the room without making eye contact. Carter opened the file he had brought from his desk and pretended to read it. Nature abhors a vacuum. He wanted her to be the one to break the stalemate.

"No matter what happens, Mr. Carter, I'm not signing anything today."

"I respect that, Lauren. You told me that on the phone. We're here to discuss the terms of a possible settlement. May I begin?"

"Go ahead."

"The goal of the settlement, first and foremost, is to protect your privacy. It will include a substantial one-time payment to you and the guarantee that you will find a comparable job in the news business. I remember the concern you expressed in my office. You will not be the next Monica Lewinsky."

"And what will be expected of me?"

"Nothing more than your silence. Are you familiar with the term NDA? Nondisclosure agreement?"

She nodded.

"Good. The NDA in the agreement will be ironclad. If you breathe a word of the settlement to anyone, you will immediately return the money that was paid to you. Now, I know this will never happen. But if litigation results, you will be responsible for paying the legal fees on both sides."

"I assume at some point you're going to tell me how much."

"Yes, I am. Upon your signing of the agreement I am authorized to wire you two million dollars. A wire typically takes twenty-four hours to complete. If you sign today, the money will be in your account tomorrow."

"I said I wasn't signing anything today."

"I heard you. I was only explaining how quickly wire transfers work."

Carter opened his folder, removed a document, and slid it in front of her. "I'm not your typical lawyer. I try to avoid the legal mumbo jumbo whenever I can. The agreement is only three pages." He glanced at his watch. "I have something I have to respond to. It will take a few minutes. Why not give it a quick read?"

Without waiting for her to answer, Carter went over to his desk, opened his laptop, and began typing. He pretended to read what was on his screen while eyeing

Pomerantz. It was working. After an initial reluctance to acknowledge what was in front of her, she was now carefully studying it.

He had labored painstakingly to avoid any word or phrase that might not be easily understood. A full five minutes passed before she finished and looked up. Carter hit a few more keystrokes, then returned to the table.

"Sorry about that. I appreciate your patience."

"Will this be treated as income? Will I owe taxes on the two million dollars?"

Carter was impressed. Clearly, Pomerantz was sharp and not to be underestimated. Her employment file indicated that she had been a double major at SMU, Communications and Economics. "At this time, no. The money you receive will not be subject to tax."

"What's that supposed to mean, 'at this time'?"

"The New York State Legislature is currently considering a bill that would change the way settlements are treated. If it passes, settlements that include NDAs will be treated as income to the recipient. A similar bill is under review in Congress. They obviously care very little about the privacy of victims. Anyone who might be in line for a settlement that includes an NDA would be wise to act sooner versus later."

Carter let his comment hang in the air. He did not mention that the intent of the proposed bills was to make it harder, or at least more expensive, for companies to protect serial abusers in their ranks. If the bills passed, settlements that include NDAs would no longer be deductible to corporations.

"Mr. Carter, I appreciate what you've done. What I read appears pretty straightforward. But this isn't a fair fight. Matthews and REL News have you, a lawyer, representing them. You obviously have experience," she pointed to the papers in front of her, "with these situations."

"Believe me, being a lawyer doesn't make you any smarter."

She ignored his attempt at humor. "Here's what I want to do. I'm not going to hire a lawyer. I just want to bring it to a friend who's an attorney, ask her to read it and make sure that I understand it and am comfortable with it."

Carter shook his head. "I'm sorry, Lauren, that's not possible."

"What do you mean? Why not?"

"My marching orders are very clear. My client wants to keep the number of people who know about the incident to an absolute minimum. I believe that's what you want as well. If you bring in a third party, the settlement offer is reduced to one million dollars."

"I just want my friend to read this and spend ten minutes answering my questions—"

"Take it from a lawyer, Lauren, that's not what's going to happen. A lawyer is going to persuade you to retain him or her. In cases such as these, the attorney will get about one-third of the award. Instead of the original two million dollars, the offer will be one million. After the lawyer's fee, what could have been two million dollars will be down to six hundred and sixty-six thousand. Even when they're on a contingency, lawyers enjoy dragging things out. Instead of possibly getting it tomorrow, you'll receive the money in a year or two if you're lucky. Your attorney's delaying actions might also give New York or Congress time to pass the bill I spoke about earlier. When that happens, you will owe an additional one-third in taxes, leaving you with a little over four hundred thousand dollars. I don't like saying this, Lauren, but I have to. It will be tempting to quietly show this to a lawyer and hope I never find out. But here's the catch. If you choose to sign the agreement in front of you, you will be swearing that you did not discuss the incident with anyone after you came to my office last week. The penalties for perjury in New York State are severe."

"I'm not a liar," she said defiantly.

"I know you're not. Lauren, do you know what the saddest part of the whole process will be?"

She looked at him but didn't answer.

"I guarantee you your privacy will be violated. Your friend, the lawyer, she's a member of a firm, right? The firm has partners who will want to know about this potentially high-profile case. They'll take the three pages in front of you and expand it to thirty. Numerous associates will work on it. Legal secretaries will print and copy the document. Can you really trust all of those people to keep their mouths shut?"

"Mr. Carter, I have nothing to hide. Maybe the lawyer I talk to will tell me I should be getting more."

"Lauren, I want to help you. Please don't make me do this."

"Do what?"

Trying to appear reluctant, Carter walked back to his desk, pulled a file from the center drawer, and sat down. He was pleased that his desk chair was higher than the ones at the conference table. It gave him the opportunity to look down on Pomerantz.

"Lauren, do you know the meaning of the word 'consensual'?"

"You've got to be kidding!"

"Somebody warned you against being alone with Matthews, but you went anyway. Didn't you?"

"I explained that to you."

"I know you did. While we're at it, explain to me again how you stopped in the makeup room before you went to see him. You wanted to look attractive, right?"

"I wanted to look my best."

"Attractive? Your best? I'm sure you'll have no trouble explaining the difference between those terms."

"You're twisting my words. I told you what happened."

"That's right. You told me just like you'll tell your lawyer, who will prep you for the first of a series of depositions where you can tell your version to the lawyers who'll represent REL and Matthews."

"It's not *my* version!"

"It is *your* version, and I'm sure Mr. Matthews's explanation regarding what happened will differ significantly from yours."

"Don't forget, Mr. Carter, I have the tape."

"Maybe."

"What do you mean, 'maybe'?"

"I'm sure Mr. Matthews did not consent to your taping the meeting in his office. It might be inadmissible."

"That's ridiculous. People tape phone calls all the time."

"Phone calls are treated differently. When a person is in his office, there is an expectation of privacy. You violated that presumption. Look, Lauren, we're bogging down, we're jousting back and forth on fine legal points. I'm trying to spare you being put through the wringer."

"I have nothing to hide."

"Really? How about I give a little preview of what's ahead of you if you go to war with Mr. Brad Matthews and REL News. And I guarantee you, it will be a war. Will that be okay, Blue Skies?"

"What did you call me?" she asked, a shocked look on her face.

"Come on, Lauren, that's the screen name you use on the dating service Tinder. You used the same name two years ago when you were on Bumble. Correct me if I'm wrong. Isn't that the dating site set up to have the woman make the first move? Have you always taken an aggressive approach to dating?" It had cost Carter $2,500 for his army buddy who worked at a credit reporting agency to compile and send him Pomerantz's MasterCard bills for the previous five years. He had given Carter the name of someone who could access the records of everyone she had communicated with when she was using the dating apps. Fifteen hundred dollars was his fee for what he deemed a rush job.

"No response to that question? Let's try another one. Tell me, Lauren, after exchanging a series of messages with a Mr. Douglas Campbell, who resides at 524 East 86th Street, you stopped using Bumble and went off the grid. Is this Mr. Campbell's cell phone?" He read the number. "Would a search of your text messages to him reveal any really racy ones? And I hope you didn't send him any explicit photos. God only knows how embarrassing that would be."

His army buddy who was at Verizon had provided her cell phone history over the past three years. When they're not together, lovers typically call each other between ten o'clock and midnight. The cell phone information had cost him another $1,500.

"That has nothing to do with what Matthews did to me," she said, lashing out. "Besides, I'm not stupid. You're not allowed to put my past on trial."

"You're absolutely right, Lauren, that would not be permitted *if* this were a criminal trial. If that's the route you had wanted to go, you'd be talking to a cop, not me. God forbid things go that far. In a civil case both sides are afforded more latitude. Way more. Your side would use all the ammo it could find to portray Mr. Matthews as a monster. And the finest legal talent money can buy will put *your* life under the microscope and find anything they can to rip you to shreds. I'm a run-of-the-mill labor lawyer. Working on my own, I found all this stuff in a few days.

"I'm sure you followed the Brett Kavanaugh circus. People in bars, people sitting at home having dinner, discussing which one is truthful and which one's a liar. Is that how you want to be remembered? Even if you win, you'll lose."

Lauren made an unsuccessful effort to beat back tears. She put her face in her hands. "I don't know what to do," she blurted out.

Using the softest voice he could muster, Carter said, "It's time to start healing, time to make the pain go away. Beatrice, the receptionist you met outside, is a notary public. After you answer one more question, I'm going to call her in and she'll witness your signature and mine on the agreement."

Ten minutes later, with the signed papers in front of him, he had his feet up on the desk. Upon further reflection he decided this office was suitable. The money he saved on office expenses could be put to better use. Beatrice, the twenty-nine-year-old, brown-eyed receptionist with her jet-black hair in a ponytail and tight, white sweater accentuating her lovely curves, had agreed to go to dinner that night.

He glanced at the paper on his desk blotter. Dallas was the city where Pomerantz wanted to work. He had to get in touch with Sherman and have him use his contacts to find something for her there.

Written below Dallas was the next project. The woman who had tipped off Lauren Pomerantz to be careful around Brad Matthews was a former REL News employee named Meg Williamson.

36

Dick Sherman was in his usual position in the left lane on Route 95 as he made his way through the Bronx on his way home from the office. What was unusual was that he was behind the wheel. At dinner last night his wife had explained that she wanted to drive her car to the city and sleep at her sister's before she and her sister caught an early flight to Bermuda from JFK. He didn't know or care what she was doing; the part that affected him was his agreement to drive her car back to Greenwich. He had told his driver to take the night off.

Sherman had just finished listening to a podcast of REL's evening news. Matthews in his folksy way sounded like the adult in the room as he reported how the Republicans and Democrats at the latest congressional hearing had spent the entire two hours shouting at each other. Matthews closed the broadcast as he usually did on a humorous note. "Ours is a system of government founded by geniuses so it could be run by idiots."

Sherman would have been making good time if it

weren't for the moron in the Toyota. The jerk was more than ten car lengths behind the vehicle in front of him. Sherman had tailgated the last mile and twice flashed his high-beams to no avail. The driver was clueless.

It had been four days since he met Carter at the Greenwich train station. He never liked carrying one cell phone, and now he had to carry his own *and* the one Carter gave him.

Ed Myers had done what he was asked to do, but that did little to allay Sherman's concern. When they passed each other in the hallway, Myers barely looked at him. Sherman recalled years ago when he had been roped into going to some stupid Boy Scouts dinner that was honoring Myers, who had been an Eagle Scout. It was torture sitting there listening to them recite the twelve points of the Scout Law. I hope Myers remembers the one about being obedient, he thought to himself. When the pressure's on, can Myers be counted on to keep his mouth shut?

His reverie was interrupted by an unfamiliar ring. For a moment he thought the sound was coming from the radio. He then realized it was the burner phone.

The Toyota in front of him finally eased over to the middle lane. Sherman swerved slightly as he dug into his right pocket and retrieved the phone that was now midway through its fourth ring. He remembered Carter's caution to not use names and talk in code lest anyone was listening. He drifted slightly toward the divider as he answered, "Hello. What's up?"

"After looking around, I've settled on a Ford. The price was right. Two bushels."

"Good job," Sherman said before considering whether that was an appropriate response to someone reporting a car purchase. "I'm happy for you," he added.

"I'm still in the market. Got my eye on a Chevy."

"That's good," Sherman answered, scrambling for how to introduce the next topic. He had decided he wanted Carter to be with him when he confronted Matthews. What was the code for doing that? The next time I see Carter I'm going to put an end to this code nonsense, he promised himself. Sherman didn't realize that he was now the one holding back traffic by going slowly in the left lane. An idea occurred to him. "I like trains. Same day and time."

"Agreed," Carter said as he disconnected.

Sherman continued holding the phone to his ear as he breathed a sigh of relief, but it proved short-lived. Flashing blue light reflected off his dashboard. He glanced to his right where a blue-and-white New York City Transit Police car was in the middle lane. The officer was gesturing at him to pull over.

"Damn it!" he shouted as he hurled the phone to the floor. Nine minutes later on the passenger's seat next to him was a summons for careless driving and illegally using a mobile device while operating a motorized vehicle.

37

"I'm sorry, honey, I must have been distracted. What did you say?"

"All right, I've had enough. We're gonna talk right now," Diane Myers said as she picked up the remote on the end table next to her husband and clicked off the football game. "Don't even bother trying to object. You probably don't even know what the score is."

Myers started to reply but then realized his wife was right. He didn't know the score or even which side was winning. So much for *watching* a game.

"Okay, dear. What do you want to talk about?"

"You, us, and whatever the hell is going on."

"Diane, I don't know what you're— "

"Ed, stop! You like to joke that patience has never been my strong suit. Maybe you're right. But whatever reservoir of patience I had is gone and it's all been used on you. Something has changed and I want to know what it is."

He sighed. "I don't know what you're talking about."

"Really? You're in a complete fog. Three days ago you forgot to call Tara for her birthday. You forgot after I called your office to remind you." Their daughter was in her freshman year at Fordham. "At dinner last night you were distracted to the point of being rude. When you got up to use the bathroom, Art and Ali both asked me if anything was wrong with you." The Grooms had been friends since both couples' oldest daughters started first grade together. "And don't take this the wrong way, but you look terrible. For somebody who never had any trouble sleeping, for the last week you've done nothing but toss and turn, and it shows."

"Diane, I don't know what to say. Things have been really stressful at work."

"I don't buy that. Not for a minute. Come on, Ed. When you joined REL News right after we got married, you told me the company was a financial mess. You'd come home joking that if you didn't call me the next day it would probably mean the phones had been shut off for nonpayment. But you never let it get to you. When you walked through the door at the end of the day, you flipped the switch. Now that the company's doing great you're feeling stress?"

"It's not that."

"Ed, be honest with me. Are you having an affair?"

"Oh God, no. I promise I'm not." He sighed. "You're right. We need to talk. Can you pour us both a Scotch?"

• • •

Diane listened intently as he told her about the unusual request from Sherman two weeks earlier and his compliance. He concluded by saying, "I signed off on REL's financial statements for the third quarter. What concerns me most are the ramifications of what I did."

"What do you mean by that?"

"Twelve million dollars doesn't simply disappear. The company, I should say, *I*, had to account for how the money was spent."

"You're saying that it was spent on M and A projects that didn't work out, right?"

"Yes. And if that were true, the money would be a deductible expense. End of story," he said.

"And if that's not true?"

He took a long sip. "First of all, skip the *if*. We know that's not true. What we don't know is how the money was used, whether it was for an expense that was deductible or not."

"Could you ask Sherman about that?"

"In hindsight I should have. In hindsight there are a lot of things I should have done differently. But he made it clear I wasn't to ask any questions. I assumed the money went to a legitimate purpose and twelve million will be deducted against REL's taxable income."

"So what does that mean?"

"It means that as CFO I've signed off on REL's financial statement. If the money was not being used for a legitimate purpose, I've broken several laws including committing tax fraud."

"Can you go back and change what you did?"

"If only it were that easy. Lots of questions would be raised. What would the explanation be? The CEO of the company asked me to do this and I did it without demanding any details? Who are Carter & Associates? Why did I okay wiring money to them? Even if I could put the genie back in the bottle, will Carter and whoever his associates are return the money or has it already been spent or disappeared?"

"Do you have any idea what the money's being used for?"

"No, I don't. Companies have had CEOs who had to be bailed out of bad personal investments, CEOs who were addicts or had gambling problems. Is this what's going on with Sherman? I don't know."

She took his hand in hers. "You've got to talk to somebody. Explain what happened and take the hit now. The longer you stay silent the worse it will be if this comes to light."

"I know, but who?"

"Is there anybody on the board you could speak to?"

"They're all Sherman's handpicked people. If Sherman denies he told me to do it, they'll believe Sherman. I'm the one who'll get fired and take the rap."

"Can you talk to Carlyle Senior?"

"He's far less engaged than he used to be. If he's capable of doing anything, the first thing he'll do is call Sherman to ask him about it."

"How about Carlyle Jr.?"

He took another deep sip of his Scotch. "That's a real possibility. He and Sherman have never liked each other. In fact they hate each other."

"Promise me you'll talk to him tomorrow."

"I will. And thanks. I love you."

38

Michael Carter was annoyed as he found himself heading for Greenwich, Connecticut, for the second day in a row, this time on a Sunday. Sherman had called him during the week and demanded a "same time, same place" meeting. He had met Sherman the previous day at the Greenwich train station. Frankly, he thought Sherman could have shown a little more gratitude for the great job he had done convincing a reluctant Lauren Pomerantz to agree to a settlement. He replayed the meeting in his mind as he drove. The CEO didn't comment on the clever ways he had delved into the young woman's personal life. Handing him a copy of Pomerantz's résumé, Carter reminded him of the commitment that was made to find her a job. "She chose Dallas," he said.

"I'm paying you a lot of money. What are you doing next?"

"I've been looking into Meg Williamson's background. I'll start the process with her over the next few days."

Sherman stared straight ahead. Carter sensed that he

was trying to resolve something in his mind and chose against interrupting the CEO's thoughts.

"Matthews has to be spoken to. He's got to keep it zipped and tell us if there are any other women."

"I agree," Carter said quietly.

"I'm thinking I should speak to him alone."

"That's your decision, but I disagree."

"Why?" Sherman snarled.

"I did these kinds of inquiries in the army. When people are confronted about serious wrongdoing, they do two things. Deny and lie. When you catch them in their lies, they feel humiliated, then very angry. It's as if the meeting is not about what he did to the women; it's about what you're doing to him. He's going to leave the meeting hating how he was treated. You have to work with him afterwards. Do you want those feelings directed at you or at me?"

"You're right," Sherman said.

Carter got the impression those were two words Sherman rarely said. It was an act of will to conceal his delight. The CEO of REL News was going to use him to take one of the most trusted men in America behind the woodshed.

"The meeting can't be at the office. I don't like hotels for this kind of thing. It would be weird to have three of us sitting in a car. Where do we go?"

"Does Mr. Matthews live in this area?"

"Stamford. One town north of here."

"Do you two belong to any of the same clubs?"

"I know what we could do." Sherman opened his

phone, went to the directory, and pushed a button. "Brad, Dick Sherman here. Something's come up related to the IPO. I'd like to talk to you about it, but not over the phone." There was a pause. "No, don't worry. All good. Let's have breakfast at the club at nine o'clock tomorrow. See you there."

Sherman turned to Carter. "We're all set. Greenwich Country Club tomorrow. Come at ten."

It wasn't lost on Carter that Sherman had not asked if tomorrow was convenient for him. "I thought you told him nine o'clock."

"I did. I'll eat with him first. You come at ten. Ask somebody to point you to the Members Grill. We'll grab coffees and go into one of the private meeting rooms where you can do your part." He looked disdainfully at Carter's blue jeans. "Do you belong to a country club?"

"No."

"I didn't think so. Go to the club website and look under 'Guests.' Make sure you're dressed properly." He glanced at the clock on the dashboard. "We're finished. I'm late for my trainer."

39

Carter turned off Doubling Road between the stone pillars that framed the entranceway to Greenwich Country Club. Majestic oaks, now mostly bare of their leaves, lined the driveway. It had cost considerably more to rent a large BMW sedan. But if Sherman asked, assuming the CEO noticed, he would have an explanation ready. "I'm not going to blend in at Greenwich Country Club if I arrive in a Honda Accord."

What had been a cold mist progressed to a steady drizzle. The temperature on this early November Sunday morning was just below forty degrees. He pulled in front of the clubhouse and was met by a bored-looking parking valet who was struggling to stay warm. "I'm a guest of Dick Sherman, meeting him in the Members Grill."

Carter descended a flight of stairs. Remembering what he had read on the website, he silenced his cell phone. He entered a near-empty room with about twenty tables. Two walls of the room were glass, allowing panoramic views of the course. Painted in gold leaf along one wall were winners of past tournaments back to 1909. A polished mahogany bar with no one behind it was to his left.

Four men who appeared to be in their late seventies and eighties were playing gin at a round table in the corner. One of the men wrote on a pad as another shuffled cards. Apparently it was considered crass to have real money on the table. Settling up would come later. On the other side, by the windows, Sherman and Matthews were seated. The egg-stained plates and juice glasses in front of them were empty. Carter glanced at his watch. Nine-fifty-nine. *Here we go*, he said to himself, trying to look confident as he casually walked across the room.

Sherman was the first to make eye contact. He waved him over. "Brad, say hello to Michael Carton. Michael's the one I told you about. He wants to go over a few items related to the IPO."

Carter didn't bother to correct him on the last name.

Matthews extended his hand. "Nice to meet you, Michael. Have a seat."

Sherman was signaling the waitress. "Marlene, bring us three coffees in travel cups."

"We can't talk here?" Matthews asked, gesturing at the almost empty room.

"You know the old expression. The walls have ears," Sherman replied.

Marlene returned with the cups. Sherman stood up. "Follow me," he said as he began to walk away.

"I guess we should humor him," Matthews said to

Carter as he got up, flashing the smile that viewers found so appealing.

Carter glanced at the waitress and then over at the gin game. If they had any idea what was going to happen to the club's most prominent member, no one let on.

Sherman led them down a narrow hallway. Framed black-and-white photos of golfers and holes lined the walls. The CEO turned left into a room with several dark leather couches and overstuffed chairs opposite a fire-place. The head of an elk unhappily stared down on the setting, a reminder of the role hunting played in the early days of the club. "We can talk here," Sherman said, as he settled himself into a chair. Carter waited until Matthews sat down, so he could choose a seat opposite him.

"Michael, I think I know why we're here," Matthews began.

Carter and Sherman exchanged surprised looks. Matthews continued before they could respond.

"When I closed the broadcast on Friday, I talked about the many great people who work at REL News, what a wonderful organization it is, and how proud I am to be one of its leaders. I've always been a news guy. I never worked in the business world per se. I know when the company's considering an IPO, you're not supposed to say anything. If I violated a rule, I apologize. But I assure you, my heart was in the right place."

His speech was followed by what the *New York Post* liked to refer to as the anchorman's ten-thousand-watt smile. The smile lingered for a few seconds, as it did at the end of every broadcast. It was as if Matthews were waiting for a producer behind the camera to count down to when he could shut it off.

Sherman was silent. It was clear that he preferred to be the spectator.

"Mr. Matthews," Carter began, "I'm here to talk to you about the IPO and how valuable you have been and continue to be at REL News. It would not be the same company without you."

"If you're worried about my retiring, don't. If it's my health, I just saw my doctor and—"

"Frankly, Mr. Matthews, I couldn't care less about what your doctor said. That's not why we're here."

Matthews turned to Sherman. "Who does he think he is, talking to me like that? What the hell's going on here?" He started to get up.

Carter stood up opposite him and said in a raised voice, "Matthews, if you don't want to spend the rest of your life drinking beer and playing golf with Bill O'Reilly, Matt Lauer, and Charlie Rose, sit down and shut up!"

Matthews looked stunned. Sherman pointed to the anchorman's chair. "Brad, please, you have to hear him out." Matthews glared at Carter as he sat back down.

Carter, back in his chair, kept his eyes on Matthews as he reached to the table in front of him and picked up his coffee cup. He took a long sip and slowly returned the cup to the table, relishing the opportunity to make Matthews sweat. It was abundantly clear who was in charge of the meeting.

"Do you know the meaning of the term 'sexual abuse'?"

"Don't insult my intelligence."

"I'll take that as a yes. But let's make sure we're all on the same page. The American Psychological Association defines it as 'unwanted sexual activity, with perpetrators using force, making threats, or taking advantage of victims not able to give consent.'"

"Don't lecture me!"

"Did you understand the definition I just shared with you?"

"Get to your point, Carton!"

"Four women have come forward and credibly accused you of making unwanted sexual advances."

Sherman looked at him, clearly surprised to hear there were four.

"I have never in my life acted inappropriately toward a woman. I have received numerous awards from women's organizations—" Matthews blustered.

"Spare me your press clippings. I assure you nobody cares about what a great guy you think you are."

"I don't know who you are, mister, but I assure you I'm at the end of my patience. I never—"

"Do you know a woman named Lauren Pomerantz?" Carter asked, reaching for his coffee cup.

Matthews flinched slightly as he turned toward the fireplace. "That name sounds familiar, but I can't be sure."

It was difficult for even good liars to maintain eye

contact when telling lies, Carter thought. He decided to let Matthews finish.

"REL News has grown so large over the past years. I try, but I can't remember the names of everybody in the News Division. Lauren, what did you say her last name was?"

"Pomerantz. Should I spell it for you?"

Keeping his eyes on Matthews, Carter reached into the vest pocket of his sports jacket, retrieved his phone, and laid it on the table. "I know I'm violating the cell phone policy of the august Greenwich Country Club," he said, "but I'm sure that under these unusual circumstances, they'll cut me a little slack. Last chance, Matthews, did an encounter between you and Pomerantz take place in your office?"

"I have no idea what you're talking about," Matthews said in a voice that lacked its earlier conviction.

"If it's not loud enough, just let me know," Carter said as he pushed a button. Matthews's voice saying, "Lauren, come right in," filled the room. The three men listened in silence to the end.

Carter stared at Matthews, who was now sitting forward, his hands clasped between his knees. "That tape may have been doctored," the anchor said weakly. "They can do that nowadays in a way that can fool even the experts."

Carter sat back in his chair, assuming the posture of a school principal dealing with a disruptive student. "Mr.

Matthews, you might not believe this, but I'm here to help you."

Matthews looked bewildered. He turned to Sherman, who spoke calmly. "That's right, Brad. It's in everybody's best interests that your," he paused, "indiscretions are not made public. We've already settled with Pomerantz."

Some semblance of color returned to Matthews's face.

Carter reached into his jacket pocket and removed a small pad and pen. "I need the names, Mr. Matthews. It's the only way I can find them, persuade them to settle and keep quiet."

Matthews hunched forward. "You have Pomerantz. The other three were Mel Carroll, Christina Neumann, and Paula Stephenson."

Carter and Sherman quickly made eye contact. It was clear to both that in failing to name Meg Williamson, Matthews was not being completely truthful. But Carter felt he had pushed as hard as he could for today. He wanted to talk to Sherman about how to go forward. The $12 million that had been wired to him might not be enough.

"Mr. Matthews, I want to thank you. We've all done things we're not proud of. It takes courage to face them like you did today. We might have to meet again. In the meantime Mr. Sherman and I are going to do everything we can to make this problem go away, but we need your help."

Matthews looked up expectantly.

"Don't make our job any harder than it has to be. No more victims please."

Matthews nodded.

"Okay, we're finished," Sherman said. The three men left the room, went outside, and waited for the valet to bring their cars without exchanging a single word.

40

Ed Myers balanced two coffees in his hand as he knocked on the half-open door. Frederick "Fred" Carlyle, Jr. was famous for the long hours he kept. He was often the first executive to arrive in the morning and the last to leave at night. He was at his desk reading a newspaper.

"Ed, come in," he said, surprised by the early morning intrusion.

"Thanks, Fred," he replied. "I was hoping to catch you before the secretaries and admins get in. I took a chance that you might be in the mood for a coffee," he said, handing him a cup.

"I already had one, but I'm ready for another," Carlyle responded while accepting the cup. "Have a seat," he said, gesturing at one of the leather chairs facing his large mahogany desk.

"Junior," as he was known throughout the company, had taken over his father's large corner office when the company founder had stopped coming to the office on a regular basis a year earlier. The move had been a surprise to many. Dick Sherman had been open about his plans to take over this office after "the old man" retired. But the CEO had shown an uncharacteristic level of restraint in not picking a fight with Junior.

The rumors about "the old man" had begun to circulate almost immediately. In the beginning Myers and everyone else had dismissed it as fatigue or being distracted. He remembered one incident in particular. In a financial meeting Carlyle Sr. had asked a marginally relevant question about the revenue generated by the cable affiliates in the Los Angeles area. Sherman had answered it and continued with his presentation. Fifteen minutes later, the founder had interrupted him midsentence and asked the exact same question. Standing in the front of the room, Myers could see the look of concern on the faces of the executives in the room.

A few weeks later Myers had been in Sherman's office when REL's head of public relations knocked on the door. John Shea explained that earlier that morning he had been prepping the Founder for an upcoming meeting with industry analysts. Carlyle Sr. twice misidentified the anchors of REL's leading news programs and insisted automobile advertising was the company's largest growth area in the current year. As they all knew, the credit belonged to pharmaceutical advertising.

The company had been unsure about what it should do. Whose job is it to tell the boss he can no longer do his job? The fact that Carlyle Sr. was a widower further complicated matters. The Founder lived alone in a stately mansion in Scarsdale. A longtime housekeeper/cook was his only companion.

It was Junior who had helped resolve the quandary. He had hand-delivered a letter to the REL board announcing his father's retirement. The retirement solved one problem but gave birth to another. Because he owned a majority of the shares, Carlyle Sr. controlled the company. Was control now in the hands of the board or Junior?

As Myers looked around, it occurred to him how infrequently he had been in this office since the Founder's retirement. Carlyle Sr. had enjoyed impromptu meetings. He would often call a group of executives to "come by for lunch." Invariably there would be a sushi spread or baby lamb chops and other hors d'oeuvres. Sr. enjoyed telling war stories about the early days of REL News and how often the company had gone to the brink financially. At the same time Sr. was a good listener. If he heard about a spouse being sick, he always followed up. If any member of the team experienced the arrival of a new child or grandchild, a handwritten, congratulatory note from the Founder along with a gift would be sent shortly thereafter.

Junior in many ways was the opposite of his father. The Founder was a born salesman. Sr. rarely took a group of advertisers to a "smokes and drinks" lunch without securing their commitment to devote an extra chunk of their budget to REL. His desk was always piled high with papers. It was nothing short of miraculous that he would somehow manage to find the document he was looking for. Dress for him was an afterthought. He often had to be reminded by his secretary to close his top button or straighten his mismatched tie before rushing to his next meeting.

While affable in his own way, Junior was far more formal. He had gone to prep school at Exeter. Sr. had been so proud that his son had graduated from an Ivy League school, Cornell, a far cry from his father, who had finished just two years at SUNY, Binghamton. Junior was liked by many but loved by none. He was meticulous about his appearance. Shirts and ties were carefully chosen to bring out the best in his Paul Stuart suits. Even on the windiest of days it was rare to see him with a hair out of place.

Sr. would have insisted that they sit at the conference table in the corner, Myers thought. Junior remained seated behind his desk, happy to gaze down on the CFO.

"So, Ed, what's so important you felt you had to get me a cup of coffee before telling me about it?" he asked with a forced smile.

"Fred, if I were more articulate, I'd do a better job explaining the circumstances that brought me here today. I'm not, so I'm just going to say it straight. I screwed up."

For the next ten minutes, Myers recounted the meeting in Sherman's office, the wiring of the money, and the potentially fraudulent tax filings. As he spoke the CFO tried to gauge Carlyle's reaction. It was pointless. Junior remained poker-faced throughout. He interrupted only once. "This Carter & Associates who received the money, do you have any idea who they are?"

"None."

"Have you made an effort to find out?"

Myers sighed, not liking how the questioning was going. "No, I haven't. I thought about it, but I was concerned that knowing more would only get me in deeper. Whatever I learned about Carter, how would I use it, would it be actionable?"

Junior sat back in his chair and folded his hands on his desk. For the second time in not even a month Myers thought he was about to lose his job. A frightening thought flickered in his mind: If he fires me and I get in trouble for what I did, will REL pay my legal bills, or will I be on the hook for them?

When Junior spoke, his voice was methodical, almost devoid of emotion. "Ed, you did the right thing by coming to me. I probably shouldn't share this with you, but you have a right to know. For several years I've suspected that Dick Sherman has been enriching himself at company expense. This latest incident confirms my suspicions."

Myers was dumbfounded. "Oh God, Mr. Carlyle, it's my job to watch the company's money. If I've missed something, I can't tell you how sorry I am."

Junior waved him off. "It's nothing you could have known about. As you're aware, in addition to being the anchor of the REL evening news program, Brad Matthews is editor in chief. He has the final say on what stories are covered and the tone of the broadcast. Companies' stocks have been known to rise and fall the day after receiving coverage on his program.

"Sherman spotted an opportunity and recruited Matthews. Through a dummy company they established, the two of them have been purchasing shares of companies in advance of REL News doing favorable stories about those companies. They've even made money from companies in exchange for favorable coverage. I'm surprised the SEC hasn't caught on yet."

"If I may ask, Fred, how do you know about this?"

Junior looked around, as if uncertain about how to continue. "I'm not sure I should tell you more, but it's hard to carry this alone. One of the companies must have assumed my father was in on the scheme. Their CEO called my father at home and complained to him that they had paid the money but REL News had not kept its end of the bargain."

"Your father told you this?"

"No, he wouldn't have wanted me to get involved. I believe my father knew that toward the end of his working days his memory was slipping. He began recording his calls so that he could refresh himself on what was discussed. I've got the CEO of Statewide Oil on tape."

"Wow! I don't know what to say," Myers exclaimed.

"Ed, I've taken you into my confidence. Don't say anything to anyone. I'm quietly conducting an investigation. The only thing I need you to do is to let me know immediately if Sherman demands more money for Carter or for any reason that doesn't pass the smell test."

"I give you my word."

"And Ed, sending money to Carter & Associates was

a lapse in judgment on your part. But it's understandable under the circumstances and can be put right."

"Thanks, Fred," he said, a huge feeling of relief washing over him.

As Myers got up to leave, he realized he had not taken a single sip of his coffee.

41

Over his second cup of coffee, brewed in the new Keurig machine he had purchased for his office, Michael Carter finished scanning the *New York Times* Real Estate section. He had circled several possibilities on the Upper East Side. Far beyond his financial reach only a month ago, under his new arrangement he felt confident he could make them work. All of these buildings, whether they were condominiums or cooperatives, had boards that heavily scrutinized would-be purchasers. They had their eye out for tenants they felt might be disruptive or, even worse, fail to pay their monthly fees on time. With New York City's notoriously tenant-friendly laws, it was time-consuming and expensive to dislodge deadbeats.

He smiled as he envisioned himself appearing in front of the board. *Let's begin, Mr. Carter, with your telling us what you do for a living.*

Dressed in his latest Paul Stuart suit, he would reply, *I like to view myself as working in the service of the public. I make it possible for Americans to enjoy their favorite TV news anchor, when in reality he should be in prison.*

Forcing himself to get serious, he recognized that it would be a challenge to come up with a satisfactory description of his occupation. But he had time to mull it over. Time, as it turned out, was something he had in abundance.

A potential new source of income had presented itself the previous day. One of his old army buddies had called his cell. Roy had been fired unfairly from his director of security job, and his employer was trying to stiff him out of eleven weeks of accrued vacation. Roy had said, "I know you're not in private practice. Can you recommend a labor lawyer?"

Carter had made the decision immediately. "I've got just the guy for you, Roy, me!"

Why not? he had asked himself. There was nothing in his agreement with REL about not having outside clients. The extra money would be nice, and it would provide a condo board a better answer regarding how he supported himself. Sherman didn't have to know, or if he did, it was none of his business.

He felt the anger burn inside him when he recalled the meeting with Sherman where he told the CEO about how he persuaded a reluctant Lauren Pomerantz to settle in one meeting. Instead of appreciation for a job very well done, he got the clear impression that the CEO felt he was overpaying him for an easy job. Carter was careful to not make that mistake a second time.

Pomerantz had admitted to Carter that Meg Williamson was the one who had advised her to be careful around Matthews. Williamson had been easy to find; her cell number had not changed after she left REL. She had resigned from the company before she had found another job. That always makes things more difficult. The potential new employer typically suspects you got fired or were forced to leave.

Carter had tried a different tack in persuading Williamson to meet with him. He had told her that REL had miscalculated on her withholding and the company owed her back pay. Holding the hand of a four-year-old, she had come to his office the next day.

The presence of the beautiful little girl who sat quietly on her mother's lap during the early part of the meeting had worked to Carter's advantage. Meg looked on approvingly as he made a fuss over her child, who answered his questions with a wide smile. Meg told him that any extra money headed her way would be a godsend. She had just finalized a divorce and her ex could not be counted on for anything.

"Meg, I apologize for misrepresenting the reason for today's meeting, but I'm sure you'll be interested in what I have to say," he had begun. A protracted legal battle against Brad Matthews, he assured her, would be tremendously stressful for her and, he added, looking at her young daughter, for Jillian.

At Carter's suggestion, Beatrice came in and took Jillian to her desk outside. Now he and Meg could talk candidly.

He had feigned interest as a tearful Meg unburdened herself describing Matthews's advances and her current, difficult circumstances. Fifteen minutes later Beatrice was applying her notary seal to the signed settlement agreements. A more composed Meg had Jillian on her lap. Overcoming her initial reluctance, Meg had admitted that she was aware of two other victims. Carter did not let on that he knew about Pomerantz or that he was hearing the name Cathy Ryan for the first time.

Completing a settlement with Williamson had been just that easy, but that was not the story he told Sherman. At their most recent Greenwich train station meeting, he had added a few elements. "Puffery," as his friend in the advertising business liked to call it, harmless, exaggerated claims about a product or service.

"It's been a knock-down-drag-out with Meg Williamson. It took multiple calls to get her to agree to meet with me. She had just made an appointment to see a therapist about what happened with Matthews. It took a lot of persuading to get her to cancel. Similar to Pomerantz, she initially insisted on bringing a friend to the meeting for moral support. I had to talk her out of that. After she said she was staying with a friend in Hackensack, New Jersey, I schlepped out there to meet her, only to be stood up. Her kid was sick, and she couldn't get hold of a sitter. I told her if she didn't sign now, she risked having the settlement be considered community property. If her ex found out about it, in theory he would be entitled to half of it. I made another trip to lovely Hackensack and got her to sign."

"Keep it up" had been Sherman's grudging compliment.

42

Jacob Wilder and Junior had become acquainted on the squash courts at the New York Athletic Club. Both in their mid-forties and both high-level players, for several years they had competed together in doubles tournaments. When Junior needed an REL lawyer to perform a discreet inquiry, the decision was easy.

"Whenever a business entity incorporates," Wilder began, "it has to register with the New York Department of State Division of Corporations, State Records, and Uniform Commercial Code."

"I assume it has to include an address."

"It does, but Carter & Associates used a PO box."

"Does the post office keep the address of box holders confidential?"

"In theory, yes. For fifty bucks, no," he said while handing a piece of paper across the desk.

"Nicely done, Jacob. Make sure you expense the fifty bucks," Junior said, smiling.

"Don't worry, boss, I'll figure something out. And one

more thing. Up until a couple months ago, we had a lawyer working here in Human Resources with the same last name, Carter. Just for kicks, I checked his file."

"And?"

"The address of the PO box holder matches the Upper East Side address where Carter lived when he was with REL."

"Excellent. Can you get me a copy—"

"I had a feeling you'd want to see Carter's file," he said, handing a manila folder across the desk. "Happy reading!"

43

Paula Stephenson didn't know what to do. She looked at the bills on her kitchen table. She was four months behind on the condo association dues and her mortgage was three months in arrears. To make matters worse, the condo had gone down in value since she purchased it. There was a letter threatening to repossess her car. Her health insurance provider had dumped her for lack of payment. Her checking account was down to a few thousand dollars.

How did I go through two million dollars? she raged at herself.

It started with the drinking, she thought as she glanced at the bottle of vodka and the glass, which were her constant—almost her only—companions. She had become the one thing she had promised herself she would avoid. Both of her parents had been alcoholics. She hated drinking, but had always wanted to fit in. When other people are drinking and you're not, you make them uncomfortable, she thought. They think you're judging them.

Not wanting to feel like an outsider, she had arrived at

a solution. She would have *a* drink, usually wine or occasionally a beer, but never more than one. That one drink would be in her hand all evening and would still have some wine in it when the party was over.

She grimaced while taking another long sip of vodka and savoring the burning sensation as the liquid went down her throat. She felt herself starting to relax.

Everything changed after what happened with Matthews, she thought while taking a long drag on her cigarette.

She had been the weather girl at a small cable station in Cincinnati. After it was purchased by REL News, she had been invited to come to New York. The hours were terrible. Weekends and overnight shifts, but she was living her dream. She was an on-air broadcaster, twenty-five years old, and loving life in New York City.

One year of a dream. Six months of a nightmare. It was at a Christmas party that he took notice of her. She had been thrilled when the great Brad Matthews called her by name. *He knows who I am!*

There was much to celebrate. REL News was finishing the year with yet another impressive gain in the ratings. Polls revealed that TV viewers regarded their middle-of-the-road coverage as more fair and balanced by a significant margin than both CNN and Fox. When the waitress came over offering champagne, Matthews took one for himself and handed her one. Touching his glass to hers, he said, "We all need to continue what we've been doing to win America's trust."

She had to fit in. The champagne tasted strange but at the same time pleasing. The rest of the evening was a blur. Another glass of champagne, a nightcap at the bar, an offer of a ride home in his chauffeured car, for whatever reason having to stop at Matthews's office first. She poured more vodka into her glass as she recalled with revulsion the feeling of him on top of her on the couch. Crying in the cab as she went home alone.

Soon after, the calls began. He wanted to see her in his office after her broadcast or before she started. She would go into his office looking perfect, her makeup and hair ready for the hot glare of the cameras. The sound of his office door closing. As he handed her a glass filled with a clear liquid, he told her how much he had enjoyed getting to know her at the Christmas party. It was the first time she had ever tasted vodka.

Usually he would leave first. That would give her a little time to compose herself. When she stopped crying, she would head back to the makeup room for a touch-up. REL insisted their on-air people, particularly the women, always look their best.

Finally, she had had enough. She hated Matthews and hated herself for what she had allowed him to do to her. She wanted out of New York. She'd quit REL a year and a half ago and accepted the first job she was offered, as the weather reporter at WDTN in Dayton. But after what happened with Matthews, something had changed, and for the worse. She had lost her self-confidence. Previously she would experience a rush of excitement when the producer counted down with his fingers and pointed to indicate when she was live on the air. In Dayton she found the green light of the live camera terrifying. And it showed.

Thanks to Matthews, she knew what she had to do to calm down. A swig of vodka before going on the air did the trick, at least in the beginning. But the feeling of nervousness crept back in and terrified her. Bigger problems called for larger cures.

It didn't take long for her producers and some viewers to notice. She slurred the pronunciation of Cincinnati several times in one broadcast.

She took another sip as she recalled the humiliation that followed. A meeting with the executive producer and a company lawyer in her small office. Her denials followed by the discovery of a half consumed fifth of vodka in her desk drawer. Her agreement to take a leave of absence for personal reasons. Who are they kidding? she asked herself. I got fired.

She didn't need to go to some stupid rehab place, she had convinced herself. It's natural to get a little nervous when you're on TV. Everything would be all right if she just took some time to pull herself together after what had happened at REL News. And besides, she was tired of it being so cold in Ohio.

And then Michael Carter tracked her down. After a meeting that lasted less than an hour, $2 million was headed her way as long as she kept her mouth shut about what had happened at REL. A year ago I had $2 million, she thought.

After receiving the settlement, she traveled for three months. Cruises around Italy and Greece. Skiing in Vale. Most people her age didn't have the time or money to go on those types of trips, so she went alone. And it was easy to meet people, particularly at the bars.

It was only a week after she had moved to North Carolina that she met Carlo. Blessed with dashing Italian good looks, he had been recruited to work for one of the many hi-tech companies in what had been dubbed Research Triangle Park near the cities of Raleigh, Durham, and Chapel Hill.

It was the first time in a long time she had felt good around a man. He was so nice to her. Unlike some of the others, he had not been critical of her drinking. They were close to getting engaged. The software he had developed seemed so promising. It was time to leave his job and go out on his own to create a future for both of them. With the right backing, the company would be profitable in less than a few months.

A few months became six and then nine. She couldn't risk losing the $700,000 she had invested, so she kept putting in more. And more. Before it was over, $1.3 million of her money was gone. So was the company. So was Carlo. How could she have been so stupid?

That was a question she had kept asking herself over recent days and weeks. But it didn't only pertain to the investment in Carlo's company. She opened the manila folder on the table that was labeled "Me Too" and again glanced over the online articles she had printed. The woman who got $20 million from one news organization. The studio magnate who settled three separate cases, each in the $9.5 to $10 million range. A woman from a TV network who had received $9 million. Two women from other networks were expected to get more when their cases settled.

What REL had paid her was so little compared to what these other women got. Twenty million dollars! That's ten times what they gave me. Whatever he did to her couldn't have been worse than what happened to me. And they tricked me into not using a lawyer, she thought bitterly.

She didn't bother to look at the settlement agreement that was on the kitchen counter. She had reread it a dozen times over the past week. If she tried to go back for more money, REL would demand repayment of the $2 million she had already received.

She looked at the phone number of Carter & Associates on the letterhead of the document. She had only spoken to that slimeball once since she signed the agreement. That was when she had called him to confirm receipt of the $2 million wire. He told her they should never speak again, with one exception. If anybody, especially a reporter, ever contacted her about her time at REL, she was to call him at that number immediately.

She knew what she had to do, but she was afraid to take the first step. It was as if the green light of the camera were shining on her again. Another sip of vodka helped her focus. She desperately needed to talk to somebody who would understand. The only other Matthews victim she knew was Cathy Ryan. By holding out and not settling right away, she almost certainly was on her way to a much bigger payday.

There was one other person she could call. One of the truly decent and caring people who was still at REL. She started to dial but then put the phone down. A sympathetic ear would be appreciated, but she really didn't want more advice, no matter how loving, that she should get help with her drinking problem.

She opened a second folder and glanced at the *Wall Street Journal* article she had cut out. It was about REL News going public. Timing is everything. Maybe my luck is changing. Maybe it is possible to get a second bite of the apple, she thought as her eyes remained fixed on the number of Carter & Associates.

44

Michael Carter inhaled the cool evening air as he walked the two blocks from the subway to his apartment. He had begun his preliminary research on the victims named by Matthews. Now that he could set his own hours, he found time to make it to the gym almost every day. The small paunch that had been starting to show around his belt was significantly diminished. His wife had given up on constantly asking him what he had been doing on the evenings he arrived home late. She had accepted his explanation that now that he worked on "special projects" for REL, his hours would be irregular. This had come in handy the previous evening when he had taken the receptionist in his rented space to dinner for the third time. He smiled as he recalled their kissing and petting all the way to Brooklyn in the back of the Uber. It would be only a matter of time before she agreed to go to a hotel after dinner.

His reverie was interrupted by a deep baritone voice that said, "Michael Carter?"

"Yes," he answered, startled.

He turned to see a large, broad-shouldered black man who was at least a head taller than he was standing next to him. He felt the man's enormous hand clamp down on his shoulder. "This way," he said, pointing toward a black Lincoln Navigator that was parked to their left with its engine running. It wasn't a request; it was a command. The man gave him a gentle push toward the car.

"Listen, if it's money you want, I can—"

Ignoring him, the man opened the back door of the car and said, "Get in."

From his standing position Carter could see someone else in the backseat, on the opposite side. He could see the man's lower arms and legs but not his face. Instead of a robbery, was this a Mafia-style hit? he thought to himself. Would they find him tomorrow floating facedown in the East River?

He felt a hand start to shove him forward. "Okay," he said. "I'll get in." He bent down and slid into the seat. Nervously, he glanced at the figure a few feet away from him.

"Oscar, give us a few minutes so we can talk alone," a voice commanded.

"Text when you need me," Oscar replied before closing the door firmly.

At first Carter wasn't sure who his fellow passenger was. But the voice confirmed it. Staring at him but not saying a word was Frederick Carlyle, Jr.

A few moments later Junior broke the silence. "Do

you prefer to be addressed as Michael Carter or 'Carter & Associates'?"

"Mr. Carlyle, if you give me a few minutes to explain—"

"Carter, I'm going to give you as much time as you need to explain why you and Dick Sherman stole twelve million dollars from my family's company. If I'm not satisfied with your explanation, Oscar and I will personally escort you to police headquarters, where I will press charges against you. Allow me to caution you, Mr. Carter," he said as he opened a manila folder on his lap. It was Carter's personnel file. "I already know a great deal about you."

Carter paused to consider his options. He could refuse to answer questions and just open the door and leave. That assumed the child locks were not in position. He pictured himself repeatedly yanking the door handle while Carlyle smugly stared at him. If he were able to get out of the car, would Oscar be there to greet him? He had an image of that huge hand around his throat lifting him off the ground. Was Carlyle bluffing about pressing charges? He had no idea.

"All right, Mr. Carlyle, I'm going to tell you the truth."

"That would be very refreshing."

Carter explained how Lauren Pomerantz had knocked on his door to share her story of being abused by Brad Matthews and how he had gone to Sherman with a plan to contain the situation. Only once did Junior interrupt.

"Who else knows about what happened to Pomerantz?"

This is a chess match, Carter thought to himself. The winner will be the one who can plan several moves ahead.

When he told Junior about Pomerantz coming to his office, he had omitted the detail that she had gone to Junior first, but he didn't do anything about it. Junior is probing to see if I know that, he thought. It won't hurt to keep an ace up my sleeve for later. "As far as I know, Matthews obviously, Sherman, myself, and now you."

"Go on. Tell me everything else."

Carter spent the next fifteen minutes recounting the settlements reached, his progress on negotiations with other victims, and the Greenwich Country Club meeting with Matthews and Sherman.

"So you believe there are more women that we don't know about?" Junior asked.

"I do. When I confronted Matthews and got him to name names, he conspicuously left out Meg Williamson. How many others he refused to admit to, at this time I don't know."

"My opinion of you has undergone a transformation, Mr. Carter. At first I thought you were a common thief, albeit a clever one. It's not easy to make twelve million dollars fall through the cracks unnoticed, but you and Sherman succeeded in doing that."

"With all due respect, Mr. Carlyle, if we were completely successful in doing that, you wouldn't be here talking to me."

"True," Junior said with a grin. "Never mind how I found out. Here's what I want you to do. Continue with your project. Keep me abreast of everything you're doing. Who you're negotiating with, settlements reached, potential new victims, I want to know everything." He slipped him a piece of paper with a phone number and email address scrawled on it.

"Two more things, Carter. REL relies on a network of well-placed sources to help us get a jump on our competitors when pursuing stories. These individuals receive monetary honorariums for their efforts. I assume I can count on you to facilitate those transactions."

"Of course," Carter responded.

"And finally, I've had my eye on Dick Sherman for several years. I won't bore you with the details, but he and Matthews have been using their positions at REL to illegally enrich themselves. I'm sure you wondered why Sherman so quickly approved your plan to save Matthews."

"That did come as a bit of a surprise to me," Carter said, knowing full well that it didn't. He had assumed Sherman was being a loyal company man doing anything he could to preserve REL's cash cow, Brad Matthews.

"A word of caution: you can't trust Sherman as far as you can throw him. Not a word to Sherman or anyone else about our meeting today or our ongoing relationship. Have I made myself clear?"

"Crystal," Carter said, repeating his favorite line from the military movie *A Few Good Men*.

"You're free to go," Junior said as he picked up his phone and began typing a text to Oscar.

45

Dick Sherman eased his Mercedes into his familiar parking space at the Greenwich train station. The slow burn that had been building inside him for weeks now felt like an inferno. *I should have followed my initial instinct,* he thought. *At that first meeting I should have wrung Carter's neck and thrown him in Long Island Sound.*

Sherman was not accustomed to feeling awkward around people, particularly employees. If he didn't like somebody, they'd have that person fired or make him (or her) so miserable that they'd quit on their own. Now when he saw Matthews in the hallways, there was no deference. After a quick, barely audible "hello," the anchorman just kept going. Myers, he noticed, also went out of his way to avoid him. With the exception of staff meetings, he and the CEO had barely exchanged a word in the last month.

But it was Carter who had set him off. The two-bit lawyer had called him on one of the stupid phones he insisted on using to say another wire would be necessary. Sherman had cut him off immediately. "Same time and place to look at trains," he had barked.

Sherman exhaled in a futile attempt to calm himself down. He had the nagging suspicion that Carter was playing him for a fool. How did he know that Carter was reaching settlements with the women? Carter said so. How did he know the victims were getting $2 million each? Carter said so. Now Carter was saying there were more victims, which meant more settlements, which meant he'd have to wire more money to guess who? Carter & Associates. If he thinks he can pull a sting on me, Sherman thought, he doesn't know who he's dealing with.

Michael Carter walked slowly across the parking lot as he approached the black Mercedes. It would be his first face-to-face meeting with Sherman since his session in the back of the car with Carlyle Junior. Frankly, he was tired of getting jerked around. He should have stood his ground with Sherman on the phone. His wife had given him a litany of complaints when he announced he would miss the last soccer game of the season. His son had a different way of showing displeasure. He refused to come out of his room to say goodbye when Carter left the apartment. I'm doing all this work to solve other people's problems, he thought, and all I'm getting in return is grief.

"Change of plans, Carter. I wired twelve million dollars to you and now you say you need more. What kind of idiot do you think I am? Starting right now I want to know everything. I want copies of the settlement agreements you've reached and copies of wire transactions you've sent to victims. I want to know who you're negotiating with and any outside expenses you're incurring. After I get all that, we can talk about whether it's necessary for me to get you more money."

Carter's first impression was that this conversation was eerily similar to the one in the back of the car with Junior. Why? He thinks I'm stealing the money, that's why, he told himself. How ironic! he thought. According to Junior, Sherman was in cahoots with Matthews to enrich themselves at REL's expense, and now Sherman was worried that somebody else was pocketing money that belonged to REL.

Chess match, he reminded himself. Think several moves ahead. He could tell Sherman, *Go to hell*, but then what? If Sherman fired him and got somebody else to pursue the settlements, he wouldn't be of any use to Carlyle Junior. And Junior had just started to use him to make payments to confidential sources. That could be a line of work that would last a long time.

"Fair enough," Carter said. "I'll get you the documents you want showing how the money was spent. While we're here, I'll give you a quick rundown on what I've been doing. You know Lauren Pomerantz settled. Pomerantz named Meg Williamson as the one who tipped her off to tape her encounter with Matthews. When Williamson settled, she gave me another name, Cathy Ryan. I've exchanged a few messages with her but progress is slow."

"Will she settle?"

"Eventually, but it's hard to tell when. When we were

with Matthews at the club, he named Paula Stephenson. I went to Ohio right afterward and settled with her. Matthews gave us two other names, Christina Neumann and Mel Carroll. I just located Neumann, who got married and is living in Montana. No trace of Carroll yet, but I'll find her.

"You asked me why I told you I'm going to need more money." Carter counted on his fingers for emphasis. "Pomerantz, Williamson, Ryan, Stephenson, Neumann, Carroll. That's six victims at two million dollars a pop. So the twelve million you sent me and more is already spoken for. And that's before my compensation and expenses. When I find these women, they're likely going to name others. Not to mention we know Matthews lied to us. At some point we'll need to hold his feet to the fire to give us the full list."

"Is there any chance you can settle with some of them for less than two million?"

"Read the papers or watch the news. Two million is cheap. Frankly, I'm surprised they're not demanding more."

"How much more and when will you need it?"

"Another six million dollars within a month. That will be enough for the time being."

Sherman sighed. "I'll get it done. We're finished."

"No, we're not," Carter responded. "If you really want to know everything I'm doing, we need another way to communicate. Use cash to buy yourself a cheap laptop. Get a new email address, obviously not using any part of your name. Use only the new computer to contact me at this email address," he said, as he finished scribbling on a slip of paper that he handed to Sherman. "When this is over, throw the laptop in the Sound or any river. Water destroys everything electronic. Then cancel the email address and no one will be the wiser."

This will save *me* some time, Carter thought to himself. Junior and Sherman both want to know everything I'm doing. I can send the same emails to each of them.

"One last thing," Carter continued, looking Sherman squarely in the eyes. "The next time we meet it will be at a time that's convenient for me at a location of my choosing. I don't want to make you late for your trainer. You're free to go."

As Carter stepped out of the car to walk toward the station entrance, Sherman resisted the overwhelming temptation to use his two-ton Teutonic vehicle to crush Carter.

One less lawyer, he thought, would make the world a better place.

46

Michael Carter stretched out in his first-class seat for the flight from Billings, Montana, to Minneapolis. After a forty-five-minute layover he would be on his way to JFK in New York.

Christina Neumann, one of the victims named by Matthews, now lived in Billings. From the time he was a little boy, Carter had always been fascinated by dinosaurs. After touring Yellowstone National Park, he had visited the Museum of the Rockies and its world-class fossil collection.

It had been an effort to get Neumann to respond to him. Fortunately, most people never change their cell phone number. For a fee, of course, his contact at Verizon had confirmed that her cell number was the same as when she was at REL and provided her current billing address.

Neumann had ignored the first three texts he had sent her. She broke her silence after he promised in a fourth text that if necessary, he would come to Billings unannounced and knock on her door. She had called him back the same day.

No, he had told her, he was not interested in her vague assurances that she had made her peace with what happened and had just moved on. His job, he reasoned, was to conclude settlements. Somebody who's content letting bygones be bygones today might feel differently tomorrow. The loss of a job, an expensive divorce, a parent goes bonkers with Alzheimer's and needs expensive care. Stuff happens; and all of a sudden dredging up the past in favor of a big payday is not such a bad idea.

He still didn't know why people insisted on sharing their deepest vulnerabilities with their adversaries. She had confided in him that she had not shared what happened to her at REL with her husband. He had confided in her that if she refused to meet with him, perhaps her husband would be more amenable. They had agreed to a date when her husband would be away on a business trip.

He smiled as he thought of sitting across from Christina Neumann. A petite blonde with a gorgeous figure, she was by far his easiest settlement to date. In and out of his rented office space in less than thirty minutes. She was not aware of any other victims. Neumann was adamant that her husband not find out what had happened to her at REL. And it was obvious that she didn't need the money. She barely read the settlement before signing it. Her instruction was that the two million dollars be wired to the ASPCA. What a dope, he thought to himself, wondering for a moment if she would follow up to assure he had sent the money.

As his army friend from Alabama used to joke, "This

is as easy as holding up the Piggly Wiggly with a gun." He was convinced that if she had been left alone, Neumann never would have come forward. But he saw no need to share that with Sherman and Junior.

Opening his laptop, he began writing the email he would send about the three days of arduous negotiations that had finally resulted in Christina Neumann agreeing to a settlement.

47

Michael Carter sighed in frustration as he made another note on the second page of his legal pad. Persuading the women to settle wasn't always easy. In his first conversation with Cathy Ryan, she had literally told him to take a hike. But he was confident he could browbeat and wear her down the way he had done the others. Finding the women and getting the conversation started had always been a snap, until now.

He looked again at Mel Carroll's personnel file. Matthews would have made the job so much easier if he'd *only* stuck to abusing Americans, Carter thought.

Carroll had been an intern in a REL News international exchange program. She had come over at age twenty-three after working for one year at REL's affiliate in South Africa.

The two women she listed as emergency contacts were no help. Both were South African nationals living in New York City. They had no idea where Carroll went after leaving REL.

The South African Consulate had tried to help. They had also given him a copy of her birth certificate, which included both her parents' names. She had been born in Genadendal.

There was some evidence she had returned there. When she resigned eleven months earlier, she left wiring instructions to send her final pay to a bank in her birthplace, a small town ninety minutes east of Cape Town. There was no guarantee she was living in that area now, but at least it was a place to start.

Carter chuckled as he tried to imagine what Sherman's reaction would be upon hearing that he would be heading to South Africa at REL's expense. To hell with him, he thought to himself. He had a job to do, and he planned to do it right. If he had a little fun along the way, that was his business. He opened his computer and typed in the SEARCH screen, "Best Safaris in South Africa."

48

Houston, we have a problem was how Michael Carter began his email to Sherman and Junior. Right from the beginning, he had recognized it as a potential flaw in his plan to buy the silence of Matthews's victims. It was a what-if? that he had never broached with either man because he didn't have a good answer regarding how to handle the situation. Truth be told, his recommendation would be more Band-Aid than solution. Twenty months after notching his first agreement with Lauren Pomerantz, he and they would be forced to confront the issue head on.

He continued typing.

> After agreeing to a settlement a year and a half ago, Paula Stephenson contacted me. She wants more money. After leaving REL she was hired as an on-air reporter at a cable station in Dayton. A few months later she resigned. In reality she had been fired for

being intoxicated while on the air. She relocated to Durham where she purchased a condominium. Shortly thereafter, she lost a large sum of money on an investment in a software company.

She is delinquent on homeowners association payments, car loans, credit cards, etc. In our conversations she cited the higher sums paid to Me-Too victims by other media companies. Although she would not share names, she claims other Matthews victims would validate her story if she came forward.

If she goes public, her accusations might be dismissed as the ranting of an alcoholic. But if in addition to her settlement document, the $2 million she received is traced to Carter & Associates and further traced to REL News, her story will be very credible.

Stephenson has agreed to remain silent until she meets with me on Monday in Durham. I suggest an interim solution. A one-year deal where each month she will receive a wire of $50 thousand. This will see us well-past the IPO and buy time to think. It will also prevent a repeat of the cycle where she squanders away a large sum of money all at once.

Your silence will be regarded as approval of this plan.

After sending the email, Carter leaned back in his chair. He had an uneasy feeling about the upcoming meeting. The sit-downs with the other victims were battles of wits, chess matches where each side had strengths and vulnerabilities. But in Stephenson he sensed a quiet defiance. He thought of the line in the Bob Dylan song. "When you ain't got nothing, you got nothing to lose." Despite being broke and a drunk, Stephenson was holding all the cards.

49

Carter had his laptop open on the desk in the temporary office space he had rented in Durham. He gave one final read to the settlement document he would discuss with Paula Stephenson. He pressed a key and heard a whirring noise behind him. The synching of his computer and the printer had been achieved.

The receptionist had buzzed a few minutes earlier to inform him that the notary public had arrived. Why did I even bother? he thought to himself. The very fact that he was here today reminded him how unenforceable these settlement agreements were. He had used the standard legal language, "now, and for all of time," to describe the signer's commitment to adhere to the terms of the contract. In Paula Stephenson's case, "for all of time" had lasted less than fifteen months.

Neither Sherman nor Matthews had responded to his email. That was both a surprise and a relief. He had anticipated incoming fire from Sherman about the prospect of paying more to someone who had already settled. He also thought at least one of them would ask why he was waiting five days to meet with Stephenson.

The answer would not have pleased either of them. After he agreed to represent his army buddy in his wrongful termination suit, he had negotiated a quick and lucrative settlement. It had led to more business. If his work for REL came to a halt, maybe he could segue into doing that full-time.

Stephenson had wanted to meet right away. He had put her off because he had two days of depositions scheduled on one of his employment cases.

"Where are you, Paula?" he said aloud as he glanced at his watch. She was now thirty-five minutes late for their eleven o'clock appointment. She had not responded to a text, and his call had gone straight to her voice mail. He checked his phone again. She had made no attempt to contact him.

When he'd told her where and when they would meet, he'd given that information over the phone. Could he possibly have misspoken? He doubted it. She had asked him to repeat it several times and she sounded reasonably sober. Even if she got the date and time wrong, why wouldn't she respond to his messages?

At noon the receptionist buzzed. Did he still want the notary to wait? "No, send her in," he said. He paid her for her time. The receptionist gave him the name of a Chinese food place that delivered.

At two o'clock he had a decision to make. Sitting here was accomplishing nothing, and he didn't want to miss his 6:30 direct flight to Newark. He clicked on his laptop and pulled up the address of Paula Stephenson's condominium. According to Waze, he could be there in twenty minutes. If she's changed her mind about meeting me, what's the point? he asked himself. But there was one viable scenario. After a night of heavy boozing, she could be in bed in a dead sleep. It's worth a shot, he thought, as he opened the Uber app.

"Don't pull in. I'll get out here," Carter ordered as the Uber driver eased to the side of the road opposite Stephenson's condominium. Across the lawn on both sides of the front entrance he could see a parked police cruiser with its overhead lights flashing. Between the two vehicles a medical technician in a white jacket was opening the rear doors of an ambulance. Two other white-coated individuals were wheeling a stretcher to a halt in back of the ambulance. A human figure with a sheet covering the entire body was motionless atop the stretcher.

Trying to look inconspicuous, Carter walked slowly down the driveway and settled in behind a group of voyeurs. He was hoping to find out what had happened without asking any questions.

"Sometimes the pressure just gets to be too much," one woman sighed. "I hear the condo association was pressing her hard to get caught up on her payments."

"Did she really kill herself?" another asked.

"I was doing work on that floor. I heard the police say

she hung herself. That's got to be an awful way to go," a man with paint splattered on his shirt and blue jeans shared. His truck, with the logo of a painting business on its side, was parked about one hundred feet away.

"Does anybody know her name?" Carter asked, trying to sound disinterested.

"Stephenson," a woman said. "Her unit was up there on the fourth floor."

Carter eased his way from the group and started to backpedal up the driveway. He made eye contact with a police officer who held his gaze. The travel bag in his hand made him feel uncomfortable. It was as if the officer was sensing that something inside the bag was linked to what happened to Stephenson. Carter gave a half smile, turned, and began to walk away. With each step he expected a whistle to blow and a loud voice to order him to stop. He reached the street without looking back and turned right. His mind was racing, and he needed the opportunity to think things through.

Problem solved had been his first thought when he learned that Paula Stephenson was dead. Another loose end tied off, this time at no expense to REL. No more worries about a drunken, loose cannon. But was there another scenario that was not nearly so rosy? The police would keep looking until they found her parents, a sibling, some relative who would volunteer to come in and take charge of her personal effects. In plain view, on top of a desk or a kitchen counter could be her settlement agreement with his name on the letterhead. What will happen if some relative shows up and takes the time to read it? Why did this group, Carter & Associates, give her $2 million?

There had been a steely resolve in Stephenson's voice when Carter had spoken to her only five days earlier. His attempt to bully her into adhering to the original settlement had gone nowhere. If anything, it had backfired. She had laughed at him, saying derisively, "If I hire a lawyer, what are you going to do, Mr. Carter, sue me?" She then mentioned three prominent New York law firms that had negotiated huge payouts for their abuse clients. She insisted on reciting the amount each woman had received. "If we don't work something out and fast, I'm going to call one of these firms." Ironically, Paula Stephenson's last words to him when they had agreed to meet at eleven o'clock were "Be on time."

It just didn't make sense. Far from being afraid, Stephenson seemed to be spoiling for a fight. How can somebody in five days go from being so gung ho to putting a rope around her neck?

Carter came to an abrupt halt as a sickening thought swept over him. "Oh my God," he said aloud. Suppose somebody else put that rope around her neck. How convenient for REL that a troublemaker, a woman who was threatening to go public with her accusation, had taken her own life.

A few minutes ago, the thought of a relative finding the settlement agreement had been a concern for Carter. Now it was far more ominous, particularly if the police got hold of it and considered the possibility that she had been murdered. He had a motive to kill her. His airline ticket and hotel reservation were in his name, so they could establish that he was in Durham around the time she was killed. The receptionist and the notary public could confirm the time he spent at the temporary office space, but that wouldn't do him any good if she were killed in the wee hours of the morning. He berated himself for taking the early flight to Durham the previous day to give him time to visit the Museum of Life and Science. If he had flown down this morning, all of his time would have been accounted for.

Stop, he said to himself. He knew *he* didn't do it. The question was, who did? There was only one choice. Sherman. After initially not wanting to know the details of Carter's work, the CEO had reversed himself and wanted to know everything. He was setting Carter up as the fall guy if the police started investigating. Sherman would be too smart to do it himself. He'd be in Connecticut with a rock-solid alibi while somebody he hired dispatched Stephenson.

A sickening thought entered Carter's mind. Killers get a morbid sense of satisfaction when they watch the police investigate the crime they committed. They often return to the crime scene, fueled by a sense of power that they alone know what happened to the victim. If the police reviewed the records from Uber, they'd find that he was driven to the building just in time to watch the body being taken away. The image of the police officer staring at him flooded into his mind.

Calm down, he ordered himself. Stop playing Dr. Phil. Any number of factors could have caused Stephenson to snap and take her life after he spoke to her. The most important thing for him was to focus on self-preservation.

50

Dick Sherman was alone in his office on the third floor of his Greenwich mansion. Tonight he was happy to have the house to himself.

Using the computer he kept in a locked file cabinet, he had just finished reading the email from Carter summarizing his trip to Durham. *Paula Stephenson dead, an apparent suicide.* Perfect, he thought to himself. Stephenson could have been a real headache for him and for REL. Now she was in a drawer in a morgue with her mouth the way it should be. Shut. He had no patience for anyone who reneged on agreements. Good riddance!

But Stephenson's trip to the Great Beyond did not solve all his problems. Not by a long shot.

Matthews's arrogance infuriated him. Instead of gratitude and cooperation, "America's anchorman" had left it to Sherman to clean up the mess he had made. I should have left that hayseed at the southern Virginia cable station where I found him twenty years ago, he sneered to himself.

Sherman still didn't trust Carter as far as he could throw him. But he'd painted himself into a corner with the two-bit lawyer. Fire him, and he'd have to hire somebody else to finish the job. And that would make Carter another person who knew too much and who couldn't be counted on to keep his mouth shut. Were lawyers the professionals who committed suicide the most, or was that dentists? he wondered.

A potentially even bigger problem was Myers. At the first sign of trouble, that Boy Scout is going to break and start singing about the wires to Carter & Associates, he thought. Even with a board that was so favorably disposed to him, if Myers and Carter started telling the same story, his support would erode very quickly.

Shoving aside the computer he used only to communicate with Carter, he opened his other laptop and clicked on the email from Junior that had turned his life upside down. He reread it for what had to be the twenty-fifth time.

> Dick, A young associate producer spoke to me today. She claims she had a me-too encounter with Brad Matthews in his office. Her description was graphic. I told her I'd look into it. How do you want to handle? Fred

Sherman got up and paced around his office. Junior has as much on the line as I do, he thought. It was an open secret that Junior was hoping to succeed his father as chairman of the board. Even after the IPO, enough shares would be in the hands of the Carlyle family to make that happen unless—

"Unless he realizes this could bring him down, too," Sherman said aloud. After Pomerantz talked to Junior, he sent Sherman the email. When she approached Junior a second time, he basically told her to go back to work. If that's all that happened, Junior might be able to wiggle off the hook. But if she played that tape for him and he let it drop after sending a note to Sherman, he was in big trouble. Women, who comprised 57.3 percent of REL's viewership, would scream bloody murder.

Sitting back down, Sherman typed a quick email to Frederick Carlyle, Jr. Would he be free tomorrow to discuss a private matter?

51

Frederick Vincent Carlyle, Jr., eased into the plush leather chair behind the mahogany desk and looked around. The corner office looked the same as when his father was the occupant. The walls included photographs of his father with the previous six US presidents, heads of state of foreign governments, and Hollywood royalty. A map of the world encased in glass showed the locations of REL bureaus and affiliates around the globe. Fourteen honorary doctorates adorned the walls. Centered among them was a "Time Magazine Person of the Year" cover.

"Junior," as he knew most employees referred to him behind his back but never to his face, was a realist. His father would always be the Horatio Alger, rags-to-riches success story, the entrepreneur whose accomplishments reminded people that America remained the land of opportunity. Junior realized and accepted that no matter what he did, he would always be viewed differently. Taking something big and making it much larger is not nearly as sexy a story as starting from nothing and making something big. He thought, as he often did, of the zinger lobbed at President George W. Bush: "He was born on third base, but he thinks he hit a triple." One industry analyst had written that Junior's sole accomplishment was being named to New York City's list of most eligible bachelors.

But the accolades would come, he promised himself. Seven years earlier, he had begun talking to his father about the advantages of transitioning the privately owned REL to a publicly traded company. "Why?" had been his father's first question. "What's wrong with the way we're doing things now?"

"Because we no longer have the luxury of slowly building our brand around the world" had been Junior's response. Using the wall map of REL's affiliates and bureaus, he had pointed to Europe and a few other locations. "Here's where we are," Junior had said. But pointing to wide swaths of Asia, the Arab world, and Africa, he said, "Look at all this area where we have zero or minimal presence. CNN is there, Fox and several European news organizations are trying to get there, and we're resting on our laurels as we focus on our business in the United States. We can borrow a ton of money to build an international presence, assuming our banks will work with us, or we can raise the capital we need by going public."

The execution to date had been flawless. Every indication from the investment bank hired to do the road show was that interest from institutional investors was very strong. Several directors had discussed with him the possibility of his succeeding Sherman as CEO or his father as chairman of the board. Avoid any missteps over the next few weeks and the idea Junior had put in motion seven years ago would come to fruition. A beep from his desktop phone interrupted his thoughts. "Mr. Carlyle, Mr. Sherman is here to see you."

"Send him in."

Junior walked around his desk and shook hands with Sherman, who declined his offer of coffee. He pointed Sherman to the conference table and took a seat opposite him. Sherman, who was never good at small talk, gave it a try.

"How's your dad doing?"

"Good days and bad. He barely recognizes me, but his aide takes very good care of him. He can speak with some clarity about his early years. Any mention of the IPO gets a blank stare."

"Well, tell him I was asking about him."

Both men immediately recognized the folly of the request. Carlyle Sr. would probably have no idea who Sherman was.

"I will, Dick. Thanks."

"Fred, I don't know if I've ever told you what a great job you did, you're doing, in shepherding this IPO process."

"I don't think you did. That's nice to hear. I appreciate it."

"The company and each of us personally have a lot to gain if this IPO is successful and a lot to lose if it isn't."

"I couldn't agree more on both counts."

Sherman thought hard, trying to find the right words

to introduce the subject. "Fred, do you remember the name Lauren Pomerantz?"

"I do."

"Do you remember her coming to your office and talking about something that happened between her and Matthews?"

"I do."

"Did she do anything besides talk to you?"

"I'm not sure what you mean by that."

"Did she show you any evidence to back up what she said Matthews did?"

"Nothing that I can recall. Why do you ask?"

"This Pomerantz situation could be a huge problem for both of us."

"What do you mean by 'both of us'?"

"You and I each were made aware of a bad situation, and we failed to act."

"That's not how I see it, Dick. As soon as I heard about it, I sent an email to the CEO of the corporation. If there's any failure here, it's yours."

"It's not that simple—"

"Yes, it is that simple. The REL Employee Handbook clearly states that on becoming aware of an accusation of this nature, the employee should immediately bring it to the attention of the employee's supervisor. That's exactly what I did. You're my boss. I sent the email to you."

"You never followed up."

"I don't have to defend myself in front of you, but right after sending that email I left for a four-week trip to

Asia to meet with potential new affiliates. I had faith in you to handle the situation. Was that faith misplaced?"

"No, it wasn't. The situation has been handled, but in a somewhat unconventional manner."

For the next twenty minutes Sherman recounted his first meeting with Carter and the agreement to go along with Carter's plan to contain the situation. When he spoke about the audiotape of Matthews's assault on Pomerantz, Sherman watched for a flicker of recognition on Junior's face. There was none.

Junior asked few questions, his face impassive. Since his meeting with Carter, none of this was new to him. He reacted sharply, however, when Sherman brought up Stephenson's death.

"Has it occurred to you, Dick, that that's one hell of a coincidence? A woman who's threatening to go public with her story conveniently commits suicide? Paying victims to keep quiet is bad enough, but at least we're in good company. Plenty of other major corporations have done the same. But if this Stephenson didn't commit—" He paused and then resumed. "How well do you know this Carter fellow?"

"He's about forty. A lawyer. Worked for us in Human Resources."

Junior got up and walked to the window. For the first time, he sounded truly agitated. "I'm not interested in his résumé. I'm asking, do you really know him?"

"I know he was in the military," Sherman answered, trying to sound confident.

"That's hardly reassuring. So was Hitler. Do you mean to say you wired this guy millions of dollars of REL's money and you don't know the first thing about him?"

"The company does thorough vetting before they hire anybody," Sherman said weakly. Junior paced around the office without responding.

"Dick, if Matthews's abuse and how it was handled, or not handled, comes to light, we're in a 'real' mess." Both men recognized the unintended pun but did not comment. "But if your guy Carter has gone rogue, do you understand you could be looking at accessory to murder?"

"Leave Carter to me," Sherman said, his confidence returning. "I've already hired an agency to dig into his background and to keep an eye on our deal maker." Sherman knew he had done no such thing, but he didn't want to give Junior any credit for inspiring the idea.

"And— " Sherman caught himself as he was about to say *Junior*, "And Fred, don't be so cocksure that sending one email to me will be your get-out-of-jail-free card. A little free advice. If the you-know-what hits the fan, you're going to look more than a little foolish defending yourself by citing the REL Handbook."

"What are you looking for, Sherman?"

"I started and I'm going to finish a plan to put this behind us." Sherman stood up. "If anybody comes to you asking questions about wires to Carter & Associates, your answer is that you approved them. Got that, Junior?"

The two men glared at each other before Sherman turned and headed for the door.

52

Michael Carter got up and walked around his office. The *Wall Street Journal* he had just read was open on his desk. Another article about REL News was above the fold, adding to the buzz surrounding the IPO and the predicting offering price of the shares.

Carter was not happy about his progress with Cathy Ryan. More importantly, neither were Sherman and Junior.

He sat back down and glanced at his computer screen. The email was addressed to Sherman. The blind copy would go to Junior.

> Had another phone conversation with Cathy Ryan. Pressed hard but she declined to set meet date. Said she's not ready to talk about what happened. Said she was leaving for vacation and wouldn't be back for six days.
>
> First thought was she's lying. One of my sources has access to credit card records. She has a round trip reservation to Aruba

> departing on October 3rd and returning on the 9th. Booked at the Americana Hotel. A plus that she's being honest.
>
> Checked out her family. Parents retired in Palm Beach. Deep pockets. One other sibling in Boston.
>
> Ryan has apartment in Atlanta and working for magazine publisher. Her trust fund in excess of three million dollars. Doesn't need our money. That makes her more dangerous. Will continue to update.

Satisfied with what he had written, if not with his progress, he pushed SEND.

53

Carter had just finished an early dinner with his wife and son. It felt good to be home, he thought to himself. Beatrice was getting to be more trouble than she was worth. A nice dinner and a hotel were no longer enough for her. Every time they got together of late she wanted him to schlep all the way to Brooklyn and be out until midnight at one of the several dance clubs she frequented. The people there were idiots, and the music was so loud that he was beginning to worry about hearing loss. Beatrice had done the impossible: she had made him miss being with his wife.

He had even volunteered to do the dishes. His son went to his room to start his homework while his wife settled in front of the TV in the living room to watch REL's evening news. He declined her offer to come and watch with her. He had seen enough of Brad Matthews to last a lifetime.

Carter went to the kitchen table, pulled his laptop out of his bag, and turned it on. The apprehension he had experienced following Paula Stephenson's death had finally begun to fade. There had been no inquiries from the Durham police, no raps on his door in the early morning hours. He had convinced himself that he had let his imagination run wild. For whatever reason, Stephenson had committed suicide. End of story.

The beat goes on, he sang to himself remembering the Sonny and Cher tune. How will she react if I just show up? he asked himself. The *she* he was referring to was Cathy Ryan. She was in Aruba now and he knew where she was staying. Before she said anything, she would probably demand to know how he found her down there. The truth, that he was monitoring her credit cards, would not do. Was there a plausible reason for him to be in Aruba, aside from, of course, the sun and the sand?

A search for Aruba's daily newspaper brought up *Aruba Today*. He scanned several articles about flower festivals and social gatherings. He hit the icon to take him to the Local section. There he came across the headline, "JET SKI TOURIST DIES IN ACCIDENT." Curious, he clicked on the link.

> *Twenty-six-year-old Catherine Ryan died when the Jet Ski she was operating plowed into a boat off the Arenas Blancas Harbor. Ryan, from the United States, was part of a tour group that had just finished lunch. Police would not confirm whether or not alcohol played a role in the tragedy.*

Carter leaned back, his head spinning. He went over to the cabinet, pulled out a bottle of vodka, poured a generous shot, and returned to the table. He felt himself calming down as the alcohol burned in his throat and down to his stomach.

I did it again, he said to himself. I set them up. He'd given Sherman all the information he needed to go down, or send somebody down, to Durham to get rid of Paula Stephenson. And he did exactly the same thing with Cathy Ryan, right down to the hotel where she was staying.

He wondered why he hadn't learned about this sooner, why it hadn't been reported in the media. Then he quickly realized why. North Korea was back to test-firing missiles, Saudi Arabia and Iran were one step short of a shooting war, the trade war with China was accelerating, and another Boeing plane had crashed. The news of an American tourist dying overseas had been lost in the shuffle.

It might be time to talk to a criminal lawyer, he thought to himself. The irony was not lost on him. He had spent the better part of the past two years convincing women that they did *not* need to consult a lawyer. Now, at the first sign of real trouble, he wanted a lawyer, another lawyer besides himself, in his corner.

Have I broken any laws? he asked himself. Using settlements to silence women who had been victimized by Matthews might have allowed Matthews to keep going. But was that a crime? He didn't think so.

He hadn't always been truthful with the women as he

strong-armed them into settlements. Was that a crime? No. It was hardball negotiating.

But the police would want to know how he learned where Cathy Ryan was staying in Aruba. They'd delve into every dollar that flowed into and out of Carter & Associates. How many times had he paid his buddy at the credit rating agency to get him somebody's credit card records? Eight, maybe ten times? And paying to get the phone records of several of the victims? Those were crimes.

A close examination would reveal that he had charged a long list of personal expenses to REL. There would be little sympathy for REL, but in using the company's money to pay his personal expenses, he was guilty of tax fraud.

And what about the bags of cash Junior had him delivering to anonymous sources? *I was only the delivery boy*, might work as a defense for a bicycle messenger. He knew, as a lawyer, he would be held to a higher standard.

And if he got disbarred, obviously that would be the end of his sideline practice helping wrongful termination clients. What would he do to support himself and his family?

Clearly, he had to keep going, but he had to do it in a way that was no longer empowering Sherman.

54

Meg Williamson sat on the couch with her feet up on the coffee hassock. It was nine o'clock. The TV was now off. A few minutes earlier she had been channel surfing and landed on REL News. And *him.* His easy smile. His signature blue blazer, white shirt, and red-and-blue tie.

A feeling of revulsion had swept over Meg. The thought of that pig's hands on her. She walked into the kitchen, poured herself a glass of Chardonnay, and returned to the couch. "Mother's milk," her grandmother used to call the two glasses of wine she would have every evening.

Meg took a long sip and allowed herself to calm down. An hour earlier she had finished what for years had been the highlight of her day. She had curled up with Jillian on her bed and announced "time to pick out a book." Jillian would scamper over to the bookshelf pretending to consider all the choices. She would then choose one of her favorite titles night after night, taking comfort and pleasure in knowing what would happen on the next page. Like mother, like daughter, Meg thought. Neither of us likes surprises.

In the six weeks since Jillian had started first grade their evening ritual had evolved. Now it was Jillian attempting most of the reading while Meg, helping when necessary, stroked her daughter's honey-blond hair. There were three classes of first graders at Ponterio Ridge Street School. While the other two teachers were good, fifty-eight-year-old Mrs. Silverman was a legend. She had taught at the school for thirty-three years. Her early students, now parents themselves, gave the school board fits with their insistence that their son or daughter be taught by Mrs. Silverman. I didn't have any clout, Meg thought to herself. This was the one time I just got lucky.

Her cell phone rang. It was beside her on the couch. The caller ID showed "Unavailable." Please be a dumb credit card solicitation, she prayed as she answered. But it was him.

"Change of plans, Meg. Get something to write with."

"Wait a minute," she said curtly as she walked over to her desk and grabbed a pad. His rudeness never failed to amaze her. God forbid he should ask, *how are you doing*? Or, *is this a good time to talk*? "I'm ready."

"You are going to talk to that reporter, Gina Kane—"

"But you said—"

"I know what I said. Shut up and listen."

"Okay," she grimaced, spitting out the word.

"You made the decision to leave REL News because you had a young child and you wanted more normal work hours. If she asks, you are not aware of any sexual harassment or bad behavior that took place at the company. Everyone you worked with, especially your male colleagues, was always courteous and professional. Are you taking this down?"

"'Courteous and professional.' Yes, I am." Again she spat out the words.

"She is going to ask if when you worked at the company you knew Cathy Ryan. Before I tell you how you should answer and what you should say about her, you may not be aware that Cathy was killed in an accident while in Aruba. . . ."

"Cathy is dead!" Meg gasped out the words. She and Cathy had gone to work at REL News at the same time. They had both just graduated college. They quickly became friends. Now an image of the girl with the long dark hair and sparkling hazel eyes filled her mind.

Carter was still talking. "Say you knew her and how sorry you were to hear about her passing. And here's what I want you to tell the reporter about Cathy's time at REL News . . ."

Meg was only partially successful attempting to stifle sobs as she wrote. Treating her like a child, Carter insisted she read the instructions back to him.

Finding courage she didn't know she had, Meg challenged him. "When I accepted the settlement, the only thing I was obliged to do was to keep quiet. There was nothing in the agreement about having to lie to reporters."

Carter's voice was icy. "Meg, be a good girl and cooperate. And recognize how fortunate you and Jillian are. Very few first-graders have a teacher as good as Rachel Silverman."

Part III

55

After dinner with Lisa, Gina slept until nine-thirty. She was in the kitchen making coffee when the phone rang. To her astonishment it was Meg Williamson.

"Ms. Kane, I'm sorry I haven't gotten back to you sooner."

"Well I appreciate your calling now. I'm doing an article—"

"I'm aware of that. I listened to your messages."

"Okay. I understand you worked for REL News for a period of time."

There was a moment of hesitation. "Yes, I did."

"I'd very much appreciate having the opportunity to visit you. I want to talk about the time you spent in broadcast media."

Again Meg hesitated. He told me to *talk* to her, now she wants to *meet* me was the thought racing through her mind. "That might be hard to arrange," she began. Grasping for words, she added, "I work full-time and I have a young daughter to take care of after that."

There was a moment of hesitation. Don't turn me

down, Gina was thinking. Get her to commit now. This might be my only chance.

"I'll do it completely around your schedule," Gina assured her. "I see you're calling from a 914 area code. Are you in the Westchester area?"

"Yes. I live in Rye and I work in White Plains," Meg said, immediately regretting that she had given out more information than was necessary.

"Perfect. I'm in the city and can meet you wherever and whenever works for you."

"I don't want to do this when my daughter's here."

"I understand. Can I meet you at work, maybe on your lunch break?"

"My schedule at work is very busy. I eat lunch at my desk."

"If Monday through Friday doesn't work, how about over the weekend?" Gina persisted.

"I don't know. My daughter is with me then." He told me to talk to her, Meg thought. "Can't we do this over the phone?"

Gina had to make a quick decision. She knew she was taking a risk, but decided it was worth the gamble. "I'm sorry," she said. "It has to be in person."

Meg panicked. *He ordered me to talk to her.* Fumbling for words, she said, "I'm dropping my daughter at a birthday party at one o'clock on Saturday."

"Then I'll come to your house at one-thirty," Gina confirmed, trying not to sound too eager.

Meg agreed and Gina jotted down the address.

56

The traffic was predictably light as Gina drove northbound on the Henry Hudson Parkway. She passed under the George Washington Bridge and fifteen minutes later had passed through the Bronx and entered Westchester County. Its roadway and mass transit system made it a prime choice for those who worked in Manhattan but chose to raise their families in a nearby suburb. A few years earlier it had had the dubious distinction of having the highest property taxes anywhere in the United States.

The Waze electronic voice guided Gina closer to her destination. Realizing she was early, she veered off and drove through the center of downtown Rye. Smart-looking shops and restaurants lined both sides of Purchase Street. Rye appeared to have escaped Amazon's devastating effect on small retailers. Every storefront was occupied. Mercedes-Benz, BMW, and Lexus automobiles were more common than their less pricey counterparts.

Enough time as a tourist, Gina said to herself as she followed the Waze directions to a small tree-lined street walking distance from downtown. Twenty-seven Pilgrim Street was a charming colonial Cape. A late model BMW was parked in the semicircular driveway. A girl and a boy who both appeared to be about ten were kicking a soccer ball on the lawn of the home across the street.

A reporter who had served as a mentor early in her career had given Gina advice about how to proceed when interviewing a potentially reluctant source for a story. Always park on the street. People feel more threatened when you violate their space by parking in their driveway, he had cautioned. They feel like you're trapping them. She wanted to do everything she could to avoid making Meg Williamson feel trapped. She eased the rental car to a halt at the curb in front of the house.

She glanced at her watch. 1:27. She had considered but decided against asking if she could record the interview. Too threatening. Notebook in hand, she walked up the driveway and rang the bell. The door opened in less than thirty seconds.

"You must be Gina. Come in please."

Meg was strikingly attractive, with dark blond hair and large blue eyes. Gina guessed she was in her early thirties.

She followed Meg into the living room and found herself admiring both the room and the way it was attractively furnished. Meg has good taste and the money to fund it, she thought as she accepted the invitation to sit down.

Pictures of a very pretty young girl, mostly alone, a few with a beaming Meg, were on the piano, the end tables, and the coffee table. Conspicuously absent were any photos of the young girl with her father, or for that matter grandparents.

Meg chose to perch on the edge of a wing chair not far from her. She did not settle down but sat rigidly straight, suggesting that this would be a short meeting.

Now that she was here, Gina intended to make the most of every minute. "Ms. Williamson—"

"Call me Meg, please."

"Thank you. Before we begin, can I trouble you for a glass of water?" It was a strategy Gina had learned from the same reporter who'd recommended against parking in the driveway. "You might need a little more time to form the question in just the right way or how to segue into the most sensitive area. Taking a sip of water, swallowing it, slowly putting down the glass gives you about ten more seconds to think while avoiding an awkward silence."

"Of course. I'm sorry for not offering," Meg said as she disappeared into the kitchen. She returned a minute later, handed the glass to Gina, and sat again on the edge of the wing chair.

"I want to thank you for making time for me. You live here with your daughter and—"

"It's only with my daughter, Jillian."

"Jillian's father?"

"Divorced three years ago. He's not," she paused, "part of our lives anymore."

"I see. Meg, I'm interested in the stories of women

like you. Women who over the past ten years entered the field of broadcast journalism but chose to leave it to pursue other careers. How did you find your way to REL News?"

"I went to Iowa State, and the university had its own TV station. I started working, volunteering would be more accurate, my sophomore year. I learned a lot. Before long, I was writing segments, producing others, doing interviews, helping edit pieces."

"Were you a Journalism major?"

"Originally Psychology. But I was enjoying myself so much that I switched to Journalism and graduated with a double major."

"So how did you connect with REL News?"

"It was through a recruiter on campus my senior year. I had filled in for one of the on-air reporters who had the flu. He liked what he saw and said REL News made it a priority to hire people who had the versatility to work both behind and in front of the camera."

"That must have been quite a transition, Iowa to New York City."

"It was. I had never been east of St. Louis."

"How long did you stay at REL News?"

"Three and a half years."

"Did you enjoy your time there?"

"It was fine. It was a job."

"Did you end up doing any on-air work for REL?"

"A little in the beginning."

It was not lost on Gina how Meg's answers were short

and clipped when talking about REL News but more expansive when recalling her college days.

"So, Meg, three and a half years later. You decide to leave. Why was that?"

"The hours were long. Because I was low on the totem pole, I had to work overnight shifts. I had trouble adjusting my sleep pattern. I had a two-year-old. What was I supposed to do? I couldn't afford a live-in nanny. And it's impossible to schedule child care when your work hours are constantly changing."

"Did Jillian's father object to the long hours you were working?"

Her answer was vehement. "He didn't care. My ex was a seldom-employed drummer. He occasionally got steady work with traveling theater shows. When he wasn't working, which was most of the time, he was hanging out in Nashville trying to get discovered."

"So the rotating work schedule and the difficulty in finding child care—are those the only reasons you left REL?"

"Yes."

Gina paused, hoping Meg would break the silence by adding more to her answer. Meg just stared at her.

"When we spoke on the phone, you said you work in White Plains. What type of work are you doing?"

"I'm an account supervisor at a PR agency, Hannon and Ramsey. It's a small firm, mostly clients in the health-care field."

"You went there directly after REL?"

"Yes."

"Meg, one of the women I was hoping to interview was Cathy Ryan." Gina was certain that it was a look of pain that appeared on Meg's face.

"You're aware of her recent passing?"

Meg nodded.

Gina continued. "Cathy worked at REL News around the time you did. Did you know her?"

"We started at REL News within a few weeks of each other. We were right out of college, both of us new to New York."

"Were you friends?"

"I'd say we were friendly. We saw a lot of each other at work. Not much outside of work."

"There's something else you have in common. You left REL News after three and a half years; Cathy stayed three years. Is that a coincidence?"

"I don't know what you mean by that."

"You left because you had a young daughter and wanted a job and lifestyle with more stable hours. Did Cathy ever share with you why she left?"

Meg appeared to be fighting back tears. Sorrow over her friend who died or something else? She collected herself. "I don't want to speak ill of somebody I was friends, friendly with. But Cathy was not well respected by most of her colleagues."

"Really?" Gina said, genuinely surprised.

"From the beginning she was difficult to work with. She was unreliable. She routinely blamed others for mistakes she had made. It pains me to say so, but she was a troublemaker."

"From your description of her, it's a wonder she lasted three years." Gina took a sip of water, using the time to carefully frame her next question. "Shortly before Cathy died, I received an email from her. She made reference to a 'terrible experience' she had at REL News. Do you have any idea what she might have been referring to?"

"I have no idea what she was talking about. Everyone at REL News, particularly her male colleagues, was always professional and courteous. It sounds like another example of Cathy just trying to make trouble."

Gina allowed the answer to sink in before continuing. "Are you aware of any women who after leaving REL News received financial settlements from the company?" Gina made it a point to look around the room at the expensive furnishings as she asked the question.

"Absolutely not," Meg answered emphatically as she stood up. "I think it's time we wrap this up."

"Just one more question," Gina said, remaining in her seat. "Did you stay in touch with Cathy after she left REL?"

"Briefly. Not really."

"How did you find out she had died?"

"Um, I read it online. I don't remember where. We're finished. I'll show you to the door."

57

After returning the rental car Gina quickly walked the eight blocks back to her apartment. Her mind was racing with ideas about the research she had to do and the people she planned to speak to before meeting with Geoff. She sent him a text: *Major progress on REL News investigation. When can I see you*? Less than a minute later he responded: *Flying back Tuesday night. 10:00 Wednesday*? She typed back, *See you then.*

Deep in thought, she grabbed a bottle of water from the refrigerator and sat at the table by the window. Following her usual pattern, she jotted down the questions she would have asked Meg Williamson if she had had more time:

When was the last time Meg had spoken to or been in touch with Cathy?

Meg had described Cathy as a "troublemaker" at REL News. Had Cathy chosen to leave or had she been fired?

Did Meg attempt to contact Cathy's family after learning she had died in the accident?

Her concentration was broken by the sound of her cell phone ringing. "Hey there," Gina said, genuine affection obvious in her voice.

"I'm glad I have pictures of you on my phone. I'm starting to forget what you look like." They both laughed wistfully.

"Well I'm not the one gallivanting around sunny California," she said. "When will I have the pleasure of your company?"

"I'm sorry to say that I won't be in until late afternoon Wednesday. Please tell me you're free for dinner that night."

"I am. I'll make a reservation."

"Pick some place really nice because we have something to celebrate."

"Really? And what is that?" Gina asked.

"I know I've bored you a lot with my investment banker stories."

"They're not boring. I like them."

"Remember how I've told you that when a private company is planning to go public, to list their shares on a stock exchange, they hire investment banks to do road shows."

"That's when they go around and present the company to the major investment funds. Right?"

"Precisely. Well our bank has been tapped to work on what's likely to be the most prestigious deal this year."

"Are you allowed to tell me about it?"

"It will be announced to the public on Monday. I think I can trust you to keep quiet until then."

"This reporter's lips are sealed."

"REL News has chosen our bank to take them public, and I'll be on the team doing the presentations."

Gina felt her knees going weak. Had she mentioned to him Cathy's email about REL News? She didn't think so. Instinctively she took a sip of water. "That's great. I can't tell you how happy and surprised I am."

"It was a surprise to me, too. I got picked over some more senior people. This is what I've always wanted to do. I feel like everything's coming together for me. For us."

"Much to celebrate on Wednesday," she agreed.

"And I hope we'll have even more to celebrate."

Gina knew what he was referring to. Before she left for Nepal, he had talked about going to Tiffany's to buy a ring for her. An engagement ring.

"Enough about me," Ted said. "What's up with you? I haven't even asked you what stories you've been working on."

If only you knew, Gina thought to herself. She hated lying to Ted, but sometimes the "greater good" theory made sense. "There's a new editor at *Empire Review*. He's tough. I've brought in a few ideas, but we haven't settled on anything yet."

"That's too bad. I liked Charlie." Gina, Ted, Charlie, and his wife had sat together at two publishing industry dinners. "I'm sure when the new editor gets to know you, he'll love you the way Charlie did."

"Let's hope so," she said.

"Got to go to a meeting. My bank doesn't acknowledge weekends. Can't wait for Wednesday. Love you."

"Love you, too."

As Gina stared out the window at the gray waters of the Hudson River, her mind was far away. It was hard to underestimate how complicated her life had become. Picking up her cell phone, she sent another text to Geoff. *Can you ask one of your corporate lawyers to join us on Wednesday?*

His response was immediate. *Will do. I assume you have a good reason for asking.*

I certainly do, Gina thought to herself.

58

"Why did you have her come to your house?" Michael Carter screamed into the phone.

"You're the one who told me to get back to her," Meg pleaded.

"I told you to speak to her, not meet her. If you felt the need to meet her, why couldn't you do it at a Starbucks or a Barnes & Noble?"

"I didn't want to take a chance someone would overhear us and learn something."

"I'm sure she learned plenty when she saw your place in Rye."

"There were no restrictions on how I could spend my settlement money and you know it. Mr. Carter, please calm down. Remember, I was a reporter. Any reporter with half a brain would be able to find out what I paid for my house."

"I guess you're right," he admitted reluctantly. "Did you tell her what I told you to say about Cathy Ryan?"

"Word for word I did."

"And what was her reaction?"

"She was taken aback. Clearly it did not jibe with the impression she had of Cathy."

"At least that's a plus."

"What do you want me to do next?"

"What are you talking about, 'next'?"

"She's a reporter. She's going to reach out to me again." It was probably the first time Michael Carter wasn't so cocksure of himself, Meg thought. He didn't know what to say.

"I'll get back to you," he said. The red circle on her iPhone signaled the connection had been terminated.

59

On Wednesday morning Gina was wide awake when her alarm clock chimed six-thirty. For the past two days she had been rehearsing in her mind the presentation she would make to Geoff. Sometimes in the solitude of her apartment she found herself speaking aloud the facts that *she* found so persuasive.

More was riding on today's meeting than the REL News story. It was one thing for Geoff to say he was a fan of her work. Those were just words. An easy compliment to give. For Geoff to put the prestige of the magazine behind the REL News investigation, she needed to convince him not only that the story was genuine, but that she had the necessary skills to pursue it to wherever the trail would lead.

Her thoughts wandered to an experience she'd had in the early days, at her first job. It never failed to ignite a burn inside her. She had accompanied a college friend to visit the friend's grandmother in a nursing home on Long Island. Suffering from dementia, the old woman drifted between reliving stories of the hardship her family endured during the Depression and complaining in the present about the shoddy care she received. Gina's friend believed her grandmother's unhappiness with the staff was the product of constant pain and a confused mind.

Gina wasn't so sure. With her friend's permission she had gone back repeatedly to visit the grandmother. In the parking lot she had talked to other families. They also had not taken seriously their relatives' similar complaints about the staff.

When Gina presented her findings to her editorial board, they were convinced the story had legs and could be an important one for the paper. So important, they decided, that their most senior male reporter was assigned to investigate and write what became an award-winning exposé. Nowhere in the series of articles was Gina's name or the work she had done ever mentioned.

As she headed for the shower, her father's advice echoed in her ears. "Live in the present, dear. That's all you've got."

After a light breakfast Gina paused in front of her closet. Business casual was the dress code at the magazine. Geoff kept a sports jacket on a rack in the corner of his office, but she had never seen it on him. At her request a lawyer would be at the meeting. Would he be dressed, well, like a lawyer? Not for the first time she lamented how much time she spent—wasted—trying to decide which were the right clothes to wear. She chose a navy-blue suit and white blouse.

Dressed and with about twenty minutes to kill before departing, Gina sent an email to Meg Williamson thanking her for being so generous with her time. I'm probably the last person Meg wants to hear from, she mused. Scanning her Inbox, she clicked on one sent from her father.

Hello Gigi.

She smiled at the nickname he would call her when she was little.

Just want to let you know your old man is doing fine down here. Took the boat over to Marco Island yesterday and had a great lobster lunch. Driving tomorrow to Lake Okeechobee to take their tour boat. Hoping to see some manatees.

Turning into a gym rat. Getting over there 4 or 5 times a week.

Friends have told me what a great time they had in Costa Rica. Seriously considering heading down there for a visit.

Will you have a chance to get down here? There's somebody I'd really like you to meet.

Love,
Daddy

So that explained the more upbeat tone and movies and dinners he'd been going to, Gina thought. Dad has a lady friend. She smiled. He's happy. At least that's one less thing I have to worry about. But she couldn't avoid the lump in her throat, missing her mother.

Gina glanced at her watch. Time to get moving. Today of all days she didn't want to be late.

60

When the elevator doors opened, Jane Patwell was waiting to greet her. She looked Gina up and down. "Looking good, honey," she said approvingly. "A little free advice. Wear skirts more often."

Gina chuckled. From anyone else she might have been annoyed. But she knew Jane meant it as a compliment.

As she followed her down the hall, Jane warned, "You might find him a little cranky. His flight got delayed and didn't land until two o'clock this morning."

"Thanks for the heads-up," Gina said gratefully.

Jane knocked and then opened the door to Geoff's office. The editor was seated at the conference table. Next to him was a silver-haired man in a dark three-piece suit and pale blue tie who appeared to be in his mid-sixties. Coffee cups and legal pads were in front of both of them on their side of the table. They stood up as Gina entered.

She declined Geoff's offer of coffee. Jane left, quietly closing the door behind her. Gina noticed that both coffee cups were less than half-filled. It was obvious their meeting had started well before she arrived.

Geoff shook Gina's hand across the table. "Gina, I want to introduce you to Bruce Brady. Bruce is our chief counsel. I've asked him to join us."

After the introductions were completed and pleasantries exchanged, they took their seats. Geoff continued, "I've taken the last fifteen minutes to bring Bruce up to speed. We're both looking forward to hearing how you fared with Meg Williamson."

Gina reached into her small briefcase and pulled out several folders. "In my original email, I should say my only email, from Cathy Ryan, she said that after a 'terrible experience' at REL News, she had been approached about a settlement. Cathy had added, 'And I'm not the only one.'

"We lost the opportunity to talk to Cathy after her," she paused, "untimely death in Aruba. But Cathy's family was able to provide contact information that resulted in my meeting with Meg Williamson four days ago.

"Ms. Williamson is twenty-nine years old, divorced with a six-year-old daughter. She went to work for REL News straight out of college after being approached on campus by a recruiter for the company. Williamson began at REL at the same time as the late Cathy Ryan. Williamson left REL," Gina glanced down at her notes, "three months after Cathy did but for different reasons. Williamson claims that she left REL News to work at a PR firm because she had a young child and wanted more stable hours and that a live-in nanny would have been unaffordable. According to Williamson, Cathy Ryan was a 'troublemaker' and difficult to work with. It's not clear whether Ryan left by her own choice or was forced out."

Geoff said, "That troublemaker business puts a different spin on things if that's true."

"Or that's certainly what REL News would want us to believe," Brady said. "Do you know anything more about what type of employee she was?"

"I was able to speak to her boss at the magazine group Ryan went to work for in Atlanta."

"Usually they won't say very much about a former employee," Brady said.

"Well, I guess this guy was unusual," Gina responded while flipping through her notes. "Milton Harsh, the associate publisher, spoke glowingly of Ryan's work at the company, how shocked they were at her passing, and how much she is missed."

"Doesn't sound like a troublemaker to me," Geoff commented.

"My feelings exactly," Gina stated. "Let's get back to Meg Williamson and let's assume she also was a victim of whatever happened at REL News. Cathy Ryan, who didn't settle, ended up dying. So where does that leave Meg?"

"She reached a settlement," Brady speculated.

"Or she's still negotiating with them," Geoff suggested.

"Both are possibilities, but based on the research I've done all signs point to her having accepted a settlement."

Gina pulled two sheets out of one of the folders in

front of her. "I assume you're familiar with the online real estate company Zillow."

They both nodded.

"This is a Zillow sales report of the home currently occupied by Williamson," she said as she handed them the sheets. "It sold just under four years ago for nine hundred ninety thousand dollars."

"Do Zillow reports show if there's a mortgage?" Brady inquired.

"No," Gina answered, "but that's where having a friend in real estate comes in handy. A Realtor who is a member of the Multiple Listing Service system can look up any property and find the name of the owner and if there's a mortgage. According to my friend, Meg Williamson is the sole owner and the property is mortgage-free."

"I assume you've looked into other ways Meg could have got her hands on a million dollars for a house," Geoff said.

"I have," Gina responded, "and they're all dead ends. Keep in mind we're dealing with somebody who is still in her twenties. Lots of young people coming out of college want to work in broadcasting. As a result, the media companies don't have to pay them very much. Remember, when she was considering child care, Meg said she couldn't afford a nanny."

"Is it possible she's making enough in her new job to account for the house in Rye?" Brady inquired.

"No way," Gina replied. "Hannon and Ramsey is a small PR firm with a modest client base, mostly small health-care companies. A woman I graduated college with works at Hill and Knowlton, one of the biggest PR firms in the world. She said an account supervisor in a small shop would be lucky to be making one hundred thousand per year. Tops."

"So she didn't earn her way to a one-million-dollar home," Geoff stated. "You said she was divorced. Did that involve a big payday for her?"

"Quite the opposite," Gina replied. "Meg told me her ex was a seldom employed musician." She opened a folder and pulled out a document. "I visited the Manhattan County Courthouse and got a copy of the divorce decree. In exchange for the father giving up all custody and visitation rights, they agreed that he would owe no alimony or child support."

"Is family money behind her?"

"I checked that out," Gina said. "Before he died from a heart attack five years ago, her father was a high school English teacher in a small town in Iowa. Her mother was a nurse's aide. She remarried less than a year later."

Gina flipped a page in her notebook. "Something Meg Williamson said to me stood out. When I asked how she heard about Cathy Ryan's death, she appeared flustered. She then said she read about it someplace online. Not too many twentysomethings experience a friend the same age dying. I'm pretty sure she would remember exactly how she found out about Cathy, if she was telling the truth."

"I agree, Gina, and that leads to a question that has

been percolating in my mind," Brady continued. "*If* Williamson took a settlement from REL News, and *if* she didn't want anyone to know about it, why on God's earth would she agree to meet with an investigative reporter?"

"And why did she ignore my early emails and phone messages and then after ten days decide to get back to me? I don't have good answers to those questions."

Geoff appeared lost in thought. He seemed to be trying to stifle a yawn as the previous night's short sleep began to catch up to him. "Gina, is there another possibility we haven't considered? Describe Meg Williamson."

"She's about five feet six, blond hair, blue eyes, slender, athletic build."

"Is she attractive?"

"Very."

"Is there any chance she's a kept woman or she has what is quaintly known as a sugar daddy?"

Gina exhaled. "Honestly, I hadn't thought of that. My first-blush reaction is to say no. She doesn't seem like the type. And she has a full-time job and a young daughter to take care of every night. I don't think she has time to be anybody's mistress."

Geoff stretched in his chair. "Excellent work, Gina. I'm convinced that Cathy Ryan's death was not an accident. I am even more certain that Meg Williamson is a victim who accepted a sizable sum of money from REL News to keep quiet about bad behavior at the firm. What puzzles me is why the sense of urgency on the part of REL News now? Cathy Ryan's bad experience happened years ago. Why was she such a threat to them that a few weeks ago they would arrange an accident to silence her?"

"I believe I can answer that," Brady interjected. "REL News just announced they're going public. If it were shown that they failed to disclose relevant facts including potential lawsuits, high penalties and substantial exposure to litigation would result. A living, breathing Cathy Ryan would have been a major problem for them."

"Mr. Brady," Gina said, "you just provided a good segue into why I asked Geoff to have you sit in on today's meeting. I'm sorry to have taken you away from your other work."

Brady waved his hand. "It's Bruce. And I assure you, what we have been discussing for the last twenty minutes is infinitely more interesting than the dull-as-dishwater legal brief I have been working on for the past two days."

Gina smiled. "Okay, Bruce, here we go. As you stated earlier, REL News is beginning the process of going public. They've hired two investment banks to advise them during the process. The man I've been dating for the past year and a half works at one of those banks and will be part of the team making the pitch to early investors."

"Oh boy." Bruce shook his head. "Have you shared anything about your investigation of REL News, even that you're considering doing an investigation? Does your gentleman friend know that?"

"Not a word."

"That's good. That gives you more options. I'm sorry for being indelicate. You and your friend, uh . . ."

"Ted."

"Do you and Ted cohabitate?"

Gina tried to hide her discomfort. "No."

Brady folded his hands together in front of his face. "That's a plus, but it still leaves the two of you with a very difficult dilemma."

"I'm sure Ted will understand if I tell him that I can't disclose what I'm working on. He can't be responsible for what he doesn't know."

Brady shook his head. "If only it were that simple. If the REL News story you're pursuing exposes serious wrongdoing at the firm, it will affect the firm's value. When investors learn that Ted was not only a member of the bank team that pitched them on the REL News investment, he was at the same time dating the journalist who broke the story, no one is going to believe for a minute that Ted didn't know what you were working on."

"But it would be the truth," Gina said emphatically.

"In litigation, the truth rarely gets the best seat in the theater."

She looked startled. "Will Ted be all right?"

"Far from it," Brady cautioned. "Odds are the bank will immediately fire him. He'll spend the better part of the next several years answering depositions from disgruntled investors suing the bank. Ted could sue the bank for wrongful dismissal, but it will be a long, ugly process."

"I don't know what to do," Gina sighed.

Brady leaned forward. "When was the last time you saw Ted?"

"Between my travel and his, not for the last three weeks. I'm having dinner with him tonight."

"Gina, think carefully. Have you ever discussed REL News with him verbally, or in an email or a text?"

"I've been racking my brain. I'm sure the only time it ever came up was this past weekend when he told me his bank had been chosen and he would be working on the road show."

Brady's eyes looked sad as he faced her. "Gina, there is one way you might be able to extricate yourself from this situation and leave Ted's career intact."

"What can I do?"

"Ted should not have shared with you non-public information before it was formally announced. But he'll be all right because I'm sure half the bankers did that with their spouses and significant others. Here's what you have to do. Immediately and without explanation, end the relationship. Refuse to see him. Send an email or a text. 'I've chosen to go in a different direction. Goodbye.'"

Gina felt her eyes well with tears. Geoff walked to his desk, grabbed a box of tissues, and put it in front of her. Then he broke the silence. "Bruce, I'm thinking out loud. I don't know if the ideas popping into my head make sense. Suppose I, with Gina's permission, assign this story to another journalist. Can Gina step back and not be part of it going forward?"

She felt a sick feeling in her stomach. It was the nursing home investigation all over again. She developed the story while someone else would get the credit.

"I'm afraid that's not possible," Brady replied. "Gina is intimately involved with this investigation. She can't stop knowing what she knows just because another reporter is going to take over."

Gina felt whipsawed by the turn of events. For the past several weeks she had questioned her reluctance to commit to Ted. She knew she loved him deeply, but committing to spend her whole life with him was a decision that frightened her. Now she was being forced to consider life without Ted. The thought was impossible!

But she needed to work this story. Young women, close to her age, had been victimized, and it was probably still going on. She felt certain that one of them had been murdered. If I walk away, how long will it take them to put someone else on the story? Will whoever they give it to pursue it the way I would have? Will there be more victims who might have been spared? This story is mine, and so is Ted. I will figure out a way to have both, she promised herself.

"I've made my decision," she said, surprised by the steely resolve in her voice. "I'll break if off with Ted." Looking at Geoff, she continued, "This is my story. I want to see it through."

It was Geoff who broke the silence. "All right, Gina. With Cathy Ryan dead and Meg Williamson reluctant to talk to you, where are you going next?"

"I have one more card to play with Williamson," she said. "Meg doesn't know that her friend Cathy Ryan was murdered."

61

"Shell-shocked" would have been a good word to describe Gina as she walked from the *Empire* offices and made her way to the subway. Operating on automatic pilot, she inserted her monthly pass and the gates flew open. She stared without seeing out the window of the train, woodenly trudged up the steps at her stop, and walked to her apartment. All that time in Nepal and Aruba and on the flights, she had agonized about what to say to Ted, how to respond to his question. Little did she know that Ted would get his answer in an email or text with the wording dictated by, of all people, a lawyer.

She absently acknowledged the doorman's greeting, but then stopped. Here's as good a place to start as any, she thought to herself.

"Miguel, I'm not seeing my friend Ted anymore. If he comes over, please don't send him up. And if he calls, please don't say whether I'm home or out." Even as the words came out of her mouth, they sounded strange to her ears.

"Oh, Miss Gina, I'm so sorry to hear that. You and Mr. Ted were very simpatico together. Of course I will give him no information about you."

Inside her apartment she numbly dropped her bag on the counter. It was approaching lunchtime, but she wasn't the slightest bit hungry. The thought of food made her think of the dinner she would not have. She dialed the restaurant and canceled the reservation. "Thank you so much for letting us know," the man said in accented English. If only Ted would take the news as well as the restaurant had, she thought as she hung up the phone.

"There's got to be a better way to do this," she said out loud as she opened her computer. She started by typing the lawyer's words as she recalled them. "Dear Ted, I've chosen to go in a different direction. Goodbye."

Gina stared at what she had typed. These were the lawyer's words except for the "Dear Ted." I'm the one who's supposedly the professional writer, she thought. I've got to be able to do better than that.

It was small consolation that the hurt she was about to administer was for Ted's own good. Hurt was hurt, no matter what the intent. If the situation were reversed, what would be less painful? Ted telling her it was over and not providing a reason or saying it was over because someone else had entered the picture?

She began typing again. "Dear Ted, I'm sorry to say this in an email. I've met someone else and I want—" She deleted "want" and replaced it with "need"—"I need to go in a different direction. Goodbye."

She read and reread what she had written and shook her head. This version raised as many questions as it answered. When did she meet someone else? Do you change your whole life around after meeting someone in the next seat on an airplane or after a single conversation in a bar? No, you wouldn't jeopardize what you have unless you were reasonably certain that the new situation offered the opportunity for a greater happiness. You'd only know that if you'd seen the new person several times, and after each meeting found yourself wanting more.

If I can think of this, so will Ted. No matter what I tell him—I'm not telling him anything in the email—he'll believe I was cheating on him, cheating on him the whole time I was asking *him* to be patient.

Gina exhaled, conceding that there was no way to conclude this in anything resembling a soft landing. She began a new email. "Ted, I've chosen to go in a different direction. Goodbye. Gina."

Tears gushed down her cheeks as her finger pushed SEND.

62

Michael Carter could not escape the feeling of foreboding. He had to admit there was also a certain irony in his dilemma. His efforts to protect one of America's foremost news organizations were potentially being undermined by a reporter or journalist or whatever she called herself. How did Gina Kane find out about Meg Williamson? He had contacted Lauren Pomerantz, who had given Meg's name to him. He'd believed Lauren's assurance that she had abided by her nondisclosure agreement, just as he'd believed Meg's. Could Paula Stephenson or Cathy Ryan have reached out to Kane? He had no way of knowing. Did one of the other victims who'd settled talk to her? Maybe a victim he didn't know about yet had opened up to her.

After viewing Meg Williamson's Rye home, Gina had to know Meg had received a settlement. But is that all she knows? Did she go beyond asking questions about Cathy Ryan's time at REL, and start digging into whatever happened in Aruba?

He considered keeping the information about Gina Kane's inquiries to himself but decided against it. Why should I be the one doing all the worrying? he asked himself.

Opening his laptop, he began typing an email to Sherman, with the usual blind copy to Junior: "Houston, we have another problem. . . ."

63

Gina spent the afternoon rereading the notes she had made from the Aruba trip a week and a half earlier, the "vacation" as Geoff had referred to it, and the ones she had jotted after her meeting with Meg Williamson. She was grateful for the periods of time, ten minutes just now, fifteen minutes earlier, when her mind focused on something other than Ted. You've got a job to do, she reminded herself. You can't let your personal life interfere with that.

She had two decisions to make regarding Williamson. Did she tell her she was 100 percent sure that Cathy Ryan was murdered? She was virtually certain someone tampered with her Jet Ski, so it was *almost* the truth, she reasoned. Gina smiled as the reporter in her kicked in immediately. She could hear herself asking, "Will you please explain to me what you mean by 'almost the truth'?"

The other challenge was how to reengage with her. Gina was convinced that Meg had been coached when she talked to her about Cathy Ryan being a troublemaker and difficult to work with at REL News. If she phoned or emailed and Meg made a date to see her again, whoever was coaching her would have an opportunity to prep her in advance. That assumed, of course, that Meg would agree to a second meeting. Gina recalled how abruptly and emphatically Meg had ended the interview at her home.

Another possibility was to surprise her and just show up, Gina thought. Show up where? Going to her house when the daughter's there would be a mistake. She was a protective mother. She wouldn't be able to focus on what Gina was saying if the whole time she was there Meg's mind was on her daughter.

Gina assumed Meg worked conventional hours and finished around five to five-thirty. She must have an after-school sitter for her daughter. That would give them a little time to talk. If she insisted she had to go immediately to pick up her daughter, Gina would be ready with a response.

The tinkling noise from Gina's phone signaled the arrival of a text. The sender was Ted! It was four-thirty. His plane must have just landed at JFK. Her breath caught in her chest as she read it.

Ha ha. Very funny. If this is your idea of an April fools joke, you're off by 6 months. Confirm where and when tonight.

Oh my God, Gina thought. Could Ted possibly believe I was only joking? She looked at his text. He would always write "Love" or include a series of Xs and Os at the end. None of these were present. Ted must have some doubt, some suspicion that her text meant what she said.

She pictured him walking off the plane and down the long corridors at JFK, his tie loosened and lowered an inch, one hand pulling his rolling suitcase, the other holding his cell phone, glancing at the screen, waiting for the message that all was well, that his only problem was that his girlfriend, the woman he wanted to marry, had a weird sense of humor.

Unable to wait, he would try phoning. As if on cue, Gina's cell phone began to vibrate on the table. She had forgotten to reset the ringer after this morning's meeting. Less than a minute later her landline sounded. She put her head in her hands as she listened to the rings. Six long, loud ones with a pause between each. Her cheerful message followed by a beep.

"Call me" was all he said before hanging up.

I can't be alone tonight, she decided. Gina dialed Lisa's cell.

"Hey there. What's up?" Lisa answered.

"If you're not busy tonight, I could really use some fun company."

"Sure, I'm free. I thought tonight was the big dinner for you and—"

"I'll explain when I see you. Pedro's at eight o'clock?"

"We're on."

"Oh, Lisa, one more thing. I told you I was working on a story about REL News."

"You did. That they might have some MeToo issues at the company."

"Have you told anybody else about what I'm working on?"

"No."

"Good. Please keep it that way. See you tonight."

64

There was far more traffic on the ride to White Plains than the previous time Gina had made the journey. Grateful that she had left extra time, she cruised past the office of Hannon and Ramsey. It was a small, glass-and-white-stone building occupied by several law and accounting practices, wealth management companies, and the PR firm. She was relieved to see that the structure did not have its own belowground parking. That would have made it trickier to spot Williamson when she exited.

After finding a meter for her rental car, she stood on the sidewalk about thirty feet beyond the front door of the building. She did not want to risk having Meg see her and use a different exit. The unseasonably warm weather made the waiting more tolerable.

At twenty after five, Meg walked out of the front door and turned in Gina's direction. She came to an abrupt halt and glared at the journalist.

"I have nothing more to say to you. You have no right to stalk me—"

"Meg, you'll want to hear what I have to say. I only need about ten to fifteen minutes."

"I don't have fifteen minutes. I have to be on time to relieve the sitter—" she said as she hurriedly walked away.

"I respect that, Meg," Gina said, striding quickly to keep up with her. "Here's what we'll do. We'll talk while we ride together in your car. Drop me off on the street before you enter your neighborhood. I'll take an Uber back to my car."

"I said I have nothing more to say to you, and I have no interest in anything you have to tell me. Just go away and leave me—"

"Cathy Ryan was murdered in Aruba. Does that interest you?"

Meg stopped in her tracks, her face betraying a level of shock and fear. "Oh my God."

"Come on," Gina said. "Let's go to your car."

They walked without talking the two blocks to the parking garage. Gina noticed that Meg's eyes were continuously darting around, occasionally turning to look behind her.

Meg clicked her key and a late model BMW coup flashed its lights. It wasn't until after Meg had paid the attendant and they were driving on the street that Gina broke the silence.

"You seemed very nervous while we were walking. Are you worried about being followed?"

"I don't know," Meg said, her fists clenched on the

steering wheel. "Sometimes they know things about my personal life that they shouldn't know."

"Who's 'they,' Meg? Who's your contact at REL?"

Meg ignored the question. "Tell me what happened to Cathy."

Gina, mindful that the fifteen-minute clock was running, quickly shared what she had learned in Aruba. She concluded by saying, "Somebody went to a lot of trouble to follow Cathy down to Aruba, to find out about the tour she signed up for, and to tamper with her ski while she was having lunch."

Meg's expression went from shock to fear.

Gina continued gently. "Meg, in her email Cathy wrote that she had a 'terrible experience' at REL News. I know you did, too. Can you tell me what happened?"

Meg shook her head as she took one hand off the wheel and used it to wipe her eyes. Gina waited, hoping Meg would break the silence. She didn't.

Gina tried a different tack. "Whoever hurt you and Cathy, would I recognize his name?"

"Yes," she answered quickly before clamming up again.

Recognize *his* name, Gina thought. *He*'s got to be one of the on-air people or a top-level executive.

"Meg, I know you accepted a settlement to keep quiet about something. You had every right to provide security for you and your daughter."

"She's all I have," Meg said, her voice barely above a whisper. "I don't want to get involved in this."

"You are involved, Meg. They used you to try to mislead me with the information about Cathy being a troublemaker at the company."

"Can't you just go to the police, tell them what you know about Cathy, and let them take over?"

"I wish it were that simple. The Aruba police have closed the case. I don't have enough proof to convince the FBI to open an investigation."

"I want to help you, but I can't," Meg said flatly. "The only way I can stay safe is to do what they say and stay out of it. I shouldn't be talking to you."

Gina could see that they were nearing Meg's neighborhood. It was time to play hardball. "Meg, you're not safe and neither is your daughter. While in the process of going public, REL News is sitting on a time bomb. Careers and hundreds of millions of dollars may be at risk. Maybe they eliminated Cathy Ryan because she refused to settle. Or maybe Cathy and anybody else who knows their dirty secrets is too much of a risk to them."

Meg turned onto a street that in another block would lead to her home. She pulled to the curb and left the engine running. When she spoke, her voice was firm and determined. "I'll help you under one condition: you promise to never contact me again."

"But how—?"

"Do you promise?"

"Yes," Gina said, while already working on how to get Meg to retract the agreement.

"There's a person at REL News who knows a lot more

than I do about the victims. I can persuade that person to contact you."

"Meg, I'll honor that agreement. I am going to find out what's going on at REL News. If I come across information that suggests that you or your daughter are in danger, do you really not want me to contact you?"

Meg stared straight ahead. "All right. But no more showing up at my workplace or my house. If we have to be in touch, email me." She glanced at the clock on the dashboard. "Time's up. Please get out of my car."

65

Ted read the email in disbelief. Yesterday, Gina had written how much she was looking forward to seeing him. Now this.

Gina was one of the most focused human beings he had ever met. She was certainly not the kind of woman who acted on impulse.

What had changed her?

Who had changed her?

There was another meeting about the REL News prospectus starting in fifteen minutes. Ted shoved the phone into his pocket then took long strides across the lobby.

As he pushed the button for the sixth floor, he could only wonder if it was something he had said or done that had made Gina drop him like this.

66

Gina felt her breathing return to normal as she slowly jogged the few blocks west from Central Park to her apartment. It was approaching seven o'clock in the evening. She tried to avoid running in the Park after dark. Tonight she had been lucky. Eight members of a running club were just beginning their six-mile loop. Safety in numbers. She had fallen in behind them. Allowing them to set the pace freed her mind to wander.

Just before she had left her apartment, a call from her father had taken her by complete surprise. While running she had replayed the conversation in her mind.

"Gina, I have to tell you something. You know how tough it's been for me these six months since your mother died. I want to thank you again for going with me on the trip. It was nice to not be alone among all the other couples."

He paused.

Gina waited, apprehensive about what might come next.

"Just before I left for the Nepal trip, I was down at the dock, doing a little cleanup on the boat."

Gina remembered smirking at the image. It had been an inside joke she and her mother shared. A few years earlier arthritic knees had forced him to stop playing tennis. Her mother's encouragement that he take up golf had fallen on deaf ears. "It takes too long," he had protested.

"Dad, you're retired, the one thing you have a whole lot of is time!" they had argued.

He had spent his career on Wall Street in the bond business, and he had landed at Chubb Insurance.

He had loved his job, but when the company was sold he retired.

The following winter a friend suggested they try renting in Pelican Bay in Naples. During their first week, on a walk around the neighborhood they had bumped into Mike and Jennifer Manley, a retired British couple in their seventies.

"Have you been to the beach to watch the sunset?" Jennifer asked.

When her parents answered no, Dr. Manley said, "We'll pick you up at five-forty-five and ride to the tram together."

The tram, an oversized golf cart that would have looked at home in Disney World, was used to shuttle Pelican Bay residents from designated parking areas through the enchanting mangrove forests to the three miles of unspoiled beach.

A few weeks later the Manleys stopped by for coffee.

Mike said, "A villa in our section is being put up for sale." Six weeks later Gina's parents became the new owners.

It was originally a place to escape the nasty New York winters, but by the second year her parents were telling her how much fun Naples was in the fall when it was less crowded. Instead of returning in early April, they stayed through Memorial Day weekend. Following the advice of their accountant, they became Florida residents. It was then that they had encouraged Gina to move into the Upper West Side apartment and treat it as her own.

Life had been so good for her parents. They loved their life in Naples. Friends from New York had retired to nearby Bonita Springs and Marco Island. Her father had become so smitten with boating that he had purchased a secondhand cabin cruiser that could sleep two. There was always something more to do on the boat, and he loved to stay busy. With Mom as his first mate, they joined groups making overnight excursions up and down the Gulf.

Then came her mother's diagnosis. What should have been another twenty plus years of fun morphed into rounds of chemo and radiation, hospice, and then the end.

And now her father, while tinkering on his boat, had met somebody. I want to be happy for him, Gina thought. But it's only six months since we lost Mom!

Gina slowed her pace and walked the remaining half block to her apartment. She was about to cross the street to her building when she glanced into the lighted lobby. Miguel was shaking his head while talking to a man who clearly appeared to be agitated. Ted! He was turning toward the door and about to exit the building.

If he looked across the street, he would see her. Gina dove to her left and crouched behind a parked Cadillac Escalade. Peering through the windows, she was able to see Ted turn and head east toward Broadway.

She wanted to run across the street, tap him on the shoulder, and at his surprised expression tuck her arm into his. But she could not. What explanation could she give him? There was none. She knew that if she ever decided to see him, there would be no way she could then stay away from him.

A brief shiver overtook her as the warming effect of her run was succumbing to the cold night air. Confident that Ted was out of sight, she started to cross the street.

Miguel approached her in the lobby and began speaking in a hushed tone. Although she knew what had happened, she allowed him to tell her about Ted's surprise visit. He insisted several times that he had given him no information about her.

On her way up in the elevator, Gina felt smothered. Her parents' apartment, now her home, had always felt like a sanctuary, a place where she had complete control. No one entered without her say-so. Safety and solitude were assured.

But now it had been compromised. If she had finished her jog a minute earlier or had been walking on the other side of the street, she would have come face-to-face with Ted, unable to answer the questions he had every right to ask. Would he try again? Probably. Definitely. He worked long hours during the week. But what would it be like this weekend? Every time she left the building, would she have to check to see if the coast was clear?

If she were to run in to him, would she blurt out that the reason she wasn't seeing him was because it would cost him his job?

Once inside the apartment, she grabbed a bottle of water while making a swift mental calculation. Whoever Meg Williamson was going to have contact her would do so by phone or email. It wouldn't matter where she was. On Friday morning she was scheduled to update Geoff but had nothing planned for that afternoon. The decision made, she picked up the phone and started dialing. He answered on the first ring.

"Hi Dad. I don't want you to be alone on your birthday. I want to help celebrate it. I'm coming down this weekend."

"That's so nice of you, but you don't have to do that. We just had that great trip together."

"I know I don't have to. I want to."

"Are you sure you can take the time?"

"Come on, Dad. That's one of the upsides of being a freelance writer. As long as I have my laptop with me, I can work. How about I fly down Friday afternoon and stay until Monday? I want to take you to dinner on Saturday."

"I guess that would be all right."

"Dad, am I hearing some hesitation? If you don't want me to come—"

"Of course I want you to come. I was just distracted for a moment."

"Okay then. We're all set."

"Text me your flight information and I'll pick you up at Fort Myers. I know you're really busy. I'll take care of making the reservation for Saturday."

"Perfect. Looking forward to it already."

"Me too. Love you."

67

Three o'clock in the morning. Unable to sleep, Carter went into the kitchen and opened up the second laptop he used exclusively to communicate with Sherman and Junior. He had no idea what their reactions would be to the news that a reporter was nosing around. Full-blown panic? Stay the course? Anything was possible.

Junior had replied first.

> Keep close eye on the reporter. If any new developments, let me know IMMEDIATELY.

Sherman's response had been similar, but it included a suggestion.

> Any chance for a catch and kill?

Carter thought about the possibility. Would the right amount of money in the right hands make Gina Kane's investigation go away? Sherman had made the suggestion, so he would certainly agree to make the necessary extra funds available.

Carter yawned. It might be worth a shot.

68

Gina exited the plane and walked through the chute, pulling her small bag behind her. Whenever she could, she preferred to travel light, to avoid the inevitable wait at the luggage carousels. It was easy to get everything she needed for a Friday-to-Monday trip into one carry-on bag.

She tapped a text to her father. *Off the plane. On my way out.* She smiled as she pictured Joseph "Jay" Kane waiting in the cell phone lot, not just on time but early, reading his *Wall Street Journal* while awaiting her text.

She walked out the door of the terminal just as her father was pulling up. He jumped out, gave her a quick hug, and dropped her bag into the trunk. Gina's first thought was that he looked great. Then she realized it wasn't just his tan that was a contrast to his full head of salt-and-pepper hair. It was something else, an undeniable spark that showed in his eyes and his voice.

After a minute of chatting about her flight, he asked the question that she had been prepping for.

"So tell me, Gina. How's my future son-in-law? It was nice of him to send a birthday email."

Dad and Ted had liked each other immediately. They were both fans of the New York Giants and Yankees. Both were center of the aisle politically while lamenting how many of their friends were right-wingers.

She hated lying to her father but couldn't share the real reason why they were apart. She chose what she hoped would be an acceptable explanation—at least for now.

"Ted and I have chosen to take a little hiatus. Before making a big decision, both sides need some time to think."

"More thinking, Gina? That's what you were doing while you were in Nepal. Let me give you one piece of advice, and then I'll keep my mouth shut on this subject. Honey, don't be a fault-finder. If you're looking to find something negative about somebody, you'll always succeed. But you'll miss out on so many positives."

Silence followed as Gina allowed her father's advice to sink in.

"Enough about me," she said. "What's new in your world?"

She did not have to wait long to get an explanation for the lift in his overall attitude. It was a forty-minute drive from Fort Myers to Naples, and her father spent the last thirty of it telling her about Marian Callow. She was raised in Los Angeles. Her father was an assistant director for one of the movie studios. She eloped when she was twenty. They broke up ten years later when she realized she couldn't have children.

After moving to New York, she worked as an interior decorator. At thirty-five Marian married a retired executive. He died eight years ago. She has two stepsons. Gina's father finished by saying he hoped Gina wouldn't mind that he had asked Marian to celebrate his birthday dinner with them.

So that explained his hesitation about her coming down and his wanting to make the reservation for Saturday, Gina thought.

"Gina, I have to tell you something. You know how tough it's been for me since your mother died. Just before I left for our trip, I met Marian. While we were away, I realized how much I was thinking about her. Then when I got back to Naples, there was a note from her asking me to come to a welcome home dinner. Since then I've been seeing her every day."

Every day for three weeks, Gina thought. Where was this going? While she was trying to decide if she wanted to marry Ted, who she'd known for over two years, he was thinking about a woman he barely knew.

"Marian is a little younger than I am," her father volunteered.

"How much is 'a little'?"

"Seventeen years," he answered sheepishly.

"Seventeen years!" Gina exclaimed. If that was your definition of "a little," what would you consider *a lot* younger? She quickly did the math in her head. She was thirty-two, her father sixty-six. Forty-nine-year-old Marian was as close to her age as to his.

"All right, so she's younger than I am," he said flatly, "but I don't think that makes a difference, do you?"

"Difference for what, Dad?" Even as she asked the question, Gina was afraid that she knew the answer.

"The way things are going, I could see us getting serious in the near future."

Her mother had been dead only six months, Gina thought. Surely after thirty-five years of a very happy marriage, her father hadn't fallen for someone else so quickly. An old expression her grandmother often used that she hadn't thought about for years crossed her mind. *Weeping widows are easily transplanted.* Did that apply to weeping widowers? she asked herself sarcastically, then chose her response carefully. "Wow, Dad, I'm happy for you. But at the same time that's pretty fast. Where are we going for your birthday dinner?" she asked through gritted teeth.

"The Naples Bay and Yacht Club."

He continued. "I know you like their food, so that's where I made a reservation for the three of us to have dinner tomorrow night."

The three of us, Gina thought to herself. That used to refer to Dad and me and Mom. And now somebody else is part of the three.

"I know it was love at first sight when you and Mom

met in high school," Gina said. "You both knew right away you'd found the right person. And from that day on you had almost fifty years of happiness with each other. But remember you met at seventeen and got married at twenty-five. That's eight years of getting to know somebody."

"Gina, when you get to be my age, you know what you're looking for. Young people have time to court for eight years. People on Medicare don't."

She reached over and touched his shoulder. "Dad, Mom isn't gone six months. You had a very happy marriage all those years. Of course you miss that companionship and want to replace it. But picking the wrong person to be with will be a lot worse than being alone."

"You've already concluded she's the wrong person. Why don't you meet her first and give her a chance?"

"Dad, I haven't reached any conclusions. Here's what I'm sure about. You're not just nice-looking; you're handsome. And you're a thoroughly smart, warm human being. You worked hard your whole life and you're financially very comfortable. In other words, you're a catch."

"Oh please," he chuckled.

"You are, Dad. I can understand why *she's* interested. Why are you so enraptured?"

Using his baritone voice to imitate Dean Martin, he began to sing, "When the moon hits your eye like a big pizza pie, that's *amore*."

They were almost at the driveway.

"Come on, Dad, I'm serious. So, when do I get to meet her?"

"Right now," he said.

As he stopped the car, the front door of the villa opened and Gina found herself staring at the woman who had so enthralled her father.

She's very pretty was the first thought that ran through Gina's mind as she took in the slender woman who was approaching them. Her silver-blond hair framed a face with even features, dominated by large brown eyes that focused directly on Gina.

"Hello, Gina. I'm so glad to meet you. Jay has told me so much about you."

"All good, I hope," Gina said, trying to force a smile.

"Nothing but." Marian's voice was hearty and followed by a laugh that Gina did not share.

There was a moment of awkward silence before Gina stepped out of the car and walked into the villa.

The first thing she noticed was that the picture of her mother and father walking past the palace in Monaco was missing. It was the last trip they had taken before Mom got sick. Her father had kept it on the mantel. She spotted it over in the corner atop a bookcase. Whose idea was it to move it?

The furniture in the living room had been rearranged. The two matching couches now faced each other, and the casual pillows her mother had crocheted were nowhere to be seen. Several new watercolors, scenes from Pelican Bay, hung on the walls. I wonder what she's done to my room, Gina thought as she headed down the hall.

It was exactly as when she had visited her father three

months ago. How long will it take for the fabulous designer to get her hooks on this room? Gina asked herself, then stopped. Dad told her all about me, she thought. It's my turn now. I'm going to find out everything there is to know about her.

69

The weekend passed quickly. On Friday evening, Gina quickly agreed to her father's suggestion that they have a drink while watching the sunset at the beach. Accompanied by Marian, they drove the half mile to the lot where they boarded the tram for the ride through the mangroves. To her credit, Marian did her best to avoid awkwardness. She insisted on sitting in the backseat during the car ride. The tram offered seating for two in each row. Waving away Gina's offer, Marian climbed in next to a woman by herself, leaving a row for Gina and Dad.

Gina could feel herself starting to relax. While still wary of Marian, she couldn't help but notice how happy her father looked. It was a beautiful night so they decided to stay at the waterside restaurant and have dinner.

Marian was very pleasant. She had taken the time to read Gina's *Empire Review* article about the fraternity branding iron and complimented her on it. She knew about Ted and started to ask questions. She let it drop when Gina mentioned the hiatus.

Gina asked about what type of work Marian had done

as a designer. “I worked in set design,” she explained. “Advertising agencies and Broadway producers used our company to create their sets and backdrops.” She’d gone back to school and landed there in the design world right after graduating from FIT. That had been her job until she married her late husband. When she met Jack, he was an investment banker at Goldman Sachs planning to retire at age fifty-five. He told her that both his father and grandfather had died young. He had no intention of keeling over at his desk, and he had made enough money to do what he wanted to do. They moved to Florida and then began taking trips. “It was wonderful,” she said. “A safari in Africa. Lots of cruises.” She wasn’t able to keep working and live the life he wanted to live, so she quit her job as a designer. Unfortunately, Jack did not escape the heart disease that plagued the men in his family. He survived the first attack but died three months later.

Her father had told Gina that Marian had two stepsons. She decided to ask about them.

“I understand you have stepsons?” Gina asked.

“Yes.”

“Do you see much of them?”

Marian paused before answering. “They have their own lives and I have mine.”

She nipped that line of conversation in the bud, Gina thought to herself.

Gesturing toward the water, Marian said, “This is the part I love. When the sun goes below the horizon and the clouds begin to glow.”

Gina glanced at her father. The glowing was not entirely confined to the clouds.

The buffet dinner the next night at the Naples Bay and Yacht Club was as good as she remembered. After a sushi appetizer, Gina treated herself to a delicious plate of veal. Knowing her father would insist that they have dessert to celebrate his birthday, Gina was grateful she had thought to pack her running shoes. *I'll work it off tomorrow morning,* she promised herself.

A number of club members stopped by the table. She was surprised by how many greeted her father, and Marian, by first name.

She had not seen Mike and Jennifer Manley, her parents' closest friends in Naples, since her mother's death. It was good to see them again, but she was disappointed to see how warmly they greeted Marian.

Gina did get a chance to speak to them quietly before they went home. "Dad seems to be getting pretty serious about Marian," she started, but Jennifer jumped right in.

"Gina, your dad was so lost without your mother. Marian is so good for him."

It was not the answer Gina was looking for. *Am I the only one having doubts about this situation?* she asked herself.

On the way to the airport early Monday morning, she and her father made small talk and then rode in silence. Gina hated the feeling of awkwardness that hung in the air. She had never hesitated to talk to her father about Ted, work, politics, anything from the momentous to the trivial. She loved their conversations. But she found herself struggling with how to introduce a topic that was so important to her, to both of them.

Sensing her reluctance, her father broke the ice. "So tell me, has the jury reached a verdict on Marian?"

"Dad, I'm not judging Marian, you, or anybody. I'm just concerned. I'm worried that you're going to move quickly to fill a void."

"Gina—"

"Please, Dad, hear me out. I like Marian. I think she's very nice. She's an attractive woman. I'm delighted that the two of you are having a good time together. But knowing a few facts about somebody is not the same as really *knowing* that person. That takes time."

"Gina, I don't think you're giving your old man enough credit. A little wisdom usually comes along with a head full of gray hair."

They pulled to a stop in front of her terminal.

"Dad, remember when you would tell me how much you liked Ronald Reagan when he was president? What he would say when he was dealing with the Russians—"

"Trust but verify," he said, smiling.

"Excellent advice. I love you."

70

Gina settled into her aisle seat for the two-and-a-half-hour flight to LaGuardia. The couple in the two seats next to her were about her age. She could not help but hear their conversation. They were planning a wedding. Holding hands as they spoke, he suggested how much easier it would be if they flew to Las Vegas and were married by an Elvis impersonator. She laughed, punched him on the arm, and leaned her head against his shoulder.

It had been a long time since Gina had felt so alone. Most of her friends envied her life as a journalist and the freedom of movement if offered. It certainly had its advantages. But there's something to be said for the familiarity of an office, seeing the same faces every day. For better or for worse, they know you as well as you know them. The sense of accomplishing as a team. Sharing a joke in the cafeteria. The spontaneous drink after work. She had been freelancing for three years. Most of that time was spent in her apartment or at a Starbucks, her laptop her only constant companion.

She didn't need a therapist to help understand why

she was feeling so gloomy. *Ted.* If things were different, he would have been the one to help sort out her feelings. She was aching to see him. She wanted to talk to him about Marian Callow. His instincts were so good. His oft-repeated joke: "There are very few problems that can't be resolved over a bottle of wine at dinner."

He had called when she was in Naples, but she had let the phone ring. She still couldn't bring herself to listen to the message he had left. The text he'd sent late Saturday evening had brought her to tears.

> *Gina, I accept that we're finished. Not that I have much choice in the matter. You always valued how well we communicated. That makes it harder to understand why, when something went terribly wrong, we can't even talk about it. Please assure me that you're okay. I hope you've found someone who loves you the way I did. Ted*

His use of the past tense to describe his love was not lost on her.

Just before the announcement came to power down electronic devices, Gina opened her phone and tapped a text to Lisa. *Counselor, please say you're free for a drink tonight. In need of your company.*

Less than a minute later the phone vibrated announcing the arrival of a text. *It's nice to be needed! DeAngelo's at 7:30.*

71

Lisa was already at the bar when Gina entered. She had thrown her coat over the back of the stool next to her to reserve it for Gina. Lisa had a *Help me!* look on her face as she was trying to be polite to an older man with the worst hair-dye job Gina had ever seen. He moved off after Gina sat down.

"Who's your new friend?" she joked.

"Oh please! Anybody who just sold his company for twenty million dollars could find somebody to do a better job on his hair than that. It looks like he used shoe polish!"

They both laughed.

"So girlfriend," Lisa began, "anything new on the Ted front?"

Lisa was the only person outside of *Empire Review* that Gina had confided in regarding her REL News investigation. When Gina shared with her the magazine's lawyer's insistence that she had to break things off with Ted immediately, Lisa had said, "I hate to tell you this, Gina, but he's right."

"I'm still getting calls and text messages," Gina said. "Of course I feel awful, but there's nothing I can do."

"I'm really sorry."

"I know you are. Thanks. But that's not what I wanted to talk to you about. Remember when I told you my father had met somebody?" Gina described the weekend in Naples, meeting Marian Callow, and her concern about her father.

"It's hard at our age, Gina, to think of our parents as sexual beings. My uncle Ken was a widower and he was dating a lot in his early seventies. He once told me, 'The call of the wild is still sounding at my age. It may not be as loud or my hearing may not be as good, but no question, it's still there.' "

They both laughed. Gina again appreciated her good fortune to have Lisa as a friend.

"Look, Lisa, I want him to be happy. I have my life up here. I like what I do. I love New York; I love my apartment. If he wants to share his life and what he has in Naples with her, who am I to object?"

A troubled look came over Lisa's face. "Gina, I'm going to put on my lawyer hat for a minute. You refer to your place on the Upper West Side as '*my* apartment.' Did your parents or your father ever legally transfer ownership into your name?"

Gina appeared stunned. "When they went to Florida, they gave me the apartment. I've lived there. I've paid the maintenance and all the expenses. It's mine, right?"

"Legally speaking, Gina, nobody cares who took care

of the maintenance or paid to fix the appliances. If the apartment has not been legally transferred to you, including paying the appropriate gift taxes, or put into a trust for you, the apartment belongs to your father. He is free to leave it to whomever he pleases."

Silence hung in the air for a few moments. It was Lisa who finally broke it. "It's always possible your parents or your father did the transfer without telling you. I can find out the owner of any piece of property in the city. I'll research it and get back to you."

"I don't know how long that will take, Lisa. I want to pay you for your time."

Lisa waved her off. "You pay for the drinks, and we'll call it even."

72

After her weekend in Naples Gina had been overdue for a good night's sleep. Worry that her father was close to making a commitment to a woman he barely knew had weighed on her the three nights she was down there. A sound sleep in her own bed would be the antidote to her feeling of fatigue. But it wasn't meant to be. Lisa's warning about the apartment served only to increase her anxiety.

It was 6:20 a.m. on Tuesday. She didn't feel rested, but she was certain that she would be unable to fall back to sleep. Pulling on a robe, she headed for the kitchen.

As she waited for the Keurig machine to brew the coffee, she tried to sort out her feelings. She had heard plenty of stories from friends and parents of friends who felt cheated with regard to what they thought they would inherit. In one family there were four siblings, two who were very successful and two who struggled financially. The parents left the bulk of the estate to their less-well-off children, believing they needed the most help. The successful children argued that hard work had made the difference in their lives. They felt they were now being punished for the sacrifices they had made.

As an only child, Gina never had to wonder about what would happen when her parents were no longer around. "What was ours will be yours someday," they had always said. It was to be a logical progression, a handoff from one generation to the next. Completely uncomplicated.

She breathed in the scent of the brewing coffee. It was already working its magic. She hadn't taken a sip, but she was already feeling a little more awake.

How did she even start the conversation with her father without coming off as really selfish? *Dad, I'm concerned that you and Marian are headed down the aisle pretty soon. Before that happens, could you kindly put the place in New York in my name so she doesn't get any ideas?*

Maybe that sounded so selfish because she was being downright selfish, she whispered to herself. Looking around the apartment, she thought, I didn't earn this. Mom and Dad did. It was theirs; now it's his. I don't have a *right* to any of this.

After several sips of coffee she felt her energy level increasing. She went to the kitchen table, tapped open her email account, and scanned the new ones. One had arrived at 6:33 a.m., seven minutes earlier. It included an attachment. She didn't recognize the sender. All that was written in the subject line was "REL." Now wide awake, she clicked and watched the email take shape on the screen.

Miss Kane,

I spoke to friend. She suggest I contact you.

I was shock when I here Cathy Ryan dead. Like you, I don't believe was accident. Paula Stephenson was another young girl hurt so bad. Like Cathy, I don't believe she commit suicide.

I have to be careful. Don't try to find me.

Gina clicked on the attachment and scanned the brief article. Thirty-one-year-old Paula Stephenson had been found hanging from her bathroom door in her Durham, North Carolina, apartment. Although they had not determined a cause of death, the police were investigating it as a possible suicide. I wonder how hard they're investigating, Gina asked herself.

There was a brief mention of time she had spent as the weather broadcaster on a station in Dayton. There was nothing about a current employer or next of kin.

The article was from June 28, four months earlier.

Gina glanced back at the name of the sender. It was a jumble of letters and numbers followed by "@gmail .com." It reminded her of one of those suggestions that are made when they want you to choose a unique password.

She reread the email. Was it from a fourth victim? The sender had been careful not to reveal his or her sex. It was also not clear if the sender was currently at REL or used to be there. Or for that matter it was possible he/she never worked there.

The multiple errors in word usage suggested that English was not this person's first language. Or maybe that was intentional, Gina thought.

Whoever sent this knew what happened to Cathy Ryan and Paula Stephenson and knows Meg Williamson. It was too early to contact Williamson for help. Meg had done what she had promised. Gina had a new lead to follow. She hoped that the police in Durham would be more helpful than their counterparts in Aruba.

73

I'm getting my money's worth out of this suitcase, Gina thought to herself as she threw the last few items in before zipping it shut. She glanced at her phone. Her flight would touch down in Raleigh-Durham at four o'clock in the afternoon.

She had tried to accomplish as much as she could in the little over twenty-four hours since she had received the mysterious email about Paula Stephenson, emailing Geoff to describe the new lead she wanted to pursue. He had texted her an hour later. *Sounds promising. Go for it. Be careful.*

Hoping the policy had changed, Gina had gone online to the Bureau of Vital Statistics, Durham, North Carolina. She was hoping to download a copy of Stephenson's death certificate. No luck. For a fee it could be mailed to her. I'll pick it up in person, she said to herself as she jotted down the address.

She had spent the previous afternoon researching online private investigators. After speaking to Wesley Rigler, she was confident she had found one who could help her. Wes was in his early sixties. Before retiring two years earlier, he had been a lieutenant in the Durham Police Department.

Earlier that morning she had received a text from Andrew, Cathy Ryan's brother.

> *Hi Gina, I know you're busy and I don't want to bother you. My mother keeps asking if there are any updates on what happened to Cathy. Is there anything you can share? Thanks. Andrew*

No matter how many investigations she did, this was the part that made her feel the most conflicted. Whether it was the nursing home abuse, the fraternity branding, or other stories she had pursued, the victims or their families had shared very private and confidential information with her. They had bared their souls and opened themselves to further pain to give her the information she needed to press forward. Most of them wanted, expected, or demanded to be kept in the loop.

But experience had taught her that sharing everything she knew could create false hopes and in some cases jeopardize the investigation. It was a balancing act. Her response via text had been:

> *Andrew, I'm sorry to say I don't have anything new on Cathy. I've spoken to another woman*

who had a bad experience at REL and have a lead on a third potential victim. Am grateful to you and your parents for your trust. Gina

She slipped her coat on, put her purse on top of her suitcase, and headed toward the elevator.

74

Gina used the electronic key to open the door of her room at the Durham Hotel on East Chapel Hill Street. Lisa had recommended it, saying her family had stayed there when they went down for her younger brother's graduation from Duke.

Ordinarily, Gina would have used the two hours of flight time to organize her thoughts, to put together a plan to make the best use of her time on the ground. There was no worse feeling—it had happened to her before—than being on the return flight home and realizing she had failed to follow up on a potential lead.

She had ample reason to feel distracted. Much as she dreaded receiving a text or an email from Ted, going several days without hearing from him produced a different kind of hurt. More than ever before, she realized how much she loved him. She envisioned his arms around her as she explained that abruptly breaking up with him was the only thing she could do to protect him. He would think of something funny and sweet to say. Gina, do me a favor. In the future, stop protecting me!

And now, only silence. She found herself hoping that his work on the REL News IPO was keeping him so busy that he would have no time to move on, no opportunity to start getting interested in finding someone else. I'll find a way to make it all work out, she promised herself.

Putting Ted out of her mind provided little respite. When her plane landed and she switched on her phone, there was a text from Lisa. *Gina, sorry to be the bearer of bad tidings. The apartment is still in both of your parents' names. Let me know how I can help. Lisa*

Gina was not surprised. She really couldn't imagine her parents or her father having done that without telling her.

Before receiving the email about Paula Stephenson, Gina had hoped to spend time looking into Marian Callow's background. She especially wanted to track down her stepsons, the ones who *have their own lives,* and hear their impressions of the woman who had married into their family.

She had said a silent prayer that things wouldn't move too quickly in Florida. Getting engaged creates a momentum all its own. She remembered talking to a girlfriend who had a short-lived marriage. "Rings are bought, the church and reception hall booked, shopping for gowns, going over guest lists, rehearsal dinner, endless photos. The plans and events were like an avalanche going down the mountain. I knew on my wedding day I was marrying the wrong guy. I just felt powerless to stop it."

The ring of her cell phone snapped Gina back to reality. It was the private investigator, Wes Rigler.

"Gina, I'm so sorry. My daughter has gone into labor two weeks early. I can't meet you tonight, but if all goes well, I'll be able to break free tomorrow afternoon. Is there anything I can help you with before I head to the hospital?"

"I want to talk to the funeral home that took care of Stephenson's body. Would you be able to find out which one that was?"

"No, but I can make the search easy for you. When the medical examiner is finished with a body, it is shipped to a local funeral home. When the deceased is from out of town, they prep it and make arrangements for the body to be transported to the home the victim's family wants to use. The City of Durham contracts with three funeral homes to provide this service. Have you got a pen?"

Gina scribbled down the names. "Thanks, Wes. I don't want to take you away from your family."

"Don't worry. Once everything's in good shape at the hospital, I'll come join you wherever you are. Keep your phone on."

"Will do. Good luck. First grandchild?"

"*Numero uno*. Can't wait!"

Gina put down the phone. The thought of a new baby arriving in the world made her think of, who else? Ted. Imagining the happy family converging on the hospital brought to mind her father, and guess who? Marian. Knock it off, she said to herself. You're not going to get anything done if you spend the whole time sulking and worrying.

75

The next morning Gina called the first and second funeral homes. Neither had a record of having made arrangements for a Paula Stephenson. With some trepidation she phoned the third. Yes, they had taken care of her. There was only one mortician at their facility, the owner, Vaughn Smith. Mr. Smith was out of the office on business but would be available to see her at one o'clock.

Change of plans, she thought to herself. She pulled a folder from her bag and opened it to Paula's obituary. The address of her condo was 415 Walnut Street. She opened her laptop and went to Google Maps. The pictures revealed a relatively small four-story building. Probably no more than sixteen units.

The Uber dropped Gina in front of a four-story structure that was set back from the road. A small parking area was in front. A painted sign welcomed visitors to Willow Farms. A set of glass double doors was in the center of the building. Looking through them, she could see a vestibule leading to a twin set of elevators.

At the moment there was no one in sight. Gina tried

opening one of the doors. Predictably it was locked. It's so much easier in Manhattan, she thought. Most buildings there had doormen. In exchange for a smile and a cash tip, most of them were happy to provide general information about the residents. Here it was going to be potluck and a lot of waiting.

Ten minutes later the elevators opened and a black man carrying a briefcase walked toward the front door. He appeared to be in his forties.

"Excuse me, sir," Gina said, "did you happen to know a Paula Stephenson, a woman who lived in the building until a few months ago?"

"I'm on the second floor. She was on the fourth. If you're here about her apartment, I'm pretty sure it was sold last month."

"No, thanks, not about that. I'm hoping to talk to anyone in the building who knew Paula. Any ideas?"

"I'm afraid not. The first time I heard her name was when the police came after her." He paused. "Passing. Sorry I can't help."

Now she knew Paula lived on the fourth floor. That was progress, Gina thought to herself.

Fifteen minutes later a taxi pulled to a halt in front of the building. A woman who appeared to be in her late seventies exited and made her way to the front door. She eyed Gina suspiciously.

"Excuse me, ma'am," Gina began.

"I hope you know there's no soliciting allowed here, young lady," the woman snapped.

"I promise I'm not here to sell anything. By any chance did you know a young woman named Paula Stephenson who lived on the fourth floor?"

"That one," she replied, almost spitting out the words. "I've never had a drop of alcohol my whole life. I don't think that one ever let a day go by that she wasn't inebriated."

"So you knew her?"

"I didn't say I knew her. Just being in the elevator with her and her breath was enough to make me feel like a drunkard. Do you go to church?"

"Yes, as a matter of fact I do," Gina answered, surprised by the question.

"If the young people today went to church, they wouldn't need to drink or take drugs, and they'd face their problems instead of killing themselves."

"I'm sure they would," Gina said as she tried to think of a graceful way to end the conversation. She could see through the doors a woman pushing a stroller headed her way and did not want to miss the opportunity to speak to her.

"Thank you, ma'am, you've been very helpful," Gina said as she kept holding the door.

"Keep going to church, and pay attention when you're there," the woman admonished her before heading toward the elevators.

Gina held the door open as the woman pushing the stroller approached. She appeared to be about her own age. Dark hair to her shoulders framed even facial features.

"Your daughter is lovely," Gina said, leaning toward

the little girl, who returned her smile. Two small teeth protruded from her lower gum.

"Why, thank you" was her mother's response, in a strong Southern accent.

"I don't want to hold you up, but by any chance did you know a building resident named Paula Stephenson?"

"Oh, I did. That was such a shame."

"Paula's friends lost track of her after she left New York. Would you mind if I ask you a few questions about her?"

"Of course not. I'm taking my little Scarlett for her walk. Why don't you come with us?"

After exchanging names, Gina followed Abbey around to the back of the building. Beyond the pool was a field. A paved path ran along a brook. "Scarlett and I walk this way every morning, except of course when it's raining."

"How well did you know Paula?"

"She lived across the hall from me, in 4A. I'm in 4B. Paula always made a fuss over Scarlett. She'd buy her gifts. My husband travels a lot for work. When Paula was going to the store, she'd knock on my door and ask if I needed anything."

"Did you get to know her?"

"I did. Lots of days we were the only ones around. She'd come over for coffee. I'd have coffee. Paula would bring her own stuff. I'm not stupid. I know she had a drinking problem. But beneath it all, she was really a sweet person."

"I agree, and I'm surprised the police are treating her death as a suicide."

"I heard that or read that, too. I'm really shocked."

"Why is that?"

"I told you we talked a lot. She was really down after her and her boyfriend broke up and she lost a lot of money. I was really worried about her then. But the last time I spoke to her she sounded a lot more positive. I remember what she said. 'I have a way to get back on track financially.'"

"Did she tell you how she was going to do that?"

"No. She said something about getting tricked the first time, but now they were going to pay up."

"Did she ever say who 'they' were?"

"No, she didn't. Lots of times Paula just needed somebody to listen and not ask too many questions."

"How did you find out she died?"

"I knew something wasn't right. We would talk or see each other almost every day, and then nothing. I was pretty sure she'd have told me if she was taking a trip. Her car was in its usual parking spot. I felt funny about calling the police, so I phoned the building manager. They're really nice. They came over and found her."

"Besides you, was Paula friendly with anybody else in the building? Did she mention any friends?"

"None that I can recall. I'm pretty sure I was the only one she talked to here."

The horseshoe-shaped path was now leading them back to the rear of the building.

Gina continued. "So you were really surprised when you heard Paula had taken her own life?"

"I was. Especially when I heard how she did it."

"Why do you say that?"

"My husband's from New Jersey. His mother freezes bagels from the store in their town and sends them to us. One day I offered one to Paula, who said no. She told me she almost choked on a bagel when she lived in New York. Somebody in the restaurant had to help her cough it up. After that she was afraid of any food that might make her choke."

"So somebody who had a fear of choking—"

Abbey finished the sentence, "doesn't seem like the kind of person who would hang herself."

"After they found Paula, did the police ask the other tenants in the building any questions?"

"About what?"

"Did anybody see someone around the building who didn't seem to belong here?"

"No, why would they?"

"It was just a thought. You've been very helpful. My contact information is on this card," Gina said as she handed it to her. "If you remember anything else about Paula, please be in touch."

"You don't believe Paula killed herself. Am I right?"

"I'm not sure what to believe right now. I'm gathering information."

Gina thanked her again, bent forward, and said goodbye to Scarlett.

76

Gina's investigation into Paula Stephenson's death had an eerily similar feel to her attempt to find out what really happened to Cathy Ryan in Aruba. She had identified anomalies—an experienced and careful Jet Skier's panic leads to a fatal crash; a woman who is optimistic about getting her life together chooses to end it in a way that would make her experience one of her worst fears. Both had bad experiences at the same former employer who was trying to settle with them. . . .

"You idiot!" Gina said aloud as she stared out the window of the Uber that was taking her to the funeral home.

"Excuse me, ma'am," the driver said, sounding somewhat annoyed.

"Sorry," Gina apologized. "I was talking to myself."

In her mind she had put Paula in the same boat with Cathy Ryan, former REL News employees contemplating settlements. Gina replayed in her mind what Abbey had shared with her. Paula was depressed after losing a lot of money and breaking up with her boyfriend. She saw a way to recover financially. She had been tricked, but now *they* were going to pay up. What if, similar to Meg, Paula had taken a settlement from REL. It made sense. Gina opened her iPhone to Zillow and put in the condominium's address. Paula had purchased it a little over a year ago for $525,000. That's a lot of money for a person in her early thirties, particularly for someone who's not working.

As she had done with Meg, Gina would try to find out if there was any family money behind Paula. Cathy Ryan and Paula Stephenson may have had two things in common. Both were balking at REL News's attempts to reach final settlements with them; both died while they were negotiating.

A soft ring announced the arrival of a text. It was from Wes Rigler. *Healthy, 8-lb Ann Marie arrived at 9:00 this morning. Mom and baby doing fine. Been busy gathering info. When can we meet?*

Gina texted her congratulations and that she was en route to the Smith Gardens Funeral Home for a one o'clock appointment. He responded immediately. *Perfect. I'm 10 minutes away. Will meet you there.*

Smith Gardens was a one-story, white-brick building with black shutters. A one-lane driveway leading to the front door cut across a well-manicured lawn. To the left of the structure was a large, mostly empty parking lot. As a result of a truck accident, what was supposed to be a ten-minute trip had taken closer to twenty. Not wanting to be late for her appointment, Gina hurried toward the door.

She stopped when a white Ford Explorer pulled quickly into the parking lot.

A middle-aged, balding man with a friendly smile and a folder in his hand hurried toward her. His sports jacket struggled to contain the wide shoulders beneath.

"You must be Gina," he said, as a large hand enveloped hers.

"I am. Nice to meet you, Wes."

"We can talk more afterwards, but I think you're going to like what I brought," he reported as he opened the door for her. Seeing no one, they walked down a hall. Viewing rooms were on either side. A man in a dark suit emerged from the one on the left and walked toward them. "Good afternoon. May I help you?"

"Yes. Thank you. My name is Gina Kane. Mr. Rigler and I are here to see Mr. Smith."

"Right this way. He's expecting you."

Vaughn Smith looked up from his desk when he heard footsteps outside his door. He popped out of his chair, introduced himself, and shook hands with Gina. He looked at Wes and said, "You look familiar, but I'm not placing you."

Wes smiled. "I was a detective with Durham PD. Retired now and working as a private investigator. I'm hoping we both can be of assistance to Miss Kane."

"Me too." Pointing to two chairs he said, "Have a seat. Let's get started."

Gina followed the same strategy she had chosen when discussing Cathy Ryan. Without identifying REL News, she explained that several young women had similar negative experiences at a previous employer. In Gina's opinion the police in Aruba were hasty in attributing the death of one of the women as the result of an accident. Now a second was dead, and despite possible evidence to the contrary, her death had been deemed a suicide.

"Do you remember," Gina wasn't quite sure how to frame the question, "handling Paula?" she asked Smith.

"I do," he said as he tapped on the laptop on his desk. "After the Durham police located the family, I was contacted by Swartz Funeral Home in Xavier, Nebraska. They sent me the authorization papers, which I took to the Medical Examiner's Office to act on behalf of the family. The body was released to me."

"Do you remember anything out of the ordinary about the injuries to her body? My understanding is that the police were investigating her death as a suicide."

"I do. When a ligature, in this case a bathrobe sash, is used in a hanging, it generally causes contusions, broken blood vessels under the skin. I recall there was something odd about the ligature marks. Over my thirty years in the business I've handled a fair amount of suicides, including hangings. The contusions on her neck were not consistent with what I usually see."

"Did you report this to the police?"

"I did, but I'm sorry to say they didn't follow up. The opioid epidemic has kept us very busy."

"Did the police do anything?"

"Not to my knowledge, but as I look at the date I can

understand why. They had their hands full at the time. White supremacists were in town protesting a decision to take down a Confederate monument. Supporters of the decision were here in force. The police were preparing for a major confrontation that fortunately did not materialize. At a time like that, it's easy for a case like this to not draw attention. With no family members screaming at the press for an investigation, no one wants to rock the boat. It slipped through the cracks."

"Did you by any chance take any photos of Stephenson's body?" Gina asked.

"No, I didn't."

Rigler interjected for the first time. "One of my former colleagues gave me these," he said as he pulled a stack of color photos from an envelope.

"Are these released to the public?" Gina asked.

"Never," he said. "I promised my friend I'd get the scene photos back to him tomorrow. I didn't bring these up sooner, Vaughn, because first I wanted to hear what you remembered."

Smith waved him off. "That's fine, Wes. Let's have a look."

Rigler spread the photos of Paula's nude body on top of the desk. He and Gina came to Vaughn's side so they could look at them together. Vaughn had pulled a large magnifying glass from his top drawer and was slowly rotating it around the neck area in the photo of Paula's upper torso.

Rigler pulled a paper from his folder and referred

to it as he spoke. "The victim was found hanging from the door on the outside of the bathroom. The sash of the silk bathrobe she was wearing was tied around her neck as you can see in this picture," he said, pointing with his finger. "The other end of the sash was tied to the door handle on the inside of the bathroom."

Smith used a pencil to trace discolorations on Paula's neck close to her jawline. "Contusions in this area," he said, "are consistent with what you would find in a hanging."

"I know I'm the novice in the room," Gina interjected, "but isn't the will to live very strong, even in a suicide victim? Once she started to strangle, wouldn't she use her hands on the knot to try to save herself?"

"The process, losing consciousness and then death, happens much faster than most people realize," Rigler responded. "The science behind it is fascinating. The rule of thumb is that after about thirty-three pounds of compression of the airway and only eleven pounds of pressure on the carotid arteries, the victim will lose consciousness and quickly die. When the ligature is pulled tight by the body weight, the victim quickly becomes unconscious due to lack of oxygenated blood to the brain. In movies and on TV shows they usually show a hanging victim that jumped off a chair or kicked aside a stool. You don't need that. Victims often successfully hang themselves by sitting up against a door, tying the ligature to the doorknob, and leaning forward."

"Isn't that how Anthony Bourdain, the CNN celebrity chef, killed himself?" Gina asked.

"Yes, it is. I had one like that only a few weeks ago," Smith replied. "Take a look at this furrow." Turning to Gina and pointing with his pencil to discoloration on Paula's lower neck, he said, "Furrows are these horizontal grooves that were made by the bathrobe sash. They're more pronounced than I would have expected."

"If this was a suicide, could the sash have scraped up her neck when she was against the door and let herself drop?" Gina asked.

"It probably did do that, but it wouldn't make marks like these," Rigler said, pointing to dark blue areas.

"If you were looking at these photos for the first time," Gina began, "what would you say happened to her?"

"Wes, I'll let you take that one," the mortician said.

Rigler continued to stare at the picture. "I would say this is a homicide that was staged to look like a suicide. And I think I know why these ligature marks don't make sense on a suicide victim. In police work when we're at a crime scene, most often we're seeing the end result. We try to imagine the series of events that took place to create this result. At first glance, this case had all the hallmarks of a basic suicide. As I studied the scene photos more closely, not everything was adding up. What scenario could have created these ligature marks? Suppose this was a homicide. The perpetrator surprised her from behind. Picture him forcing her down on her bed face first. Her face against a mattress would muffle an attempt to scream. He yanked the sash off her bathrobe and slipped it around her neck. With his knee against her back, he pulled hard upward to get her to stop struggling. That would explain the prominent horizontal furrows on the lower neck. He then took the sash, tied it to the bathroom door handle, looped it over the top of the door, tied it around her neck, and released her into the position where she was found."

"Does that explain something else?" Smith asked. "The bruising on her upper neck closest to the ligature is less severe than one would expect following asphyxiation from hanging. There may have been less blood in the affected area—"

"Because she was already dead?" Gina interjected.

"Precisely," Rigler answered.

Gina broke the silence that followed. "Did she leave a note?"

"No note," Rigler responded.

"Does that mean anything to you when you're trying to determine if this was a homicide?" she asked.

"Not at all," he replied. "Contrary to popular belief, most suicide victims don't leave a note."

Gina flipped through the pictures. The bed was unmade. Newspapers and magazines were piled haphazardly on a table in the living room. Toiletries were stacked on the vanity in the bathroom. Dishes were in the sink. A Kentucky Fried Chicken bag was on the kitchen table next to a half-empty vodka bottle. Four empty vodka bottles, a plastic water bottle, and three Diet Pepsi cans were on a corner of the kitchen counter. It looks like she was behind in taking out the recycling, Gina thought to herself.

"Is there anything else you see that sways your opinion one way or the other?" she asked.

Rigler thought for a moment. "Gina, do you own a terry-cloth bathrobe?"

Surprised by the question, she answered, "Yes, I do. Why do you ask?"

"Because most women do and most women are remarkably consistent in the way they commit suicide. They choose a comfortable place, typically at home. They care a lot about how they'll look when they're found. That's why it's rare for women to use a gun or anything that will leave them disfigured. That includes bruises around the neck. Women who use a rope or electrical cord usually put a towel around their neck first to avoid leaving marks.

"If I were the investigator on the scene, I would have gone through her closet. A terry-cloth bathrobe sash would have been her first choice. It would have left fewer marks than a silk sash."

"Is it too late to check her wardrobe?"

"It is. With the exception of the bathrobe, the sash, and any undergarments she might have had on, the police by now will have released all personal property to her family."

"Is there anything we can do to have the police reopen the case?"

"I still know the guys on the detective squad, but we have an uphill climb ahead of us."

"Why?" Gina asked.

"Because we just put together a theory of what we

think happened," Rigler explained. "Somebody else could look at these pictures and insist that everything we're looking at is consistent with a suicide."

"I'm sorry. I'm a little confused," Gina said.

"Let me be devil's advocate and argue the other side. There was no forced entry into the apartment, no signs of foul play, no indication of a struggle. Was the victim a substance abuser, alcohol, drugs?"

"A neighbor who knew her well told me she had a drinking problem," Gina said quietly.

"That tips the scales even more toward a suicide conclusion."

"Although not this severe, I've seen similar marks on necks that did not result from homicides," Smith added. "Some people take a perverse joy in having their lover almost fatally strangle them during sex acts."

"*De omnibus dubitandum*," Rigler stated.

"All is to be doubted," Gina replied.

"I'm impressed," Rigler said.

"I went to an all-girls Catholic high school, mandatory two years of Latin."

"That phrase was told to me by an old detective who helped train me. If you're going to have an investigator's mind-set, you have to enter the scene with an open mind. If you don't, you'll only find stuff to support your preconceived notion. It looks like that's what happened here. They rugged it."

"Rugged it?" Gina asked.

"The police came in believing this was a suicide,

found ample evidence to support that, and anything that didn't fit was swept under the rug."

"There's got to be something. The bathrobe and undergarments. Might there be DNA evidence they can follow up on?" Gina asked.

"Possibly," Rigler answered. "But that's expensive and time-consuming. The cops on the Durham force do a good job. But remember, this did not appear to be a crime scene. It was an apparent suicide. It's been about four months."

"I want to speak to the family," Gina said quietly.

"I can help you with that," Smith said as he began typing on his laptop. A few seconds later the printer ejected a sheet of paper that he handed to Gina. "This is the contract with the funeral home in Nebraska. It includes the family contact information."

Rigler insisted on driving Gina back to the hotel.

"I'm sorry to make you work so hard on your first day as a grandfather," Gina said.

"Oh, I almost forgot," Rigler said while reaching into his pocket. He pulled out a cigar with a little pink ribbon tied at the end. "Do you like cigars?"

"No," Gina laughed. "But I'll take one for my dad if that's okay."

"Absolutely," he said, handing it to her.

"If you were at the hospital all night, you must be exhausted."

Rigler smiled. "No big deal. I'll catch up on sleep tonight. I love what I do. It's like solving puzzles. It's a challenge to figure out how all the pieces of a case fit together."

Without naming REL News, Gina gave him a more detailed account of her investigation into Cathy Ryan's death than she had shared at the funeral home. She told him about the email that had suggested she look into Paula's death. He listened intently before responding.

"As I said earlier, Gina, I'm going to try to get the PD to take a fresh look at the Stephenson case. I'll keep you posted. In the meantime I want to give you some advice. Be careful. If you're right about the two victims, and I think you are, the killer is smart and has access to resources. Stephenson would have been easy to track down and kill. As to the Ryan girl, he found out when she was vacationing outside the country, where she was staying, and what activities she was doing, before making his move. You don't look like the type to commit suicide, but I don't want to find out that you've become the victim of a tragic accident."

77

Michael Carter spent the balance of the afternoon at his computer trying to learn as much as he could about Gina Kane. Wikipedia gave references to the fraternity branding iron story and several other pieces she had written for *Empire Review.* He had originally intended to quickly scan through the fraternity article. Captivated, he had carefully read all twenty-nine pages. In addition to being an excellent writer, she was a formidable investigator.

In the section about her education he noted her undergraduate years were at Boston College. The late Cathy Ryan had gone to BC and would have been on campus two of the years Kane was there. Coincidence? Maybe not.

He went to the CBS website and pulled up the *60 Minutes* interview she had done. If Kane had been nervous, it didn't show. She exuded confidence as she answered Scott Pelley's questions.

He had overcome his initial reluctance to call his

friend at the credit rating agency. Spying on the records of private citizens is not that big of a deal, he thought. But doing it to a reporter ups the ante. They'll all scream bloody murder and go hunting for scalps if word of this leaks out. The answer was to make sure there were no leaks.

The email he was waiting for arrived with attachments. He printed out the last several months of Gina Kane's MasterCard and American Express records. Almost all of the activity was on the MasterCard. Using a yellow Hi-Liter, he began to go through the transactions.

She's quite the traveler, he thought, as he came across numerous charges related to a trip to Nepal. I wonder who she went with, he asked himself.

"Oh God," he said aloud as he put a line through the airline reservation from JFK to Aruba. Any possibility that was a coincidence was nixed when he saw that Kane had stayed at the same hotel as Ryan.

The trip to Naples could be relevant or maybe not. He made a note to try to find out where Cathy Ryan's family was from, or more precisely, where her parents were living now.

Carter reviewed to the end of the statement. Either Kane had not used her credit card over the last two weeks, which was unlikely considering that she used it at Starbucks almost every day, or his friend had sent him the previous monthly bill without updating the record to the present. He fired off an email requesting the extra information. Knowing his "friend," Carter was certain he would charge again for going into the system and conducting another search.

He thought of the catch and kill idea Sherman had suggested. What would happen if money, lots of it, were offered to Kane to walk away from this story? Carter asked himself. She was only thirty-two. A couple million bucks could make a big difference at that stage of life. There was an outside chance she would accept it, pocket the cash, and bury the story. But that was a long shot and a risky one at that. Millennials were notoriously "me-oriented," he thought, recalling the younger soldiers he'd served with. At the same time they were also oddly idealistic. They hadn't had the life experience that teaches some hills aren't worth dying on.

Was there more than one way to kill this story or at least delay it for a while? Intrigued by the possibility, Carter called up the *Empire Review* website and searched for the name of the editor in chief. After finding the name, he checked into the background. "Maybe Geoffrey Whitehurst is a bloke I can do business with," he said aloud in an attempt to mimic a British accent.

78

Gina stretched as she sat at the desk in her room, her laptop open in front of her. She had welcomed the opportunity to eat alone at an Irish bar and grill that was walking distance from her hotel. The handful of notes she had scribbled on a pad while eating had expanded to three typed pages on her computer.

She had texted Geoff, who had agreed to meet with her the next morning. Again she would go straight from the airport to the *Empire* offices.

In addition to Geoff, there was someone else she needed to update on what she had learned in Durham. That was Meg Williamson's contact who had suggested she look into Paula Stephenson's death. "Deep Throat" was the nickname Gina had assigned to her mystery source, borrowing the moniker of the FBI agent who had secretly aided the two young *Washington Post* reporters in the early stages of the Watergate investigation. After opening Deep Throat's previous email, she hit REPLY.

> Found strong evidence that Paula Stephenson's death may have been a homicide. Will continue efforts to get Durham police to reopen the case. Am concerned that I still don't have enough to convince my publisher to confront REL. Need names of other victims.

Gina searched for the right words to encourage Deep Throat to come out of hiding.

> Victims may be in grave danger. If we meet, I can go faster. I guarantee your identity will be kept confidential.

Unsure what else to add, Gina tapped SEND.

79

Pulling her wheeled suitcase behind her, Gina stepped off the elevator at *Empire Review.* As usual Jane Patwell was waiting to greet her. "I'll take that for you," Jane said, taking hold of Gina's suitcase. "Pick it up at my desk on your way out."

While riding in the cab from the airport, Gina had read that one of the magazine's largest advertisers, Friedman's, a department store chain, had just filed for Chapter 11 bankruptcy.

Jane knocked on the editor's door and pushed it open slightly. When he saw Gina, Geoff gave her a quick smile and directed her to the familiar conference table. Jane closed the door behind them and pulled the suitcase down the hallway.

Geoff sat down opposite her and opened a manila folder he had brought to the table. He glanced at it for a few moments and then said, "So tell me, Gina, was it a good decision for me to pay for you to go to Durham?"

Gina was taken aback by the question. A round-trip

to Durham and one night in a hotel was hardly a budget buster. Had the loss of Friedman's really put that big a chill in the air? So much for the editorial being separate from the business side of the magazine. I'm glad I'm not here today pitching the Aruba trip, she thought, wondering if that would come up later in the conversation.

"As far as the REL News investigation goes, yes, it was an excellent decision." Gina recounted her interviews of the neighbors at Paula Stephenson's apartment complex. He listened, but then began what Gina felt was an interrogation.

"So Paula told the other neighbor she'd found 'a way to get back on track financially.' How do you know that wasn't a new boyfriend with another foolish investment?"

"I seriously doubt that," Gina said evenly. "Somebody who just lost most of her money in investment number one is hardly in a good position to back investment number two."

"A fair point," Geoff conceded. "When Stephenson said, 'they're going to pay up,' why are you so convinced that the 'they' she was referencing was REL News? How do you know she wasn't planning to sue her former boyfriend and the other members of his company? Is it possible that's who she was referring to when she said, 'they'?"

"Possible, but unlikely," Gina said, her frustration building.

"Oh, and I once choked on a cucumber. According to you, that's good news. I'm an unlikely candidate to hang myself."

He laughed loudly at his own joke. Laughter is often contagious, but not this time. When he settled down, Gina said evenly, "Should I continue?"

Geoff's hand gesture suggested the affirmative.

Occasionally glancing at her notes, Gina walked him through what had been discussed when she met with the detective and the mortician at the funeral home. Even as she was talking, she found herself mentally preparing for the zingers that would be fired at her when she concluded. When she was a teenager, her mother often said, "Gina, when you're stuck and no one will help you, you always find a way to blow into your own sail to keep going."

But now she felt vulnerable. Working alone was hard; even harder when the fruits of one's labor were scoffed at by a presumed ally. She considered whitewashing or eliminating entirely Wes Rigler's contention that another detective could look at the evidence around Paula's death and confidently conclude it was a suicide. But facts are stubborn things. When you start discarding them because they don't neatly fit your narrative, progress is always faster, but toward the wrong conclusion.

Gina concluded her summary of the meeting at the funeral home by repeating verbatim Rigler's belief that Paula's death could have been a suicide. The editor was sitting back in his chair, arms folded across his chest. Gina got the impression he was patiently allowing her to finish, his mind long since made up. His opening words confirmed her suspicion.

"Gina, I know how hard you've worked on this REL

News piece. But as journalists, sometimes we have to face the fact that we're seeing things that simply are not there. You put together an interesting case that the girl in Aruba was murdered. But it's equally plausible that she drank too much, panicked, and the crash that killed her was an accident. Same with the Paula Stephenson case. Possibly a murder, but just as likely a suicide. If you were writing the story as a novel, it would make a good read. I'm sure a lot of publishers would be interested. But we're not in the fiction business."

"What about Meg Williamson?" Gina protested. "We know she got a settlement."

"Probably true, but isn't that the same Meg Williamson who is refusing to talk to you anymore?"

"I've reached out to the source who told me to look into Paula Stephenson. If she provides additional leads, what then?"

"I'll tell you what then. As editor, I have to allocate our precious resources to stories that I believe will one day appear in the pages of our magazine. I still have confidence in you, but we're not going to waste any more time or effort on REL News."

Gina wondered if she looked as stunned as she felt. How could events have turned so quickly? A story she felt so strongly about was being cut loose because some big advertiser folded? I never even liked their clothes, she thought to herself.

"What am I supposed to say," Gina sighed, "but okay?"

Geoff's climbing to his feet announced the meeting

was over. "I'm sorry it ended this way, Gina. I don't have time to go into it now, but there's another project that I want to assign to you. I'll be in touch."

Gina nodded. Without saying anything, she got up and headed for the door. For the second time in the last few weeks she was leaving this office feeling shell-shocked. The first time was in the early stages of an investigation so electrifying that she was willing to risk losing the love of her life to pursue it. Now Ted was gone, and along with him, the REL News story.

80

Dick Sherman felt his stomach in a knot. One of the expressions he had often used to instruct underlings was: *Some people when they're in a hole climb out of it; others ask for a bigger shovel.* It was becoming clear that he had failed to follow his own advice. Given the chance, he would turn the clock back to the Saturday morning Carter had called him at home. Who knows? Maybe he could have survived with an apology for dropping the ball and failing to take action after the email about what Matthews did to that woman Pomerantz. But he'd chosen to go along with Carter's plan and now, two years later, there was no turning back.

The previous evening he had stayed late, until after Matthews completed his evening newscast. The anchor was a creature of habit. When his program was over, Matthews would go back to his office, pour himself a Scotch, and watch the half-hour broadcast from start to finish. On-air reporters and their producers who did an exceptionally good job received emails lavishing praise. Similarly, he felt no qualms about providing quick feedback to those correspondents whose work disappointed him. He also paid scrupulous attention to the work of the two cameramen who were responsible for the close-up shots of him. He believed it was his duty to the millions of Americans who watched him every weeknight to look his very best.

Sherman had waited until Matthews's longtime secretary had left. He knocked on the anchorman's closed door, pushing it open as he did so. A bizarre thought had leaped into Sherman's mind at that moment. What would he do if Matthews were in his office molesting another young woman? Fortunately, that was not the case. He was seated behind his desk, tie loosened, Scotch in hand, watching himself on a flat-screen TV affixed to a wall. On the wall behind his desk were portraits of Edward R. Murrow and Walter Cronkite. The two appeared to be smiling down on their worthy successor.

Matthews looked surprised and more than a little uncomfortable. Using a remote, he turned off the TV. He broke the silence by saying, "Would you care to join me in a Scotch?"

Having a drink with Matthews was the last thing Sherman wanted to do. But a little preamble before a difficult discussion might not be a bad idea.

"Why not?" he said as he slid into a chair opposite the anchor. He reached forward to accept the glass.

Sherman had repeatedly rehearsed in his mind the conversation he wanted to have. But he was mindful of the quote from the military, *The best laid plans go out the window when the first bullet is fired.*

"Brad," he began, "we both deserve an awful lot of credit for bringing REL News to where it is today. Twenty years ago this place was a backwater, a junkyard of marginally profitable cable TV stations. Now it's a juggernaut, the envy of the industry."

"It's been quite a ride," Matthews agreed after taking a sip of his Scotch.

"Yes, it has, and you and I have been well rewarded along the way. As good as things have been, Brad, they're about to get a lot better. If this IPO goes as intended, a very lucrative payday awaits both of us."

Sherman waited for a reaction. Not receiving one, he continued. "Billions of dollars are at stake. It's critically important that we avoid any situation that would dampen the enthusiasm of the investment community."

"I couldn't agree more," Matthews said amiably.

"Brad, I'm going to speak candidly. Finding the money to pay settlements to the women you," he paused, "had misunderstandings with is a greater challenge than we anticipated. Every dollar we spend is being scrutinized by investment bankers to determine just how profitable we are. I'm sure you'll recall Michael Carter, who met with us at the club. He just told me he needs another six million dollars to continue his efforts. The question is, where do we get the money?"

Matthews poured himself another drink. Sherman had barely touched his and declined the offer to have it topped off. "Tell me, Dick, what's the answer to that question?"

"The six million is going to be used to solve problems you created. That will be on top of the twelve million REL has already anted up. This time, it's only fair, the six million is going to come out of *your* pocket."

Matthews smiled his anchorman's smile. He took a long sip and used his finger to wipe his lips. "No, Dick, I don't think so. When, or should I say, *if*, this IPO goes through, *you* are projected to pocket over sixty million dollars. *That's* a lot of money. In fact it's more than twice what I'm slated to get. You're right. We've both got a lot to lose, but you've got more at stake. Way more. So if you and your bean counters over in accounting can't figure out a way to come up with the money, you write the check."

Sherman got up to leave, the fury building inside him, and heard a voice behind him.

"Dick, not so fast." Matthews grabbed a pen, scribbled on a piece of paper, and handed it to Sherman. "I've had some time to think since that ambush you pulled at the golf club. Tell your errand boy Carton to make a deal with these two girls. Now get out of here."

Sherman turned and Matthews called to him again.

"Dick, two more things. Be sure to close the door when you leave. And the next time you want to talk to me in my office, make an appointment."

Sherman complied by slamming the door so hard that the window blinds in Matthews's office gently rattled.

• • •

Sherman ordered himself to focus on the task at hand. He picked up the phone and dialed the extension for Ed Myers's secretary. Wasting time on pleasantries was never his thing. "Is he in his office?"

"Yes, Mr. Sherman, do you want—"

"Does he have anybody in there?"

"No, should I—"

"Don't do anything. I'm on my way over to see him."

Two minutes later he was at Myers's door. He entered without knocking and closed it behind him. Myers, who had been on the phone, appeared startled to see him. "Something's come up that I have to tend to right now. I'll call you back," he said as he hung up the phone.

"Ed, I need another six million to go to Carter & Associates. When will you send it?" Sherman remained standing, looking down on his CFO.

Myers leaned back in his chair, removed his glasses, and began to chew on one of the rims. "I know better than to ask any questions. The numbers for this quarter are really good. It will be better to take the hit now. I'll get it moving by tomorrow."

"I knew I could count on you, Ed. Thanks."

It was a rare expression of gratitude that Myers would have welcomed if the circumstances had been different. As Sherman was heading for the door, Myers asked, "Dick, do you have any idea how much more money this Carter group is going to need?"

Sherman stopped, turned around, and faced him. In a voice that was devoid of its usual bravado he responded, "I'm hoping this will be it."

Myers waited a full minute before he picked up the phone and dialed the extension of Frederick Carlyle, Jr.

81

Gina trudged woodenly out of the elevator, fumbled for her key, and unlocked the door of her apartment. To say she was in a daze would have been an understatement. While walking to the subway after her meeting with Geoff, she had been oblivious to a DON'T WALK traffic signal. She had stepped in front of a taxi that swerved to avoid hitting her. The driver had blared his horn while shouting at her in a foreign language. In all likelihood whatever he said was not complimentary.

She pulled a bottle of water from the refrigerator and plopped into a chair at the kitchen table. The overwhelming feeling of fatigue that washed over her had little to do with having gotten up early to catch her flight. She felt like a marathon runner who collapses after completing a grueling 26 miles, with only 352 yards to go and the finish line in sight.

She glanced at her phone and saw that five new emails had arrived. One was from Andrew Ryan, Cathy's brother.

> Hi Gina, I'm sorry to reach out to you again. My mother calls me twice a week to ask if there's anything new in your investigation of Cathy's death. I know I've said it before, but I can't tell you how grateful my parents and I are to you. No matter what you find, it will be a great comfort to know what really happened to my beloved sister. You have our eternal gratitude. Andrew

Geoff's pulling the plug on the REL News story denied her the thrill of the chase, the exhilaration that results from being the first to see what no one else saw, the privilege of shining a light on truth that had been left to rot in a dark, anonymous grave. She had imagined the accolades that would flow in her direction when the REL News saga was published. More than once she'd fantasized about a Pulitzer Prize. Andrew's email was a sober reminder of the young women whose lives had been unfairly taken or irreparably altered by a monster sheltered and protected by a corporation, and now they might never get justice.

Gina glanced around the small kitchen. The new appliances and quartz countertops and shiny, glass-tiled backsplash had given her unit a brighter and more modern look. The new master bathroom was an absolute joy with its walk-in shower and new tiles. But these amenities had not come cheap. While adding to the value of the apartment, the improvements had significantly diminished her savings.

Geoff had said he had "another project for her." When would that start? Next week? Next month? Three months from now? This was the first time she had been shut down in the middle of an investigation. It was ambiguous how much she would be paid for the work she had done. With everyone fretting about Friedman's bankruptcy, clearly now was not the time to ask. Some of the advance she had been given was not yet spent, but that was to work on the REL story. The balance would have to be returned.

Empire Review is not the only game in town, she thought to herself. Several other magazines published investigative journalism. A few had reached out to her in the past. But the way forward would be tricky at best and fraught with difficulties. She would have to disclose that she had developed the story while working for *Empire*. Why did *ER* pass on the story? Would an editor at a different publisher choose to see things the way Geoff had: an accidental death and a suicide, period.

Another question occurred to her that made the situation even more murky. *ER* had given her a monetary advance. Even though the magazine declined to pursue the story, did it retain any ownership interest? She was tempted to call the lawyer Bruce Brady and ask him to clarify the situation, but she decided against it. Brady was a nice guy, but at the end of the day he worked for *ER*. His job was to protect and get the best outcome for his client.

Assuming the REL News story belonged to her, would it be feasible to pursue it on her own? When she thought about it, there was only one lead that would cost some money to follow. Did Paula Stephenson's parents know anything that might be helpful to her? The paperwork from the Durham funeral home indicated that Paula's body had been shipped to Xavier, Nebraska. A quick search on her phone revealed Xavier was an agricultural community seventy miles from Omaha, the nearest major city. It would be plane fare, a rental car, and maybe one night in a hotel, she thought to herself. Why is it so easy to spend somebody else's money and so difficult to part with your own?

Gina knew her father wouldn't hesitate to lend her money, but she didn't want to go that route. With extra time on her hands, she wanted to take a close look at Marian Callow's background. The thought of borrowing money from her father and using some of it to investigate his girlfriend gave her a queasy feeling.

"God, I miss talking to him," she said aloud as she stared at the small, round, solitary refrigerator magnet. Ted's mother had given it to her after they visited his parents at their vacation home in Cape Cod. She had snapped the picture as Gina and Ted were standing on the deck overlooking the bay, watching the sunset. Even though Ted was gone, the picture offered a faint hope. Despite everything that had happened, at some point in the future they would hold hands and watch the sun slowly dip below the horizon.

82

There were no direct flights to Omaha. She chose a Delta flight out of Newark that included an eighty-three-minute layover at O'Hare in Chicago. By departing at eight-thirty in the morning, she could get to Omaha by three-thirty. By the time she picked up her rental car and drove seventy miles to Xavier, she would arrive around five o'clock. That gave her a half-hour cushion before she was scheduled to meet Paula Stephenson's mother at five-thirty. It would be too late to fly back the same day. She decided against booking a hotel room in Omaha. Not knowing what to expect, she wanted the flexibility to stay in the Xavier area.

"God, I hope this isn't a waste of time and money," Gina said aloud as she finished inserting her credit card information. She stared at the blue box that read "Book This Flight." In for a penny, in for a pound, she thought as she tapped on the box and Expedia processed her $831 reservation. Before I die, I wanted to be sure to see Nebraska, she mused.

Twenty minutes earlier she had spoken to Lucinda Stephenson. Paula's mother had been initially hesitant when Gina said she was a journalist. Her mood brightened considerably when Gina used the word "reporter." "Yes," Lucinda responded in answer to Gina's question, Paula's personal items, including clothes and papers, had been boxed and shipped to Xavier and she had not gone to Durham. A nephew in the Marine Corps who was stationed at nearby Camp Lejeune had taken care of cleaning out the apartment and getting it ready to sell. No, she had not had a chance to go through the boxes he had sent. She had no problem letting Gina look through them. It was agreed that Gina would pick her up and they would go to dinner.

She glanced at the time on her phone: 7:30 p.m. After sulking at the kitchen table this morning, she had actually managed to put together a productive day. The receipts for the Aruba and Durham trips and car rentals to see Meg Williamson had been tallied and submitted to the magazine. She had put a check in the mail to return the advance money that hadn't been spent.

Throwing caution to the wind, Gina had sent another email to Deep Throat. Some sources had to be nurtured and coddled. The time for that was over.

> *Empire Review* is no longer supporting my efforts to pursue the REL News investigation. They claim the evidence that Cathy Ryan and Paula Stephenson were murdered

> is not strong enough. I have not given up and for the time being will continue on my own. If you have information that will help me, I need it NOW. I'm trusting you and expect the same in return. It's critically important that we meet.

If Deep Throat didn't respond, she could always go back to Meg Williamson, Gina decided.

She had also spent time laying the groundwork for her discreet inquiry into the background of Marian Callow. Jack Callow's obituary had been in the *New York Times*. Survivors included his beloved wife, Marian, and two sons, Philip and Thomas. No mention of any surviving parents or siblings, she noted. Jack and Marian had been living in Short Hills, New Jersey, at the time of his passing.

Jack was sixty-three. His sons were probably late twenties to early thirties. They could be anywhere. Whitepages .com was no help. Most people in that age group don't bother with landline phone numbers. Gina's source inside New Jersey's Department of Motor Vehicles had recently retired. If the boys had New Jersey driver's licenses, he would have been able to help her find them.

Telling herself the worst he could do was hang up on her, she had called a friend of Ted's who was an investment banker at Goldman Sachs. After exchanging a few awkward pleasantries that included no mention of Ted, she asked a favor. He called her back twenty minutes later. Former employee Jack Callow's personnel file included two emergency contacts, a Marian and a Philip Callow. He gave her both numbers.

A late afternoon run in Central Park had helped clear her head. Gina was tempted to ask Lisa about meeting for dinner but decided against it. She was already feeling the effects of her early start this morning. Tomorrow was going to be a long day that would begin with her alarm set for 5:30 a.m. She went into the bedroom and replaced the clothes she had used in Durham with fresh items. After a dish of pasta and a Chardonnay, she called it a night.

83

Corn, beef cattle, corn, dairy cows, corn, and then more cornfields was the view that greeted Gina as she sped west along pancake-flat Interstate 80. Her flights had been on time and she had been able to doze a little on the way to O'Hare. There had been no wait at the car rental counter. Now she was enjoying the seventy-mile-per-hour speed limits, a rarity in the Northeast. She glanced every few minutes at her phone to assure herself the Waze app was working. It was. The silent message was, *just keep going straight*.

It was a mixed blessing that Paula Stephenson's mother had not gone through the boxes sent from Durham. It would be more work for Gina to sift through them, but it reduced the chance that any key evidence had been thrown away. What exactly was she hoping to find? She didn't really know. If Paula was communicating with somebody about increasing her REL News settlement, Gina was crossing her fingers that at least some trail still remained.

She exited off the highway and came to a sign welcoming her to Xavier, population 1,499. A mile later she came to a downtown area comprised of a diner, several granaries, two gas stations, and a small grocery store. While stopped at what appeared to be the lone traffic light, she looked at a two-story office building to her left. Two doctors, two lawyers, one dentist, one accountant, and one insurance office peacefully coexisted under one roof.

Gina glanced at her phone. It was a few minutes before five o'clock. She decided she would drive the remaining three-quarters of a mile to locate the house before doubling back to the diner for a cup of coffee. She wanted to be alert when she spoke to Paula's mother.

The downtown area ended almost as quickly as it began. Small houses, most in need of paint jobs, were spaced widely apart on each side of the road. Pickup trucks of varying sizes rested on the unpaved driveways.

The voice from the navigation system announced, "You have reached your destination." Gina slowed to a halt and glanced to her right. A small home that looked like an oversized packing box was set back about seventy-five feet from the road. Three uneven steps led up to a covered porch that spanned the front width of the house. The front lawn, if the term applied, looked as if it had not seen a mower in months. To the right of the front door the number "8" was hanging straight while the number "2" dangled at an odd angle. An ancient pickup truck, rust protruding from its crooked back fender, was hibernating at the top of the gravel driveway.

The door opened and a stocky woman with straight gray hair stepped out onto the porch.

"Are you Gina?" she yelled as Gina lowered the passenger's-side window.

"Yes," Gina answered as she shut off the engine.

"You're early," the woman shouted back. Before Gina could apologize, the woman continued. "Give me about ten minutes," she said as she disappeared back into the house.

There goes my cup of coffee, Gina thought to herself, as she pressed the button to put the window back up.

Fifteen minutes later Lucinda Stephenson walked down the driveway, pulled open the passenger's front door, and slung herself into the seat. She pulled the door shut and with effort scrambled to extend the seatbelt over her substantial frame. Her straight graying hair hung loosely to her shoulders. Despite the chilly weather, she had no topcoat. She wore a faded Cornhuskers sweatshirt adorned with the University of Nebraska logo. Soiled blue jeans and worn black sneakers completed the ensemble. Whatever tasks had taken fifteen minutes inside her home, applying makeup was not one of them.

Her first words were "I hope you don't mind driving."

"No, not at all," Gina said as she tried to ignore the smell of alcohol that seemed to grow stronger each time her passenger exhaled.

"Do you know Barney's Steakhouse?"

"I'm afraid I don't. This is my first time in this area."

"That's all right. It's about ten minutes from here. I'll direct you. Start by turning around."

Barney's was in a converted barn. About ten tables were spaced around the almost windowless structure. A bar with seating for six was on the left. A Hank Williams tune played softly from an ancient jukebox.

After they seated themselves, a waitress came over, greeted Lucinda by name, and handed them menus. "Can I get you anything from the bar?"

Lucinda looked at Gina. "You're buyin', right?"

"Yes, I am," Gina responded, once again wishing the magazine was covering her expenses. Lucinda ordered a Scotch while Gina contented herself with a Pinot Grigio, the only white wine they carried.

"I know what I want," Lucinda said. "Why don't you take a look so we can order when she comes back."

Gina glanced at the menu then put it down. "I want to thank you again, Mrs. Stephenson, for agreeing to meet me on such short notice—"

"Call me Lucinda. Everybody does. My daddy named me that because he loved to play 'Lucinda Waltz' on his accordion. It was about the only song he knew," she said breaking into a loud laugh.

"Okay, Lucinda it is. We spoke briefly on the phone last night. Are you familiar with the MeToo movement?"

"They talk about that a lot on TV."

"That's right. They do. For a lot of years women who were taken advantage of, abused, in the workplace either suffered in silence or left the company and never shared their story with anyone. They thought correctly that the deck was stacked against them and no one would believe them."

"Did this happen to my Paula?" Lucinda asked in a voice now filled with sadness.

The waitress placed their drinks in front of them. Gina ordered the eight-ounce filet; Lucinda the twenty-six-ounce prime. They continued after the waitress walked away.

"I'm almost certain it did. But thanks to MeToo, women who come forward with complaints are now being listened to. In most cases, their accusations are taken seriously. All companies hate bad publicity. Many choose to make confidential cash settlements with the victims to keep everything quiet and make it go away."

"Are these big settlements, more than a hundred thousand dollars?"

"Yes, they are."

"That explains it."

"Explains what?"

Lucinda caught the eye of the waitress, jiggled her now empty glass, and turned back to Gina.

"My son Jordan, Paula's baby brother, three years younger, he got caught up in the opioid mess."

"I'm so sorry. Is he," she paused, "all right?"

"He's doing much better. The treatment, if you can find it, is so expensive, more than I could ever afford."

"When did this happen?"

"Last year."

"Did you reach out to Paula for help?"

"I did, but not right away. Paula and I loved each other in our own way, but we didn't always get along. She was a neatnick. I was the opposite. She wasn't but twelve or thirteen when she started getting on me about drinking too much. We fought about that a lot. Maybe I should have listened to her."

"I haven't heard any mention of Paula's father. Is he in the picture?"

Lucinda took a long sip and slowly put the glass down on the table. "He's gone, thank God. He drove his truck into a ravine two years ago. Of course, no seatbelt and drunk as usual. It's because of him Paula and me stopped talking."

"What happened?"

"Paula was always smart as a whip. She got herself a full scholarship to University of Nebraska in Lincoln. She was a beautiful girl and was working at the college TV station. Her senior year she came home for Christmas break. Her father and I had stopped," she paused searching for the right words, "being husband and wife a while ago. Lloyd came home late, I'm sure really drunk, went into Paula's room and tried to get in her bed. There was a lot of yellin' and fightin'. Thank the Lord nothing really bad happened."

"What did you do?"

"Lloyd said he just made a mistake about which room he was in."

"And you believed him?"

"It's not easy when two family members who hate each other are both asking you to take their side."

"What did Paula do?"

"She took off the next morning, went back to Lincoln to finish her senior year. She left me a note saying she was never coming home again. Don't bother to look for her."

"Did you ever see her after that?"

"No, but when her brother was going through his troubles, I tried to find her, hoping maybe he'd listen to her. A friend who was visiting relatives in Dayton saw her on the TV. She wouldn't take my calls or answer any messages so I wrote her a long letter about Jordan's problems."

"Did you finally connect with her?"

"Yes and no. Next thing I know a lawyer from town comes knocking on my door and met with me and Jordan. Paula had sent the lawyer a check for one hundred thousand dollars. The money could only be used for Jordan to go to a facility to get himself clean."

"Did Jordan do that?"

She smiled. "He did. I told you Paula was smart. She set it up so that if after treatment Jordan made it to one year of sobriety, he could keep the rest of the money for himself. Jordy made it. Now he's working and using it to finish college at night."

The waitress arrived with their orders. Lucinda pointed at her empty glass. "I'm ready for another. How about you?"

Knowing that she had a lot of work ahead of her, Gina declined in favor of a club soda.

"In New York they'd charge forty to fifty dollars for a steak like this," Gina announced while savoring her first bite.

"Get out of here!" Lucinda responded.

"I'm not kidding. Tell me, Lucinda. Did you grow up around here?"

For the next twenty minutes Lucinda shared details of her life growing up on a farm, getting married at eighteen, and having her first child a year later. Motherhood in the early years was a happy experience; 4H clubs, school plays, and barn dances were pleasant memories. The whole town would show up for high school football games. Jordy was the quarterback and star player.

There was no conversation during the first half of the drive back to the house. Lucinda broke the silence by asking, "I know I asked you last night, but what are you hoping to find in those boxes?"

"If I can, I want to find out who Paula dealt with when she agreed to her settlement. Even more important, I want to confirm my belief that she was in the process of renegotiating, and if she was, who she was talking to."

"My Paula was a good girl," Lucinda said, as much to herself as to Gina. "She saved her brother's life. After she died that same town lawyer came knocking on my door. After her condominium was sold, almost two hundred thousand dollars was left. In her will she left half of what she had to the trust the lawyer made up for Jordan. The other half she left in a trust for me. Same deal. If I get treatment and get sober for a year, I get to keep the rest of the money."

"What are you going to do?"

"You may not believe me after tonight; I owe it to my little girl to give it a try," she said, wiping a tear from her eye.

As they approached the driveway, Lucinda said, "When those boxes arrived, I just shoved them in Paula's bedroom. After you called last night, I slit them open. Most of them have clothes, books, dishes, and the like. I separated the ones with papers and put them by the door. I'd invite you in, but I'm a little embarrassed. I'm not much of a housekeeper."

"It's okay. I'd rather take them to a hotel room where I can spread them out and sort through them. I'll drop them back off in the morning."

"If I'm not here, just leave 'em on the porch."

Five minutes later four boxes were in the trunk or backseat of the rental car. After saying goodbye to Lucinda, Gina tapped on her phone and made a reservation for a hotel thirteen miles west on Interstate 80.

84

Rosalee Blanco reread the letter from her mother. My poor family, she said to herself. My poor people.

She had just turned thirty when she emigrated from Venezuela almost fifteen years ago. That was before things really started to go bad, before the dictators Chávez and Maduro destroyed what had been the country with South America's highest standard of living. Her father and mother had run a successful grocery store in Coro, a city that at one time was the capital, before that title went to Caracas.

The grocery store, along with most of the businesses in Coro, was forced to close. After they were ordered by the government to sell items at below the cost of acquiring them, before long there was no money to buy new inventory. Instead of feeling sympathy, the authorities had arrested Rosalee's father. Shuttering his store, they claimed, was proof that he was working with foreign powers against the government.

Using the precious American dollars Rosalee sent,

her mother was able to bail him out. Her parents spent their days scrounging for food. With all of their neighbors doing the same thing, it was hard to find any. They would have been able to afford to buy more, but they insisted on using most of the money to buy Rosalee's brother's asthma medication.

Trained as a hairdresser in Venezuela, Rosalee had quickly found work in New York City. She worked six days each week and split her evenings between taking English classes and learning to do makeup. She dreamed that one day she would move to Hollywood and work on movie stars.

The salon that employed her was on the Upper East Side. Through word-of-mouth recommendations she counted as clients half a dozen women from REL News. One day a woman in her forties came to her for the first time. When Rosalee finished working on her, the woman gave her a business card with a number written on the back. "That's my cell. Call me when you get off duty."

A week later she had an interview with this woman, who was assistant director of human resources at REL. Two weeks after that she was working as a hair and makeup artist for the company. "The people I work on are not in the movies, but they are on TV," she had proudly written to her mother.

But it wasn't only the people one saw on TV who would come to her. Of course they were the first priority. When she wasn't busy, the young girls would often come by when they'd finished their shift, to freshen their look before heading out for the evening. She loved getting to know them. They were the daughters she would never have.

It was almost two years ago that the *mal*, the evil had begun. She would see the young women, the pretty girls, smiling as they walked past her area to the executive offices. When they came out, the smiles had been replaced by tears, eye makeup running, blouses in disarray. Often alone at that hour, she would call them to her, hold them while they sobbed, sometimes even rock them on her lap. She would redo their makeup and hair to help them recover a little piece of their dignity.

Most of them would leave the company, their spirits wounded, the optimism that comes with being young having been ripped from them prematurely.

She had been tempted to meet with the reporter, had even sent another email, but of late the *mal* had stopped. She thanked God for taking care of the problem and not forcing her to put her family at risk.

85

After checking in, Gina drove around the side of the hotel and was fortunate to find a parking spot opposite her first-floor room. Pulling her suitcase behind her, she used the electronic key to open the door and flipped on the lights. Her first glance confirmed that she had received what she had requested. Two double beds. She wanted as much surface area as possible to spread out and go through the papers. She took a few minutes to unpack her bag and put her toiletries in the bathroom before making four separate trips to the car to lug in the boxes.

A wide yawn reminded her of the very early start she had had that morning. She was grateful that she had chosen a late afternoon flight to return to New York the next day. Even if she ran out of energy tonight, she would still have several hours tomorrow morning to conduct her search.

She sat on the bed and rubbed her eyes. She had never met Paula Stephenson, but that did not prevent her from experiencing genuine heartache over her fate. Through sheer will and determination Paula had not only survived but thrived in a household with two alcoholic parents. She was ultimately driven away by her father's attempt to sexually assault her. After escaping halfway across the country to begin a new life in New York, what was her fate? Being sexually assaulted. It's no wonder that Paula succumbed to the disease that had ravaged her family, Gina thought.

The familiar question about how much information to share with family members again weighed heavily on her. In her conversation with Lucinda, they had spoken about Paula's death but neither of them mentioned the word "suicide" or alluded to Paula taking her own life. Although Gina had been tempted, she had held back. In her own way Lucinda had come to terms with losing her daughter. What good would it do to rip open a scab, to create uncertainty by introducing the possibility that she was murdered? I have no right to do that, Gina thought, at a time when I don't have answers for her. Or for that matter, when I don't even know if I'm about to walk away from this investigation.

Gina looked around the drab hotel room, with its cheap window blinds, worn carpet from another era, and disposable cups wrapped in cellophane atop the desk. The glamorous life of a journalist, she said to herself as she pulled the desk chair next to one of the beds, used her car key to slit open the first box, and dumped its contents on the dingy bedspread.

• • •

By seven-thirty the next morning Gina was back at it. She had managed to go through two boxes the previous evening before being overtaken by fatigue. Feeling refreshed after eight hours of deep sleep, she had jogged on a treadmill in the fitness center, showered, and gone to a room off the lobby for a continental breakfast.

Paula may have been a "neatnick" in her early days, but the habit did not carry over to her recordkeeping. The boxes Gina had gone through included three-ring binders and bound documents prepared by legal firms related to her investment in Capriana Solutions. Presumably, that was the boyfriend's company. Randomly among the pages were old phone and utility bills. Paula had the habit of writing unrelated messages in the margins and on the back of the pages of the Capriana documents. Wanting to be thorough, Gina examined the front and back of every page. Paula's spidery, hard-to-decipher handwriting further impeded progress.

At eight-forty-five, Gina stood up and stretched. Three down, one to go, she thought, as she looked at the cardboard boxes.

Her cell phone rang. The electronic screen identified the caller as *Empire Review.* Surprised, Gina answered.

"Hi Gina, I hope I'm not calling too early. Are you home?" It was Jane Patwell.

"Actually, Jane, I'm in Xavier, Nebraska, watching the corn grow. What's up?"

"Sounds exciting," Jane said. "Two things. I received your expense summary. I approved it and sent it to Accounting. But that's not why I called. Did you hear the news?"

"No, but I'm all ears," Gina responded, smiling.

"Geoffrey Whitehurst resigned yesterday."

"Oh my God! I had no idea," Gina said while wondering if this was an aftershock following the loss of the Friedman business.

"Neither did anybody. We're all stunned. He already cleaned out his office and is gone."

"Any idea who's going to run things until they find somebody else?"

"None. It would have been Marianne Hartig, but she just went out on maternity leave."

Gina knew the deputy editor from the time they worked together on the fraternity branding iron story.

"Thanks for calling, Jane. I'm as surprised as you are. Out of curiosity, do you know where Geoff's headed next?"

"He didn't tell anybody, but I found out. I went to put a message on his desk. My hand must have brushed the keyboard and it got his computer out of sleep mode."

Gina smiled broadly at the image of Jane "accidentally" seeing a message meant for her boss.

"I guess he's one of the people who've decided there's not much of a future in magazines. He took a job at a REL News station in London. Got to go. Say hi to Nebraska for me."

Gina slowly sat down on the bed, her mind reeling. Think things through, she ordered herself. Could

Geoff's going to REL be a coincidence? Not a chance. Somebody at REL got to him. In exchange for an offer of employment, Geoff pulled her off the REL investigation. But wouldn't they have been better off leaving Geoff in place? When Gina found out he went to REL, they'd know she would suspect—She stopped in mid-thought. She wasn't supposed to find out he went to REL. It was a fluke that Jane saw it on his computer and mentioned it to her.

How could they know about my investigation? she asked herself. Am I being watched? The answer dawned on her. It made sense. The victims who settled almost certainly agreed to contact REL if any reporters came nosing around. She remembered the magazine's lawyer, Brady, commenting that he was surprised Meg Williamson agreed to meet with her. Meg wasn't acting on her own. She was told what to do.

An all-encompassing feeling of being alone gripped Gina. *What should I do*? She opened her phone to Contacts, selected Ted, and quickly typed a three-word text. She pushed SEND before she had the opportunity to convince herself it was the wrong thing to do.

Gina took several deep breaths to calm down. What would Ted say if he were here sitting next to me? Her eyes alighted on the lone box she had not gone through. He'd say, *Get to work*.

86

Gina glanced at her watch: 9:45. Check-out time was eleven o'clock, but most hotels, upon request, would give you a little extra time. But she didn't want to cut it too close. When she finished here, she still had to drive the boxes back to Lucinda's house, make her way to the airport, and turn in the rental car. If she missed her flight, it could mean a substantial change fee and paying for another night in a hotel room.

A half hour earlier she had come across the first pieces of the evidence she was looking for. Scattered inside several manila envelopes were articles about abused women who had received settlements from major corporations. Paula had printed out a story about a reporter at Fox News who had received a $10 million settlement. *5X what I got. Next time a lawyer!!* was scrawled in the margin. The name of the attorney for the woman had been circled. Was it possible Paula had contacted her? Gina entered the name in her laptop.

Wanting to give her eyes a break, she used the machine in the room to make a cup of coffee. It was warm, weak, and predictably foul-tasting.

Paula settled for $2 million without using a lawyer, Gina thought. She ultimately lost most of the money on a boyfriend's bad investment. If Meg Williamson received a similar amount, that would explain the mortgage-free house in Rye on a modest salary. Cathy Ryan came from a wealthy family. Maybe it was harder or impossible to tempt her with money.

Gina sat back down and resumed the task of going through Paula's records. She flipped through documents related to the purchase of the residence. In the next folder was a wide array of late notices from credit card companies, utilities, an auto leasing firm, and the phone company. There was correspondence from a law firm representing the condominium association threatening to commence foreclosure procedures. Paula's final days were anything but peaceful, Gina thought. She had ample motive to try to get more from REL.

A white 8.5-by-11-inch envelope was the last item in the box. Only one word was written on the outside. *Judas.* Gina undid the metal clasp and pulled out a three-page document. The letterhead was from Carter & Associates. Oddly, there was no business address, only a phone number. Trying to contain her excitement, Gina read the settlement agreement Paula had signed a year and a half earlier. There was no mention of counsel representing Paula. The only names on the signature page were hers and that of a Michael Carter and a notary.

Gina flipped over the document and recognized the familiar spidery handwriting. *6/24 left message. 6/27 11:00 at 123 Meridian Parkway.* The dates immediately triggered a memory. She opened her laptop and called up the police report she had scanned into her computer. Paula's body had been discovered on Monday, June 27. She knew the police would try to use whatever they could find in the apartment to determine the approximate time of death. According to the police investigation report, "a flier dated Friday, June 24, announcing a condominium association meeting that would be held on Wednesday, June 29, was found on the kitchen counter. According to the president of the condo association, the fliers were distributed to the door of each resident on the afternoon of Sunday, June 26."

So if Paula took in the flier, she was alive at least until that Sunday afternoon, Gina thought. Whoever was scheduled to meet Paula on Meridian Parkway on Monday afternoon could have killed her Sunday evening or into Monday morning. Finding out where she lived would have been easy. She had purchased the condo in her own name. The information was in a public database.

Gina typed the Meridian Parkway address into her computer. The building offered temporary office space. She needed to find someone there who would share with her which companies/individuals were renting space on June 27.

On the assumption that Michael Carter was a lawyer, she went to the New York Bar Association website and tried to conduct a search. Only members could use that option. She emailed Lisa and asked her to do it.

Gina held the three-page settlement in her hand and considered what to do. If she was right, this could be a key piece of evidence in a murder trial. Using her phone, she took pictures of the three pages and the back page where Paula had written notes. She emailed the pictures to herself to assure she could retrieve them in case anything happened to her phone.

After hustling down to the lobby, she was told there was no business office in the hotel. The clerk agreed to make a copy for her. He found it strange but agreed that Gina could accompany him to the copying machine in the back office. She didn't want any gaps in the chain of custody. He refused her offer of $10 to let her borrow a roll of masking tape.

Back in her room she put the original back in its envelope and box, used the tape to seal all four boxes, and carried them to her car. After leaving them on Lucinda's porch, she eased onto Interstate 80 East for the drive to Omaha.

As Gina gazed past the endless rows of corn, she thought to herself, I'm on the trail of a great story, but I have no idea who's going to publish it.

87

Theodore "Ted" Wilson finished shaving in the bathroom of his Beverly Wilshire hotel room. He toweled off his face as he walked into the bedroom, pulled on and buttoned a starched white shirt, and chose a tie. Conducting the road show for the REL News initial public offering was an exhilarating experience. It was also a grind. The PowerPoint presentation to the private equity groups and pension funds in Chicago had gone well, but the Q&A period had run significantly longer than they had anticipated. There were a lot of questions about to what extent the profitability of REL News was linked too strongly to Brad Matthews. What if he had a heart attack? Suppose he chooses to retire? Did any other on-air personality have the gravitas to slide into Matthews's chair if for any reason it became available?

Ted's team had missed their scheduled departure to Los Angeles and had been forced to scramble onto other flights. Instead of first class, he had found himself sandwiched in the middle seat between a young man who should seriously consider a career as a sumo wrestler and a woman with a squirmy two-year-old on her lap. By the time they checked into the hotel, it had been one o'clock in the morning.

Most team members were looking forward to the end of this traveling and the long hours, to having a chance to reconnect with spouses, children, and significant others. Although Ted would welcome the chance to catch up on lost sleep, part of him dreaded a return to normalcy. For the past few weeks work had filled the void in his spirit, the empty space in his life that had been created by Gina. The thought of trying to find someone to replace her was more daunting than simply being alone.

The delay in reaching the hotel hadn't changed their plan. Breakfast at 7 a.m. Today at ten o'clock they would make their pitch to CalPERS, the California Public Employees' Retirement System. The largest public pension fund in the United States, CalPERS managed the assets of over 1.6 million public employees, retirees, and their families. CalPERS was considered a bell cow in the industry. Get them to commit to a significant investment in REL, and many other pension funds would follow their lead.

CNBC was on the television. The federal investigations into the alleged monopoly power of Google, Amazon, Apple, and Facebook were plodding forward. All four companies were major clients of Ted's bank.

He had just finished knotting his tie when he heard his cell phone vibrate, signaling the arrival of a text message. He walked over, glanced at the screen, and almost felt his heart stop. It was from Gina. *Please trust me.*

Ted tapped on the screen to go into his text message file. This has to be the first line of something much longer, he thought. But no, this was the entire text. *Please trust me.*

Slowly, he sat down on the bed. The alarm clock read 6:53. In minutes he would have to head downstairs.

What does she mean? he asked himself. For a moment he was angry. She had no right to do this to him. Disappear with no explanation and then send a cryptic message to further toy with his emotions. But the resentment passed almost as quickly as it had appeared. Any contact with Gina, even these three words, was infinitely preferable to heartrending silence. In the early days of their separation, he would jump at the arrival of a text, believing this one had to be from her, offering some explanation for what happened and a path leading them back to where they had been. But there were only so many times one could be disappointed. Hope can sustain, but at the same time it can make one feel like a fool and act accordingly.

Why would she ask me to *trust* her? Is it possible there's some reason she broke it off, but can't share it with me?

Ted's mind raced through the time they had spent together, searching for any hint of what Gina was trying to communicate. He recalled a company dinner he had brought her to early in their dating relationship. Taking him into her confidence, she had shared with him that she was working on a story about a major charity in the

New York area that supported veterans wounded from their service overseas. The charismatic founder, who had lost a leg in Afghanistan, had been widely hailed for his fund-raising prowess. But he had a darker side. Two former employees had confirmed to Gina that he had child pornography on his computer. Their discreet complaints to the board had gone nowhere. Her article would expose him and force his resignation.

"Not a word about what I'm working on," she had warned Ted several times before the dinner. One of the partners at Ted's bank sat on the board of the charity.

It was as if a light had been switched on in his brain. "Of course, that's got to be it," he said aloud. There was only one story that Gina could be working on that would make it impossible for her to trust him. Why? Because merely by letting him know what she was doing would put him in a compromised situation. It was clear as day. Gina had uncovered wrongdoing and was now investigating *his* bank!

88

Gina pulled on a bathrobe and slippers and, eyes filled with sleep, made her way to the kitchen. Her flight to Newark had been delayed by four hours. Bad weather on the East Coast followed by mechanical problems on the ground had resulted in her touching down at 2 a.m. It was after three-thirty that she finally fell asleep.

More out of habit than needing the guidance, she had used Waze during her drive to the airport in Omaha. It had completely drained her cell phone battery. She had resisted the temptation to use a charging station at the airport. A cybersecurity expert spoke at a dinner she had recently attended. He warned that airport charging stations could have devices implanted by hackers to download the information stored in the phone. Never, he stressed for the same reason, accept an Uber driver's offer to charge your phone.

Under ordinary circumstances Gina would have been salivating to get to the meeting with her editor at *Empire Review*. She had what she considered to be proof that Paula Stephenson had reached out to REL to renegotiate her settlement. Paula's life had ended at precisely the same time she had agreed to meet someone from Carter & Associates.

It was the time when she and her editor would talk strategy. At what point should they share what they know with the police? She had a contact number for Michael Carter. They would listen together on speakerphone as they called the number, shared some of what they knew, and tried to gauge the reaction of the person on the other end. The other scenario for them to consider was how to respond if Michael Carter contacted her. She had used her cell phone to communicate with Meg Williamson. Her number undoubtedly had been passed to Carter.

But at a time when she most needed the help, the editor's chair at *Empire* was empty. An idea occurred to her. She could call Charlie Maynard, her former editor, for advice. She glanced at the clock on the refrigerator: 8:45. 5:45 was way too early to call the West Coast, particularly when the person was retired.

She pulled her cell phone from the pocket of her bathrobe and plugged it into the charge cord atop the kitchen table. A small red line indicated the battery was working its way back to life. A vibrating noise announced the download of a text message. It was from Ted! How would he respond to her cryptic *Please trust me* message? His answer caused a wave of relief to wash over her. "Thank God," she said aloud, as she stared at his reply, marveling that six letters could lift the shadow that had hung over her for weeks. *Always* was his response.

89

Michael Carter was grateful he had thought to bring an umbrella. What had started as a light drizzle had quickly progressed into a steady downpour. His wife and son had gone to bed early and were fast asleep. No explanation had been necessary regarding why he was leaving the apartment at 11:25 p.m.

It had taken Junior less than ten minutes to respond to his text. *11:30 tonight. Same place.* He was tempted to walk back under the awning of his building when he saw a black Lincoln Navigator turn onto his block and slowly pull to the curb opposite where he was standing. Oscar stepped out and peered under the umbrella until he could see Carter's face. Satisfied, he opened the passenger's rear door. Carter shut his umbrella and slid into the backseat. Oscar closed the door behind him and disappeared.

"Sorry to bring you out on a night like this, Mr. Carlyle."

"I should apologize. You're the one who was standing in the rain. By the way, call me Fred."

"Okay, Fred, I'll get right to it. Three months ago Paula Stephenson who wanted to renegotiate her settlement all of a sudden commits suicide."

"I'm aware of that. I read your email."

"And then Cathy Ryan who was refusing to negotiate with us dies in an accident."

"Both terrible tragedies," Junior said, his voice somber.

"Tragedies with something in common. Both Matthews victims who refused to cooperate have left this world prematurely. Nothing happens to the victims who settle and keep quiet. But the ones who won't settle or stick to the settlement, that appears to be very bad for their health."

Junior exhaled loudly and buried his face in his hands. "What a mess!" he sighed. "Michael, I have a confession to make. Until tonight, I was concerned that you had something to do with Paula Stephenson's death—"

Carter's objection was immediate and fierce. "I assure you I had absolutely nothing to do with that. I can prove that I—"

Junior held up a hand to cut him off. "Michael, I know. You don't have to convince me. I should have known better than to listen to Sherman."

"While you're at it, you should ask Sherman why he's doing it. You and I know that the two deaths are not a coincidence. What's going to happen when somebody figures it out?"

"I don't know," Junior said. "I have to think about that. In the meantime, Michael, you be careful. I know that

Sherman's hired somebody to look into your background. I wouldn't be surprised if he's having you followed."

"Fred, I want to lay low for a while. With Ryan," he hesitated, searching for the right word, "gone, we've tied off all the loose ends that we know about. There's one in South Africa, but I don't think she'll be a problem. I'll keep doing the money drops—"

"We're not quite finished with the victims," Junior said quietly.

Carter turned to him. "We're not?"

"A few days ago Brad Matthews called me. He said he wanted to visit my father and asked if I could be at the house at the same time. Apparently even he has a conscience. When we were alone, he opened up to me, apologizing for what he had done. He didn't want to deal with Sherman or you so he gave me the names of two more women who he said should receive payments.

"Even more surprising, he said he had personally reached out to the women. They accepted his apology and agreed to the settlement. All you have to do is meet with them and sign the papers. Nothing needs to be discussed," he said as he handed him a slip of paper. "This is their contact information."

"All right. I'll do it. But after that, I'm finished."

"Agreed. And a word of caution. No need to share this with Sherman. There's enough venom already between Matthews and Sherman."

"But two more victims. That's another four million dollars. How will I—"

"You'll get the money via wire. Let me worry about that."

"Okay."

"Michael, I'm sorry you're in the middle of all this. I know you have a family. Be careful."

Carter opened the door and stepped out. The rain was coming down hard, but he didn't bother with the umbrella as he trudged toward his building.

90

"All dressed up and no place to go," was how Gina felt as she contemplated her next move. There was no longer any doubt in her mind that both Paula Stephenson and Cathy Ryan had been the victims of foul play. What was going on at REL News went beyond an abuse scandal! Women were being murdered.

She considered but rejected the idea of contacting Carter & Associates. As a lone investigator she was far more vulnerable than she would be if she had the weight of a respected national magazine behind her. She had spoken to Jane Patwell, who reported that no progress had been made in naming a successor to Geoff. An ad hoc committee was scrambling to put out next month's edition. Jane had promised to call her if anything changed.

The email she had sent to her mystery source, Deep Throat, had gone unanswered. Gina's involvement in this case began, she recalled, when Cathy Ryan sent her an email, but after responding, she never heard from Cathy again. She shuddered at the thought that Deep Throat had met a fate similar to Cathy's.

There was one small benefit that flowed from her REL News investigation being on hold. She opened her laptop and retrieved the phone number she was looking for. I have to do this, she said to herself. But that didn't prevent a feeling of guilt as she started dialing. It was answered on the third ring.

"My name is Gina Kane. I'm hoping to speak to Philip Callow."

"You got him."

She had given a lot of thought to what she would say next. Part of her wanted to blurt it out in frank terms. *Your gold-digger stepmother has set her sights on my much-older, retired father. Am I right to be concerned?* But the situation called for subtlety.

"My dad is a widower, retired in Florida. He and your stepmother, Marian, have become very close. When I met Marian, she spoke about you and your brother, Thomas. I'd really like to meet both of you."

"Why?"

It was the question she had anticipated. She was ready with her answer. "Because the way things are going, I believe they're going to get married. If that's destined to happen, I'd rather meet the new members of my family in advance versus waiting for the wedding day."

There was a pause. "I guess that would be okay."

"Excellent," Gina said. "I'll be happy to come to you. Where do you live?"

"Buffalo."

"All right," Gina replied. "Is your brother also in Buffalo?"

"We live together. When do you want to meet?"

"Any time and place that's convenient for you and your brother."

"Tomorrow afternoon? One-thirty?"

"That works for me."

He gave her the name of a restaurant.

She had two thoughts as she ended the call. If Philip and his brother can start lunch at one-thirty, they must have flexible work hours. She wondered if they were thinking the same thing about me. Her second thought was how long does it take and how much does it cost to fly round-trip to Buffalo?

About ninety minutes and $351 were her answers.

The next day, she rode in an Uber to the restaurant. Gina had passed on the chance to catch an early morning flight and take the fifteen-mile ride to Niagara Falls. She and Ted had once talked about going there. She would wait until she could do it with him.

Maria's, the restaurant Philip had chosen for lunch, was more of a diner, and a dingy one at that. Old circular stools with faded red seats were below a countertop that spread out almost the length of the building. Tables were on either side of the front door. Booths were in the far corners.

A waitress carrying a handful of menus walked up to her.

"By yourself?" she asked.

"No, I'm meeting two men."

"If it's Phil and Tom, they're over there," she said, while pointing to the booth in the left corner.

Gina made her way over to where the two were seated on the same side. "Philip and Thomas?" she asked.

"That's us," one answered while the other said, "Have a seat." Neither stood up to greet her. Each had a half-filled coffee cup in front of him, suggesting they had been there for a while.

The brothers appeared to be in their mid-thirties, a little older than Gina. Both were on the paunchy side. Neither had bothered to shave that morning, perhaps the previous several mornings. Although it was chilly out, each wore a faded short-sleeved shirt. One had an Ace bandage on his wrist. Each had pronounced deep, dark bags under his eyes.

Gina slid into her seat, wondering how to start the conversation. Before she could say anything, the waitress appeared and placed plates in front of the brothers.

"We were hungry, so we ordered. I hope you don't mind," Philip said.

"Of course not," Gina said, while taken aback at how rude they were.

"How about you, honey, you know what you want?" the waitress asked, looking at Gina.

"I'll start with an iced tea. I haven't really looked at the menu." She glanced across at the brothers' plates. Each had a stack of pancakes, eggs, and bacon, with a generous side of home fries. Not your typical lunch choice, she thought to herself. "A hamburger sounds good," she said. At the waitress's urging, she ordered the deluxe.

"I appreciate your taking the time to meet me," Gina began.

"That's all right," Philip murmured.

"I hope I'm not taking you away from work."

"You're not," Thomas volunteered.

"What kind of work do you do?"

"We're entrepreneurs," Philip said.

"In the gaming field," Thomas added.

"Gaming?" Gina asked. "I'm not sure what you mean by that."

"Competitive video gaming is a huge industry that's growing like mad around the world," Philip stated. "Tom and I had a successful company until Mommy Dearest persuaded our father to pull the funding out from under us."

"By Mommy Dearest, I assume you're referring to Marian."

"The one and only Marian," Thomas said with a scowl as he used his hand to wipe a piece of pancake off his chin.

"I'm sorry to hear that. What happens now that the funding is gone?"

"We're trying to find other backers," Thomas said. "It's a slow process."

"Do you ever see Marian?"

"Once in a while," Philip answered.

"Do you talk to her?"

"Every now and then," Thomas replied.

It's like pulling teeth to get any answers out of these two, Gina thought. Subtlety is not getting us anywhere. She decided to ask a question that she hoped would get them to open up. "I've met Marian. She seems very nice. You know her better than I do. It's clear you have a lot of resentment toward her now. What were your feelings when you first met her and what happened along the way?"

If Gina was hoping to light a conversational fuse, she succeeded. For the next half hour, the brothers tripped over each other to describe a woman who at first seemed so sweet. But given time, Marian had completely dominated their father's life. His estate, and it was substantial they insisted, was supposed to go to them. By the time he died, Marian had convinced their father to leave everything to her. "We got nothing," Philip said, while Thomas nodded in agreement.

When the check came, neither brother made a move. Nor did they thank Gina for paying. On the way to the airport a thought occurred to her. Neither of the brothers had asked a single question about *her*.

91

Michael Carter was back in his office after back-to-back trips. He had taken a day trip to Portland, Maine, earlier in the week. After returning to New York, the following day he had flown to Phoenix, where he had spent one night. He sat back and glanced at the email he had written to Junior about the trips. Satisfied, he sent it. He noted this was the first time he was sending an email to Junior but not to Sherman.

The women in Portland and Phoenix were the ones whose names had been provided by Junior, the ones Matthews confessed to. Carter still had a hard time picturing Matthews unburdening himself to Junior. When Carter, Sherman, and Matthews met at the club in Greenwich, the anchorman didn't have an ounce of remorse over what he had done. He lied when he failed to identify Meg Williamson as one of his victims. For all Carter knew, Matthews was still at it, adding to the list.

Junior had told him that Matthews had personally reached out to the latest two victims and persuaded them to settle. Whatever he told them, it must have hit the spot. Each woman had come to the rented office space, asked no questions, barely read the agreement, signed, and almost run out the door.

The second time they met in the car, he had told Junior he needed a break. Junior had agreed that time off was in order after he settled these two women, but that was not going to be the case. Far from it.

92

Gina returned from an early morning run to find her cell phone ringing on the kitchen table. A glance at the screen revealed it was her father.

"Hi, Gina. Just wanted to call and see what my little girl is up to."

If only you knew, Gina thought to herself. "The usual, Dad. I'm still pitching that story to *Empire*. There's been some turnover in the editor's chair so the decision-making wheels are turning slowly."

"I'm sure it'll all work out," he said.

"What's going on in Naples?" Gina asked, almost reluctantly.

"A group of us are going bonefishing for a few days in the Bahamas. We're leaving tomorrow. It's stag, guys only. Don't worry, dear. I'm not running off to elope."

"All right, Dad, I get it. How is Marian?"

"She's fine. In fact, she's up in your neck of the woods. She has some business to take care of in New York. I took her to the airport this morning."

Probably arranging to have this apartment put in her name, Gina thought, but then scolded herself. "Dad, if Marian has any free time, I wouldn't mind having a drink or dinner with her while she's in town."

"That would be really nice. I know she'll be there for a few days," he said and then gave her Marian's cell number. She didn't let on that she'd already obtained the number through Ted's friend at Goldman Sachs. "I really hope you get to know Marian better."

"I promise I will, Dad. You don't have to worry about that. Catch a lot of fish!"

93

Life's funny, Gina thought to herself. Over the course of her career she had interviewed a lot of powerful people, many of whom resented that circumstances had forced them to sit and answer her questions. It was natural to feel a little nervous before these sessions started. "We all have butterflies," a veteran reporter had advised her. "As long as you can keep yours flying in formation, you'll be fine."

This evening was different. The calculus was turned upside down. If she succeeded in exposing Marian Callow as an opportunist preying on older men, that would be a win. But would it prove to be a Pyrrhic victory? If, in order to protect her father, and herself, she ended up breaking her father's heart—

Her reverie was broken by Marian, who, after making eye contact, waved and began to make her way to the table. Gina had chosen a small Italian restaurant on the Upper West Side. Unusual for a New York restaurant, the tables were a comfortable distance apart. Gina did not want to have to shout to be heard, and she certainly didn't want their conversation to be audible at neighboring tables.

"What a lovely place," Marian said as the maître d' pulled a chair out for her. "How did you find this?"

Marian was wearing an obviously expensive navy-blue suit with a red-and-white scarf around her neck. Gina realized again how very attractive she was.

"A friend ate here and gave it two thumbs-up," she replied. That friend was Ted, but she didn't want to sidetrack the conversation to *her* love life. That's not why they were here.

Gina ordered a bottle of Pinot Noir, and Marian insisted that Gina order the entrees for both of them. The two women engaged in small talk as they went through their first glass. Several reasons had brought Marian to New York. She was staying with an old friend who had worked with her at the design studio. They had seen *To Kill a Mockingbird* the previous night, and it had been fabulous. Tomorrow she would have lunch with the two brokers who managed her money. They had been her late husband's friends at Goldman Sachs before leaving and setting up their own shop. "Of course, we're not doing anything that we couldn't do over the phone, but every now and then it's nice to look into the eyes of the people you're trusting with your money."

I couldn't agree more, Gina thought, as, trying not to be too obvious, she stared into Marian's eyes.

Unlike her stepsons, Marian showed genuine interest

in Gina. She asked about what Gina was working on now but was respectful when Gina apologized for not being able to share details. She asked if anything was new with her and Ted. When she said she hoped Gina could get down to Naples more often, she seemed to really mean it.

The food came and it was as delicious as ever. There was a friendly quality, a feeling of warmth in Marian that Gina had not noticed in Naples. She could see why her father was attracted to her, why men found her so captivating.

After they finished eating, Gina gently introduced the reason she had asked Marian to dinner. "After Mom died, Dad was a lost soul. He and my mother had been together since they were kids. I was really worried about him. That's why, when I heard he'd met someone so quickly, I'll be honest, I had mixed feelings."

"I can certainly understand that, Gina. If I were in your position, I'd also be asking questions."

"Marian, you're very nice. I feel like a heel for even having this conversation. But with my mother gone, Dad's the only family I've got. I feel an obligation to . . ." She paused, searching for the right words.

"Watch out for him?" Marian volunteered.

"For lack of a better term, yes," Gina said.

Marian smiled. "You're very lucky and so is your dad. He's a wonderful man. You're both so fortunate to have someone watching over you." She took a sip of wine. "Like you, I'm an only child. Both of my parents are gone. I had eight great years with Jack. He was a terrific guy."

She paused. "Jack was older. I knew I'd probably outlive him. But I thought we'd have more time than we did."

"I'm very sorry about your loss," Gina said sincerely.

"Thank you," Marian said. "I'm sure you know what it's like to lose someone you were very close to."

Gina wasn't sure if Marian was alluding to her mother or Ted or both.

"I like you a lot, Gina. Regardless of what happens between your dad and me, I want us to have a good relationship. I know you have questions for me. I'm ready. Fire away."

"Marian, I really appreciate your making this easy for me. I'm going to lay my cards flat on the table. When I was in Naples, I asked how often you see your stepchildren. You responded, 'They have their own lives.' I'll be honest. That was a huge red flag for me."

"Do you want to talk to them?"

"I already did."

"How did you find them? Never mind. Considering what you do for a living, it doesn't surprise me that you were able to track them down."

"I not only talked to them, I flew up to Buffalo and had lunch with them."

"You're doing better than I am."

"I'm not sure what you mean," Gina said.

"They refuse to even see me. I'm sure they told you I'm the Wicked Witch of the West. I turned their father against them. I stole all the money that should have gone to them. Did I leave anything out?"

"They said you convinced their father to stop funding the company they had founded."

Marian smiled and sighed at the same time. "Where to begin. Those boys broke Jack's heart. From day one Jack was an achiever, a hustler. He played sports in school but always had a job on the side. His parents didn't have any money, so he put himself through SUNY Buffalo. He somehow got an interview at Goldman at a time when they were only interested in Ivy Leaguers. Once he got his foot in the door, he outworked everybody. He'd leave for work early, get home late, and was overseas more than half the time."

"So I gather he didn't get to see much of his sons when they were growing up."

"No, he didn't, and that's a regret he carried to his grave. His wife was a good person, but a shy, timid type. She'd claim to be on board with Jack's plan to get tougher on the boys and make them earn their way, but as soon as he left, she'd let them do whatever they pleased. She was always worried about putting too much pressure on them. Her attitude was that their sitting in their rooms playing video games was better than being out on the street doing drugs. She didn't see any harm in it."

"That must have been tough."

"It was. Jack and she got divorced. He was making a good income so a big chunk went to her in alimony and child support. Jack paid for both of them to go to SUNY Buffalo, but neither finished. In fact, they rarely showed up. They were in their rooms playing video games."

"It sounds like an illness, an addiction almost."

"I agree with you, except for the 'almost' part."

"Is their mother still in the picture?"

"No. She was prone to depression and it got worse as she got into middle age. She eventually had to go to assisted living. She's still there."

"What happened to the boys after that?"

"By this time, they were men, in their mid-twenties. Their mother left her money to them, which was the worst thing she could have done. They fancied themselves competitive players. In less than three years they squandered five million dollars."

"What a waste," Gina said.

"Of money and lives," Marian agreed. "It took their going broke for Jack to finally regain some control over the situation. He begged them to go to therapy. A growing number of experts are saying that video game addiction is every bit as destructive as gambling addiction. Of course, they wouldn't go. Why would they? They insisted they didn't have a problem."

"What did Jack do?"

"They refused to even speak to Jack. When they lost the house in New Jersey, he got a place for them in Buffalo. He wanted them to be close to their grandparents. The house is in a trust he established. The trust pays for everything, including a high-speed Internet line for their games. It provides each of them a car, a monthly living allowance, and health care. If they ever agree to go for therapy, it will pay one hundred percent of the cost."

"That's so sad."

"It is. It's the only thing Jack and I ever had a fight over."

"You were against the trust?"

"Just the opposite. I agreed it was the only thing he could do under the circumstances. Neither of us wanted to see them end up on the street."

"Then what was the fight about?"

"The grandparents were getting on in years. He insisted I be the trustee. I didn't want the job."

"But you ended up taking it?"

"Not right away. When Jack was around and healthy, there was no sense of urgency to resolve the dispute. But when he got sick," she paused, a tear forming in her eye, "he was never going to be at peace until he was sure that somebody he could count on was taking care of his sons. I didn't want him on top of everything else to be worried about the trust. So I agreed."

"How did Philip and Thomas react?"

"Predictably. With Jack no longer around to blame for their problems, I became the new bad guy."

"It sounds like a thankless job."

"'Thankless' isn't the word."

"They told me you persuaded Jack to stop funding a company they started."

Marian chuckled. "Their idea was to put together a team of gamers to go around the world to compete in tournaments. I didn't cut off the funding. There never was any funding. Jack wouldn't put a nickel into it."

"Marian, would it do any good to tell you how badly I feel for having misjudged you?"

"Gina, you were protecting somebody you love. You have nothing to apologize for."

"I'm so glad we had this chance to talk."

"There's one more thing we have to talk about."

"There is?" Gina asked, a hint of concern in her voice.

"I'm dying to have an amaretto and I hate drinking alone."

"So do I. Let's make it two."

94

Gina walked into her apartment, dropped her purse and keys on the kitchen table, and grabbed a bottle of water from the refrigerator. She felt as if an immense weight had been lifted from her shoulders. The purpose of the dinner had been to find out what kind of person Marian was. She now had the answer. Gina found herself actually hoping things would work out between Marian and her father.

For at least the tenth time she opened her phone to the one-word text Ted had sent. *Always.* It never failed to give her a sense of comfort and belonging. She battled the temptation to call him, just to hear his voice. I can't do that yet because—

She found herself at a loss to finish the sentence. Because the investigation I'm doing is more important?

She sat down, put her elbows on the table, and rested her head on her hands. I just want this to be over, she said to herself. I want my life back. I want Ted back.

Absentmindedly she tapped her computer and watched

the screen come to life. She went to her email account and clicked for new messages. There was a response from Deep Throat.

> Miss Kane,
>
> I'm sorry not answer more soon. Very afraid.
>
> Can't lose my work. My family depend on money I send.
>
> They did terrible things to young girls. You can make stop.
>
> I can meet you. You promise never say my name.

Gina checked the time. The email had been sent a little over thirty minutes earlier. She wanted to respond immediately to avoid giving the sender a chance to change his or her mind—she was convinced it was a her—and use words that would be easy to understand.

> I promise I will never tell anyone your name. I will meet you any place that you feel safe. We have to talk NOW.
>
> You were right about Paula Stephenson. She did not kill herself. I need you to tell me the names of other girls who were hurt at REL.
>
> Thank you for being brave. With your help, I will stop them.

Gina
212-555-1212 cell phone

Getting my life and Ted back will have to wait a little longer, Gina thought, as she headed for the bedroom. She was going to see this through.

95

Michael Carter was seriously considering getting new office space. He had ended his fling with Beatrice. There was no drama, no fight; there were no speeches. He had just stopped asking her out. When she suggested they do something, his response was always that he was too busy. She had pouted for about two weeks. Her new tactic was to completely ignore him. This morning he had stopped at her desk to report that one of the overhead lights in his office was not working. She never looked up, pretending she didn't hear him. I need this like I need a hole in my head, he thought to himself.

He opened his phone. He had put in place a Google Alert to flag any stories about REL News. The headline caught his eye immediately. *REL News Executive Found Dead.* He clicked on it, and his lower jaw dropped as he began reading.

> Edward Myers was declared dead after police recovered his body from the Harlem

River shortly after dawn this morning. Myers, fifty-three, had spent his entire career at REL News and was currently serving as the company's Chief Financial Officer.

A jogger who was not identified called police to report a male body floating in the water. According to a department source, initial identification was made when a wallet was found in the deceased's clothing. A family member, believed to be his wife, confirmed that the body was that of Myers.

An unnamed source at REL revealed that there was concern among top executives at REL that Myers had been despondent of late. The source suggested that the grueling hours Myers worked preparing the company for its IPO may have played a role.

Myers was last seen leaving REL's midtown headquarters the previous evening. Police are reviewing security camera footage from buildings in the area. A department spokesperson stated that the cause and manner of death is pending further police investigation.

Many industry analysts over the years gave credit to Myers's deft handling of REL's finances, particularly in the early years, as having laid the groundwork for the company's meteoric rise. REL is currently

> in the final stage of going public. It is not clear what, if any effect, Myers's death will have on the IPO process or the value that institutional investors will ultimately assign to its shares.
>
> In addition to his wife, Myers leaves behind a college-age daughter.
>
> A media relations spokesperson at REL indicated the company will issue a statement later today.

Carter got up, walked over to the window, and stared down at the vehicles and pedestrians sixteen floors below. When my time comes, he asked himself, will it be an accident or a suicide? A vision of himself splattered on the pavement below filled his mind. He turned away from the window, fighting off a sensation of vertigo and a sick feeling in the pit of his stomach.

Why Myers? he asked himself, but then it all made frightening sense. A CEO, even one as powerful as Sherman, couldn't just wave his hand and have over $12 million of REL's money sent to an entity such as Carter & Associates. Checks and balances were in place to prevent that from happening. Sherman needed Myers to sign off on sending the money. Who knew what Sherman had told him, or maybe he didn't tell him anything and just bullied him into doing it.

How convenient for Sherman, Carter thought. Sherman would have been careful to ensure there was no paper trail linking him to the money. A waterlogged Myers was not going to shed any light on the subject. As far as Carter knew, Sherman was not aware that Junior was privy to what was going on. If all this became public, investigators would track down the money Carter had disbursed from Carter & Associates. No trace of Sherman there. So who was left as the only living, breathing person who could tell of Sherman's involvement? "Moi," he said, unconsciously putting a finger to his chest.

For the second time he thought seriously about calling a criminal lawyer. He was confident that he could explain—and a jury would believe him—that when he sent emails to Sherman about Cathy Ryan and Paula Stephenson, it was to report his progress toward settlements, not to give Sherman their locations so he could get rid of them. And that was the truth, if that mattered.

Could he somehow assure Sherman that he'd always keep his mouth shut, that he wouldn't turn on him? The folly of that idea became clear to him as he tried to imagine the conversation. *Hey Dick, don't take this the wrong way, but if you're considering ways to arrange my death, it's really not necessary. You can trust me to be a good soldier.*

He thought of the old Arab words of wisdom: *The enemy of my enemy is my friend.* He fished through his notes until he found the phone number Meg had provided for the nosy reporter, Gina Kane.

96

Brad Matthews was in his office sipping his third Scotch watching himself on that evening's broadcast. It was almost midnight. He wasn't happy. Far from it. Whoever set the lighting had made his high forehead absolutely glisten. I look like Joe Biden, he lamented. Page Six of the *New York Post* was already making fun of him, referring to him as "Botox Brad." This will only give them more ammunition, he feared.

He also didn't like what they had persuaded him to do with his hair. For years he had parted it on the left side and combed it across his head, the long strands covering much of his increasingly bald scalp. This new comb-it-straight-back look was "more distinguished," they said. As far as he was concerned, it just made him look older.

He was having that feeling again. In recent months he'd been able to avoid it either by heading home early, going to the gym, or making a date to meet a friend at a restaurant. But for whatever reason tonight the urge was really strong. He could usually count on the Scotch to dampen it, to put out the fire; this time it had made it stronger.

He opened the door of his office and looked around. His secretary had long since gone home. The other offices near his were empty. He could see down the hall to the makeup area. The artist on duty, Rosalee, was reading a magazine. At the moment none of the on-air people required her services. Matthews closed the door and went back to his desk.

He had first noticed her a few weeks ago. She had been promoted from desk assistant in syndication to associate producer on his evening newscast. Opening his top drawer, he pulled out her employment file: from Athens, Georgia, a Journalism major at Vanderbilt. Sally Naylor was petite, with long, dark auburn hair, full lips, and bright white teeth accentuated by a slightly olive complexion.

He picked up the phone and paused a moment, cataloguing in his brain the myriad reasons why this was a bad idea. "The spirit is willing but the flesh is weak," he said to himself as he dialed her extension.

"Hi, Sally, this is Brad Matthews. I'm glad you're still here. I need some fact-checking to be done on one of the stories we ran tonight. Can you come to my office for a few minutes?"

"Of course, I'll be right over."

Matthews smiled and drained the last of the Scotch in his glass. There's something about a good-looking girl with a Southern accent that really sends me.

A minute later he heard three soft knocks on his door.

97

Rosalee heard the sound of footsteps moving quickly on the tile hallway, followed by an unsuccessful attempt to stifle a sob.

"Sally, *aquí*, here," she said, mixing Spanish and English as she often did when she was agitated.

She put her arms around the girl, who began to cry and shake uncontrollably. "*Bastardos*," she whispered to herself as she stroked the girl's hair and felt the moisture of tears on her shoulder. "*Hermosa niña pequeña. Lo siento. No he podido protegerte*," she said softly. "Beautiful little child. I'm sorry. I have not been able to protect you."

Rosalee held Sally, rocked her back and forth, and ran her hand up and down her back. "*Querido Jesús, dime qué hacer.* Dear Jesus, tell me what to do."

The *mal* had come back, and this time she was going to do something about it.

98

Michael Carter was becoming increasingly distracted, and it showed. He'd spent the morning at a deposition for his client Sam Cortland, who had been sued for violating a noncompete agreement after he left his previous employer. Twice during the interrogatory he'd had to check his notes to remind himself of the name of Sam's erstwhile supervisor at the firm. It was even more embarrassing when he stumbled over his client's last name, referring to him as Sam "Kirkland."

"Are you all right?" a concerned Sam had asked during a break.

"I'm fine" was his reply. Truth be told, he was anything but fine.

Every facet of the REL News situation was taking a toll on him. The previous evening he had delivered a cash honorarium to an administrative supervisor in the New York State Attorney General's Office. On a Zip drive she had given him transcripts of what was supposed to be secret grand jury testimony—after he had sat cooling his heels in a Starbucks until she arrived three hours late.

How do you resign from a job you don't officially have? he asked himself. A letter to Junior saying he was retiring from being REL's bagman? A letter to Sherman stating he was leaving his position as secret settlement negotiator?

There was still a million and a half dollars of REL's money in his attorney trust account. Would returning it raise awkward questions? If he used it for his own expenses, on top of everything else would he face charges of theft? Maybe it would be best to just leave it in his attorney trust account until—Until when? he asked himself.

The idea that he had been dealing closely with a murderer increasingly unnerved him. Sherman had access to his personnel file at REL. He knows where my family and I live. Anytime he wants to he can—Carter didn't finish the thought.

He had reached out to his friend at the credit rating agency yet again. The invoice this time was for double the usual amount. The note in the email explained why. *Your boy Sherman has four cards in his own name and two joints with his wife. No charge for the additional info on Gina Kane.*

Hi-Liter in hand, one account at a time, Carter now scanned through Sherman's charges during the previous eighteen months. Despite himself, he chuckled as he came across numerous charges at Madelyn's. It was an innocuous-sounding name for a high-end strip club in Midtown.

When he was finished, he stood up, stretched, and closed his eyes. They felt strained after a sleepless night.

He hadn't found any entries that would put Sherman in the vicinity around the times when Ryan and Stephenson were killed. But the exercise provided little comfort. If Sherman wanted them dead, he had the resources and probably the brains to hire somebody to do the dirty work.

Sitting back down, he clicked on the attachment that included the most recent three weeks of Gina Kane's MasterCard charges.

The American Airlines charge leaped out at him. Gina had flown from LaGuardia to RDU, which he remembered was Raleigh-Durham airport. She had spent one night in a hotel, and there were two Uber charges.

Two and a half weeks later she went from Newark to ORD, which he recognized as O'Hare in Chicago, and then to OMA. "That's got to be Omaha," he said aloud. She had rented a car and eaten at a restaurant. The next day she had paid for a hotel and for gas.

He opened Paula Stephenson's personnel file to confirm what he already knew. She had graduated from the University of Nebraska.

After trekking down to Aruba to investigate Cathy Ryan, this Gina Kane went to Durham to check out Paula Stephenson. And then she went to Omaha, presumably to talk to Stephenson's family.

It's Junior's company, Carter thought angrily. Let him figure out what we should do. He reached into his travel bag and pulled out the computer he used exclusively to communicate with Junior and Sherman. A four-word email was sufficient. *We have to meet.*

99

"All right. Would you please tell him Gina Kane called?" Gina spelled her last name. "There's a story I've been investigating. I believe *American Nation* will be interested in learning more about it."

"Our policy is that you send an email first. Include a synopsis—"

"I don't mean to interrupt you or be rude, but that's not my policy. Please ask Mr. Randolph to be in touch as soon as he returns from vacation."

Gina put the phone down. Putting all my eggs in the *Empire Review* basket may have been a mistake, she thought to herself. But she had believed it would be easier than this to get started at another publication.

Cheer up, she told herself. It's been a really good twenty-four hours.

An early morning run in the Park had helped clear her head. She was tempted to call another magazine on the list she had made when she heard her cell phone vibrate. The screen identified Charlie Maynard, her former editor.

"Charlie, what a great surprise." She glanced at the clock. "It's not even ten in New York, so it's before seven in LA. I thought part of being retired was sleeping in."

"I've been up for a while," he said. "Gina, I'm going to talk fast. They just called my flight. *Empire* asked me to come back and fill in until they can find a new editor. I accepted. I was going through the stories that are in development and I was surprised to read that you had pulled the story you were doing on REL News."

"I did no such thing."

"That's what I figured. Do you still like chicken with garlic sauce?"

"Yes, I do, and egg drop soup," Gina said, laughing as she recalled past impromptu dinners with Charlie.

"I'll get in at three-thirty. I've got meetings starting at five. You come over to the office at seven-thirty. We'll eat and you'll tell me what's going on at REL."

"I'll be there, Charlie. It's great to have you back."

"Don't tell Shirley," he said, referring to his wife, "but it's great to be back. Got to go. See you tonight."

100

A big hug from Charlie Maynard was Gina's welcome when she entered the interim editor in chief's office. They spent five minutes getting caught up on their personal lives before Jane Patwell brought in the Chinese food. For the next twenty minutes, between bites of chicken, Gina outlined her pursuit of the REL story. Charlie mostly listened, asking a few questions along the way.

"The CFO at REL, the one they just fished out of the river, how does he fit into all of this?"

"I have no idea," Gina said. "Scenario number one: He was the one doing the abusing. Concerned that he might be publicly identified, he commits suicide to avoid the embarrassment. Number two: He wasn't the abuser, but he was part of the cover-up. Kills himself to avoid public shaming."

"Number three," Charlie interjected, "is that the same person or people who got rid of Ryan and Stephenson arranged his suicide because he knew too much."

"Believe me, I thought of that. But I'm trying to avoid

the temptation to see a conspiracy behind everything that happens."

"Have you had any more contact from your mystery emailer, the one you referred to as Deep Throat?"

"In my last message I expressed in pretty strong terms that it was time to come forward. But so far, nothing."

"And the only victim who'll talk to you is Meg Williamson?"

"She's the only 'living' victim we know about. It's a bit of a stretch to say she'll talk to me."

"So where do we go from here?"

"I'm wondering if we have enough to get the police involved."

"I was thinking the same thing," Charlie said, "but the question is where to start."

"Our stronger case is Paula Stephenson. Shortly after demanding that REL News renegotiate her settlement, she dies in a questionable suicide."

"If your retired detective, Wes Rigler, is onboard, things will move a lot faster if he goes with you to make the case to the Durham police. If you try to do this yourself, you'll end up talking to a bored desk sergeant."

"Agreed. But how do we get them to look into Cathy Ryan?"

"If the Durham police believe the Stephenson death should be further investigated, the Cathy Ryan situation would be further evidence that something strange is going on with women who used to work at REL. One case would support the other. The FBI would at least listen if they were approached by the Durham police. The Bureau, of course, is the only agency with the resources to conduct an investigation in Aruba."

"I don't know," Gina said. "We need something stronger."

"Yes, we do," Charlie agreed, "and for another reason as well. I have tremendous respect for the FBI and the work they do. But their decision, justified or not, to investigate a major news organization is going out on a limb. It will open them up to an avalanche of criticism."

"I hadn't thought of that," Gina sighed. "We definitely need something stronger."

Charlie tried to stifle a yawn.

"You must be exhausted," Gina said.

"It has been a pretty long day. Submit your expenses on the Nebraska trip and we'll cover them. Keep going, Gina, but be careful."

101

Gina left the subway station and began the four-block walk to her apartment. Lisa had texted her while she was meeting with Charlie. She and some friends were meeting for a drink at the Sugar Factory. Did Gina want to join them?

I behaved myself this time, Gina thought to herself. She had limited herself to one glass of wine.

She turned off Broadway and was one hundred yards from her apartment when she heard her cell phone ring. The call was from a number she didn't recognize. She was tempted to ignore it, knowing in all likelihood it was yet another annoying robocall. Despite her misgivings, she answered.

"Miss Kane?" a heavily accented voice asked.

"This is Gina Kane," she replied, forcing herself to be civil.

"I am friend with Meg Williamson. I send you email about Paula Stephenson."

Gina stopped in her tracks. She pressed the button to

put the call on speaker, to allow her to hear better. She held the phone in front of her face.

"Thank you for calling me. I won't ask your name. Are you ready to meet me?"

"*Me temo que*, I'm sorry, I'm afraid. If they find out—"

"It's okay," Gina said soothingly. "We don't have to meet. Let's just talk. I know Cathy Ryan, Paula Stephenson, and Meg Williamson were victims. I need more names. If several women come forward, we can stop them."

"No tell these girls I talk to you."

"I won't. I promise. Please give me the names."

Gina didn't want to make her wait while she fished for a pen. She pressed the RECORD button on her iPhone and watched the red light go on. She listened as the caller slowly spoke seven first and last names.

"*Ayer*, they hurt another beautiful young girl," the caller said, clearly on the verge of tears.

Gina recognized *ayer* as the Spanish word for "yesterday." "I wish I knew what to call you."

"Martina, *mi madre*'s name."

"Okay, Martina. I will make this stop. I need to know who is hurting the girls."

"*Que un cerdo*, what a pig. Brad Matthews."

Gina felt herself reeling as she stared at the phone in disbelief. America's most trusted anchorman, this generation's Walter Cronkite, was a serial abuser. She was trying to process Martina's revelation when she heard the sounds of running footsteps behind her. A hand brushed against hers and snatched away the phone. In the same motion the attacker put his shoulder into her back, sending her sprawling on the sidewalk. Gina gasped loudly as she used her arms to push herself up. “Stop!” she yelled. “Help!” All she could see was a tall figure in a hoodie and blue jeans sprinting away from her.

Rosalee heard the gasp and the screams. “Gina, Gina, are you okay?” About ten seconds later the call disconnected. Rosalee slowly settled down on the couch of her South Bronx apartment. She buried her face in her hands and sobbed. “The *mal* has taken another young girl,” she said to herself, “and it’s my fault.”

102

An officer in a patrol car volunteered to drive Gina back to her apartment. Someone had heard her cry for help and had called 911. The police had arrived within minutes. She had refused their offer to take her to an emergency room. They had taken her to the 20th Precinct on West 82nd Street to file a complaint. It was almost one o'clock in the morning by the time she was inside her door.

While waiting at the precinct, she had jotted down three of the victim names "Martina" had provided. She had racked her brain but couldn't recall the others.

The police had told her the odds were very much against getting her cell phone back. Worst case, whoever stole it would download the information and sell it to a hacker. The more likely scenario was that everything on the phone would be erased. Hers was the most current generation of iPhone. It could be resold for $350 on the black market.

Although it would be a nuisance, she knew she could

recover the Contacts from her phone. They were stored in the Cloud and could be retrieved. What she didn't know was whether or not the recording of the conversation with "Martina" was somehow salvageable. She was pretty sure she would be able to recover the number the woman had used to call her. But there was no guarantee she would answer. Gina tapped on her computer. The Verizon store five blocks away opened at nine o'clock. She would be its first customer.

103

When Gina woke the next morning, her back felt stiff as a result of the shove. Her wrists were still sore from having used her hands to break her fall. Fortunately, the scrape marks on her palms and her right knee were not deep.

Her visit to the Verizon store accomplished half of what she had hoped. After providing her phone number and pin, she purchased a new phone. Fortunately her Contacts were stored in the Cloud. In a matter of minutes the sales assistant was able to download the information, and as if by magic, her emails and texts populated the new phone.

When she asked about retrieving the recorded conversation she had been having with Martina, the sales assistant was unsure. "I don't know if things get stored in real time. I'll ask the manager."

The manager came over and introduced herself. She was a pretty black woman who Gina guessed was about forty. After introductions were made, the manager said,

"I've been here for twelve years and I never had that question. Let me see. Your recorded conversation would have to have been backed up to be in the Cloud. That usually happens when the phone is charging and connected to WiFi. If your thief was really stupid and he charged your phone in a WiFi zone, you might be in luck. When you go home, check your Apple iCloud account. If it doesn't show up in a day or two, I'm afraid it's gone."

The first thing she did after getting back to her apartment was to check her iCloud account. No recording. She then called her editor. When Charlie didn't pick up, she left a message filling him in on her phone contact with "Martina" and the incident on the street. Next she dialed the number "Martina" had used to call her. An electronic voice began, "You have reached . . ." After waiting for it to finish, Gina left a detailed voice mail message explaining what had happened the previous evening and imploring "Martina" to contact her. She sent the same message in a text and then in an email. *Ball in her court*, Gina thought to herself, wondering if she would ever again hear from the frightened "Martina."

I have to assume I'm never going to get that recording back, Gina thought to herself. The only option left to her was to work with the names she had.

She glanced at the list she had made while waiting at the police precinct. *Laura Pomerantz, Christina Newman, Mel Carroll.* Each name presented a problem that was going to make her search more difficult. She wasn't certain if Pomerantz's first name was Laura or Lauren.

There were a number of ways to spell Newman. The name "Carroll" could begin with a "C" or a "K," and Mel didn't sound like a name that would appear on a birth certificate. Short for Melissa? Melanie? Carmela? She didn't know.

An additional complication was the heavy Spanish accent of the woman who called herself "Martina." Did she say "Christina Newman" or "Christine Anaman"? Gina asked herself as she opened Facebook on her computer and began her research.

A full day of work had produced a list of leads that filled four pages on a legal pad. As she had thought from the very beginning, any woman who was victimized at REL would remove all references to the company from her Facebook page. Not a single name on Gina's pad had any direct link to REL.

A late-afternoon run in Central Park helped reduce some of the stiffness in her back. She showered, cooked some pasta, and was ordering herself to get back to her research when Charlie Maynard called on his cell. He began by asking if she was okay, and then apologizing for not getting back to her sooner. After marathon meetings all afternoon, he was going in for a session with the publisher.

He told her he had done some checking. After killing her story, Geoffrey Whitehurst had taken an on-air job at a station REL owned in London. "I detest journalists who sell out," Charlie said. "After your article breaks, Gina, I'm going to see that the closest he ever gets to working in journalism again is delivering newspapers."

Charlie had a concern about her cell phone incident. "Are you sure that doesn't have any connection to your investigation?"

"I got a brief look at the guy. He was a kid," Gina assured him. "I've been waiting, hoping for weeks for my mystery source, Deep Throat, to call me. There's no way anybody could have known she was going to do it last night."

"All right, be careful. Keep me posted on any new developments."

104

Michael Carter stood on the street in front of his apartment. Unlike the previous times he had met with Junior, there was no place along the curb to pull over. Precisely at 9 p.m. the black Lincoln Navigator slowed to a halt where he was standing. Oscar opened the back door and Carter climbed in.

"Oscar, find a place where you can pull over," Junior ordered. Turning to Carter, he said, "Then we'll talk."

They rode in silence for two blocks. Junior stared straight ahead. *This is my third time in this car*, Carter thought to himself, *but the only time when it's been moving*.

Oscar pulled over to the curb in the NO PARKING area in front of a church. Without any conversation, he left the engine running, got out, closed the door behind him, and walked away.

In Japan, Carter mused, *underlings show deference by letting the person with higher status speak first*. They were a long ways from Japan, but it might be a good idea—

"How did we ever let it come to this?" Junior asked, his voice filled with anguish, his eyes red and on the verge of tears. "Carter, you created a monster," by now he was screaming, "and I was foolish enough to get involved with your plan!"

Carter didn't know what to say. He didn't know that people who were as rich as Junior could get this angry. For the moment he thought it would be better to let him vent.

"My father spent a lifetime building REL News. Part of me is relieved he's too ill to see what's going to happen to his company. As a tribute to him I wanted to elevate it from America's best news organization to the best in the world. And now, thanks to you and your . . . 'schemes,'" grimacing as he said the word, "my family's company will be mired in scandal. All because I put my trust in a hack labor lawyer."

By now Carter had had enough. In the army he had been forced to listen as higher-ranking first sergeants and sergeant majors vented their spleens, blaming those in lower ranks for their shortcomings. This wasn't the army, and he didn't have to take it from a jerk whose only accomplishment was being born into the right family.

"You know something, Junior, you're right. That's one hell of an organization your father built. The face of the company is an out-of-control sex maniac who can't keep his hands off the young female employees. Your CEO, when he's not busy running the business, is a murderer whose victims include the company's CFO. I was only at REL a short time. I'm sorry I didn't get to meet all the other fine people who work there.

"Let's make one thing clear, Junior. I didn't create the mess at that cesspool family business of yours. I devised a plan to clean it up, a plan Sherman backed, a plan you backed as soon as you found out about it."

"You're convinced that Sherman was involved in Myers's death?" Junior asked.

"You're damn right I am. Using the information I gave him, he got rid of the women who were troublemakers. Now he's eliminating anybody who could point to his involvement in the settlements. If I go for an unexpected swim in the river, the only one who'll know anything is Matthews, and God knows he'll keep his mouth shut."

Junior paused and then spoke slowly. "I'm afraid you're right about Sherman. I went to Security and reviewed the footage from the night Myers died. Sherman left the building five minutes before Myers did."

"So he could have been waiting for Myers outside."

"Precisely. And if Sherman asked him to go for a walk with him or to get in his car, Myers would not have suspected anything."

"Until it was too late."

"That's how I see it."

"You fancy yourself a leader, Fred. Here's your chance. Lead! Tell me where we go from here."

Junior was silent for a few moments. Then, in a calm voice, he said, "You're right. There'll be time later to sort out who's at fault for all this, but for now . . ." He stopped.

Struggling to find the right words, he asked, "Is there any chance that we can keep a lid on everything that's happened?"

"Slim to none," Carter replied. "I doubt the reporter, Gina Kane, went all the way to Nebraska to have a good steak. If she got access to Paula Stephenson's personal papers, she knows about the settlement and about Carter & Associates. She's met Meg Williamson. If she applies enough pressure, Williamson might cave. If Cathy Ryan and Stephenson were in touch with other victims, has Kane tracked them down and spoken to them? Another unknown is the late Ed Myers. Did he talk to his wife or anybody else in the company about sending the wires? For all we know, an internal investigation is already going on."

"I'm on the board. If there were an internal investigation, I'd know about it. But you're right. This is not going to stay quiet. Our best chance is to get ahead of the story."

"It's a little late for that. How do you propose to do it?"

"We have to meet with that reporter, Gina Kane, and make it clear to her that your actions and mine were confined to achieving settlements with the victims. We played no role in," he paused, "what Sherman did to Ryan, Stephenson, and Myers."

What Sherman did, Carter thought to himself. Junior still can't say the word "murder." "That's our best option and our only option," Carter said. Again he began thinking about which criminal lawyer to call. "I'll set up the meet."

"There may be a better way," Junior said. "My family

name still carries a lot of weight. Arrange for her to meet with you. I'll show up in your place and assure her that top management at REL is behind getting the truth out and fixing the problem. You can then join us and explain the effort that was made to reach amicable settlements."

"Fred, by the time this is over, the legal bills are going to run into seven figures. That's not a burden for somebody like you, but for me—"

"You're right, Michael. Help me take control of the crisis, and I'll take care of your legal fees."

Carter felt relieved. He didn't know how he would come out of this, but at least he wouldn't be broke.

"Find out where she lives. Tell her you'll pick her up in an hour. Oscar and I will get her, then drive back here and get you. The three of us will go over to REL, sit in a conference room, and," he paused, "do what we have to do."

Carter, for the first time, felt admiration for Junior. "If it's any consolation, Fred," he said, "you're doing the right thing."

With the phone on speaker, Carter dialed the cell number Gina had given Meg Williamson. She recognized his name immediately. After he explained that he and a member of REL's board wanted to meet with her, she quickly agreed and provided her address.

105

Minutes after Gina finished speaking to Charlie, her phone rang again. She tried to contain her excitement that she was speaking to Michael Carter of Carter & Associates. She was initially taken aback by his request to meet him in one hour. After she agreed and provided her address, she phoned Charlie's cell. He probably had it off or silenced while he was in with the publisher, she thought. She left him a message about her Carter meeting.

She was about to start making a list of the questions she would ask Carter when her landline phone rang. The caller ID showed "NYPD."

"Gina Kane, please."

"This is she."

"I'm Sergeant Kevin Shea from the Twentieth Precinct. Miss Kane, we recovered your cell phone—"

"Do you have it there now?"

"Yes, it's on my desk."

Gina glanced at the clock on the refrigerator. There would be barely enough time. If she could get her hands on the phone, she would know if it had the recording of the seven names. Armed with that information, she would have a much stronger hand to play with Carter.

"Sergeant Shea, I'm on my way over right now to get it," she replied.

"Okay, but—" He heard a click as the call disconnected. People are funny sometimes, he thought to himself as he looked at the phone. It was dry now. A pedestrian had found it in a puddle and given it to an officer in a squad car. A business card taped to the back of the phone showed Kane's numbers. What was the big rush to come over and pick up a useless phone?

He got up, walked the phone to the front desk, and said the owner was on her way over to pick it up.

Gina felt her chest heaving up and down after jogging the seven blocks from the police precinct back to her building. It was two minutes before ten o'clock. She wanted to see if the recording was in the phone, but she also wanted to be waiting outside when Carter arrived. Her attempt to turn on the phone was unsuccessful. If the Record mode had been left on, that would have run down the battery.

She spotted the doorman behind the desk and hurried over to him. "Miguel, you use an iPhone, don't you?"

"Yes."

"Do you keep a charger handy?"

"Right here," he said as he pulled it out of a drawer, plugged it in, and extended it to her. She attached the phone and waited. Nothing. She unplugged and tried again. Same result. She looked at her business card attached to the back of the phone. Some of the ink was smudged. It must have been in water, she said to herself. It's ruined.

Trying to stave off her disappointment, she shoved it in her jacket pocket and went outside to wait.

106

Gina looked at her new phone. Ten o'clock. If she'd had more time to plan, more time to think things through, she probably would have insisted on conditions before agreeing to this meeting. Maybe at a quiet table in a public place such as a Barnes & Noble, or she would have insisted on bringing somebody with her. But every fiber of her being wanted to bring this investigation to a conclusion. She wanted to stop Brad Matthews before he could prey on another young woman. Another reason, she admitted to herself, was personal. Once the story broke, she could bring Ted back into her life forever.

A black Lincoln Navigator proceeded slowly down her block before coming to a halt in front of her building. An African-American man who looked like a football player stepped out of the driver's seat and walked toward her.

"Gina Kane?"

She nodded.

He opened the rear door, allowed her to climb in, and then closed it behind her.

A console separated her from the other passenger. The man, who appeared to be in his mid-forties, was in the backseat on her opposite side. He had on a white collared shirt. His tie was loosened at the neck. In his hands was a legal pad atop a manila folder. Her eye was drawn to the cuff link at his left wrist. Even in the dim light she was certain the initials on the link were a small "F," a large "C," and a small "V." The "C" could be Carter, but the other initials did not match.

Gina felt the car begin to move. The feeling that something wasn't right grew stronger, but she forced herself to stay calm. We're probably going over to the REL building to talk there, she reassured herself.

It was clear that if the silence was to be broken, the burden fell on her to do it. "Mr. Carter, I appreciate your reaching out to me. I want the story I'm going to write to be as accurate as possible. Our talking now can go a long way to make that happen."

He turned and looked directly at her for the first time. She wasn't sure why, but she was certain he looked familiar. "Before we talk, let's establish the rules of the game. No recording permitted," he said crisply. "Hand over your cell phone." He extended his hand, palm up, across the console.

The alarm bells in Gina's brain grew louder. The Michael Carter she had spoken to on the phone had a thin, nasally voice with a distinct New York accent. He would have said, "yaw" cell phone. The man in the car with her now had a cultured voice that was closer to a baritone.

"All right," Gina said. She had begun to shift in her

seat to reach into her back pocket when she stopped. Reaching instead into her jacket pocket, she pulled out the phone she had retrieved from the police and handed it over. She breathed a silent sigh of relief as the man slipped it into a bag at his feet.

"We've established we're not recording," Gina said, trying to maintain an even tone in her voice. "I'd like to start by asking—"

"What they tried to do to my company is an abomination!" he snapped, clearly trying to contain the anger he felt building inside him.

"My" company, Gina repeated to herself. His next words confirmed her suspicion.

"My father worked his whole life to build REL. It is my destiny to guide it to its place among the world's great news organizations. Can't anyone understand why that is so important?"

It was Frederick Carlyle, Jr., who was sitting across from her. He never looked at her as he spoke. He had the air of a Shakespearean actor in a soliloquy, trying to resolve a consuming internal dispute.

Gina glanced out the window. They were driving east, heading toward Central Park. Clearly they were not taking the most direct route to the REL building.

"Mr. Carlyle," Gina began. If he had any reaction to her now knowing his identity, he didn't show it. "There's no question that the company your father," she paused and in an attempt to pacify him added, "and you, built is an extraordinary achievement. It's natural you want that to be recognized. But a light also has to be shined on horrible things that happened at your company. Innocent young women—"

"The women were treated fairly," he said. "They were generously compensated, including those who didn't even ask for money. No harm came to any of them who stuck to their agreements."

Gina was astonished that Carlyle was defending the behavior that had led to settlements. This was the man who, it was rumored, would become the chair of REL a few years down the road? she asked herself. Time to confront him head on.

"Tell me, Mr. Carlyle, what happened to Cathy Ryan, who wouldn't settle, or Paula Stephenson, who wanted to renegotiate her agreement? Explain to me how they were treated fairly."

"Paula Stephenson was a drunken waste of a human being," he said and scowled, clenching his hands into fists. "Complaining while she lived on other people's money, demanding more money because *she* made bad decisions. What is it about women like that and their fondness for vodka?" he demanded, his head turning away from Gina, looking out the window.

Gina froze, recalling the picture of the half-empty vodka bottle on Paula's kitchen table, the empty bottles on the counter, and Wes Rigler's insistence that the police never release the crime scene photos to the public.

"Did you ever meet Stephenson when she was at REL?" Gina asked, trying to make her voice sound casual.

"No. I'm happy to say I never had the pleasure."

That confirms it, Gina thought, while trying to control her nerves. The only way Carlyle could have known that vodka was Stephenson's alcohol of choice was if he had been in her apartment!

Grateful that the console provided a small visual barrier, she leaned forward slightly and used her right hand to ease her cell phone out of her right back pocket. Noticing that Carlyle was beginning to turn toward her, she slipped it under her left thigh and clasped her hands together in front of her.

"So Gina, what do you think you're going to get out of all this?"

It was imperative to keep him talking. "I'm not sure I understand the question."

"Well let me put it in simpler terms that even a woman can understand."

She turned away from him as if in disgust over his chauvinistic comment. She glanced down at the phone, tapped it, and in a quick glance watched the screen titled "Recents" light up. Who was the last one to call her? That number would be on top. Was it Charlie Maynard or Michael Carter? Using her memory to picture the screen she used her left index finger to touch what she hoped would be Charlie's number.

107

Michael Carter was sitting alone in the living room of his apartment, grateful for the solitude. His wife had taken their son and one of his friends to see the latest Disney movie. The boys had probably prevailed on her to take them for ice cream afterward, he speculated.

As he waited for Junior to pick him up, he found himself envying ordinary people who were leading ordinary lives. They worried about cranky bosses, nagging wives, pushy in-laws, and their kids getting Cs in school. His concerns were more profound. *No matter how this plays out,* he thought, *I'm almost certainly looking at jail time.* Glancing around the living room, he tried to imagine how big a jail cell was and what it would be like to share it with someone he didn't know. And the toilet with no privacy. He didn't want to think about that.

His cell phone rang. He had put Gina Kane in his contacts. It was her number on the screen. He answered, "Hello," but got no response. "Hello," he said for a second time. He could clearly hear Junior and Kane talking in the background. You'd think a reporter would be more careful not to make a "butt call," he thought, before deciding to listen. Maybe it would give him some advance intelligence about how to answer the journalist's questions.

108

"What did you think was going to happen, Gina? You would publish an article in your magazine, ridicule my company, destroy me and any chance I had to be my father's successor? And while REL was going down in flames, you would prance over to *60 Minutes* and do another interview?"

"Mr. Carlyle, I'm not the one who will destroy your company. It was rotting from within. I became aware of the stench, and I will write the story. Isn't it your own Brad Matthews who is fond of saying, 'Sunlight is the best disinfectant'?"

"Don't take this the wrong way, Gina, but in a sense I admire you. You're courageous to the end. I don't know if Cathy Ryan was that way. I was on another pier, watching through binoculars when she went for her last ride. I couldn't see her face. Paula Stephenson was facing the other way when she went to that great distillery in the sky." He turned and stared directly at her, his pale blue eyes cold and lifeless. "It's fascinating to look at someone in the final moments of her life and try to imagine what she's thinking."

Forcing back her feelings of terror, Gina responded in a voice that was calm but deliberate. "I find it fascinating that you're a big enough fool to think you can do something to me and get away with this. *Empire Review* knows what I've been working on, and they'll pursue the story. They know I was meeting you tonight."

Junior smiled condescendingly and said, "Gina, you're right and you're wrong. Your magazine will pursue the story. I'm counting on it. But there will be zero connection to me. The late Ed Myers can be counted on to remain quiet. All the evidence will point to Dick Sherman, who will make a pathetic, unsuccessful attempt to involve me. And remember, you arranged to meet Michael Carter tonight, not me."

"You're confident Carter won't talk?"

"I'm scheduled to meet with him later tonight. To answer your question, I am one hundred percent confident Carter won't breathe a word to anyone. After tonight, he won't breathe at all," Carlyle said in a deadly calm voice.

109

Michael Carter remained transfixed as he listened to the conversation between Junior and Gina Kane. He was certain he could not be held accountable for playing a role in the murders of Cathy Ryan and Paula Stephenson. When he had provided information about their whereabouts, there was zero evidence that he was dealing with a killer.

From the moment he began suspecting Sherman might be behind the murders, Junior had encouraged him in that belief. How could he have been so gullible? he asked himself. He had accepted without question Junior's story about Sherman leaving the building at the same time as Myers the night the CFO disappeared. He had tried to link Sherman to the murders by reviewing his credit card transactions. It had not occurred to him to do the same analysis with Junior's cards.

He felt himself barely breathing when Junior revealed his plan for him, "After tonight, he won't breathe at all."

Nervous beads of perspiration forming on his forehead, Carter got up and began to pace around the small living room. A few minutes earlier he had been considering the possibility of making a run for it, literally fleeing the country. He had a little over a million in his attorney trust account and almost as much in his personal account. He could wire money to a new account he would establish in the Cayman Islands. He could look on Google to find out which countries didn't have an extradition treaty with the United States, then go online to find the next available direct flight to one of those countries out of JFK or Newark.

As his mind raced forward with the plan, a heavy dose of reality put a wet blanket on the idea. Wiring money took time, probably forty-eight hours, particularly when you have to open an account first. Were Beverly's and Zack's passports in the apartment or in the safe deposit box at the bank? If the latter, he wouldn't be able to get them until nine in the morning. Would she agree to go? If she didn't, would he leave his son behind?

When the police found Kane's body, one of the first things they'd do is examine her cell phone. If they couldn't find it, they'd go to her carrier and get a record of her calls. It would show the call Carter made to her earlier in the evening on a phone registered in his name. For that matter, it would show the call he was listening to right now! He would quickly become a Person of Interest and be placed on a watch list. Any attempt to use his passport would trigger questions and his arrest.

I can be the good guy here, Carter thought to himself. I can be the one who saved the reporter's life. Maybe they'll even portray me as a hero. The moment I heard her life was in danger, I didn't think about the consequences for me; I called the police. Satisfied, and more than a little proud of himself, he dialed 911.

Four minutes later a dispatch went out to all units in Manhattan: "Be on the lookout for a black Lincoln Navigator, plate number . . ."

110

Feelings of despair filled Gina's mind. Where were the police sirens that would have ensued if she had successfully dialed Charlie? They would have been able to trace her movements through her cell phone signal. Who knew what Carter would do if he were listening to this? Maybe he was in on the plan to trick her into getting in Junior's car?

She mourned the life she would have had with Ted and their children who would never be born. She wondered how or if her father would survive the loss of another family member. At least Marian would be there to help.

Snap out of it! she ordered herself. If I'm meant to go down, I'll go down swinging!

"So what's in store for me, Mr. Carlyle, an accident or a suicide?"

He smiled. "Oh, Gina, nothing as creative as that." He leaned over to the bag by his feet, pulled out a pistol, and pointed it at her. "When they find your body in the Park, the only question will be whether Dick Sherman was behind it or were you the victim of a senseless mugging?"

Junior looked toward the front seat and said, "Oscar, it's about a half mile ahead on the right."

Time is running out, Gina thought. What can I use as a weapon? There was a pen in the bag on the floor by her feet, but it would be so obvious if she reached for it. There was one other possibility.

Junior was alternating between looking at her and searching forward for a spot he had chosen. The gun was in his right hand, about three feet from where she was sitting. Gina slipped her left hand below her left thigh until she felt her phone. She leaned forward slightly as she slid the phone behind her back. Using her right hand, she eased it along the seat until she had a firm grip on it with her right hand.

There was the faint wail of a siren in the distance. Junior pointed the gun at her as he looked around trying to discern from what direction the sound was coming.

Gina recognized her chance. Throwing herself in his direction, with her left hand she grabbed the barrel of the pistol and pointed it away from her. With her right hand she lashed out at his face while gripping the cell phone. It struck home. She heard a yelp of pain as the hard edge of the phone shattered his nose. Blood spattered on both of them.

Still wrestling with her for control of the gun, he tried to bring it lower and turn it in her direction. She forced it level. A deafening sound filled the car as the pistol discharged.

Suddenly, the vehicle began to accelerate. Glancing forward she could see Oscar's head slumped to one side. She could feel her wrists aching from having used them to break her fall to the sidewalk the previous evening.

Junior's strength was prevailing against hers. She could feel the bumping as the SUV ran over an obstacle. Outmuscling her, he maneuvered the barrel of the gun until it was almost at her chest.

Next came the crash. Gina and Junior were thrown forward into the backs of the front seats as the SUV plowed into a tree trunk and came to an abrupt halt.

Gina was semiconscious, at first unable to move. Every part of her body hurt. She saw Junior stir, lean forward, and reach for something on the floor. Lacking the strength to fight again, she struggled to open her door, almost falling out as she did so. She turned back to see Junior raising the gun toward her again. Then she felt a strong hand pull her from the vehicle and force his body between her and the backseat of the car.

"Police! Don't Move!" the patrolman screamed at Junior as he pointed his firearm at him.

Gina staggered toward another cop who was running to the scene. She had her hands over her ears in an attempt to silence the ringing in them. I'm safe, she thought. Thank God I'm safe.

Epilogue

Four months later

Gina and Ted held hands as they climbed off the trolley that had taken them through the mangroves to the bar on the beach in Pelican Bay. Marian waved and gestured them to the table she and Gina's father had reserved.

After hugs and handshakes Marian said, "I want to see that gorgeous ring your father told me about."

Gina held her hand forward, proudly displaying the engagement ring Ted had given her on Christmas Eve.

After they were seated and had ordered cocktails, Gina's father said, "We've been following some of it in the papers, but bring us up-to-date on what's going on with those scoundrels at REL."

Gina laughed. "Where to begin. Of course you know Brad Matthews was fired the day the story broke. Losing his job is the least of his problems. Fourteen women have filed sexual abuse suits against him and REL."

"Frederick Carlyle, Jr., is in even bigger trouble," Ted added. "He's been indicted for three murders that he's trying to blame on his chauffeur. And of course," he looked at Gina, "for attempted murder."

"The chauffeur never made it to the hospital alive, so he's not around to defend himself," Gina said.

"Dick Sherman, the CEO, got fired. He's insisting he's entitled to his huge severance package. REL disagrees. The lawyers are going to have a lot of fun with that one," Ted said.

"What's going to happen to the one who was going around scaring the women into taking settlements?" Marian asked.

"That was Michael Carter. From what I hear, he's trying to cut as many deals as he can," Gina responded. "He's agreed to testify against Carlyle Jr. and a slew of others."

"The editor who tried to get you to stop investigating, I hope he got what he deserved," Gina's father said.

"REL fired him as soon as they found out he had taken a bribe to kill the story. He's suing and, of course, the lawyers are fighting," Gina replied.

"There it goes," they heard a woman from a neighboring table say.

Their attention turned toward the water. There was near silence as they and other patrons beheld the wonder of another magnificent sunset over the Gulf of Mexico. As the sun dipped below the horizon and the orange glow began spreading outward across the distant clouds, Gina glanced over and saw her father's hand cover Marian's. At the same instant she felt the warm caress of Ted's hand on the back of her neck. The moment was punctuated by the words of a song that had been written almost one hundred years earlier:

There's a somebody I'm longin' to see
I hope that he turns out to be
Someone who'll watch over me

Simon & Schuster
Proudly Presents

Piece of My Heart

AN UNDER SUSPICION NOVEL

Mary Higgins Clark & Alafair Burke

Available in hardcover and eBook
in November 2020 wherever books are sold

Please turn the page for a preview of
Piece of My Heart . . .

Prologue

Five Years Ago

"If I only could, I'd make a deal with God."

Roseanne Robinson heard that old song lyric playing at the back of her mind as she tried to do precisely that—make a deal with God. *Please, I'll be a better wife. I'll be a better person. I'll do good deeds every single day for the rest of my life. Anything if you spare my husband. Send him back to me.*

She raised her head from her ongoing prayers when she spotted a doctor in surgical scrubs emerge through the double doors into the hospital waiting room. She held her breath expectantly, but her hopes fell when he locked eyes with an older woman in the corner who had been wiping away intermittent tears since Roseanne had arrived. A sorrowful wail followed only seconds later.

That poor woman, Roseanne thought. *Please don't let that be me.*

Roseanne was only thirty-one years old but could not imagine life without her husband. They started dating during college, and then remained serious while he launched his architectural career and she added accounts to her digital marketing firm's growing roster of clients. He had bought the motorcycle three years earlier, two weeks after their second wedding anniversary.

That stupid motorcycle. That's what brought us here.

She had made her disapproval clear. She even appealed to his older brother, Charlie, thinking a police officer would talk some sense into him. But instead, she had gotten a lecture from her brother-in-law about "letting a man be happy."

Despite the risks, part of her had been relieved at the time by the purchase. For months, her husband had seemed distracted. Inattentive. Bored. She wondered if he disapproved of her decision to go back to the firm, if only part-time. She wondered if he enjoyed being a father. Worst of all, she wondered if maybe their marriage was fundamentally broken. But once he had that motorcycle, he seemed more like his usual happy, charming, and hilarious self. Apparently whatever early midlife crisis her husband had experienced had been fixed by a shiny new two-wheeled gadget. It could be worse, she had told herself.

But now here she was, waiting to hear how his surgery had gone.

The police officer who called her had reported the news with icy detachment. There had been an accident, he explained. A delivery truck had blown through a red light. The motorcyclist—her thrill-seeking husband—was unconscious, even though he had been wearing a helmet, as she had implored him to do, so many times.

She looked at her watch. 11:55 a.m. Bella would be out of preschool in five minutes. Their neighbor, Sarah, would be picking her up along with Sarah's own daughter, Jenna. Bella would enjoy an afternoon playdate with her best friend, but at some point, she'd want to know where her mother and father were.

Please, God. How can I possibly explain to my daughter that Daddy won't be coming home?

Another doctor emerged through the double doors—this time a woman, her hair still covered by a blue surgical cap. "Roseanne Robinson?" she called out.

This was it. Her and Bella's futures would turn on whatever news was about to be delivered. They'd either keep rolling down the path that was their current life, or find themselves on an entirely different route. Door Number One or Door Number Two.

She rose from her chair. "I'm Roseanne Robinson."

Or Ro-Ro, as most of her friends called her. That nickname had been the primary reason she kept her maiden name when they married. *If you live, my love, I'll change my last name, the way you always wanted me to.*

"Please, just tell me," Roseanne pleaded. She squeezed her eyes shut, bracing for the impact of a pronouncement that would change her life forever.

"Your husband's alive."

The hug that followed was automatic, a pure display of the gratitude Roseanne felt in that moment.

The doctor outlined the treatments that would follow—additional skin grafts, physical therapy, rehabilitation. As Roseanne absorbed every last piece of data and envisioned every single medical appointment, she could not stop thinking about how lucky she felt. Her family had been spared.

But as the weeks and months passed, reality set in. The rehab. The recovery. The resentment. Life would not go on, at least not as they had once known it. Every day brought another domino, toppling forward.

Then one day, five years later, she'd get a phone call to learn that all the dominoes that fell would end with a little boy named Johnny Buckley.

Be sure to check out the entire

UNDER SUSPICION SERIES

Available wherever books are sold or at SimonandSchuster.com

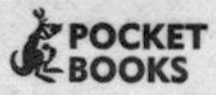

75631